DARK GOLD

"Imbued with passion, danger and supernatural thrills."
—*Romantic Times*

"Wish I had written it!" —Amanda Ashley

DARK DESIRE

"A very well-written, entertaining story that I highly recommend." —*Under the Covers Book Review*

DARK PRINCE

"For lovers of vampire novels, this one is a keeper . . . I had a hard time putting the book down . . . Don't miss this book!" —*New-Age Bookshelf*

THE SCARLETTI CURSE

"The characters and twists in this book held me on the edge of my seat the whole time I read it. If you've enjoyed Ms. Feehan's previous novels, you will surely be captivated by this step into the world of Gothic romance . . . Once again, Ms. Feehan does not disappoint."
—*Under the Covers Book Reviews*

DARK SYMPHONY

CHRISTINE FEEHAN

JOVE BOOKS, NEW YORK

THE BERKLEY PUBLISHING GROUP
Published by the Penguin Group
Penguin Group (USA) Inc.
375 Hudson Street, New York, New York 10014, USA
Penguin Group (Canada), 90 Eglinton Avenue East, Suite 700, Toronto, Ontario M4P 2Y3, Canada
(a division of Pearson Penguin Canada Inc.)
Penguin Books Ltd., 80 Strand, London WC2R 0RL, England
Penguin Group Ireland, 25 St. Stephen's Green, Dublin 2, Ireland (a division of Penguin Books Ltd.)
Penguin Group (Australia), 250 Camberwell Road, Camberwell, Victoria 3124, Australia
(a division of Pearson Australia Group Pty. Ltd.)
Penguin Books India Pvt. Ltd., 11 Community Centre, Panchsheel Park, New Delhi—110 017, India
Penguin Group (NZ), 67 Apollo Drive, Rosedale, North Shore 0632, New Zealand
(a division of Pearson New Zealand Ltd.)
Penguin Books (South Africa) (Pty.) Ltd., 24 Sturdee Avenue, Rosebank, Johannesburg 2196,
South Africa

Penguin Books Ltd., Registered Offices: 80 Strand, London WC2R 0RL, England

This is a work of fiction. Names, characters, places, and incidents either are the product of the author's imagination or are used fictitiously, and any resemblance to actual persons, living or dead, business establishments, events, or locales is entirely coincidental. The publisher does not have any control over and does not assume any responsibility for author or third-party websites or their content.

DARK SYMPHONY

A Jove Book / published by arrangement with the author

PRINTING HISTORY
Jove mass-market edition / March 2003
Special $4.99 edition / October 2007

ISBN: 978-0-515-14417-8

JOVE®
Jove Books are published by The Berkley Publishing Group,
a division of Penguin Group (USA) Inc.,
375 Hudson Street, New York, New York 10014.
JOVE is a registered trademark of Penguin Group (USA) Inc.
The "J" design is a trademark belonging to Penguin Group (USA) Inc.

PRINTED IN THE UNITED STATES OF AMERICA

10 9 8 7 6 5 4 3 2 1

This book was written, with love, for my youngest daughter, Cecilia, who has managed to inspire more than one character for me! And also for Beverly Gladstone and her son, Tony. Wishing you both all the best in the world.

Author's Notes and Acknowledgments

Special thanks go to Alicia Miller, owner of Kat Avalon Habit of Perfection FCH, daughter of Celt. She is a member of the Borzoi Club of America and was invaluable to me in the writing of *Dark Symphony*. Alicia was so very generous with her time and knowledge and support. Without her, I would never have discovered the incredible breed of the borzoi.

CH Avalon Celtic Cross is owned and bred and very much loved by Sandra Moore. Sandra Moore is the owner of the real Celt, a wonderful borzoi with outstanding qualities. She is a member of the AKC, the Borzoi Club of America, and many regional clubs as well. She also has had nationally ranked borzois for many, many years.

Sandra Moore
avalonbz@usit.net

Avalon Borzoi on the Web
http://www.geocities.com/avalon_borzoi/

Last, but not least, I must thank my daughter Denise, for coming up with the lyrics for Josef's immortal rap song!

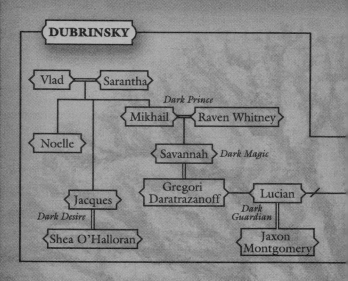

DUBRINSKY

Vlad — Sarantha

Dark Prince
Mikhail — Raven Whitney

Noelle

Savannah — *Dark Magic*

Jacques
Dark Desire

Gregori Daratrazanoff — Lucian

Shea O'Halloran

Dark Guardian
Jaxon Montgomery

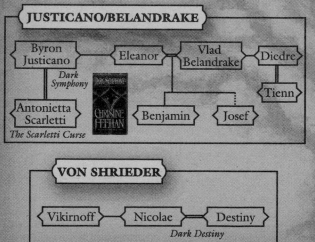

JUSTICANO/BELANDRAKE

Byron Justicano — Eleanor — Vlad Belandrake — Diedre

Dark Symphony

Antonietta Scarletti

The Scarletti Curse

Benjamin — Josef

Tienn

VON SHRIEDER

Vikirnoff — Nicolae — Destiny

Dark Destiny

THE CARPATHIANS

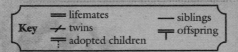

Key
≡ lifemates   — siblings
⟍⟋ twins   ⊤ offspring
⋯ adopted children

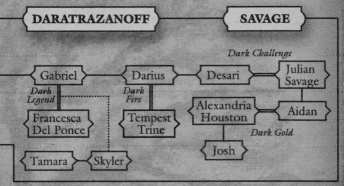

DARATRAZANOFF   **SAVAGE**

Dark Challenge

Gabriel — Darius — Desari — Julian Savage

Dark Legend

Dark Fire

Francesca Del Ponce — Tempest Trine

Alexandria Houston — Aidan

Dark Gold

Josh

Tamara — Skyler

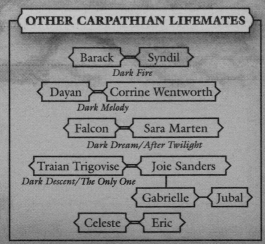

OTHER CARPATHIAN LIFEMATES

Barack — Syndil
Dark Fire

Dayan — Corrine Wentworth
Dark Melody

Falcon — Sara Marten
Dark Dream/After Twilight

Traian Trigovise — Joie Sanders
Dark Descent/The Only One

Gabrielle — Jubal

Celeste — Eric

1

Fog, *thick and* dense, blanketed the sky, muffling every sound. Muffling the sound of conspiracy. Of murder stalking the night. Of dark, ugly intentions hidden within the white, swirling mists and the deeper shadows. The fog was the perfect cover for the predator as he moved silently across the sky, searching for prey. He had been alone too long, far from his own kind, fighting the insidious call of power, of evil, that whispered to him every waking minute of his existence.

Far below him were the humans, his prey. His enemies. He knew what they would do to one of his kind, should they discover him. He still woke choking from his slumber, trapped for those first waking moments in his past. His body would always bear the scars of torture, though it was nearly impossible to scar his kind. He was Carpathian, a species as old as time, with tremendous gifts to hold dominion over the weather, the land, even animals. He could shift shape and soar high, run with the wolves, yet without the light to his darkness, he could so easily give in to the whispers of temptation, the call for power, and turn wholly evil. He had the potential for becoming the undead, as so many of his kind had chosen to do.

He traveled the world, hunting the vampire, seeking to maintain a balance of life in a world of bleak loneliness. Seeking to maintain honor when he felt he'd lost it. And then he heard the music. It was playing on a television set in one of the stores he passed late in the evening, and the music caught him as nothing else had. Ensnared him. Mesmerized him. Wrapped his soul in golden notes until he thought only of the music. He could only hear the music playing in his head. It was so powerful it even dulled the relentless hunger that was ever present in his life. He traveled to Italy, drawn by the music. And he stayed for other, much more compelling reasons.

He flew across the sky with silent stealth, pulled in the same direction on every awakening. With his acute sense of smell he caught the scent of salt from the sea and the fuel from a boat tossed about on the rolling waves. The wind also brought him the scent of man. For a brief moment his lips drew back in a silent snarl, and he felt his incisors lengthen in hunger. In distaste. Most humans had become his enemy, although he sought their protection. Humans used him as a trap to draw others of his kind, nearly succeeding in killing the lifemate to his prince.

The stain of shame would always be on him. Would always keep him from being completely comfortable in his homeland and with others of his kind. He would never be able to bear their forgiveness. He could not forgive himself. His self-imposed penance had been service to his people. He actively hunted their mortal enemy, the vampire, engaging in battle after battle when he had never been a warrior. He went from country to country in a relentless, merciless hunt, determined to rid the world of the evil stalking his kind. Every kill brought him closer to the edge of madness. Until he found the music.

The night enfolded him, embraced him as a brother. In the darkness, his eyes glowed the fiery red of a predator on the hunt. Far below him, he glimpsed the lights of the villas dimmed by the thick bank of fog, houses crammed close to one another set precariously on the hillsides. In the distance he could just make out the Scarletti palazzo, a work of art created so many centuries before.

The music originated there, in the great palazzo. Concertos and operas were composed and played on a perfectly tuned piano. He stayed close by to hear the beauty of the masterpieces created and performed. The notes soothed him and gave him a sense of hope. He had even gone so far as to purchase several CDs and a machine on which to play them, keeping his treasures deep beneath the earth in the lair he kept to be close to the woman he knew belonged to only him.

Her family knew he was dangerous by looking at him. They sensed the predator in him, but Antonietta thought herself safe with him. And she was the only one he wanted. The one woman he would have.

Antonietta Scarletti stared blankly toward the elaborate stained glass window of the palazzo. Outside the walls of the villa, the wind shrieked and moaned. She touched the glass with her sensitive fingertips, tracing the lead and the familiar patterns. If she tried, she could remember them, the vivid colors and frightening images. She laughed aloud at the thought. As a child she had certainly been frightened by the gargoyles and demons decorating the fifteenth-century palazzo, now she simply appreciated their beauty, although she could only see them through her fingertips.

Her home had been modernized many times over the centuries, but the Gothic architecture had been preserved as closely as possible to the original. She loved every secret passageway with the Machiavellian traps and every carefully cut stone that made up her home. Strangely, she was sleepy. Most nights she wandered, wide awake, through the large hallways or played her piano, the music moving through her and onto the keys, to pour out the torrent of emotion that sometimes threatened to overwhelm her. Tonight, as the wind howled and the sea pounded on the cliffs, she plaited her hair into a thick rope and thought of a dark poet.

Tasha, her cousin, had commented at dinner that threads of gray were already beginning to appear in her mass of long hair. Antonietta knew she was vain about her hair, but it was her only call to glory, and now with the gray beginning to appear, it was only a matter of time before that small vanity would vanish. Her self-mocking laughter was soft as she moved without hesitation across the room, unerringly to the piano. Her fingers slid across the keys, immediately responding to the laughter in her heart.

She loved her life, blind or no. She lived it the way she wanted to live. Music flowed into the night. A summons. She knew the music called to him. Byron. Antonietta thought of him day and night. A secret obsession she could not get over. The sound of his voice touched her like she imagined his fingers on her skin would. A caress of sound. He was her only regret. Her money and fame allowed her to lead the life she wanted in spite of her loss of sight, but it also provided a barrier between her and every man. Even Byron. Especially Byron. His quiet acceptance, his continuing interest—so completely focused on her—threatened to involve her emotions as well as her body, and that, she couldn't afford.

Antonietta seated herself at the bench, her body leaden with unexpected fatigue. Her fingers raced over the ivory keys. The music flowed into space, unrequited love, boundless passion unanswered. Heat. Fire. A hunger that would never be sated. Byron, the dark poet. Brooding. Mysterious. A man for fantasies. She had no idea of his age. He often answered the summons of her music. Ever since the day four months earlier when he saved her beloved grandfather from a car accident, he would suddenly appear in the room with her, somehow getting past the security to sit quietly while she played. It was a degree of her obsession that she never questioned him, never asked him how he managed to get into her home, into her music room.

Antonietta always knew the moment Byron entered the room, although he never made a sound. Her family had no idea how often he came, appearing in the great music room late at night and staying up till all hours with her. He rarely talked, just listened to the music, but sometimes they played chess or discussed books and world affairs. Those were the times she loved best, sitting and listening to the sound of his voice.

He had courtly, Old World mannerisms and spoke with an accent she couldn't quite place. She imagined him a chivalrous prince coming to call whenever she allowed her girlish imagination to get the better of her. He rarely touched her, but he never objected when she touched him, reading his expressions. He took her breath away each time he came into the same room with her.

The music swelled beneath her fingers, rose to a crescendo of rioting emotions. Byron. Her grandfather's friend. The rest of her family were wary and on edge around him. Most left the room soon after he entered. They thought him dangerous. Antonietta thought he might be, despite the fact that he was unfailingly gentle with her. She sensed behind Byron's calm exterior a predator hunting. Watching. Waiting. Biding his time. It only added to his allure. The unattainable fantasy. The dangerous, dark prince lurking in the shadows . . . watching . . . her.

Antonietta laughed again at her own fanciful nonsense. She presented a certain image to the world: a confident, renowned concert pianist and respected composer. She dreamed her passionate dreams and turned each of them into soaring notes of music to express the fires burning deep inside where no one could see.

Her fingers raced across the keys, fluttered and coaxed, so that the music took on life. There was no warning whatsoever. One moment she was lost in her music, and the next, a rough hand clapped over her mouth and dragged her backward off the piano bench.

Antonietta bit down hard, reaching back to pound at the face of her assailant. It was then she really noticed how leaden her body felt, sluggish, almost unwilling to follow her orders. Rather than striking hard, she barely tapped the man. She had the impression of strength. He smelled of alcohol and mints. He thrust a cloth over her nose and mouth.

Antonietta coughed, thrashed in an effort to be rid of the foul-smelling material. She felt dizzy and lost the ability to move, sliding down, down toward semiconsciousness. At once she stopped fighting, slumping like a rag doll, pretending she was already unconscious. The cloth disappeared, and her assailant lifted her.

She was aware of being carried, of someone breathing hard. Of her heart pounding. Then they were outside in the biting cold and piercing wind. The sea raged and thundered loudly, and sea spray reached her face.

It took a few moments to realize that they were not alone. She heard a man's voice, slurred, incoherent, asking something. A chill went down her spine. Her grandfather, frail at eighty-two, was being dragged up the path to the cliffs right along with her. Determined not to allow anything to happen to him, Antonietta fought her way back, breathing deeply to draw oxygen into her laboring lungs, gathering her strength, biding her time. In her mind she began to chant his name, using it as a prayer, a litany of strength: *Byron. Byron. I need you now. Hurry, hurry. Byron. Where are you?*

Byron Justicano circled above the small city before winging his way toward the palazzo. As he moved across the sky, hunger crawled through his body, demanding he feed, but he ignored it, answering the sudden uneasy feeling churning in his gut. Something was wrong. Some intangible vibration in the air made him aware of the drama unfolding on the rocks below. A snarl exposed his fangs. Eyes glowed a frightening red in the dark of the night. A savage, bestial growl escaped his throat as he increased his speed, hurtling through the sky over the towering palazzo with its many stories and turrets and battlements.

Above the many terraces and lofty stories loomed a high, rounded tower where it was rumored more than one woman had been murdered in the murky past, earning the palace the dubious name of Palazzo della Morte. Winged gargoyles stared blankly at him out of the heavy, white fog, looking almost real as the creatures seemed to swarm up the side of the villa. Sitting on the craggy cliffs above the raging sea, the sprawling castle was dark and foreboding with the blank eyes of the statuary always watching.

The heavy forests that had once grown wild, a refuge to a multitude of animals, were long gone, replaced by groves and grapes. Byron preferred the freedom of the forests and mountains of his homeland, where he could run with the wolves if he desired, but the need to protect the occupant at the palazzo had become all consuming.

Alarm spread, a premonition of danger he couldn't shake.

Byron increased his speed, streaking through the sky, flying low over the sprawling estate. The palazzo rose up out of the fog, architecture belonging to an era long gone, made of stone and stained glass, almost alive in the swirling mists. Byron ignored the ancient statues and the gleaming windows piercing the fog like so many eyes.

He first heard the voice whisper in his mind. *Byron. Byron. I need you now. Hurry. Hurry. Byron. Where are you?* She had never used a telepathic connection to him before. He had never taken her blood, yet he heard the words clearly and knew her need must be great to reach out to him.

Wicked forks of lightning whipped from cloud to cloud, anger he couldn't contain. She was in danger! Someone dared to threaten her. The sky roared, thunder splitting open the heavens to reveal a fury of flame. He took a breath, fought to control the elemental fear for her. The ground was reacting, rolling and buckling in answer to his mounting anger.

Byron hurried out toward the cove and the jagged rocks with his pulse pounding to the beat of the sea. The wind shifted and brought the haunting echo of a scream. His heart nearly stopped beating in his chest. It was the sound of despair, of death itself.

He swooped even lower over the sea, uncaring that he might be seen and discovered for the predator he was. Waves leapt toward the heavens, foamed, and collapsed with an angry boom, greedy for a living sacrifice.

"Byron!" This time she called his name aloud, her only chance while the clouds spun dark threads and the fog thickened in an attempt to cut off all escape. "Help us." The wind whipped the cry out over the roiling waves, straight to him.

There was a plea in her voice, soft and musical and alive with awareness. She knew he was close, as she always seemed to know. Antonietta Scarletti. Heiress to the Scarletti fortune. Composer of the most beautiful music the world had known in a long time and owner of the priceless Scarletti palazzo. The Palazzo della Morte, palace of death. Byron feared the curse of the palazzo would bring death to Antonietta, and he was determined to stop it.

Her voice brought alive the colors of the night, sharp and vivid and focused, where for so long there had been nothing but bleak gray. His heart stuttered, stammered, as it always did at the unexpected gift. It was that way each time he heard her voice, when she spoke his name in velvet tones. When she lit his world with colors and vivid details he had long ago lost.

Byron flew so low the churning waves splattered him with water as he raced over the choppy surface straight toward the sound of her voice. Through the swirling mists Byron saw Don Giovanni Scarletti in the greedy sea, clawing desperately for a purchase on the slick boulders. The waves slammed the old man hard, tossed him as if he were a small string of kelp, nothing more. The foaming water closed over the gray head and took him under.

"Byron!" The call came again. Haunting. Unforgettable. He knew he would hear that voice echo forever in his dreams.

She was up in the jagged rocks, near the edge of the crumbling cliffs, struggling with a large man. Below her, the water slammed against the rocks, reaching higher and higher as if to drag her down. It was only the increasing fury of the storm, the earthquake sending shocks through the cliff that prevented Antonietta's attacker from flinging her into the sea. The man staggered, nearly fell, even as he wrestled with her. Lightning exploded around them, whips of energy rained hot, glowing sparks. Thunder crashed so loud the man yelled in fear.

Fangs exploded in Byron's mouth, black venom swirled in his gut. He was on them in an instant, uncaring of his enormous strength, catching Antonietta's assailant by the nape of his neck and wrenching him backward, away from her. With the ferocity of his animal nature, with the rage of his human side, he shook Antonietta's attacker, his hands crushing the throat. An ominous crack was loud, even with the sea roaring in accompaniment to his rage.

Byron dropped the body carelessly, allowing the empty carcass to crumple to the ground. He turned quickly toward Antonietta. She was moving to get away from them, her arms stretched out full length to try to feel her way. There was nothing but empty space in front of her and the sea below, swelling and booming with relentless fury.

"Stop! Don't move, not a single step!" The command

thundered through the night air, reached her atop the cliffs. Trusting she would obey that merciless compulsion, Byron plunged straight into the sea. Diving deep, down into the cold, dark abyss until his fingers found the material of the old man's collar, and he grasped it hard in his fist, kicking strongly to bring them both to the surface.

Byron shot from the sea, straight into the air, dragging the leaden body against his own as he headed for the top of the cliffs. The white mist thickened and swirled around him like a living cape, creating a shield from prying eyes. The old man choked and gasped for air, for life. He clung convulsively to Byron, not quite aware of his surroundings, not able to believe he was hurtling through space. Don Giovanni, grandfather to Antonietta, had his eyes tightly shut while his chest heaved and saltwater spewed from his mouth. The water poured from their clothing and hair, adding to the droplets of mist in the air as Byron alighted on the ground.

The old man began to pray loudly in his own language, calling on the angels to save him, but he never once opened his eyes.

Antonietta turned toward the sound, but her feet remained perilously close to the edge of the cliff, exactly where they had been when Byron roared his command. His heart in his throat, Byron carefully stretched the old man out on the ground, well away from the edge, and rushed to gather Antonietta into his arms. Into safety. Holding her tightly, knowing she was safe, he forced air through his lungs, forced down his rage and fear to allow the violent storm to calm.

Despite the fact that his clothing was soaked, she burrowed close to him, her hands finding his face unerringly, mapping his features with loving fingertips. "I knew you'd come. Our guardian angel. My grandfather? Is Nonno going to be all right? I heard him fall into the sea. I couldn't get to him. I couldn't see to get to him." She turned her head toward the coughs and grunts the older man was making, tears glistening in her huge, dark eyes.

"He will be fine, Antonietta," Byron assured her. "I will not allow him to be anything else." And he meant it. He couldn't bear the sight of tears in her eyes.

"You saved him, didn't you, Byron? That's why you're soaked. You always come to us when there's trouble. *Grazie,*

I cannot live without my grandfather." She stood on her toes, her body soft and pliant, melting against his hard strength, oblivious to his soaked clothing, and she pressed her mouth to the corner of his.

That small tribute shook him to the very core of his being. Fire streaked through his veins. Every cell in his body reacted, reached for her. Needed. Hungered. His arms tightened possessively for just a moment. He made a conscious effort to remember his own strength, to remember she had no idea who or what he was.

Byron swung her up, cradling her body close. She was shivering in the biting wind. "Did he hurt you? Are you injured, Antonietta?" It was a demand, pure and simple.

"No, just frightened. I was so frightened."

"What were you doing on the cliffs?" His voice was much harsher than he intended. "And where is the rest of your family?"

Her fingers moved over his face, an intimate exploration. She had read him many times, but this seemed different somehow, or maybe he was far too aware of her. "Someone put a cloth over my mouth and nose and dragged me outside. I was so afraid for Nonno. I could hear the sea." The pads of her fingers sent tiny flames dancing over his skin as she mapped his face. As she traced his frown. "The sea sounded angry, much like you sound right now. I couldn't get to Grandfather, and I heard him fall over the cliff." She was silent a moment, dropping her head to his shoulder. "I was struggling with the man who dragged me out here. He was trying to throw me into the sea, too." Her voice was shaking, but Antonietta struggled for composure.

"Did he say anything to you?"

She shook her head. "I didn't recognize anything about him. I'm certain he's never been to the palazzo before. No one said anything to us, they just tried to throw us into the water."

Byron set her carefully on the ground beside the old man. "I want to take a look at your grandfather. I think he swallowed half the sea. Do not move. It is dangerous up here. You are on the high cliffs, where the edges are crumbling, and the fall could kill you." He couldn't look at the innocence on her face, the childlike trust there. He knew she belonged to him, yet he had once again failed to keep safe those he was sworn to protect. "You do not realize it, Antonietta, but you are in shock. Do not move, just sit here and breathe for me."

He came from an ancient race, a species that could claim immortality. He had seen the passage of time, witnessed his race nearing extinction. Without women and children, it was impossible to live anything other than a bleak, soulless existence. Unless one was lucky enough to find his lifemate. Antonietta Scarletti was his lifemate. He knew it unerringly. She came from a long line of psychics, people gifted with talents beyond mere sight. Byron had listened often to the history of her family. He knew that many of Antonietta's ancestors, both male and female, were strong telepaths and healers. Only a human who was psychic could be lifemate to one of the ancient Carpathian race. Antonietta Scarletti was a very strong psychic.

Don Giovanni struggled to sit up, his chest heaving while he gasped for air. He caught at Bryon's wide shoulders with gnarled hands. "How did you know to come? The sea claimed my life, but you brought me back." His teeth were chattering with cold, his thin body shaking uncontrollably. "That is twice now that you have saved me."

Byron held him gently. "Do not talk so much, old friend. Let me see what I can do to take the chill from you."

Antonietta couldn't see Byron, but as always, the sound of his voice intrigued her. It was beautiful and compelling, much like the symphony of music always playing in her head. She wanted to think of him as her grandfather's friend, but it was a difficult task when she listened for the sound of his voice and hungered for the slightest physical contact between them.

Antonietta learned years earlier that she was not the kind of woman men looked at for reasons other than her fortune. She had far too much Scarletti pride to be loved for her money. She didn't believe in buying a man, although she knew many women in her position did so. She was no young girl to dream of white knights. She was fully grown, with a woman's voluptuous figure and a face scarred by the blast of an explosion that had robbed her of her sight. There was no handsome lover on a white charger ready to whisk her away for endless nights of romance. She was a practical woman, a successful pianist and composer, who poured all of her dreams into her music where they belonged.

Antonietta carefully ran her hands over her grandfather, to see him, to assure herself he would survive his escape from the sea. Her hands encountered Byron. She rested her fingers lightly on the back of his hand. He never showed annoyance when she touched him. He never acted repulsed or impatient with her. He simply continued with what he was doing, while her hands rested on his. She could hear the steady rhythm of his breathing, slow and uniform, so that her breath, moving in and out of her lungs with such frantic intensity, slowed to follow his lead.

Byron's hands generated tremendous heat. She could feel it flowing like a fine wine into her grandfather's veins, slowly warming him. She didn't dare speak, but she *felt* him. Heard his breath, his heart. She saw things without her eyes that others couldn't see. She knew Byron was far more than a mortal man. Right now he was a miracle worker. She saw him so clearly, yet it was only through her fingertips resting so lightly on the backs of his hands.

Byron closed his eyes and shut out all the sounds and scents of the night. It was difficult to get beyond the touch of the woman he was always so aware of, but his examination had detected something in the older man's lungs. Don Giovanni was too old and fragile to fight off infection or pneumonia. Byron separated himself from his body, setting his spirit free to enter the aging man lying so cold and helpless on the rocks. Healing in the way of his kind, from the inside out, Byron made a thorough inspection, determined to give Antonietta's grandfather as many years of life as possible.

The wind rushed across the cliffs, pierced right through Antonietta's clothing in spite of the fact that Byron had positioned his body between hers and the wind. She could feel the warmth radiating from Byron into her grandfather. But there was something much more, something even more rare. She understood it, and she believed in it. Byron Justicano had left his own body and entered that of her grandfather's. She didn't need eyes to see the miracle of a natural healer. She *felt* him. Felt the energy and the heat. She knew it required total concentration, so she did nothing to distract him. She sat in the biting cold and thanked the heavens Byron had come to her family to watch over them.

"There is poison in his system." Byron's grim voice startled her. "Small amounts as if he is being fed them, but it is in his muscles and tissues."

"That can't be," Antonietta denied. "You have to be wrong. Who would want to harm Nonno? He is much loved by the family. And how could such a thing happen accidentally? You must be mistaken."

"When I was young and impetuous, I made mistakes, Antonietta. Now I am much more careful in the things I say and do. In the things I covet or seek to call my own. I am most careful in my friendships. Don Giovanni has been poisoned, much like his ancestor before him. Is that not the legend of the Scarletti family?"

Antonietta shivered, lifted her hands away from Byron in hopes he wouldn't notice her reaction. "Yes, centuries ago, another Don Giovanni, an ancestor of ours, and his young niece were poisoned. The healer was sent for, and Nicoletta arrived to aid them. He chose her as his bride. I don't believe in curses, Byron. There is no curse over my home or my family." She slipped her arm around her grandfather.

"I tell you there is a poison in his system that will eventually kill him if more accumulates. There is also the remnant of a drug to make him sleep. When I examine you, I am certain I will find the same thing."

"Do you suspect my chef of trying to kill me?" Antonietta gripped her grandfather hard, hanging on to her poise by a mere thread. "That is ludicrous, Byron. He would have nothing to gain. Enrico's been in our family since I was a child, and he's completely devoted and loyal to every member of the Scarletti family."

"I did not mention your chef, Antonietta," he replied patiently. "That may be your best guess, but it is not mine." When she remained stubbornly silent, he sighed his exasperation. "I must remove the poison from your grandfather. Then I will attend to you." His teeth gleamed very white in the darkness, but she didn't see, she could only hear the promise of menace in his voice.

It made her shiver, aware that she knew very little about

him. "Byron." She said his name to keep calm, to remind herself he had always been gentle with her. A guardian watching over them. Antonietta had always been safe with him. She wouldn't allow the aftermath of the attack to weaken her nerves and make her fear the very man who had come to her rescue. "It is true that accidents have always plagued the lives of the Scarletti family. There have been intrigues, political and otherwise. Our family has always had a great deal of power and money."

"Your own parents were killed when your yacht exploded. You were blinded, Antonietta. It was only luck that a fisherman was in the vicinity and got to you before the sea swallowed you."

"An accident." It came out a whisper when she wanted to sound certain.

"You want to believe it was an accident, but you know better." There was a distinct bite to his voice. She had the impression he wanted to shake her.

She would not talk about the explosion on the yacht that had blinded her and left her an orphan. There was guilt and fear and too many other emotions. She kept that door firmly closed in her mind. "Who is he?" She knew her assailant was dead. It should have frightened her that Byron had killed so swiftly, so efficiently, but truthfully, she was grateful.

"I have no idea, but he could not possibly have done this alone. Someone had to have drugged you both, someone within the palazzo. And it would take two people to bring you both up here. It isn't that far, but the path is steep, and with both of you drugged, it wouldn't have been easy. It would have made better sense to heave you both into the sea. One of them must have been in a hurry to do something else."

"What of my family, Byron?" Antonietta's fingers plucked at his sleeve. "They are perhaps helpless, drugged in their beds, awaiting their fate as we speak. Please go to them."

"It is more likely they are searching for something, not intending to murder your entire family."

Antonietta gasped, one hand going to her throat. "We have many treasures. Priceless art. Jewels. Artifacts. Our ships carry classified cargo, the manifest is usually kept in the offices at the palazzo rather than in the offices on the dock because the security system is so much better. They could be after anything."

"Go, Byron," Don Giovanni encouraged. "You must see to it that my family is safe. Scarletti is an old and revered name. We can't have any doubt on our reputation. Make certain nothing has been taken from the office."

"You want me to leave you both here, unprotected on the cliffs? That would be far too dangerous." Byron simply stood, lifting the old man, drawing Antonietta up as he did so. "I will take you both to the palazzo with me. Put your arms around my neck, Antonietta."

A protest welled in her mind. She was too heavy. He couldn't carry both of them. He had to hurry. Sensing his impatience, Antonietta remained silent and did as he instructed, circling his neck with her arms. Her body pressed close to his. Byron's muscular body was as hard as a tree trunk. She had never felt more feminine, more aware of how curvy and soft her form was. She simply melted into him.

Antonietta was thankful it was night and the darkness hid the faint blush stealing under her skin. She should have been thinking of the honor of her family name; instead, she was thinking of him: Byron Justicano. She clung tightly to him. One of his arms wrapped securely around her waist. Almost at once she felt her feet leave the ground. Her grandfather cried out in fear, thrashing against the restraint. Byron murmured something softly to him, something she didn't catch, but his tone was commanding. Her grandfather subsided, going so quiet she thought he must have fainted.

She turned her face up to the wind, relaxing, wanting to savor every moment. She was blind, but she was alive. She lived in a world of sounds and textures, rich and wonderful, and she wanted to experience everything life could offer. She was moving through space, across the sky, with the sea boiling and thundering below her and the clouds roiling above her. And she was safe in Byron's arms.

What should have been the worst night of her life had turned into the experience of a lifetime. "Byron." She whispered his name, an ache in her voice, thinking the wind would take the sound far from them, out over the ocean where no one would hear her most secret desire.

Byron buried his face in the fragrance of her hair as they

soared across the sky. There was no fear in Antonietta. He rarely detected fear in her. Because her brain patterns were so different, it was difficult to read her mind, where he could most humans. Now that his heart had settled back to a natural rhythm, he could admire the way she fought for her life there on the cliffs. She was an extraordinary woman, and she belonged to him. She just didn't realize it yet.

Antonietta had a strong personality and a determination to control her life and her business. Claiming her in the way of his people, Byron suspected, would not only make her resistant but would cause her great unhappiness. Years earlier, he had learned a hard lesson of attempting to take something too fast, for his own benefit, without thought of consequences.

Antonietta was his world. He could put aside his own needs and urges and the terrible hunger to give her the things she needed. He would have her, he knew that. There was no other choice for either of them, but he wanted her to come to him willingly. To choose him. To choose his life, his world. And even more, he wanted to give her all the things he suspected she had never had in her life. He wanted her to know her own worth as a woman. Not a Scarletti. Not a pianist. Not a shipping magnate. A woman.

"Are you afraid?" He whispered the words, half aloud, half in her mind. Knowing she wasn't and wanting her to acknowledge what they were doing. He hadn't protected her from their method of traveling. She might be blind, but she was more aware than any other human he knew.

Antonietta laughed, the sound one of joy. "How could I be afraid, Byron? I'm with you. I'm not going to ask how you do this until my feet are safely on the ground." She answered him as honestly as she could. There was a wild exhilaration in her heart. If she was truly afraid, it was only of the unknown. Soaring through the sky was a dream, a fantasy come true. Her childhood dreams of flying had been so vivid she often believed she had soared across the night skies. "I do wish I could see the view." There was a wistful note she couldn't keep from her voice, and she was ashamed that he heard it. "I wish you had the time to describe it to me."

"There is a way you could see what I see." His heart was

pounding now. The moment he noticed, he allowed it to seek the rhythm of hers. To connect them, heart to heart.

Antonietta's grip tightened around his neck. For the first time, she turned her face into his throat. He could feel her breath warm on his throat, and his body tightened in reaction. In anticipation. "What are you saying?" Now it was her heart that was pounding. He could work miracles. Heal. Hear a call for help across the raging sea. Dive deep into roiling surf and pull a drowning man from the depths, carrying him to safety. Soar through the night sky while carrying two adults as if they weighed no more than small children. She dared not hope for the impossible.

Her voice was low, but her lips were pressed against his skin. Against his pulse. Byron's body burned with heat, throbbed with need, with hunger. She seemed unaware of his reaction. He fought the nearly overwhelming urge of his kind, keeping his face turned from her, from the temptation she presented. He couldn't answer her with his incisors lengthened and his body craving hers.

Fortunately, they were close to the great palazzo. Byron turned his attention to finding the location of every human in the area. He scanned the villa and the surrounding region. The aftermath of violence still vibrated in the air, but if the other conspirator had rushed back to the villa to find the manifest for cargo or the Scarletti family treasures, he had already managed to do so and was long gone, or he was in his bed feigning sleep. Byron could detect no foreign enemy present within the walls.

Family members were sleeping peacefully in their own beds. The entire household seemed to be unaware of the attack on Antonietta and Don Giovanni. Suspicion found its way into his heart.

2

Byron *did not* put Don Giovanni or Antonietta down until he entered the old man's room.

"The alarms should be going off," Antonietta said. "Intruders should have triggered them. How did they get in? How do you get in?"

"Not the same way they entered," Byron replied with absolute conviction. "There is no intruder present in the palazzo at this time."

"You can't know that," Antonietta pointed out. "There are over a hundred rooms in our home. They could be hiding anywhere. You haven't even checked the office."

"I will conduct a search later, only to see what they have been up to. There are no intruders, only your family in their beds," Byron repeated patiently. "Don Giovanni is freezing from the seawater and chilling wind. His temperature is dropping at an alarming rate. Go to your room and take a hot bath, Antonietta," he said, his tone abrupt and clipped as he began stripping the elderly man. "You are shaking with cold."

"I don't much care to be ordered about," Antonietta responded. Her teeth were chattering, although she tried desperately to stop them. She was cold through and through. "Don Giovanni is my grandfather and my responsibility."

"Then give him the dignity he deserves." Byron's voice had gone so soft it was black velvet. And it made her shiver.

Antonietta took a step backward. For a moment a lump welled up in her throat, threatening to choke her. Her eyes burned. She hadn't cried in years.

His fingers caught her chin in a firm grip. "I do not mean to sound abrupt, but I have little time for necessities. If I have offended you, I am sorry. Your grandfather's heart is weak, and his resistance is low, even with my earlier ministrations." He bent his head to hers. Touched his mouth to hers. Feather light, a mere brush. She felt it all the way to her toes. Heat curled in the pit of her stomach. For a moment she couldn't think clearly, couldn't think why she wanted to cry.

"Because someone tried to kill you and your grandfather," he answered for her. "Someone poisoned him and most likely you and also drugged you both. You are tired and cold, and I was curt in my manner of speaking. Anyone would cry, Antonietta. I will see to Don Giovanni while you take a hot bath and get in a warm bed."

Byron sounded so tender her heart turned over and tears burned behind her eyes. His hand dropped away from her, and she turned to go, compelled by the beauty of his voice, his soothing logic. She even took a step away from him before she realized what she was doing. "*Grazie*, Byron, but Nonno may need my assistance in the bath. I can't see him, I'm blind, you know." Byron was the only person who made her feel as if he never noticed she was blind.

Byron tossed Don Giovanni's sodden shirt to one side. "You do not have to do everything, *cara mia*. Go now. I will attend him in the shower and get him settled."

"Go." Don Giovanni waved a trembling hand toward the door. "Do as he says, Toni, go to your bath. I will be fine. In fact, both of you go. I want you to look after her for me, Byron. See to it that she changes into something warm."

"Nonno!" Antonietta was shocked. "I may be blind, but I assure you, Byron is not. I don't think he can attend me in my bath."

"I want her protected. Suppose they come back?" Don Giovanni ignored his granddaughter's protest. "You stay with her at all times."

"It will not matter, Don Giovanni, whether they come back or not. They will never again put their hands on your granddaughter."

Byron leaned into Antonietta, and for the first time she felt his body tremble. Rage was a living, breathing entity in the room with them. The air thickened into a heavy mass, a dark cloud of roiling energy until it was difficult to breathe.

Deep inside Byron, the demon roared for release, called for retribution. Demanded he take her away where no harm could possibly reach her. "It is far safer in your bath alone than with me standing guard at the moment, *cara*. Allow me to attend your grandfather in peace." His voice hissed out between his teeth. A promise. A vow. An absolute conviction.

Trying to be dignified with her teeth clacking together and her body shivering uncontrollably was difficult, but Antonietta was a Scarletti. She lifted her chin. "The authorities must be notified. I think there's a body on the cliffs."

"A body?" Don Giovanni sank onto a chair while Byron gently removed his saturated shoes and socks. "Whose body?"

Byron shrugged casually. "One of them was trying to throw Antonietta into the sea. I may have wrenched him a bit too hard. I was angry and afraid for her, and I was not thinking of my own strength."

Don Giovanni shook his head. "Better the body go into the sea, and we know nothing of what happened to him. You struggled, he fell. It is better not to take chances with the authorities in the matter of death."

"Nonno!" Antonietta was shocked.

"If you keep standing there with wet clothes, shaking like a leaf, I am carrying you up to your bath and putting you in it myself," Byron said. "I will not be responsible for what happens after that. Do not make the mistake of thinking I am jesting."

Her heart jumped, began to pound at his words. She did her best to look irritated before touching her grandfather's hand as she swept from the room.

"You never take your eyes off of her," Don Giovanni said approvingly. "That is good. I wanted a man like you for her. She's strong-willed, Byron." The red-rimmed eyes regarded him steadily. "You could hurt her."

"Not me, Don Giovanni. Never me." Byron helped the old man to stand. "Lean against me, and we will make our way to the shower."

"I'm too weak to stand by myself," Don Giovanni admitted, ashamed.

"I will not drop you, old friend," Byron encouraged gently. He allowed the man to take staggering steps to cross the room to his private bath rather than arbitrarily lifting him. Instinctively he knew Don Giovanni's pride would insist on that small independence, even if his body were too weak to walk without assistance. "It has been quite a night. You are aware, of course, that both your life and that of your granddaughter are in danger. She needs protection, as will you."

Don Giovanni sighed as he reached with gnarled fingers for the glass door to his shower. "She's a stubborn one. I've relied too heavily on her, and she feels responsible for all of us now. She won't want to hire a bodyguard."

"I know." Byron helped the old man shed the last of his clothing and adjusted the temperature of the spray. "But it will be necessary. I cannot be here during most of the day. Why would someone want you both dead?"

Don Giovanni turned his face up to the spray while jets of water helped to heat the rest of his body. Byron was very matter-of-fact about standing with him in the shower, allowing the old man to hang on to him while the water poured over them. He waited until the don had stopped shivering so violently before he turned off the hot jets of water and enfolded the elderly man gently in a towel.

Carpathians regulated their own body temperatures, and it took a heartbeat to dress in dry clothes. The don hardly noticed as Byron helped him to put on his pajamas and crawl into bed. "Go to her, Byron. See that she comes to no harm."

"I will," Byron assured. "Sleep now, and do not worry." He used his hypnotic voice to persuade the don.

"What of the others? My other grandchildren? You were going to check on them for me. And my great-grandchildren?" Don Giovanni slurred his words.

"Sleep now." Byron gave him another gentle push with his mind. He drew the covers up to the older man's chest.

Because the elder Scarletti was restless even in his sleep, Byron chanted the ancient healing ritual aloud as he worked on ensuring all traces of poison were driven from Don Giovanni's body. It took longer than Byron thought it would, mostly because he worked on strengthening internal organs. "You cannot die for many years, old friend," he murmured as he rose. He looked around carefully, allowing his senses to flare out and reach the corners of the suite of rooms. "I have only recently met you, Don Giovanni, but you are important to me and to your granddaughter. I have great respect for a man such as you." He leaned very close, put his lips close to the don's ear. "You will live and be strong."

Someone had been in Don Giovanni's room recently. Someone who may or may not be of Scarletti blood. The scent permeated the room. Byron took his time, thoroughly canvassing the room for anything that could be lethal to Don Giovanni. He detected no living thing, not even a poisonous spider. The intruder had dragged the don from his bed. It would have taken only moments to overpower the old man. The intruder must have returned to the room after he had flung Don Giovanni from the cliff. And he was either a family member or servant, sleeping in the palazzo, although the scent wasn't familiar, or the intruder had left immediately after returning to the room, which didn't make sense.

Byron shifted shape, taking the form of a large wolf with dark reddish-brown fur. He lifted his muzzle to scent the room again. At once his lips drew back in a snarl. The odor was subtle but there. Wild. Feline. A predator. That explained the quick escape. Was a vampire involved in some act against the Scarletti family? A vampire would have taken the old man's blood, not simply thrown him into the sea. Vampires were wholly evil, wanting those around them to suffer endlessly.

The wolf began to search throughout the palazzo. How had the intruder come into the house without triggering the elaborate alarm system? Byron simply became mist in the way of his people and streamed through a partially closed window in one of the many unused rooms. Any vampire could do the same. The wolf trotted up the curving staircase on the east side of the palazzo where Antonietta's cousins made their home.

Antonietta shoved open the door to her rooms with the flat of her hand. She had moved much too quickly and was grateful the children hadn't left their toys out where she could trip over them. Ordinarily, they were very good about such things, but little Vincente sometimes forgot. More than once Antonietta had suffered a minor bruise and damaged pride stumbling over one of his trucks. Once, she would have tumbled down the stairs if Justine hadn't been with her to catch her. Vincente denied he was playing with his toys on the forbidden stairway, but his father, Franco, had punished him all the same. Marita, Vincente's mother, wrung her hands together and wept aloud for the terrible treatment of her son, but for once, Franco prevailed, furious that Antonietta had nearly tumbled down the marble stairs.

Thoughtfully, Antonietta closed the heavy door to her suite and leaned against it as it occurred to her that Vincente might have been telling the truth. Someone else could easily have put his toys at the top of the stairs in the hopes of causing an accident. *Darn you! You have me thinking conspiracy.*

There was a small silence. Byron was shocked that she had used the intimate form of communication between lifemates so easily. She was a strong telepath—and more. She often called him to her with her music, yet she seemed unaware of it. *You are finally coming to terms with what is happening around you. Deliberately closing your eyes to a possible threat is not wise.*

Antonietta began to slowly slip the small pearl buttons from the fastenings on her blouse. Her fingers were shaking with cold and maybe fear, so it was difficult to manage.

I could come and help you.

Antonietta gasped, looked around her room as if she might glimpse him there in her world of darkness.

His laughter was soft. Flirtatious. *The night belongs to me. I come out of the shadows. I can be anywhere. Even there in the room with you right now, helping you to undress.* There was a drawling caress in his tone that sent liquid fire racing through her body and pooling low into an aching need.

I always know when you're in the room with me, and you're not at this moment. Antonietta realized she was beginning to stop trembling, and she was smiling in spite of the events of the evening and the serious situation. Byron was deliberately warming her, making her relax. *I don't think helping me undress is a particularly good idea. What are you doing?*

The idea of helping you undress takes my breath away.

There was a short silence. Antonietta draped her blouse over the back of a chair. Her fingers trailed over the silk, wishing she were touching Byron's chest. The idea of him helping her undress robbed her of breath, too. Of speech. She couldn't think straight. Dragging the tie from her hair, she began to pull out the weave as she crossed to her bathroom.

I am searching the palazzo to see what the intruders were up to and examining your cousins to make certain they were not fed poison or drugged. A much more interesting question is, what are you doing?

I'm taking the braid out of my hair.

Byron closed his eyes and inhaled sharply as if he could drag her scent deep inside his body. *There is something very erotic about a woman letting down her hair. Have you removed your slacks?*

My blouse. She admitted it without hesitation. It was part of her dreamworld. He was far away and it was a harmless game. And it distracted her from thinking about the terrors of being nearly killed. Of someone hating her enough to want to kill her. Antonietta's fingertips moved across the swell of her breasts. She ached for his touch. She had never wanted a man more. *It doesn't make sense.*

It makes perfect sense.

She had never talked with any man this way, not even a lover. She had never blushed or stammered or deliberately tempted a man. Byron never once had given her an indication that he was interested in her as other than a friend. She might even be making a fool of herself, but it didn't matter. He was an obsession.

As she made her way across the tiled bathroom floor, colored images leapt in front of her eyes without any warning. Shades of vivid red and yellow. She cried out, closing her eyes instinctively. The colors were so intense they hurt her, made her feel ill.

What is it?

She was disoriented, frozen to the spot, unable to tell exactly where she was in her own bathroom. *I see something. Colors. Red and yellow. Like heat images.*

Take a deep breath, your heart is beating too fast. It is nothing. Let the images go. You may have been seeing what I was seeing. Our connection is strong. Byron bit back the ominous growl in this throat, hackles rising. He shifted shape back to his human form and bent over her sleeping cousin.

Cautiously, Antonietta opened her eyes and saw the comforting darkness. *That made me sick to my stomach. How strange.* Rather than use the centuries-old bathing pools, now modernized, Antonietta filled her private bathtub and tossed in scented salts. She wanted to feel beautiful tonight. She needed to feel beautiful.

Where are you? She didn't want to be alone. In spite of her bravado, she was frightened by the events of the evening and wanted the comfort of Byron's powerful presence. She peeled off her damp slacks and laid them carefully on the vanity. The simple act of removing her lacy bra and panties made her feel sexy. A tempting siren.

She stepped into the bath, sank into the blessedly hot water, and allowed her head to fall back against the side of the tub.

I am standing over your cousin Paul. He is sleeping deeply, and I do not think it is a normal sleep. I must spend a few minutes examining him. Are the windows in your rooms closed and secured?

Her breasts floated on the scented water as she relaxed. *I didn't think to check. I will before I go to bed.*

Have you smelled a strange odor? A wild cat. Large breed.

Antonietta sat up straight, the water beading, rushing down her skin. *Why would you think that? What made you ask me that?*

Byron was silent, analyzing her voice. There was fear in her tone. Fear in her mind, but her barriers were intact and strong. For a moment he considered pushing through to get the information he needed, but she was his lifemate, and he had learned, all too well, the danger of trying to force and manipulate. Patience, he reminded himself. Above all, a Carpathian male could endure.

Antonietta could not escape him, now that he found her. He had not counted on danger in her own home.

Byron? Why would you think I would smell a wild cat?

She sounded very anxious. For the first time he wished he could see images around her through her eyes. He felt textures through her, but there were no images to aid him. He had to use feelings. Emotions were still somewhat alien and overpowering. It made him dangerous and near the edge of control.

I smell a cat here, in this room. And also I smelled the same creature in your grandfather's room. He answered truthfully because she was his lifemate, but his instincts told him she knew something he did not.

Are you with Paul or Franco?

Paul.

There was another long silence. He tuned his acute hearing to finding her room. Bathwater splashed as if she were agitated. He closed his eyes with a small groan, picturing her lush body naked and floating in the scented water. Her silky hair would be surrounding her, an allure he would never be able to resist.

His entire body tightened, hardened to a painful ache. Antonietta. How much he wanted her. How difficult it was to wait. He savored every moment with her. And his creativity, so long gone, was returning, thanks to her.

Is it Paul? Does he have the scent of a cat? There was reluctance to her voice, as if she might be betraying someone . . . or something she held dear. And there was an underlying note of fear. She tried to hide it, but it was there.

Byron leaned over Paul, examining every inch of him, paying attention to his fingernails, his arms, looking for scratches, for any telltale sign that would indicate he had been a party to the attack on Don Giovanni and his granddaughter. There was one long scratch along the inside of his left forearm. It looked raw and angry.

Byron! Please, does he have the scent of the cat?

The Scarletti palazzo and the family dwelling there had nearly as many secrets as his own people. Byron inhaled deeply. The scent of the cat permeated the room. It was difficult to tell if Paul had the scent or not. *I have no idea. It reeks in here of the scent. If it is not Paul, the cat has been here. Do you keep large cats or know someone who does?*

A slight noise downstairs distracted him immediately. Byron's head snapped up, and his black eyes flashed with instant menace. Someone was making their way up the long, curving staircase. Soft, stealthy footfalls. Furtive. The whisper of material against the thick banister sounded overly loud to Byron. A small, wolfish smile softened the hard edge to his mouth. Not bothering to scan, he simply waited in the darkness for his prey to come to him.

Of course not.

The footsteps were at the top of the first landing. Whoever it was hesitated, then turned toward Paul's suite of rooms. Byron shrank back into the shadows. His lengthened incisors were exposed, and when the door opened just a crack, the dim light from the hall turned his eyes a fiery bloodred.

He knew her instantly. Antonietta's trusted assistant, Justine Travis, stepped cautiously inside the room, closing the door behind her. She took several steps into the middle of the room but stopped, not attempting to cross to the bed.

"Paul?"

Silence greeted her. The man in the bed didn't stir. Byron was certain he had been drugged, but it was necessary to check him. Either way, it didn't make him innocent. A smart man might try to commit murder and drug himself to make it appear as if he were in danger, too.

Hunger stirred, a dark and terrible need that welled up sharp and overpowering. Byron had not fed, and he had used considerable energy saving Don Giovanni from the cold depths of the sea. Healing had drained him, driving out the poison from the fragile system, and now he craved and needed. He could hear the call of the rich, hot blood rushing through veins bursting with the life his shrunken cells needed. He moved, a blink of the eye, no more, and he stood behind Justine. Her hair was drawn up into a simple ponytail, pulled away from her neck and leaving her throat exposed. He could see her pulse beating rapidly.

Justine sighed and wrung her hands together in obvious agitation. "Paul, wake up. I have to talk to you. I'm sorry

we fought, but you have to understand I can't risk my job."
Justine touched her throat with her palm, a defensive movement as if she sensed the predator so close to her. "You know
I'll do anything to help you. We'll find another way to get
the money. I'll help you, I will."

Paul didn't respond but continued to lie motionless on the
bed.

Justine sobbed softly. "I didn't mean it when I said we
were over. I'll find a way to help you, Paul. Don't do anything rash until I figure things out. You know you would feel
so awful if you did anything that would harm or betray your
family." She waited a moment. "Please, Paul, answer me."
When Paul didn't answer or turn toward her, Justine jammed
her fist into her mouth to muffle her weeping.

A dark shadow fell across her so that Justine shivered and
half turned, her eyes widening with terror. The predator in
the shadows spoke softly to calm her, whispered a command
even as he enfolded her in his arms. She tilted her head and
gazed up at him with blind rapture.

Byron looked down into her face. Her mind was chaotic,
filled with thoughts of Paul. Of how she loved him, how she
didn't want to betray Antonietta but . . . He smiled, and there
was no humor in that smile, only a showing of fangs. "It is
in you to be treacherous, and you have chosen the wrong
alliance." His voice held a whip of contempt so that even
under his dark enthrallment, Justine winced. Byron bent his
head, teeth sinking into soft flesh, and drank.

Antonietta stepped from the bath, wrapping herself in a thick
towel. It was precisely ten steps to her vanity, and she sank
into the chair and reached for the brush that was always in
the right corner. The handle was cool and smooth and fit in
her hand as if made for her. It was an heirloom from the
past, but she loved it and used it nightly to brush her hair.
As she pulled the brush down the length of her hair, her neck
throbbed and burned right over her suddenly wildly pounding
pulse.

Startled, Antonietta dropped the brush and covered the
spot, reaching for Byron automatically. She found not her
calm, tranquil poet but a beast, raging with demonic hunger,

feasting, drawing energy and vitality from a warm, living creature. From a human . . . Abruptly, the connection was broken.

Antonietta choked, her hands fluttering to guard her throat while her mind tried to grasp the implication of the dark, shadowed beast roaring for release. Had she somehow connected with the wild cat Byron had scented in her cousin's room? Was her imagination simply playing tricks on her?

She was tired and frightened and wanted comfort. Where was he? Why hadn't he come to her? *Byron!* She called him sharply, terrified of needing him so much and torn between wanting him to come to her and hoping he would stay away. She was weak tonight, she might not be able to resist him. The last thing she wanted to do was destroy their friendship by making a fool of herself.

Byron heard Antonietta's beloved voice echoing through his mind. Touching his heart. Pulling at his soul. Awareness of where he was and what he was doing hit him. Immediately, he swept his tongue across Justine's throat to close the tiny pinpricks and slowly lifted his head, making every effort to pull back from the heady rush the infusion of fresh vitality gave him. For Antonietta's sake, because Justine was someone she cared for, he was gentler than he might have been as he lowered the woman to the floor and helped her to rest against the wall.

I am here.

Antonietta couldn't believe the relief sweeping through her body, through her mind. *For a moment I thought something was terribly wrong.* She felt along the floor for her brush. Her fingertips found the smooth handle. The towel unraveled, leaving her body exposed to the cool air. Outside, the rain began to pour against the stained glass windows. Antonietta walked across the floor. The marble tiles were cool on the soles of her feet. Her body was hot and flushed at the idea of him walking in on her unexpectedly. She had no idea why just the sound of his voice made her feel sexy. Made her want to tempt and entice him. He was always so cool and calm, and she wanted to drive him out of control.

I find I'm edgy and moody tonight, Antonietta admitted. She stood naked in front of the stained glass window, listened to the rain pouring down, and lifted her arms upward as an offering to the gods of fantasy. Of dreams. "Bring him to me. Let him come this night. Let me know he has looked at me as a woman and not as a bank account."

You should be in bed. Beneath the warmth of your covers, not flitting about your room. The idea was to keep you healthy.

How could a mere voice affect her so much? Set her body on fire, aching and needing and craving just one man. It made little sense to her. Antonietta turned from the window and moved unerringly to the tall dresser. Some time earlier in one of her moods of generosity, Tasha bought her a white lace nightgown, one Antonietta had never worn. It slithered over her skin, almost alive, heightening her senses and her body's terrible needs. It was a gown meant to lure. To tempt. It clung to every curve and showed off her skin. It made Antonietta feel a beautiful temptress.

Keep me healthy? How very prosaic.

You are edgy and moody. So am I. That could be a dangerous combination.

Antonietta braided her hair, reveling in the way the lace material caressed her skin. *Do you think so? You're probably right. I'm in a strange mood and hardly recognize myself.* She sighed as she pulled back the covers and slipped between the sheets.

Byron leaned down to check Justine's pulse. She was fine, just dizzy. He whispered to her, a soothing chant, planting the idea to go back to her room with no memory of her visit to Paul. Justine obeyed like a sleepwalker, falling under his hypnotic spell and going out, even quietly closing the door behind her.

It is no wonder, Antonietta. I am certain you will be unsettled for some time to come, and rightly so. Byron once more bent over Paul. Her cousin. A betrayer who might be plotting to take Antonietta's life. For a moment the urge to crush him beneath the strength of his hands rose up and nearly overwhelmed him. He bent closer, his incisors lengthening as he neared the pulse beating strongly in the neck. If he took Paul's blood, it would be easy enough to read his mind.

Byron! Antonietta's voice was sharp and frightened. *I have a terrible feeling you are going to hurt my cousin. Promise me you aren't.*

Byron closed his eyes, took a deep, calming breath to settle the demons roaring for release. There was too close of a connection. She would know. She would feel him. *Your imagination is running away with you, Antonietta.*

Why is it you always call me Antonietta? Everyone else calls me Toni.

Byron concentrated on the sound of relief in her voice. Antonietta, his lifeline to sanity and control, when his emotions were as powerful as the raging sea. *Your family calls you Toni. Everyone else calls you Signorina Scarletti, a title of great respect.*

That does not tell me why you won't call me Toni.

Antonietta is your name, and it is beautiful. He said it simply, with no embellishment.

Antonietta allowed her lashes to drift down. She was tired, and the steady rhythm of the rain was making her sleepy. Byron didn't say anything particularly romantic or brilliant, not even poetic, but she thought of it that way. *Your voice is hypnotic. I could listen to you forever.*

That is a good thing. It is nice to know we are making progress.

Well, I don't know why I'm suddenly telling you. I knew it the first time I heard your voice. I could just sit and listen to you forever. And after you leave, I hear the music playing in my head and through my body, and I know it's your music. It belongs to you more than it belongs to me.

That is the nicest compliment anyone has ever given me. Byron left Paul's room and made his way to the third floor where Franco Scarletti resided with his wife and two children. *I have decided you need a dog, Antonietta.*

Antonietta burst out laughing. *Only you would think I need a dog. I'm blind. How would I care for a dog? And don't suggest a Seeing Eye dog. I don't know the first thing about animals. They've always shied away from me.*

He could hear the interest in her voice in spite of herself, and he smiled. *You have not met the right dog. The animal world is unique and astonishing. The right dog is an invaluable companion. They can be devoted and loyal. The right dog picks you, bonds with you, and works with you.*

What kind of dog do you suggest is right for me?

Byron bent over the little girl sleeping so innocently and peacefully in her bed. The thought of an intruder harming the child had a snarl rising in his throat. The scent of the wild cat was strong in the room. Once Byron determined there were no drugs or poison in her system, he examined the windows for points of entry. Someone could have rappelled from the battlements above. Or a cat might have leapt from the battlements to an open window. He could find nothing to indicate entry in either child's room. He moved to the parents' room, taking the precaution of becoming unseen to the human eye.

The borzoi, of course. They are renowned hunters, and the breed has stayed true throughout centuries. They have been owned by royalty and certainly would be at home here in the palazzo. The borzois hunted wolf packs. Once, as a young Carpathian, not quite yet in full power, practicing his shape-shifting with Jacques, his best friend, two borzois had spotted them as they shifted to wolves in a field. The borzois were swift and silent hunters, running them down relentlessly. Neither were very fast at shifting at the time, and they barely made it to the trees, managing to clumsily shift shape and scramble for the high branches. Jacques had nearly fallen out of the tree laughing. It had taken them both several minutes to slow their heartbeats and connect with the borzois. Byron had a high respect for the animals ever since that time. They had the heart of a lion and the gentle nature of a lamb.

He had never seen an animal quite like the borzois and thought Queen Victoria very smart for wanting the creatures in her royal palace. It saddened him immensely when there was a wholesale slaughter of the intelligent, lethal, though gentle animals when the peasants rose up to destroy anything that could possibly have the mark of royalty. Perhaps he identified with them, as his species was hunted and they, too, could be both lethal and gentle. Byron didn't know the reason, but the borzois had always remained in his mind. More than anything, he wanted Antonietta to experience the bonding and loyalty as well as receive the protection of such a fine animal.

He couldn't very well tell her his own history with the borzois, so he chose another. *I saw a male one time protect its owner from everyone simply because she had an injured foot. He moved in close when she was limping, took her weight while they walked, and refused to leave her side the entire day, even giving up a hunt, which they are born and bred for. Hunting is in their bones, yet his devotion to his companion came first. They are extraordinary animals, and I do not say that lightly.*

Do you own dogs?

If I did, I would own borzois. I travel too much, and it would be unfair to the dog but if I ever am lucky enough to call a place home, I will have several. Franco Scarletti was turned toward his wife, one arm flung around her as if to hold her to him. Marita, his wife, faced away from him and even in her sleep looked unhappy. The air in the room was cold and Byron found the open window immediately. In spite of the wind, he could still scent the cat. It had visited Franco and Marita as well as the others.

With a soft, threatening growl, Byron made his way to Tasha's suite of rooms. She had the wing encompassing the dreaded tower where it was said a Scarletti male had strangled his wife and beat her lover to death. All of Tasha's rooms reeked of cat. The animal had spent some time in her wing of the palazzo. Like Franco and Marita and their children, Tasha showed no signs of either poison or drugs in her system.

The kitchen and the chef were next. The cat's stench invaded his lungs, clung to every part of the chef's private quarters and in the kitchen.

Antonietta? She was drowsy, and for some reason he found that more sensual than ever. He pictured her lying in bed, waiting for him. Her body already hot and wet and hungry for his. A soft groan escaped. Antonietta might flirt with him from a distance, but she had always remained aloof from him, even during their many quiet talks together. She didn't flirt often with men, which was a good thing, given that he found he had a jealous streak.

I'm still awake, thinking about having a dog. I don't know if I could care for it properly, but it would be nice not to feel so alone all the time.

Yes, it would. His answer was heartfelt and came directly from his soul. He was glad she was awake. He still had much to do. The body couldn't stay on the cliffs. Don Giovanni was right. It wouldn't do to give the authorities too much to think about. Yet Byron wanted to see Antonietta. He *needed* to see Antonietta. To touch her. To feel her warm skin beneath his fingers. To know she was alive and well.

3

"**H**ow did you get in here?" Antonietta wouldn't scream, although he had startled her from her sleep. It had always seemed a useless, pitiful reaction to an intruder. In any case, she knew exactly who was sitting on the end of her bed. She was more concerned that she had no dark glasses to hide her hideous scars and that the thick rope of hair was a mess from squirming restlessly. Waiting. Hoping he would come to her to tell her of her grandfather's condition. Certain that he wouldn't. It was one thing to carry on a long-distance conversation with him, flirtatious or not, and something altogether different to have him solid and real in her bedroom. Alone in her bedroom. Now that he was really there, her white lace gown seemed a ridiculous choice. She didn't want him to think she wore it on the chance that he would come to her, although of course, she had. She would *not* search for her robe and cover up the fine lace, drawing more attention to her lack of attire.

"You should be afraid of me, Antonietta," Byron reprimanded. "You have no sense of self-preservation whatsoever."

Antonietta cautiously sat up, gasped when his arm brushed her full breast as he reached past her to straighten her pillows. Her entire body went warm. He didn't apologize for the contact. Instead, his hands dropped lower to settle in her hair. She could feel the small tug on her braid. Her breath caught in her throat at the intimate contact. She was certain it was an accident, so she sat quietly with folded hands. To keep from feeling her burning body, she tilted her chin and concentrated on looking regal.

"I have plenty of self-preservation," she denied. "I had the presence of mind to call you when my grandfather fell into the sea."

"He did not fall into the sea, Antonietta. He was pushed. You know someone drugged the two of you and dragged you up onto the cliffs. And you know the man was hired to kill you both. This cannot be allowed to go on. I won't let it." There was resolution in his voice. "You cannot wish this attempt on your life away."

Something in his beautiful voice sent a chill down her spine. Byron was always so quiet. She thought of him as a dark, brooding, mysterious angel, sent to watch over her and her grandfather, yet he sounded dangerous. Antonietta forced a smile. "I don't wish things away, Byron, I deal with them. I run the palazzo, and my people believe in me. I don't let them down by pretending or wishing."

"Then stop closing your eyes to the possibility that someone wants you dead."

"You're reprimanding me as if I were a small child. I can't remember the last time anyone dared to do so. You even had the audacity to send me off to bed in my own home, which no one has dared to do since I was a child."

"You were freezing, Antonietta, and the temptation to put you in a hot tub and thoroughly bathe you was getting the better of me."

Her heart jumped. The sound of his voice was a caress, a stroke of fingers down her body. She felt it all the way to her toes. For a moment she couldn't think, let alone breathe. Antonietta held tightly to her fingers to keep them from trembling or to keep from reaching for him, running her hand over his chest. "That would have been quite an experience, Byron." She tried another carefree laugh, very much afraid it came out a husky croak. She could feel the intensity of his gaze burning over her face. A slow smolder began in the pit of her stomach.

"You have no idea what an experience it would be." His tone held a blatant sexual appeal. There was no mistaking it.

He was flirting with her. The idea was both exhilarating and frightening. "I need my dark glasses." She couldn't bear the thought of him staring into her dead eyes, seeing the scars, while she was going up in flames at the sound of his voice.

"Why? It is dark in your room. There is not even a small sliver of moon able to get through the clouds this night. And it is just me here with you." His fingers brushed her face. Feather-light. Tracing her high cheekbones, her wide, generous mouth. There was possession in the way he touched her, a man's clear interest.

Antonietta inhaled sharply, pressed back against the pillows, afraid she had made a fool of herself. "What are you doing?"

"Touching you. Feeling your skin. Maybe tonight did not scare you, but it terrified me. I have to know you are safe, so just sit there and let me do this."

"Byron, you're not making any sense. Of course I'm safe. I'm here in the palazzo, safe in my bed, thanks to you." She tried to be practical. Antonietta was always practical, even in her bed in a frivolous white lace nightgown.

He caught the nape of her neck, pulled her toward him. His mouth settled on hers and the earth moved. Shifted. Stilled. Antonietta melted. Byron burned. The kiss deepened into something molten; it was tender, hot, and merciless, all at the same time. The world exploded into a sizzling heat neither could recover from. Sparks leapt over skin, arced through them. Lightning danced in their veins.

Antonietta simply merged with him. She belonged. Had always belonged. Lord Byron, her dark, brooding poet with his black velvet voice and his mysterious ways. She gave herself up to him, embraced the magic of the moment, pouring the fiery passion welling up inside of her into her response, matching him heartbeat for heartbeat, flame for flame.

Byron growled deep in his throat, sounding more beast

than man. He lifted his head just inches away from her. "Do you have any idea what you do to me?"

His breath was warm on her skin. His lips brushed the corner of her mouth. A caress? A tease? An accident? She had no idea which. Antonietta shook her head, touching her burning lips to make certain she wasn't locked in a dream. "How could I possibly know? You have never said anything to indicate you're attracted to me." It was difficult to talk. To maintain any semblance of normalcy when she wanted him with every fiber of her being.

"Attracted to you?" There was a derisive note in his voice, self-mocking. "I hardly call what I feel, when I am anywhere near you, attraction. I burn for you. Every waking moment, I burn for you."

Antonietta shifted back away from him, pushing deeper into the pillows. She pressed her trembling fingertips to her lips. She could still taste him. She could still feel him deep inside her as if he'd burrowed into her skin and wrapped himself tightly around her heart. "You've never said anything. Never."

Music was rioting in her mind, clear melodic notes begging to be given freedom. She clearly heard the sharper notes. The off-key tones. The sudden clashing of the cymbals, striking a discordant note. "After all this time, you suddenly decide you want me? I'm to believe it has nothing whatsoever to do with who I am? Just my good looks?" She forced the ugly accusation out, even when everything inside of her screamed at her to stay silent, to take what he offered for whatever his reasons. She might have done so had he been anyone other than Byron.

She felt the movement as his weight left her bed, but she couldn't hear a sound. The silence stretched until she wanted to give in to the tears burning behind her eyes. She lifted her chin and waited instead. Damn him for letting her make a fool of herself.

"I never once considered you might be a coward." His tone was thoughtful, not accusing. "You have such confidence in yourself. I have watched you perform in front of ten thousand people. You even walk onto the stage alone, without an escort."

Antonietta could hear the note of admiration in his voice.

He must be standing by the stained glass window, turned away from her, where the clear resonance of his tones was slightly muffled. She had deliberately worn the white lace in hopes of enticing him, and she was angrier with herself than with him for his reaction. Was she a coward? She never thought of herself that way.

"The first time I saw you was at a concert. I could not take my eyes off of you. You were so beautiful with the lights on your shining hair. You walked with perfect confidence, without hesitation, straight to the piano. You took my breath away, and you had not played a single note."

His voice moved away from the window, toward the door. Antonietta's heart beat loudly in reaction, terrified he would leave her and not return. She knew almost nothing about him. Byron. Man of mystery. The man filling her dreams. "My hair is streaked with gray, and I'm hardly beautiful, Byron, but thank you for the compliment." Her hand fluttered to her throat to hide her rapidly beating pulse. He said the sight of her robbed him of breath, yet his words alone left her breathless.

He laughed. It was a shocking reaction and the last thing she expected, given her precarious emotions. "Why would you think your hair is streaked with gray? Your hair shines like a raven's wing. If there is silver, it only adds to the depth and richness of your color. No one else has such beautiful hair. Surely you know that."

Antonietta squirmed under the sincerity of his words. She searched on the nightstand for her dark glasses, feeling more naked without the eye covering than with the lace barely skimming her body. Byron didn't help her as he normally would have. He was always the perfect gentleman, opening doors and placing her things close to her fingertips without a word.

"How is my grandfather?" She should have asked him immediately instead of reacting to his presence like a schoolgirl. She needed a way to get the spotlight off of her and her all too noticeable reaction to him. "You spent a long time with him."

"Don Giovanni is fine. I removed the poison from his body, and he is sleeping peacefully. I also examined the other members of your household."

Behind her dark glasses, Antonietta closed her eyes, feeling more foolish than ever. She could walk onto a stage and take command, but here, in her own home with this one man, she felt foolish. He had the strangest effect on her. She didn't want to think of him alone in a bedroom with her cousin Tasha. She fought to keep her voice cool. "Had any of them been poisoned?" She fought to keep from imagining Byron bending over Tasha in her bed when so many men were so vocal about her cousin's perfect body.

"Strangely enough, yes. Your cousin Paul had traces of the same poison in his system. Very small amounts. He also had been drugged just as Don Giovanni, and, I suspect, you had been. Not that it makes him innocent. In fact, it is interesting that he was drugged yet not dragged to the cliff."

Byron was closer to her. She couldn't stand being in bed, sitting there helplessly while he prowled like a great tiger around her bedroom. She tossed the covers to one side, intending to stand up, but with the terrible silence of a stalking cat, he was at the side of the bed. She could feel the bulk of his body, feel the heat radiating from him. Her hand accidentally brushed the hard column of his thigh. Her entire body clenched in reaction. Heat spread and pooled into a sweet ache. It was just possibly the worst night of her life. At the very least, the most embarrassing.

Antonietta swallowed hard. "Paul was drugged and poisoned? Are you certain?" She was uneasy with the soft growl to his voice when he said Paul's name. He sounded almost threatening, and it frightened her.

"Yes he was. I want to check you, not only for the drug, but for poison. I think you are going to have to consider that this was a personal attack on both you and your grandfather and possibly Paul, although why he was not thrown into the sea I cannot fathom. He would represent more of a threat than you, I would imagine. I also searched the palazzo. Someone went through the drawers in your office, leaving everything a mess, but I suspect it was to keep the police from finding out that what really happened here tonight was an attempt on your lives."

"I was awake still, I do remember being sleepy, although normally I go to bed in the early hours of dawn." She couldn't prevent the faint blush stealing into her cheeks. Byron would know her sleeping habits better than most. "Perhaps they broke in expecting us to be drugged and Grandfather and I were both still up. Maybe they tried to kill us out of fear."

"You do not believe that. The first time I met Don Giovanni, his car had gone off the cliffs and was falling onto the rocks below. I only managed to get him out seconds before the car hit the rocks and was mangled. He was lucky I happened by."

"His brakes failed. It happens, Byron." But she was beginning to believe he might be right. "Why would someone want to kill Nonno? He's loved by everyone."

"Money. It has been my experience with humans, it is nearly always about money. And you and your grandfather have far more than most people."

My experience with humans. She had come to know Byron for all his mysterious ways. He had used the expression deliberately. Just as he was deliberately crowding so close to her body. Just as he had deliberately brought up her grandfather's impossible rescue. She remembered the story well. Don Giovanni told everyone who would listen the absurd and totally unbelievable tale of the rescue from his vehicle as it fell over the cliff. The door torn from the hinges in midair and being pulled out to find himself on the cliff with Byron, his newfound friend. Byron merely smiled when the story was related, neither confirming nor denying the impossible story. Antonietta had come to believe it.

Tonight he carried her through the wind and clouds. She felt the rush of air on her face and her feet had not skimmed the ground. As ridiculous and as impossible as it was, she was certain he had carried her through the sky. If he could do that, he could pull her grandfather from a car plunging onto the rocks. A fairy tale. But she lived a fairy tale, so she knew all things were possible.

Antonietta rubbed her temple, forcing herself to marshal her thoughts and focus on the threat on her life and that of her grandfather. "You are implying someone in my own family, someone I love, would try to kill *mio* Nonno? Would try to kill me? Maybe even Paul?"

Byron's fingertips skimmed her forehead, tucked stray tendrils of hair behind her ears, removed the dark glasses. Found her temples and lingered for a moment until the throbbing had ceased. "I think you have to at least entertain the possibility, Antonietta. No one likes to suspect their loved ones of such things, but avarice and jealousy are sins that have led many to murder." His hand dropped to her shoulder, gently but deliberately pressing her back against the sheets. "Your grandfather runs a very successful company. You inherited your father's stocks, his entire estate, so you actually own more shares of stock than any other family member. It is no secret that your grandfather relies heavily upon your advice. Your cousin Paul has taken no interest in the company. Your cousin Franco works hard, but he committed a grave error when he listened to his wife and she poisoned his mind with her constant nagging. Your grandfather has never trusted him since it came to light that he took a great deal of money in exchange for inside information into the bidding for contracts. That is common knowledge, *cara mia*, it was a very public scandal. Tasha has no interest in the company, would sell it in a heartbeat and spend the money within the first year. Again, it is no secret your grandfather intends to leave everything to you. If he does that, you would own more of the company than the others, unless they could get together and combine their stock."

"Have you forgotten I'm blind? It would be difficult for me to run the company efficiently with such a handicap. I would have to rely tremendously on others."

"It is not a handicap for you, Antonietta, it is an asset. In the boardroom you sit quietly without speaking. They treat you as if you are deaf as well as blind, and you are able to glean information that way. You use it to your advantage."

"How do you know these things?" Her hand went defensively to her throat, covered the telltale pulse beating so rapidly there. What other things did he know about her? There was much she did in her grandfather's boardroom, using methods best not known or spoken of to get the results they needed.

"And then you have Justine Travis. She is your eyes and ears and seemingly completely loyal to you."

"Justine is a treasure," Antonietta agreed. "I went through hundreds of applicants for an assistant, and I'm so grateful that I waited to hire the perfect person." She tilted her head, frowning as a sudden chill went down her spine. The air in the bedroom stilled. The palazzo held its breath. "What do you mean, seemingly loyal? There is no question about it. I pay Justine an enormous salary, and that aside, she's my friend and confidante, has been for years, and I trust her implicitly."

"Is she? Does she confide in you? Does she tell you her personal life?"

She could hear the wind rise, rattle the great stained glass windows. An ominous sound in light of the conversation. "Justine is a very private person, as am I. We don't share every detail."

"Were you aware she is in a relationship with Paul?" He asked it quietly, watching her face, knowing he was hurting her but having no other way to make her see she was surrounded by people she loved who had reasons to betray her. Even he had a hidden agenda, one she would not like but he knew was necessary.

Antonietta felt the twist of pain in the region of her heart, but she kept her chin up. She could feel the weight of his stare, knew he registered every small nuance of her expression. She didn't want him to know he'd scored a hit. She had an acute sense of smell. More than once she had been certain Paul was in the room when he hadn't been. She realized his scent must have been on Justine. "My assistant is entitled to any relationship she chooses to have. And that includes Paul."

"Even if that divides her loyalty?"

"I trust Justine. She's been with me for years. I might point out I have known you only a short while."

Again he laughed softly, his response unexpected. He didn't seem to take offense but was amused by her reaction. "I think you have a built-in radar for people who are allies, which is one of the reasons your grandfather prefers to have you in on every major deal."

"If you think that, Byron, then it is unnecessary to tell me things about my family and the people I regard as family." In spite of her intention to keep her tone neutral, she sounded faintly haughty, even to her own ears.

"Oh, but your family is an entirely different matter. You refuse to listen to your warning system."

"I have a warning system?"

"Absolutely you do. I suspect you have other gifts as well that are an asset to you." His hand on her shoulder still held her in place, preventing her from rising as his intention was to examine her body for the aftereffects of drugs and to see if she had the same poison in her body as her grandfather.

It was a measure of how Byron managed to mesmerize everyone and everything that she didn't protest his pinning her to the bed. She would never allow anyone else to dictate her movements, yet she couldn't manage to voice a protest. And how could he know such things? "Who are you, Byron?"

There was a small silence. The room seemed filled with the fragrance of flowers. She inhaled the scent, took it deep into her lungs. Several candles were burning, she could tell by the faint odor of the wick along with an unfamiliar aroma.

"Right at this moment, *cara*, I am your healer."

Antonietta lay all the way back against the pillows at his urging. She couldn't help but put her hand over her eyes.

"Why do you do that?" Byron gently removed her hand and stroked her eyelids, stroked around her eyes.

For one heart-stopping moment she was certain he was tracing the lines of her scars. She didn't dare breathe. The earth stopped spinning in just the way it had when he kissed her. She reached up to catch his wrist. "I don't like people to stare at my scars."

"Scars? You mean these small, thin lines one needs a microscope to see?" Byron shifted closer to her, leaning down so that his breath was warm on her face. She knew he was peering at her eyes, but all she could think about was how close his mouth was to her skin. "I have scars much worse than those. Do physical imperfections bother you?"

There was silence. His lips, velvet soft, brushed her eyes. Brushed the corners with exquisite tenderness. For a moment she couldn't find her voice. She forced air through her lungs. "No, of course not, how could any physical imperfection possibly bother me? I can't see, Byron." She hated that he might think she would be so shallow as to care about someone else's scars. "I know my face is a mess from the accident." She shrugged, trying to look casual. "It happened a long time ago, and I've learned to live with it."

Byron settled his weight on the bed beside her. He was beginning to understand. "Someone told you that you had scars." He didn't want to think how difficult it would be for a little girl to lose her parents and her eyesight and be told she had terrible scars.

"I wanted to know." She excused her cousin.

"She lied to you. You do not have to tell me who told you such a lie. I know who it was. Tasha has a malicious mouth on her when she thinks another woman is getting too much attention. I can see that she would have a difficult time with you. You are beautiful and talented and unafraid of hard work." His fingertip brushed along her skin again. "You have several very thin white lines along the outside edge of your right eye. The lines are not at all noticeable unless you are looking for them. Around your left eye, you have several small white lines, again barely visible. There is one larger scar running from your temple to the corner of your eye. It is not unsightly, but it is wider than the other scars." Byron deliberately kept his tone clinical. He had a sudden urge to go to Tasha's room and bare his fangs, allow her to see what could make an unattractive scar. He traced the longer line, showing Antonietta the slight curve. "In some countries, when an item is made for a home, a small flaw is added because it is believed that if something is too perfect, evil will be drawn to the maker."

Antonietta smiled. "I'm hardly flawless, Byron."

"Perhaps others do not share your opinion."

She wasn't touching that. "What do my eyes look like?" She didn't know whether to believe him or not about the scars. He had such a way of speaking, it was nearly impossible to think he could lie, even to make her feel better. But would Tasha keep up a lie for years? Antonietta never asked her grandfather about her face after Tasha had screamed in alarm, crying out that the scars were hideous. "I was told the plastic surgeon hadn't fixed the damage to my face." A lump formed in her throat at the painful memory of that outburst.

"You have large, very black eyes. Your eyelashes are an extraordinary length. I am particularly fond of your eyelashes." Byron studied her enormous eyes, trying, without success, to be clinical. "You have high cheekbones and a beautiful mouth. I have had my share of fantasies about your mouth."

Antonietta's entire body blushed. She grew hot with the thought of him fantasizing over her mouth. "Why are you suddenly telling me these things?"

Byron shrugged, uncaring that she couldn't see. "Maybe because you scared me tonight. Maybe because there should be honesty between us, and my silence could be construed as a form of deception. In any case, I cannot be with you during the days. I would very much like you to consider hiring a personal bodyguard."

Antonietta stiffened. Byron's hand moved from her silky hair to her shoulder with exquisite gentleness. "Before you protest, hear me out. You are capable of doing research and finding a bodyguard yourself. If you do not want to go to the trouble, allow me. I have a few connections. I am willing to spend my evenings and nights here with you, watching over you, but I cannot possibly be here all the time. If you do this, it will go a long way toward alleviating my worry."

Antonietta knew instinctively he was not telling her everything. There was a warning note in his voice. Something she couldn't quite put her finger on. She was a Scarletti, and Scarlettis had a way of seeing things others did not. Byron was delivering an ultimatum. He didn't like doing it, but he was resolved on some path she couldn't fathom. And one she was certain she wouldn't agree with.

She lay quietly, feeling the weight of his body as he leaned over her. Feeling his heat. "You aren't quite human." The words slipped out before she could censor them. Before she could stop herself. A challenge. A demand. A mistake.

The silence lengthened. Grew. She knew it was deliberate, a reprimand for her audacity. Her dark poet didn't like questions. Outside the windows the wind blew against the stained glass. Whispered ominously. Always sensitive to vibrations, a chill swept through her.

Antonietta curled her fingers in the bedcovers but kept her expression serene. She was unshakable. She had no regard for authority or threats. She was a law unto herself. Let him glare his disapproval.

"You are a Scarletti. I doubt if you are entirely human

either. What are you?" His hands slipped to her throat, stroked her rapid pulse.

His touch was mesmerizing. It dazzled her, threw her off balance when she needed to keep her senses about her. "Well, there is the tale told to all of our children," she replied, trying to introduce a lightness to their conversation. She wanted to believe the howling wind rattling with such persistence at her windows caused her chill. "Perhaps you would care to hear that explanation. There are some carvings in the hidden passage and obscure references in the diaries, enough to make it seem a grain of truth might be in the absurd tale." She hoped to distract him. Hoped to keep him with her just a bit longer. And she was revealing things she shouldn't.

"Tell me this tale."

"Are you going to let me sit up?" Let him think it an amusing bedtime story.

His hand remained resting on her throat, his fingers splayed wide. The heel of his hand rested on the soft swell of her breasts. The lace was stretched over her breasts, barely covering them, and she could feel the heat of his hand with every breath she took. It was becoming difficult, nearly impossible to breathe.

"No, I am going to kiss you."

The words were said against the corner of her mouth. She felt his warmth, the anticipation, the clenching of her muscles and the thousand butterfly wings suddenly brushing at her stomach. Her breath caught in her lungs, was trapped there. Was she really going to lie there like a Sabine captive and wait for his mouth? Wait for him to take possession of her heart and soul? Instinctively she brought both hands up to push at the wall of his chest. Her palms touched him. Felt hard muscle. Felt heat.

There was no way to push him away. Her strength was gone in an instant, her body melting with desire so intense she shook with it. She wanted him with every breath she took. The hunger rose up out of nowhere to consume her, to take away her every good sense and replace it with need. She made a single sound of protest. Or a plea for his dark embrace. She honestly didn't know which it was. She only knew she was born for him, born to be in his arms. He was forbidden, just by nature of who she was, what she was. By who and what he was. But it didn't matter. There in the dark of her bedroom, with the wind shrieking a protest, Antonietta simply gave herself into his keeping. And took what she wanted.

She turned her mouth into his neck. Tasted his skin. Inhaled his scent. Her mouth trailed, featherlight over his neck, over his throat. Daringly, her teeth nibbled on his chin. She felt his body's reaction, hardening, thickening against her, molded as they were together.

His hands tightened on her, caught in her hair and dragged her head up to his. "Are you sure this is what you want?" He demanded the truth from her. Compelled the truth. "There is no going back, Antonietta. I will not give you up. I refuse to go back to being your grandfather's friend and sharing only polite conversation with you."

"I want you to kiss me, Byron," she said, more certain than she'd ever been of anything else in her life. "I dreamt of your kisses." And God help her, she had.

His mouth was hot and hard and possessive. It was everything she had ever dreamed of. Perfect heat. A perfect fire blazing through him, through her. He devoured her, kissing her as if he would never get enough of her. She could lose herself in his smoldering passion. She knew she could. Simply go up in flames and rise into the wind and clouds and night sky where she would soar free from the daily intrigues and dramas in the palazzo.

"Byron." She whispered his name into the silken heat of his mouth, her hands in his thick, long hair, tangling there, every bit as possessive as he.

His hand closed over her breast, and flames licked her skin, seared her belly, and drove the breath from her body. His mouth left hers, trailed little kisses to her throat. His tongue swirled over her pulse, while his palm cupped her breast through the fine lace and his thumb stroked her nipple into a hard, aching peak.

Antonietta gasped with pleasure, with excitement. How long had she dreamt of him? Longed for his touch? From the first moment she heard his voice, she knew he would be a perfect lover. Be an instinctive lover.

His mouth roamed lower, his tongue replacing his thumb,

laving her nipple, until her hands gripped fistfulls of hair in reaction. His mouth was hot and wild, suckling strong at her urging. She heard her own moan, a soft whisper of need that spread from her aching breasts inside her body, thickening her blood. Hunger and need were sharp and terrible, so much so that she was afraid. She had never been so on fire, her body ruling her mind. She couldn't stop herself from thrusting deeper into his mouth, from making the small, urgent noises that escaped her throat.

His mouth left her breast, and she cried out with bereavement. His arms tightened around her, pulled her fully into his arms. His heartbeat was strong and fast. Her heartbeat followed the rhythm of his. She cried out with longing when his teeth began to scrape teasingly back and forth over the telltale pulse beating so frantically in her neck. Desire pounded through her blood when she felt the tiniest of nips. She had never expected such a thing to be so erotic.

He whispered to her. Antonietta could not catch the words, but she felt them. She was restless and edgy, her body ached for relief. For the possession of his. She moved in his arms, unable to be still when every inch of her was inflamed. Still, he took his time, his mouth roaming lower until he reached the swell of her breast. She felt his teeth again, and a thousand butterfly wings fluttered in the pit of her stomach. Hot liquid desire trickled along her thigh. Her muscles clenched.

Then there was white-hot lightning, a flashing pain that gave way to sheer pleasure. Instinctively she cradled his head to her, feeling as if she belonged to him. As if they were two halves of the same whole, and they were merging, skin to skin, blood to blood. She heard his voice whispering in her head, soft words in an ancient dialect she couldn't place, although she spoke several languages. The actual words didn't matter to her, just the sound of his voice as it slipped past her guard and branded his name on her heart. On her soul.

She didn't want his name on her heart. She wanted a lover with no strings. The terrible enchantment he cast was wrapping her up in something she couldn't afford. For a moment she did her best to struggle, to come up for air, to find a way for her melted brain to function again.

Byron swept his tongue across the pinpricks, whispered to

her, commanded her so that she ceased her struggles and fell deeper into his enthrallment. Her head lolled back against his shoulder, and he couldn't resist the temptation of her neck. She tasted the way he knew she would. A woman of courage and sweetness. A conflicting mixture of confidence and self-doubt. A contradiction of innocence and experience.

He shifted her in his arms, his body hardening to the point of pain with the knowledge of what he was about to do. He opened his shirt, stared at his hand until one fingernail lengthened, razor sharp, and he swept it over his chest and pressed her mouth tightly against his skin, whispering another command.

At the first touch of her lips, he threw back his head in ecstasy, shaken by his reaction to her touch. To the sight of her face, so beautiful in the darkness. To the fall of her hair, shimmering like a dark cloud. Byron knew he had learned patience over the last years, a steady, carefully cultivated trait he guarded. Antonietta shook his self-discipline. He wanted her—worse, needed her. He had taken his time to learn everything he could about her, and he knew she had no thought of a permanent relationship. She wouldn't mind taking him as a lover, but she didn't think in terms of marriage or eternity.

His first thought was to simply take her, but he dismissed that impulse immediately, refusing to be selfish, refusing to make a mistake that might cause her to suffer in any way. He had been determined to court her until the moment he had seen her struggling for her very life on the cliffs. Safety came first, and he was of the earth, impossible to protect her during daylight hours. So he had to tie them together before she was ready to accept what he was.

His entire body shook with the effort not to say the ritual binding words that would tie them together for all time. She had to stay above, and he would have to return belowground while the sun was high. Trembling with need, Byron stopped the exchange at just enough to complete a true bond between them.

With most humans, scanning and reading thoughts was relatively easy, but Antonietta and many members of her family were more difficult to read. It was not only the Scarletti family but also a few people in the city and some of the servants in the palazzo. Their brain patterns weren't normal. If he simply pushed beyond the barriers, they would know he was there, reading their minds, taking their memories. He needed to work out their strange brain patterns before he attempted to do something he might regret. He had no idea what other differences the people in the region had. With the blood bond he established between himself and Antonietta, he could find her easily anywhere and touch her mind at will. There was no way she could escape him, and he had a better chance of protecting her should there be need. It was the only real solution and the only safe thing he could think to do to ensure her protection.

"Wake, Antonietta," he ordered softly.

She blinked up at him with her enormous, dark eyes, almost as if she couldn't quite focus on him. The pads of her fingertips found his lips unerringly. "I've never had anyone kiss me quite like that. I'm afraid if we went any further, I'd go up in flames."

"We cannot have that. The night is almost over, and I have yet to examine you for poison. When I make love to you, Antonietta, I want time to do it properly."

Her eyebrow shot up. "When? Not if?"

"I do not think there is much doubt we both want the same thing." He placed her gently back on the bed, his hands stroking the soft swell of her breast. "Lie quietly and allow me to ensure no poison remains in your system and no drug lingers."

Antonietta wished she could see him. She had the impression of great strength, of a tall, broad-shouldered man. She knew from Tasha that Byron was handsome and wore his hair long. Her cousin had particularly mentioned his chest and his firm backside. Strangely, she felt different. Her hearing, always so acute, seemed even more so, as if she could hear his very breath moving through his lungs. She was even more aware of Byron, of his every movement, of his exact location in the room.

"Sleep, Antonietta. Tomorrow your family will make their usual demands on you, and you must be rested."

Her eyelashes drooped down, almost as if he compelled it. She felt him gathering energy, felt heat and power, knew the precise moment he entered her body to find if she had been poisoned along with her grandfather. "Byron." She whispered his name because she was sliding into sleep despite wanting to stay with him. She didn't want to let go of her magical night.

"Do not worry, *cara*, no one will be allowed to harm you or your grandfather. Sleep now and be at peace."

A small smile tugged at the corners of her mouth. "I wasn't in any way thinking of either of us being in harm's way. I was thinking only of you." She succumbed to the lure of sleep with his name on her lips and the taste of him in her mouth.

4

"**A**ntonietta! *Wake up!* If you don't wake up, I'm call-ing the doctor!" Natasha Scarletti-Fontaine shook her cousin over and over. "I'm not fooling around, wake up right this minute!" There was panic in the voice.

Antonietta stirred. Her lashes lifted partially, indicating she was awake. "What is it, Tasha?" Her voice was drowsy, and her lashes simply dropped down, covering her sightless eyes. Her head settled back into the pillows, and she burrowed beneath the covers. She was so tired, far too tired to get up. Everything in her urged her to sleep at least two more hours. It couldn't be sunset yet. . . .

"No you don't! Antonietta Nicoletta Scarletti, you wake up this instant!"

Recognizing the absolute resolve in her cousin's voice, Antonietta made a supreme effort to shake off the need for more sleep. "Oh for heaven's sake, is there a major catastro-phe I don't know about?" She rubbed her eyes and struggled to sit up, desperately trying to understand where such an absurd thought as waiting for sunset had come from. "What is wrong with you?" She felt slightly disoriented and hazy, as if there were a veil over her mind, and she couldn't quite remember important things. She wanted to sleep forever.

She pressed her hands over her ears. Her hearing was so acute, she could hear the steady beating of Tasha's heart. Like a drum. It threatened to drive her crazy. Tasha's breathing sounded like a rush of wind. Outside, the sea thundered and the rain poured down. Antonietta put her pillow to her ears in an attempt to muffle the sounds before she identified the whispering as actual conversations being carried out throughout the palazzo.

"Wrong with me?" Tasha was outraged. "I'll have you know it's nearly four in the afternoon, and none of us could wake you. Nonno told us about the break-in and said both of you had been drugged. He said your attackers threw him from the cliffs. What utter nonsense to think Byron Justicano saved his life by pulling him from the sea. No one could do such a thing. Nonno is getting senile. The authorities have been waiting for your account, and you just lie here sleeping the day away like nothing was wrong! And if that's not enough to have to deal with, the cook has gone missing, just up and left without a word, and we had nothing suitable to eat. The housekeeper is having hysterics."

Antonietta could not imagine the housekeeper, reliable Signora Helena Vantizian, in hysterics. The housekeeper was a steady, patient, matronly woman, well in command of the palazzo. "Why would Enrico have gone missing?" Cautiously she took the pillow from her ears, deliberately trying to turn down the volume on her hearing. It helped enough that her eardrums weren't ringing.

"How should I know what that silly man is thinking? And it's just like you to choose the most uninteresting and unimportant thing to deal with. The *authorities* came. Didn't you hear me? They waited all day."

Antonietta had a mad desire to laugh but wasn't altogether certain the impulse stemmed from mirth. She might have found it amusing that it was perfectly normal for Tasha to sleep until noon every day or perhaps the problem was she was slightly hysterical due to the strange phenomenon with her hearing. For a moment, she actually tracked an insect scurrying across the floor. She forced her mind to focus on her cousin's distress. "Are they waiting now?" Things were coming back to her, crowding into her mind. Not the details of attempted murder, but pure sensual pleasure. Byron.

"Nonno sent them away. He said you needed your rest after your ordeal last night. He can be so utterly rude sometimes. I wish you'd talk to him."

Antonietta recognized the petulant note in Tasha's voice. "You know perfectly well Nonno is as sharp as a tack." Although he could be quite abrupt if he thought someone was acting like an idiot. He was often abrupt with Tasha. "For a minute there, I thought you were worried about me."

"For a minute there, I thought I was, too, and I don't appreciate the worry one bit, Antonietta. I absolutely do not want to get those hideous worry lines you *serious* types get. And why is it you always get the adventures? Why can't someone try to kill *me*?" There was a rise to her voice now, a hint of a wail that forced Antonietta to shield her sensitive ears. "It makes no sense to waste it on you. You're so *you*. Look at you sitting there just as calm as you please. I could be such a *perfect* victim and look pale and brave and *interesting*. You don't look as if a single thing out of place happened."

"Believe me, Tasha, it wasn't a particularly fun experience. You don't need to have someone try to kill you to look interesting. You always manage that nicely. You don't need to be pale and brave, you're beautiful, and you know it."

Tasha waved the obvious away. "I know, I know." She sighed. "Mere beauty isn't always enough to capture attention, Antonietta. Some men are only interested in silly things like *murder*. What am I supposed to do? Hire someone to kill me just to get a little attention?" She stood up and paced across the floor with quick, angry steps. "It's utterly ridiculous to think of that man spending hours with you, and you can't even see him! It doesn't bear thinking about."

"Byron?" Antonietta tried desperately to follow her cousin's thinking and at the same time control the volume of her hearing. The sound of Tasha's shoes reverberated through her head.

"Oh that odious man! Not *him*. You know I can't stand to be in the same room with him. He's rude and obnoxious, and I hate him." Tasha stared at her reflection in the mirror of the vanity. "Why would you have a mirror in here? I've never understood that." She turned sideways and held her breath, checking her flat stomach.

"It came with the furniture," Antonietta said. "What man are you talking about? I don't spend hours with any man." She turned away from her cousin to hide the sudden color she knew was spreading into her face. She couldn't think too much about the time spent with Byron. About her reactions to him.

"The policeman, Antonietta," Tasha snapped impatiently. "For heaven's sake, follow along. This is important."

"This is all over a policeman?" Antonietta sighed with a mixture of relief and exasperation. "Tasha, you're engaged to be married. You have a fiancé, a very wealthy fiancé, I might add."

"What does that have to do with anything? I'm going to marry Christopher, but he's so boring. And he's so jealous. It's tiresome. His entire life is his family and church and business. All he can think about is ships and religion."

"His family does own the second largest shipping company in the world, Tasha," Antonietta said. "And Italian families are nearly always close."

"Mama's boys," Tasha sniffed, "or in Christopher's case, a daddy's boy. They insist I have to go to church with him."

"You knew going into the betrothal he wanted you to convert to his religion."

"I didn't realize I was supposed to take it so seriously. He brings that horrible priest over every week, and I'm supposed to *study*. All I should have to do is go and sit with him during the services. I don't need to know all the mumbo jumbo that goes along with it. I doubt if anybody else really knows it. In any case, why can't he just be a Catholic like everybody else? Who cares which religion is the true one and who broke away from what? It's just silly."

Antonietta sighed again. "You can't have a fling with a policeman when you're engaged to one of the more powerful men in the world. I think the tabloids would get wind of it."

"Who mentioned a fling? I could really fall for him. He has the most wonderful chest you've ever imagined. Even Byron doesn't have a chest like his, well, not as perfect anyway." She made a rude noise. "Why do you like him?"

Deliberately Antonietta misunderstood. "I've never met

your policeman, Tasha, so how could I possibly have an opinion?"

"You know very well I was talking about Bryon!"

"Why don't you like him?" Antonietta countered.

"He doesn't look at me. Never. That's just not normal," Tasha said. "All men look at me. And he's scary. There's just no other word for him. His eyes are flat and cold, and he stares at people like he sees inside of them. He never smiles." She shivered. "He reminds me of a tiger I saw at the zoo one time, pacing back and forth in its cage and watching me without blinking."

"He smiles."

"He bares his teeth, it isn't the same thing." Tasha gasped loudly. "Antonietta! What is on your neck? You have a love bite."

Antonietta could feel the sudden burning, a throbbing on her neck that caused an instant reaction in her body. Fire smoldered in the pit of her stomach. There was an answering throb between her legs. For a moment she could actually taste him in her mouth. Wild. Untamed. A dark, erotic dream better left for night yet persisting into daylight hours. The throbbing spread to include a spot on the swell of her breast. She tried not to blush, remembering the feel of Byron's mouth, hot and wet and wild on her skin. She covered her neck with the palm of her hand, captured his kiss there, holding him to her with that small caress.

"It *is* a love bite! He was here last night with you!" It was an accusation, nothing less, as if Antonietta were on trial for criminal behavior. "You took Byron Justicano into your bed! Look at you, what you're wearing!" Tasha was nearly hysterical. "That lace barely covers you! Have you no decency?"

"Tasha." Antonietta forced herself to remain calm when she wanted to order her cousin out of the room. "You bought me this gown. I sleep in it because it is comfortable, and I have always considered you to be the epitome of good taste."

"Well, yes, I am, it is true." Tasha was somewhat mollified. "But I didn't mean you to wear it for that horrible man. He's a fortune hunter, out for your money all along. All this time pretending to be friends with Nonno, but in truth he was willing to seduce a blind woman."

"Must you be so dramatic all the time, Tasha? I'm thirty-seven years old. Did you think I never slept with a man? This may surprise you, but you don't have to have sight to share sex with someone." Antonietta dragged on her robe and shoved her dark glasses over her eyes. "And I don't appreciate you telling me I have hideous scars when they are barely noticeable." She swept past her cousin toward the enormous bathroom. She should have slept with him. She'd been an absolute idiot *not* to sleep with him. It was all so hazy. She had wanted Byron to make love to her. Had she fallen asleep in the middle of it all? The idea was humiliating.

Tasha followed her. "That was years ago, Toni, you know it was. And the scars were much worse then. And you were getting so much attention from everyone. Poor little orphaned girl. It was like a movie. Just imagine what I could have done with that role."

"It wasn't a role, Tasha." Exasperation crept into Antonietta's voice in spite of her resolve to be patient. "I lost my mother and father. It was horrible. A tragedy."

"I know. I was born for tragedy."

"You have suffered tragedy."

"Not that I can talk about." Tasha sniffed indignantly. "And no one's thought about your scars in years."

"I thought about them every time I went out in public."

Tasha studied one perfectly manicured fingernail. "If you weren't so vain, thinking about your looks all the time, you wouldn't have even remembered."

Antonietta bit her tongue to keep from pointing out that Tasha spent half of her life in front of mirrors. "You should have told me they weren't that bad. Not being the center of attention your every waking minute is not a good enough reason to hurt me."

"Oh for heaven's sake, Toni, you know I'm sorry, it was *years* ago. And you know I can't help my need for constant affection. My shrink said it's Daddy's fault. He paid Paul all the attention."

"He showered you with presents," Antonietta contradicted. "You were his little princess. He gave you anything you ever wanted."

Tasha sank into a deep-cushioned chair. "Presents can never make up for parental affection, and you know very well Daddy's entire world was the polo fields. I couldn't stand getting my shoes dirty, and he never forgave me. And he took Paul everywhere with him." Her perfect pout was always wasted on Antonietta, so Tasha didn't bother with it.

"You certainly know how to rewrite history. Poor Paul couldn't do a thing right. He tried to please your father for years." Paul and Tasha's father had been obsessed with women, not with the polo fields, but Antonietta refrained from correcting Tasha's version of history.

"And then Paul gave up and began gambling and drinking and doing everything he could to embarrass our family," Tasha pointed out. "He went through every cent he inherited, first from Mama, and then Daddy. And then he lost all of my money. Daddy was perfectly right about his weak character all along."

"That isn't true. You went through most of your money yourself and then insisted on that investment Paul came up with. I told you it wasn't sound. You knew it was throwing money away, but you did it anyway."

Tasha jumped to her feet. "Ooh! How would you know what it's like? Everything you touch turns to gold. You don't have to sell yourself to a man who's about as cold as a fish."

"You and Paul have plenty to live on, Tasha, and you always have a home here, you know that. You don't have to sell yourself, either. I told you not to invest your money. As I recall, I was adamant about it, but you wouldn't listen." To prevent further argument, Antonietta firmly closed the bathroom door.

She took her time showering, hoping Tasha would be gone by the time she dressed, although she knew it was unlikely. Her cousin was tenacious when there was a man in the picture, and apparently the authorities had made the supreme mistake of sending a handsome officer. She couldn't imagine where the palazzo chef, Enrico, had disappeared to, but a distinct chill was working its way down her spine in spite of the hot shower. Byron was certain that someone was introducing poison into the food. Could Enrico's disappearance have something to do with that?

She turned her face up to the hot water spray above her head. Byron had killed her assailant. She was certain he had. And the body had been dropped on the cliffs, carelessly, with little thought of what the authorities might think. What did she think? She knew things others didn't. She could do things others couldn't. And she knew Byron wasn't quite human. She accepted it as she accepted it in herself, yet he had killed easily, swiftly, without hesitation. He claimed he hadn't been suspicious of Enrico. Had he found evidence linking Enrico to the poison?

For a moment Antonietta leaned her head against the shower tile, allowing the spray to pour over her. Byron was many things she didn't quite understand, but he would not have murdered Enrico. She was not going to allow Tasha, with all her drama, to make her suspicious. With a little sigh she turned off the hot water and dried the beads of water from her skin. The towel lingered over the one spot on her breast that felt hot and throbbed for attention. She dressed with great care, braided the thick mass of hair, and swirled it into an intricate knot to give her more height. To give her added confidence.

Tasha was still in her bedroom. Antonietta could smell her distinctive perfume and hear the continual rustle of clothing. Tasha was not a patient or restful person, and waiting would have been difficult for her. Antonietta forced a smile. "You're still here. It must be important."

"Finally! You could have hurried, Toni." Tasha caught her arm. "This is important, you don't know how important. You have to talk to Nonno. I must be allowed in the room when the authorities return to question you."

"I'll speak to him, Tasha," Antonietta agreed.

There was a moment of silence while Tasha searched for the right words. "Don't get upset with me. You know I always look out for you. You're not nearly as worldly as I am, although, of course, you're *much* older."

"Have you forgotten we share the same birthday?"

Tasha hissed out a soft whisper of aggravation. "I don't know you in this mood, Toni. Do you see? Already he is driving a wedge between you and your family!"

"I'm not having this conversation with you, Tasha. I don't interfere in your personal life, no matter how bizarre I think it. All I ask is the same respect. What I do is my business, no one else's. Don't you dare bring up Byron to the rest of the family."

"Are you really going to talk to Nonno for me?" Tasha asked.

"Yes, I said I would."

A knock on the door was loud. Antonietta recognized Marita's distinctive way of announcing herself. Marita tried very hard to come across with authority and importance, even in minor things. "Come in, Marita." In another few minutes, all of her cousins would be crowding into her room.

"My husband, Franco, has sent me out of concern for your well-being, Antonietta." Marita made the announcement formal and loud. "You have never slept this long in all the time we can recall."

"You've been married to Franco for ten years, Marita," Tasha said with exasperation, "we know he's your husband. Do you have to announce it every time you walk into a room? You do have your own identity. If you'd just see Dr. Venshrank, you wouldn't need to identify so strongly with Franco."

Marita stuck her chin in the air. "Just because I've managed to stay married and happy for ten years and you've gone through two husbands and three fiancés doesn't mean I need to see your doctor, Tasha. Franco is a good man, and I'm *proud* to be his wife. In any case, it reminds you I am a member of the family, too, if only by marriage."

"You are so insecure," Tasha said, rolling her eyes in disgust. "You've been in the family for ten *long* years, you have two children, and you'd think you'd get over the fact that you had totally inferior breeding and no social status whatsoever when Franco found you. We all have."

"Don't start, you two. I have to speak with Signora Helena immediately and find out what is happening, or you may not have food for the next few days." Antonietta was exasperated with the both of them, grown women always feuding.

"Marita would live just fine for a day or two, but I wouldn't survive." Tasha patted her flat stomach lovingly.

Marita nearly screamed in frustration. "My stomach is a badge of courage, two *bambini*, and you with none."

"Enough!" Antonietta nearly yelled it. "I don't want you to ever say that again to Tasha in my presence, Marita."

"I'm sorry, forgive me, Tasha. Toni is right, I shouldn't have said such a thing."

"I don't pay attention to anything you say," Tasha said belligerently, but her voice trembled.

Marita turned her attention to Antonietta. "Toni, I really needed to talk to you about Franco. He's in a meeting with Nonno. I don't want you to interrupt them. You must see he deserves another chance. It is time Nonno realized his worth and paid him accordingly. He should be vice president and respected by all."

"You know I have no say in what Nonno's decisions are, Marita."

"Just promise me not to ruin Franco's chance. I must insist, Antonietta. You know he works hard and deserves so much more than Nonno gives him. One little mistake should be forgiven."

"It wasn't a *little* mistake, as you well know, Marita. You pushed him until he was bitter and angry and wanting your respect. He *betrayed* his family and our company. He was lucky charges weren't brought against him and that Nonno listened to Tasha's and my pleas to allow him to stay here. If you're pushing him again to do something he will later regret, think hard, Marita. Nonno won't forgive another betrayal, not even for the children, and Marita, neither will I."

"He *turned down* a *huge* offer from Christopher's company to join with them. A merger would be good for both companies. Franco has proved his loyalty even though he knows the merger would make us all wealthy."

Antonietta sighed. "We are wealthy already, Marita, and there is no advantage to our company from a merger, only on the Demonesini side. You know very well Christopher's father even tried to court me in hopes of a merger."

"The families will merge when Christopher marries Tasha."

A loud crash followed by a bloodcurdling scream of pain interrupted the two women. There was no mistaking a child's continuous scream of agony. Tasha turned toward the sound instantly. "That's little Margurite!" She was already racing from the room as she called out the warning.

The screams emerging from the lower story were appalling. Antonietta had never heard anything like it. "Something is really wrong with Margurite."

"She just wants attention." Marita pressed her hands over

her ears. "Tasha should make her stop that noise, no Scarletti should make such a scene. That's Tasha's influence. If Franco hears her, he'll rush to her side instead of keeping his mind on business as he should!" But she was running even as she complained.

Antonietta listened to her tone, not the words. Marita was terrified, her breath coming in ragged gasps. Antonietta took her hand as they hurried down the wide hall toward the sound of the screams. She had to slow down on the sweeping stair-case, not wanting to chance a misstep. Marita suddenly pulled her hand away, pressing back against the wall.

Antonietta could hear Tasha soothing the six-year-old girl. "There, there, Toni's here now, and she'll see to it that the doctor comes. He'll fix you right up. Your *madre* is here. It's going to be all right now." Antonietta judged by the direction of the voice that Tasha was sitting on the floor beside the child right at the bottom of the stairway. She stepped cautiously off the last stair and stopped walking, careful not to trip over them.

Marita screamed, a terrible sound, adding to Margurite's cries of pain. There was a thud as her body crashed to the floor.

"What is it? What happened to her, Tasha?"

"Don't mind Marita. She fainted like she always does in a crisis. Here, Toni." Tasha caught her hand and guided her to the floor beside the crying child. Already the screams were becoming sobs as Margurite tried to regain control. "It's her right leg. Tell me what you think. Hold still, *piccola*, it will take only a moment to examine you, and Antonietta is always so gentle. Your *madre* is fine. She just fainted. You've seen her do that before." Tasha kissed the curly head over and over, brushing at the tears running down the little face. "Watch yourself, Toni, there's rubble everywhere."

Antonietta ran her hands gently over the thin leg. Her breath caught in her lungs when she felt the jagged bone protruding. "Tasha is right, *cara mia*, we need the doctor immediately for you. You're so brave to stay here with Tasha." She raised her voice, knowing her assistant would be close, drawn by the screams. "Justine! We must have an ambulance at once." Justine Travis had been her assistant for thirteen years, and she acted as her eyes and ears in the ever-changing household.

"Right away, Miss Scarletti!" Justine answered from where she hovered in the hallway. "Helena is calling straight-away."

"Tell them to hurry, it's most urgent!" Antonietta kept her voice calm, not wanting to alarm Margurite. "Try to wake Marita. And get Franco in here."

Marita moaned. *"Bambina. Mia bambina.* How could this happen?" She kept her face averted, allowing Helena to help her to her feet. "There's so much blood, and the bone. She'll be crippled for life."

"Marita!" Tasha hissed her name. "That's not helping. Go to Vincente. He must be frightened by Margurite's cries. Franco will attend her."

"Yes, yes, you're right, Tasha." Marita pressed a hand to her stomach, turned her head, and was sick. *"Grazie*, take care of my poor *bambina."*

Franco gathered Tasha and his daughter into his arms. "Helena, take Marita up to the room. She's ill, and this is too much for her."

Helena complied, wrapping her arm around Marita while one of the maids immediately began to clean the floor.

Tasha rocked back and forth in an effort to soothe both the child and herself. "Do something Toni, I can't stand to see her in such pain," Tasha begged in a whisper. "How did such a thing happen?"

"Hurry, Toni, take the pain from her," Franco urged.

"Describe for me what you see."

"The Scarletti coat of arms above Nonno's door has come down. Didn't we just have that inspected and secured? Mar-gurite was coming out of Nonno's room, and it came right down on her. She could have been killed." There was a sob as well as anger in Tasha's voice. "She went to visit Nonno but he was gone."

Antonietta stiffened. The palazzo was undergoing repairs, and she had been with the inspectors when they had gone through her grandfather's wing of the house. She knew they had paid particular attention to the Scarletti coat of arms, due to the heavy weight of it. "Don't touch anything. We'll let your policeman take a look around."

All at once the home Antonietta loved, the home with which she was so familiar, took on a sinister atmosphere.

Margurite lay against Tasha, keening her distress softly while her father caressed her hair and face, murmuring how much he loved her. Tasha's fingers tightened around Antonietta. "Do something, take her pain away, Toni. Do it right now, I can't stand her being in so much pain."

"The ambulance will be here soon," Antonietta whispered back, but her hands were still on the little leg. She took a deep breath and concentrated, blocking out the sounds of weeping, blocking out the overwhelming emotions of everyone in the room. She let everything flow through her, around her, finding the deep well inside of her where she could free the energy that was so strong, so much a part of her and her heritage.

Antonietta knew Byron Justicano was capable of healing because the ability to heal was also a part of her family legacy. She couldn't heal in the same way he did, but she could diagnose a problem, lessen the pain, and speed her people onto the path of recovery. She felt the heat building, spreading, moving through her body to her hands, to the child's leg.

Almost at once, Margurite became quieter, her sobs reduced to sniffs and small shudders. Antonietta felt most of the tension leave Tasha's body.

Franco leaned over and kissed his cousin. His face was wet with tears.

"*Grazie,* Toni. I wish I could do that." Tasha hugged Margurite closer to her.

"The ambulance is on the way, Antonietta," Justine said as she picked her way carefully through the mess. "I also notified the authorities. The bolts holding the Scarletti shield are completely sheared through. This was no accident." Before her employer could protest, she hastily reassured her. "Don't worry, I was careful not to touch anything and leave fingerprints. I've seen enough movies to know you're not supposed to do that." She crouched down close to Antonietta. Almost protectively. "This was no accident, and coming on the heels of last night, I don't think you should take any chances."

"I believe you're right, Justine," Antonietta agreed.

"Please give Joie Sanders a call and let her know I need an appointment. Ask if she would be willing to come here to the palazzo."

"I'll set it up immediately. Sanders is renowned for her security measures, but she's very hard to get. She might be able to recommend someone to us though. Shall I cancel your performance at the local charity event next week?"

Antonietta shook her head. "No, it's for a good cause. But I want Nonno protected, too; that's important, Justine. See to it that our security people keep a close eye on him until I can work something out with Sanders."

Don Giovanni hurried into the hall, his breathing heavy from trying to run. "What is it, what has she done? Franco, is she going to be all right?" His usual authoritative voice trembled.

"We'll take her to the hospital, Nonno," Franco said gently. "They will fix up Margurite's leg in no time."

"Sit down, Nonno," Tasha said, concerned. "Toni has taken some of the pain away, and Margurite is much more comfortable." Quickly she hugged the child's shoulders in reassurance. "You're so brave, *cara mia*. Isn't she brave, Toni?"

"Very brave." Antonietta kissed the top of the child's head, still keeping contact with the little leg in hopes of keeping the pain at bay.

The child fumbled until she managed to clutch Antonietta's sleeve. "Am I a true Scarletti then?"

Tasha made a single sound, turned her head to glare at Franco, angry that Marita's continual nagging made the child insecure. "You have always been a Scarletti, Margurite. You are brave and wonderful and a joy to us all. Isn't she, Toni? Franco?"

"Margurite, you are a Scarletti through and through," Antonietta agreed instantly.

"You have always been just like me, Margurite," Franco said, kissing the top of the child's head. "Hasn't she Nonno?"

"You have your father's eyes and his sunny disposition," Don Giovanni assured.

"Signorina Scarletti, the ambulance is here," Helena announced. "This way." She waved the attendants through.

"*Grazie,* Helena," Antonietta acknowledged. She trusted

Justine to guide the medics around the debris and to the child.

After an examination and a brief discussion with Franco, it was agreed they must move Margurite to the hospital where her leg could be properly looked after.

"Please make certain there is no pain," Tasha pleaded, hugging the child protectively. "We've waited a long time for you, and she's very frightened."

"We will see to it that she does not hurt more than necessary," the attendant assured. "We can give her pain medication to help while we move her."

Antonietta waited until Margurite was settled in the ambulance with her father and Tasha and was on her way to the hospital before attempting to sort out the damages. "Justine, make certain the area is cordoned off so no one touches anything and none of the maids attempt to clean this up before the police have a chance to take a look at everything."

She knew her housekeeper was close by the faint perfume. "Helena, tell me of Enrico. What do you know of his disappearance?"

"Nothing, signorina, he was simply not in his room. Nothing has been taken, his clothes and personal belongings are there. He prepared today's menus last night, and we discussed what we needed for the kitchen so I could send the boy this morning. We had a glass of wine together about ten, and he retired to his apartment as he always does. This morning he did not appear to prepare the morning meal, and I sent one of the maids to check on him. He was not in his room. When she told me this, I immediately went to his room myself. I did not see anything out of place."

"Has anyone heard from him? Does he have a woman?"

"No." Helena's sigh was loud, and Antonietta could not turn down the volume. Everything seemed overly loud, even the sound of shoes on the highly polished floor. It was a bit distracting. She could hear insects buzzing and creaks and groans in the house. Thunder rumbled ominously in the distance and outside, the rain was steadily drizzling.

"Would he just go off like that? He's never done such a thing in all the years he's been with us. This is his home. Surely someone knows where he would have gone. His friends? Someone outside the palazzo."

"I'm sorry, signorina, but Enrico stayed only here. The

people here are his family. This is his home. He didn't go other places," Helena insisted. "I know this to be true. Enrico told me often he preferred the palazzo. At night he sometimes wandered the grounds and looked up at the sculptures. He loved the architecture and felt it was a privilege to live in such a place."

"Have the grounds been searched? He could have become ill and is lying somewhere hurt."

"I should have thought of that, signorina," Helena said. "I'll have the servants search the grounds immediately."

"One of my cousins should have thought of it," Antonietta corrected. Sometimes she wondered what her family was thinking. That the palazzo magically ran itself? Not even Don Giovanni had thought to do a search of the grounds for poor Enrico. She could not imagine her chef had walked off leaving behind all of his possessions. "*Grazie,* Helena, as soon as you hear anything, please let me know. Meanwhile, who do we have that can help out in the kitchen? I know you're already way too busy, and I don't want you to fill in. Justine can hire a temporary if we don't have an assistant that can manage."

"I'll move Alfredo up until Enrico returns," Helena said. "He's a decent chef and has worked with Enrico for the past seven years. He likes his way and is a bit difficult, taking to his bed with headaches and spasms, but I'm certain he'll do fine until Enrico returns. And my nephew, Esteben. You remember we hired him to work in the kitchen as an apprentice chef some time ago? He has been working out well. He can step into Alfredo's position for the time being."

"Are you certain, Helena? Alfredo will need someone to be fast and efficient. There were one or two complaints about Esteben. I thought he didn't care for the job."

"Oh, no, no, signorina. Esteben is most grateful for the job. He had the big date and wanted time off, and Enrico refused him. They had words, but Esteben was only trying to impress his *amore.* He understands the importance of his work."

Antonietta nodded. "Justine, please tell the bookkeeper to compensate them accordingly."

"Yes, of course, I'll make a note of that. You really must go to your grandfather. He was very agitated. I don't know if he took his heart medication, but he was upset."

"Very well." Antonietta placed her hand lightly on Justine's arm. "Thank you for all you do for me, Justine. I hope you know I consider you invaluable, both as my friend and as my assistant."

"I know, Toni." Justine was less formal when they were alone. "I love this job and the palazzo. I love that I can travel all over the world with you. Most of all, you've become the family I never had, so it is mutual." She led with confidence, moving quickly around any object in their path, and Antonietta didn't hesitate to follow her. "I was appalled at the rumor that you were attacked. Is it so?"

Antonietta inclined her head. "Yes. If it weren't for Byron, Nonno and I would both be lost. I have bruises from the struggle."

"Why would someone want to harm you or your grandfather?"

"Why would someone want to harm my parents?" The words slipped out before she could stop them, hung in the air between the women while they moved through the twisting hall toward the wing where the offices were located.

"I've never heard you say that," Justine said. "Not once. I thought the explosion was an accident. Wasn't it ruled an accident?"

"No." The single admission came out a whisper. No, it hadn't been an accident, but she would never admit it, not to herself, not to anyone else. Someone had rigged their yacht to blow in the open sea. The explosion hadn't managed to burn or sink all the evidence. A fishing boat had been close and managed to pluck a blind five-year-old girl from the water. Antonietta had never demanded to see the report, had never thought it was necessary. If the authorities couldn't find out who had destroyed her family, what could a child do? And when the child was grown, she had not wanted to look back.

"I'm calling Joie Sanders right away," Justine said, a hint of panic in her voice. "Do you think you're in immediate danger? I'm not leaving your side."

Antonietta caught the fierce, protective note in Justine's tone and found herself smiling. It was the exact same tone Tasha had used over Margurite.

"Don't worry, we'll get to the bottom of this," she assured. "I'll have plenty of protection. I'm more worried about the children now."

5

"**H**ow is she, Franco? Toni?" Don Giovanni asked anxiously. "Poor little Margurite. I should have gone with you all to the hospital."

"Nonno, there was no sense in all of us going. Franco and Tasha were already there and Marita, Justine and I made it a huge crowd. She's asleep, and Marita will stay with her through the night."

"The doctor thinks she will be able to come home tomorrow," Franco added. "There's no need to be upset."

Don Giovanni glared at his grandson. "Don't treat me like I'm an old man, Franco. I'm upset that someone broke into my home and tried to murder my granddaughter and me last night. And I'm upset that my baby great-granddaughter was injured in what probably wasn't an accident. And I'm upset that you're trying to steal my company out from under me."

Franco sighed and stalked across the room to pour himself a drink. "It's been a long evening, Nonno. I'm not certain I'm up to arguing. Toni, are you feeling all right after your horrible experience last night? You should have woken me up immediately. And then when you didn't wake up. You scared me."

"At least Franco is making sense now. Toni, don't go scaring us again," Don Giovanni said severely.

"I didn't choose to fight a man out on the cliffs, Nonno. I would have preferred my nice, warm bed." She tried to turn the pending argument aside with a joke. Franco was exhausted after the ordeal of seeing his child so injured. Don Giovanni was upset at himself for not having the strength to accompany his beloved great-granddaughter to the hospital. "I could use a drink, too, Franco." The moment she asked, her stomach lurched at the idea. "Just water, please."

"While you were sleeping up in your room, your cousin was threatening me. What do you think of that, Toni? My own grandson, a treacherous viper."

"You know very well I didn't threaten you, Nonno," Franco objected.

"Nonno," Antonietta said patiently, "Franco would never threaten you. Tell me why you're so upset. It isn't good for your heart."

Don Giovanni threw his hands into the air in disgust, nearly hitting his granddaughter with his wild gesture. "This talk of mergers. Of ousting me as president. That's the kind of loyalty this boy shows after I took him back. He utterly disgraced our name, sold out our family, and I welcomed him back to the fold, and yet once again he is the viper at my throat."

"I never said any of those things," Franco denied. "Toni, I never said any of that. I merely pointed out that if we disagreed over so large an issue, we should ask the rest of the family their opinions. And I've more than made up for past indiscretions. I've worked day and night for very little in return." He held up his hand to stop his grandfather's sputtering. "I know I deserved to be thrown out and to work for nothing to make up for the past, but I've done that. This is an entirely different matter. The family feels strongly on this issue of the merger."

Don Giovanni snarled his disgust. "You reason with him, Toni. How can he run a company if he's afraid of taking control? If he has to consult the rest of the family? What kind of leader would he be? Why, we'd lose the entire business in a month!"

"That's not fair, Nonno, you never once said there was a chance I would control the company. If I thought I had a chance—"

"What?" Don Giovanni demanded, "You'd do your job? You'd wait until I die and ruin everything I've ever worked for? You'd sell out to the pirate Demonesini? *The demon seed?*" He spat out the insult to his closest rival.

Antonietta intervened quickly. "Nonno, calm down, you're going to have a stroke if you keep this up. There is no way to oust you as president without my votes, and I would never do such a thing. Franco doesn't want to oust you either; he'd just like you to listen with an open mind to someone else's opinion besides your own."

She took the glass from Franco, her fingertips judging the amount of liquid to prevent spilling. Out of nowhere she became aware of Byron. He was close by. She could feel him. It was a strange sensation to know he had risen. He was no longer sleeping but moving steadily toward her, as if they were so connected she could know the moment he opened his eyes.

Good evening. Are you well? I have missed you. She heard the words clearly. They brushed along the walls of her mind like tiny butterfly wings. Her muscles contracted, clenched in anticipation. In reaction. His voice was like velvet rubbing over her skin. She heard her cousin and grandfather arguing as if in the distance, but her body, her entire being, was acutely aware of Byron's approach.

It didn't startle her that he would continue to talk telepathically to her, but it was very unsettling to have such a physical reaction to the intimate feel of his voice. She reached for him in her mind, followed the path of his voice to find him. To feel him. To connect strongly as she needed.

The palazzo is in an uproar. There was a terrible accident. Poor little Margurite went to visit Nonno, and the family crest fell on her leg. She has a compound fracture and was taken to the hospital. Marita is there with her now. Justine thinks the bolts were sheared straight through. And our chef has gone missing.

There was a small silence. She found she was holding her breath.

I will be there soon, Antonietta. I know you are upset over young Margurite. I will visit her in the hospital late this night and see if I can aid her in some way.

Grazie. She was in so much pain. Everyone is upset. I had the grounds searched for Enrico, but there is no sign of him. Antonietta took a cautious sip of water, finding she was not in the least hungry for food or drink.

I do not like that your chef is still missing after what I found last night. Someone had to be feeding you poison over a period of time.

You knew Enrico was missing last night?

He was not in his room.

She didn't want to have this conversation with him. She wanted to know if he had thought of her. If he burned for her. If he woke up consumed with need for her.

Yes, I did. He answered her thoughts in a smoldering tone. *And I still do. I cannot wait to be at your side. I must feed first. I wish to be at full strength when I come to the palazzo.*

She found herself smiling right in the middle of her grandfather's and cousin's squabbling. Byron was gone, yet he wasn't entirely. She felt she had only to reach for him in her mind, and he would be with her. She hugged the thought to her, astonished that it mattered so much. Astonished that Byron mattered. Astonished that he could make her feel that everything would be all right.

"Are you paying attention, Toni?" Franco demanded. "This is becoming a serious issue, and Nonno has no choice but to address it. He may not want to pay me a decent salary, but he has to listen to reason."

"I don't have to listen to anyone, boy. I've guided our company through stormy waters more than once, and we've come out better than ever. There is no advantage on our side to this merger. If you were a true Scarletti, you would look deeper, look past the lure of fast money, and see what this offer is really about."

Antonietta deliberately stepped between her grandfather and cousin. "The Demonesini Company needs a bailout, and they're looking to us to do it, Franco. It's that simple. I've thoroughly investigated their company. They run on a very small cash flow, and they took a large loss when they lost one of their freighters."

Antonietta could feel the thick tension in the room. She turned her back on her grandfather and deliberately smiled at her cousin, determined to change the subject. "Franco, have you any idea where Enrico could have gone? Helena says he has no woman and rarely left the palazzo."

Franco shook his head. "I spoke to the servants and to the authorities when they came this morning. They were allowed to search Enrico's room."

A soft knock on the door heralded Helena's arrival. "Pardon me, but Signora Marita is on the phone, and young Margurite would like to say good night to her father. Signora Marita says Margurite is sleepy from the medicine, Signor Franco, and I'm afraid she will fall asleep if I ask her to wait for you to call back."

"No, no, Helena, you did the right thing, *grazie*. Forgive me, Nonno, I know this meeting is important, but I must speak to *mia bambina*. I don't want her to go to sleep without giving her my love."

"I understand completely," Don Giovanni said and waved him out of the room.

There was a moment of silence. "That is the one thing that makes that man endearing. I can't help but love him for that. I still cannot quite believe he betrayed us."

Antonietta slipped her hand onto her grandfather's arm. "Franco has many wonderful qualities, Nonno; he just had the poor luck to fall deeply in love with a woman who is never satisfied."

As she spoke she thought of Byron. Wanting to touch him again. Wanting to feel the fluttering in her mind, in her stomach. What was he? A stranger with a commanding voice and a quiet, self-sufficient air, who had come out of the storm-drenched night when they needed him most. She had no idea where his home was, had no idea where he was staying. Even if he had another woman somewhere.

"Franco is strong-headed, Toni," Don Giovanni said. "He has ambition. And he has a greedy wife. That combination can be deadly."

"Nonno," Antonietta tried desperately to keep her mind on the conversation. "Franco made a mistake, and he knows it. It was years ago, when he was young and impressionable. He was crazy about Marita and would do anything she said. Stefan Demonesini and Christopher certainly can be charming and persuasive. Franco simply fell into the trap of thinking they were his friends."

Don Giovanni sighed heavily and sat in a chair. "And Tasha has invited the serpent into our home."

"Nonno." There was amusement in her voice. "You're being melodramatic. We grew up with Christopher. He played here as a child and has been at every one of our family events. He isn't a serpent, and he works very hard."

"Tasha doesn't have good sense. He isn't suited to her at all. And she knows how uncomfortable you are in his father's presence."

Antonietta could hear the concern and worry in her grandfather's voice. He sounded tired and even old. "I'm used to seeing him, Nonno; he's at every charity event and every function we attend. He will always see me as the woman who spurned his advances when every other woman was thrilled to be at his side."

"He offered marriage," Don Giovanni reminded, hearing the note of distaste in her voice. "You always thought he was after your money, but he had plenty. Why didn't you ever think it was a genuine offer?"

How could she explain an aversion that made no sense? "I thought I was scarred, overweight, and ugly, Nonno, it never occurred to me a man would want me for me."

"That's utter nonsense!"

"But it was how I felt at the time. I was very insecure."

The housekeeper knocked politely on the door a second time. "Signorina Scarletti? The authorities are here, and they are demanding to speak with you. I've shown them into the garden room."

"Thank you, Helena. I will come immediately."

"Signorina Tasha is entertaining the men as we speak." Although she spoke in the most even of tones, it wasn't difficult to pick up on her alarm and dismay at leaving Tasha alone with the authorities. Tasha was unpredictable, and the entire family and every one of the servants knew it.

"I didn't get a chance to talk to you about last night," Don Giovanni protested. "You have no choice but to go. If we allow Tasha to entertain the authorities, we'll all be locked up."

Antonietta patted her grandfather's leg. "Be nice, Nonno. She wore herself out at the hospital. She was wonderful with Margurite."

"She does love the children," Don Giovanni agreed. "Did Byron happen to mention to you whether or not he would be here today? I don't know his address, and the authorities wanted to hear his account of what happened. I don't think anyone believed he would dive into the sea to pull out a drowning old man."

Antonietta could not prevent the small smile. "Oh, I'm certain he will be here soon, Nonno." She leaned over to kiss her grandfather. "Anyone would do anything to save you. You're the family treasure."

Byron settled the young man against the wall of the building where he remained, dizzy and unaware of what had transpired, but uninjured. At full strength, Byron took to the sky, shape-shifting on the wing, something he could never have done even twenty years earlier. Hunting vampires had given him a hard edge, a coolness under fire, and complete confidence in his ability to handle a tight situation, but it hadn't prepared him for a woman like Antonietta.

Of course, his first impulse had been to carry her off, claim her with the ritual binding words, and let nature take its course. But he had been cautious, after learning from a lifetime of being impetuous. After having been captured and tortured and used as bait in an attempt to murder the prince and his lifemate and destroying his relationship with his best friend, Jacques Dubrinsky, Byron now believed in caution and patience and thinking puzzles all the way through. With a lifetime of mistakes behind him, he wasn't going to chance any more.

He was determined to know Antonietta. Unfortunately, the members of the Scarletti family had a built-in protective barrier in their minds. He couldn't simply scan their thoughts and learn all there was to know. He took his time, infiltrating the palazzo through his friendship with Don Giovanni. Waiting. Watching her. He realized she needed to feel in control.

She needed independence. She needed to be courted and won if he were to make her happy.

Byron sighed softly, allowing the wind to carry the sound out to sea. The murder attempt had changed everything. He needed to know she was protected, day and night. He needed to be able to touch her mind at will, needed to be able to know what was happening to her at all times.

Once more he dropped from the sky to the ground where he had left his gift for her. He knew Antonietta well enough to know she would take his present whether she liked it or not. Antonietta was far too polite to reject anything given to her by another.

The dog was the picture of noble elegance. From the moment Byron had seen the animal, he had admired the sheer poetry in its flowing lines. The borzoi was always graceful, whether in motion or standing perfectly still. Byron knew the accepted theory was that borzois had been around six to eight hundred years. He knew from personal experience that time line was a bit off. The breed had endured, refined perhaps, but stayed true. Byron bent over the dog, took the intelligent domed skull between his hands, and stared down into the dark, gentle eyes.

"This is your new home, Celt, if you would like it to be. She is here. The one who can be your new companion and one who will love and respect you as you deserve. She will admire you in the way I do and understand it is your choice to stay or go." They understood one another, the dog and Byron. He knew the animal was gentle but possessed a ferocious heart.

Celt was as fine an example of the borzoi as Byron had ever seen. The dog's head spoke of intelligence, his jaws were long and powerful and deep. His fur was pure black, his coat the texture of silk. And Celt's eyes reflected the true heart of the breed.

"You will have to wait out in the garden until I see her," Byron explained aloud. "I know it is raining and you are uncomfortable, but I will protect you from the elements for however long it takes. You know some there will be unkind to you." His hand stroked across the great head, found the silky ears and scratched. "I trust none of them, and neither should you. Look only to her protection. Be cautious of offers of friendship."

He felt the animal answer, the understanding and affection that passed between them, and he was doubly grateful to Antonietta for giving him back his emotions.

Byron's tall, broad-shouldered frame shimmered for a moment, nearly translucent in the rain, then he simply disappeared, droplets among the steady downpour. He found entrance into the house through a narrow gap in one of the second-story windows. At once he felt the terrible tension in the great palazzo. Fear and anger vibrated throughout the spaces, all the way to the great ceilings, up to the battlements, and along the traces.

Byron glided silently through the wide, marbled halls, down the sweeping staircase to inspect the damage near Don Giovanni's private room. Two people were collecting evidence, carefully putting bolts in plastic bags. He knew at once this was no accident but a deliberate attempt to harm someone, most likely the old man.

He could hear the boy, Vincente, crying softly for his sister, alarmed at her absence. Franco soothed the boy, singing softly to him, reassuring the child that little Margurite and his mother would return in the morning.

Byron, more than anything, wanted to see Antonietta. There was a strange, anxious feeling in the vicinity of his heart. Emotions were dangerous, he was discovering. Exhilarating, but quite dangerous.

Unerringly, he found Antonietta in a spacious room filled with plants and surrounded on three sides by glass. A large fountain dominated the center of the room and was surrounded by comfortable benches and several small chairs and tables positioned for conversations among the greenery. Outside the glass, the night was dark, with winds lashing rain against the panes and the roar of the ever-moving sea accompanying the distant growl of thunder.

A man in uniform stood unnecessarily close to Antonietta. Short, stocky, very muscular, his handsome face bent toward hers. His dark eyes were moving over her with obvious enjoyment. Byron snarled, a low, nearly nonexistent sound. The man lifted his head and searched the room with suddenly wary eyes.

Antonietta smiled, her head going up, inhaling, as if drawing Byron's scent into her lungs. "Please do sit down, Captain, there's really no need to be quite so formal." She walked with confidence through the labyrinth of plants and furniture, knowing where every obstacle was placed and making her way gracefully around it. Her fingers curled around the back of a chair and she slipped into it, folding her hands neatly in her lap.

"Signorina Scarletti, I trust you are well rested after your ordeal last night?" There was a caress to the man's voice that had Byron's incisors lengthening. "I am Captain Diego Vantilla at your service." He took Antonietta's hand and bent low, his lips skimming her skin.

Electricity sizzled, arced up the back of her hand, a small whip of lightning that zapped his lips loudly. Diego leapt back, dropped her hand, and pressed his palm to his stinging mouth.

Hidden behind lacy ferns, Byron leaned one hip against the wall in the midst of several leafy plants nearly as tall as he was, crossed his arms over his chest, and eyed the policeman with great satisfaction.

Tasha glared at her cousin. "Do sit down, Diego. I know this is impossibly bad manners, but may I call you Diego? It is so much easier than Captain Vantilla." She sent him a flirtatious smile and offered her hand as she sat in the chair beside Antonietta. "My cousin was very shaken by the events of last night and needs me to comfort her." She had wished for a few more precious minutes alone with the handsome officer, but Antonietta had arrived nearly as soon as Helena summoned her.

Diego nodded. "That is understandable, Signora Fontaine."

Tasha smiled sweetly. "*Scarletti*-Fontaine, but *you* may call me Tasha. All my friends do."

"*Grazie, signora,*" Diego acknowledged, his focus clearly on Antonietta. "I really must get your account of what happened last night. Don Giovanni was convinced there were two assailants and that both of you were drugged and dragged up to the top of the cliff."

Antonietta nodded. "I was playing the piano, but I felt strange. Unusually tired, my arms and body felt heavy. I heard a noise, and then someone put a cloth over my mouth. I struggled until I realized the chemical on the cloth would knock me out, so I pretended it had done so. At once I was carried outside the palazzo. I heard the other man dragging my grandfather. I couldn't tell who they were, their voices and their scents were unfamiliar to me. Once I meet someone, I nearly always recognize them again, but these men were strangers. I called for Byron. I don't know why, but as I began to struggle, I called for Byron Justicano."

"And why did you call for this man? Did you know he was near?"

Antonietta heard the sharp, alert note in the voice, and she smiled. Tasha's policeman was not up to playing cat and mouse with a man like Byron. She shrugged. "I just called his name as a talisman. To keep me safe. He's like that. He makes me feel safe."

Tasha sniffed her disdain loudly, drawing the officer's interest. "I see," he said when he clearly did not. "Please continue."

"I heard my grandfather go into the sea, and I fought harder, although how I could aid him, I didn't know. But then Byron came. He fought with the man who attacked me and then he told me to stay still. I could hear the wind shrieking and the waves thundering. The storm was furious, and even the ground shook and rumbled beneath us. And then Byron had my grandfather safe and was helping him to breathe, to get the water out of his lungs. They were both soaked with seawater and we were all so cold." She shivered at the memory. "I can't help you with a description of these men, although the one carrying me was tall and very muscular. His hair was short, and he was enormously strong."

"And where is this man now? Where is the man who attacked you?"

"I believe he is dead. I don't know for certain."

There was a short silence. "I do not see how this man, this Byron Justicano, was able to get your grandfather to shore. It is many feet from the cliff to the sea below. I doubt if it's possible to live through a dive into the sea at night. And last night the waves were high, and the storm was great."

There was a small silence. The air thickened. A shadow grew over the room. Tasha and the officer exchanged uneasy glances. Even the hair on the backs of their necks stood up in response to the sudden menacing atmosphere. Tasha rubbed her arms against a sudden chill.

Antonietta shrugged tranquilly as if she didn't notice. "You asked me what happened, and I told you. It's up to you whether or not you wish to believe me."

"Why weren't we called immediately?"

"You were called. I called the doctor to assist my grandfather, and I went to my quarters to shower and warm up. It was nearly dawn. I'm sorry I went to sleep, but we were both exhausted. Surely the housekeeper allowed you access to the music room and showed you where my grandfather was taken and also the site at the cliff."

"Yes, she did, but we could not wake you or your grandfather to speak to you, and the cliff site raised more questions than answers. There is evidence of a struggle, even of someone going over the cliff. We could see where your grandfather lay and evidence of someone kneeling beside him. But it is impossible, Signorina Scarletti, for a man to pull a drowning man from the sea and bring him all the way to the top of the cliff again. Why was your grandfather taken all the way back up the cliff? That is the question."

"Perhaps because a blind woman who was alone in a raging storm at the edge of that cliff needed help, too?"

"I think I can help, signor," Tasha said, her voice a soft invitation. "This man Nonno speaks so much of, Byron Justicano, he is a stranger to us. A fortune hunter out for my cousin's wealth. She is worth so much, the palazzo, the shipping company, her private trust. This is common knowledge. He seems to turn up at the most opportune times. How could he rescue a man from the sea? How could he save Antonietta at the same time? Do you see how ridiculous this story is? Of course he must be involved. And you heard Antonietta admit she thinks her assailant is dead. Dead by Byron's own hand and perhaps drowned in the very sea that nearly took my cousin." Tasha allowed a small sob to escape and reached to take Antonietta's wrist. "He is a seducer of innocents and a master criminal. You must save us all from this man. I must count on the kindness I see in your magnificent eyes, otherwise, there is no hope to save my dearest cousin from this man."

Antonietta would have laughed if she could have found her voice. She opened her mouth, but no sound emerged. Tasha so easily made up stories to suit her mood or her cause. She had just delivered Byron as a suspect to her handsome policeman. And she had betrayed Antonietta's confidence without a single thought.

Antonietta turned her head in Byron's direction. *You're here, aren't you? You heard my cousin tell the captain these lies about you. I'm sorry she's caused you trouble. She wants him to see her as a woman.*

Do not distress yourself over me, Antonietta. I am perfectly capable of taking care of myself.

There was a bite to his voice, the impression of strong teeth snapping together. The image was so strong in her mind, Antonietta envisioned a great shaggy wolf eyeing prey. She knew he was in the room, her every sense was on full alert. How could Tasha be so careless as to condemn him while he stood right in the same room with them?

Byron sauntered into one of the many alcoves, materializing behind the thick, wide fronds of several potted trees. He emerged from the greenery slowly, scanning the policeman as he did so, planting memories of an introduction and sending waves of warmth. He didn't bother to cover up for Tasha. She had the intricate Scarletti pattern in her brain. And he wanted her to be startled and uncomfortable, simply because she had upset Antonietta.

"Good evening," he greeted formally as he glided forward. "I am afraid Tasha's insecurities are showing, Captain. She is easily upset, and tonight the young child was injured." Deliberately stopping in front of her, Byron took Antonietta's hand away from Tasha and raised it to his mouth. He opened her fingers and pressed a soft kiss into the exact center of her palm. A slow, unhurried movement. Calm and deliberate and blatantly possessive. He lingered there for a moment, his thumb sliding over her skin.

Byron turned his head slowly and looked at Tasha. For a moment, in the dim lighting of the solarium, his eyes appeared to glow a fiery red. His teeth gleamed an amazing white and appeared, just for that second in time to Tasha, sharp and long, much like a wolf. She blinked and saw he was smiling, bowing low in a courtly, charming gesture.

"Tasha, my dear, I am sorry that your poor nerves suffered so on your cousin's behalf, but there is no need for hysterics. She is truly safe, and the captain and I will keep her that way." His voice was velvet soft, a blend of slight male amusement and arrogance, yet very compelling.

Byron turned the full force of his hypnotic voice and his mesmerizing eyes on the captain. "It is not so difficult to believe, with the evidence supporting every word Don Giovanni and Antonietta say. They are, of course, above reproach, and you have no trouble believing them. You are most concerned with protecting them. As we are good friends and you know it is my greatest concern, you wish to join with me, sharing with me all you know about this attack on them and aiding me in their protection." His tone held such purity and goodness, it was impossible to do other than agree.

Tasha stared at the two men in utter horror. Byron bared his teeth at her again.

Diego clapped him on the shoulder in a comradely way. "It's good you were here, old friend, or we might have had a grave tragedy. Signora Scarletti-Fontaine, surely you can see Byron has saved your grandfather and your cousin from certain death. Your family owes him a great deal."

Antonietta couldn't help but be swayed by Byron's velvet voice, but she noticed she couldn't quite remember his exact words. Only the tone. The perfect, pure tone. Her chin lifted. *Do you do that to me?*

What to you?

The laughter in his voice set her teeth on edge. Male amusement could wear thin very fast. *Mesmerize me with your voice so you get full cooperation.*

I try to mesmerize you with my kisses. My voice does not work on you. If only it would. My fondest dream would come true.

She wasn't touching that. It was far too unsettling to be sitting with others yet carrying on a private, intimate conversation that was flirting with sensuality. "Do you have the information you need, Captain?" She spoke to the officer, but her focus was on Byron. Every cell in her body was aware of him. Obsession. It was an uncomfortable feeling and one she didn't care for.

I feel the same way. It was a deliberate reminder that he

could read her thoughts. Antonietta had a great deal of pride, and Byron was well aware that craving a man would make her feel vulnerable and unsettled.

Tasha leapt up, her hands on her hips. "That's it? That's all the questions you're going to ask him? Byron Justicano is not at all what he seems. How did he get into this house? How does he ever get in? Why don't you ask him that!"

Byron swung his head around, his dark brows raised. Again she caught that fiery red glow, a devil's warning when he looked directly at her. "I turn into tiny molecules and seep under the doors. Take care you do not leave your window open, you never know what might creep in." He laughed softly, and the captain joined him.

Antonietta went still. She had no idea how Byron defeated their state-of-the-art security system. He often simply appeared in a room. She knew he was there immediately, even though others didn't seem aware of his presence. His entrance was always silent and instantaneous. She couldn't remember him coming through the door unless he met them on the grounds. *How do you get in? I thought I knew what you were, but even then, you couldn't just appear in a room.* Antonietta had the impression of laughter, yet there was no sound. And he didn't answer her.

"That isn't funny, Byron," Tasha snapped, "and it isn't an answer. Where do you live? What's the address? How come no one knows where you live?" She tapped her foot impatiently as she glared at Diego. "Do you even have his address down? Could you find him if he did turn out to be part of a plot to get my cousin's fortune?"

"Byron wouldn't inherit if I died, Tasha," Antonietta said. She stood up, knowing they would make way for her on the path winding through the flowers and shrubs. "You do. I doubt if Byron would gain from my death at all, or Nonno's."

Tasha shrieked. "What are you saying? What are you accusing me of doing? Did I drag you to the cliffs and throw you over? What are you saying?"

"I'm saying leave Byron alone. He risked his life to save Nonno and me. There is no need for you to pursue this any further."

Few people argued with Antonietta when she was serious. Not even Tasha. Glowering, Tasha left the room, two bright spots of color on her cheeks and her eyes promising retaliation.

Byron reached for Antonietta's hand. "Do you need anything else, Diego?" His voice was friendly, filled with camaraderie. "Please do tell us what you know."

"It isn't much, I'm afraid." The captain responded instantly to Byron's tone. "We don't even have the body of the man you pulled off of Signorina Scarletti. It isn't on the cliffs, although it is possible the sea has swallowed it."

"I thought he hit his head as he fell. He did not get up, but I had to carry Don Giovanni to the palazzo, and I did not check him as I should have." Byron spoke easily with a casual shrug of regret. "It all happened very quickly."

"That is usually the way of it." Diego sighed and stared after Tasha. "She is a beautiful woman."

Byron felt Antonietta's fingers tighten around his. "Yes, she is," she responded. "Tasha loves children, and she is very distraught over little Margurite's accident. Do you think that ties into this attack on us?"

"I am certain your grandfather was meant to be harmed," Diego said.

"What of the security cameras? Is there nothing on tape to show how they got in and how they could move about so freely in the palazzo without triggering an alarm?" Byron asked quietly. He felt the small shiver that ran through Antonietta, and he drew her beneath the shelter of his broad shoulder.

"They had to have known the code to get into the house, and they knew where the security room was to shut down the system."

There was a small silence. Antonietta did her best not to sag against Byron. Not to reveal her emotions when she wanted to cry out at the betrayal. Someone in the palazzo, someone had to have aided her assailants. She rested her head against Byron. Behind the dark glasses, she closed her eyes tightly against the pain piercing her heart. Her family. She loved them desperately with all their idiosyncrasies. The thought that any of her family could possibly be involved in a plot to murder Don Giovanni was inconceivable.

The one thing that I have learned in this long life is to never jump to conclusions.

The voice purred in her mind, stroked heat and hope deep inside where a great, gaping hole had been torn. Just like that. With a few simple words and a magic voice, Byron had managed to heal her.

"Signorina? I believe you must be very careful until we find who is behind this attempt on your life and that of Don Giovanni," Diego warned.

Byron noted how often his gaze strayed to the hallway where Tasha paced just outside the solarium. He leaned closer to the man, looked him directly in his eyes to reinforce a powerful feeling of friendship and trust. "That is a good idea. Antonietta, I think being careful is very much in order. Are we finished here, Diego? Perhaps Tasha would be willing to provide you with a cup of tea while you talk to the kitchen staff about the disappearance of Enrico." He pulled Antonietta beneath the protection of his shoulder.

"I'm certain she would," Antonietta agreed. More than anything she wanted to be alone with Byron. She needed to be alone with him.

"I think that would be best," Diego said immediately. "*Grazie*, for your time, Signorina Scarletti. I will be in touch."

Antonietta allowed Byron to retain her hand, although normally she made it a point to walk on her own. It was forbidden to move furniture in the palazzo, and she knew where every plant, chair, and table was. Byron Justicano was under her protection. She wanted to make it very clear to her family that they were to accept his presence in her home and in her life.

"Please come this way, Captain. Tasha is just outside." It was easy enough to identify the restless pacing. And she knew her cousin. Tasha wouldn't have gone far when she was so interested in the policeman.

Byron opened the door and stepped back to allow Antonietta to proceed him. As she went past, he whispered in her ear, "I brought a surprise for you."

Tasha swung around instantly as they emerged from the solarium, her large, dark eyes resting on Diego. "Do you have any idea who would do this?"

"Not yet, signora."

"Tasha!" Her lips formed a perfect pout. "If you don't call

me Tasha, I'm afraid I won't answer. Signora Scarletti-Fontaine is so formal." Ignoring Byron, she stepped close to Antonietta and kissed her cheek. "I'm sorry, cousin. You know why," she whispered. Her voice was low, but Byron's acute hearing heard the words clearly.

Antonietta nodded. "Tasha, would you have time to take the captain to the kitchen and tell the staff to be most co-operative? Byron brought me a surprise, and I was hoping you wouldn't mind showing Diego whatever else he needs to complete his report."

Tasha's entire face lit up. "Of course I'll show him around, Antonietta. Diego, please do come with me." She tucked her hand in the crook of his elbow and gave him a smile designed to keep him focused on her.

6

"**I would really** like you to check on Margurite tonight,"
Antonietta said. "She'll be in the hospital overnight. I
know she's asleep, and they're probably giving her painkill-
ers, but if you can speed the healing process, I'd really like
you to try."

"I'll go to her," Byron agreed, "but at the moment her
mother is with her, and it would be better if I went in when
she was alone. I cannot heal her in front of her parents or
even doctors. They would think I was the devil."

"I suppose that's true," Antonietta conceded with a faint
smile.

"I think you should take a look at my surprise. He's been
stuck out in the weather all this time waiting."

"You brought someone?" For a moment her heart jumped.
Did Byron have a son? She knew very little about him, al-
though he visited often. Tasha had brought up a good point.
No one really knew where Byron lived.

"In a manner of speaking," Byron replied enigmatically.
"The garden entrance . . . he's waiting there."

"You should have brought him inside," Antonietta said.

"Well, I brought him for you and hope you feel the same way when you meet him." Byron opened the door and signaled to the borzoi.

Celt walked in majestically. True to his word, Byron had protected him against the storm, so his coat was completely dry. He went straight up to Antonietta and, as if knowing she was blind, thrust his head beneath her hand. His gaze was already fixed on her devotedly. Byron smiled. "I knew you would like her immediately," he said to Celt.

Antonietta's fingers sank into the silky fur in amazement. "A dog? You brought me a dog?"

"He is not just any dog." Byron closed the door against the lashing rain and wind. "Celt is a companion and protector. He knows how to stay out of the way yet will always be with you, completely devoted. As long as this dog is with you, should there be need, I will be able to aid you, even if I am a great distance away." He watched her face carefully for any indication of unease at his words. It wasn't logical for Antonietta to accept his differences so easily, yet she never seemed to question him.

Antonietta dropped to her knees as she ran her hands over the dog's powerful chest and down its back. "He's very large. And he seems built to run. How will I ever be able to give him adequate exercise?" She wanted to keep the animal. The moment she touched the dog's warmth, the moment she felt his long nose, gentle in her palm, she knew there was a connection. The dog was meant to be hers. She was desperate to have him, but at the same time she was aware of her limitations. "I want you to be happy."

"Celt. His name is Celt. Borzois do not stay with people who make them unhappy. It is his choice, and judging by the way he has taken up position at your side, I would say he has made it. He needs rest and to regain his strength. His former owner was quite abusive. Apparently, Celt was owned by a young lady who had the misfortune to marry the wrong man. He was locked in a tiny pen where he could barely stand, and he was starved."

"How awful. I feel his ribs." Antonietta rubbed the silky ears. "We'll get him strong again. *Grazie*, Byron. Truly. You make me want to cry that you would think to bring me something so wonderful. How ever did you find him?"

Byron shrugged casually. "I heard his call. He is a powerful dog but extremely gentle. He will obey all commands from you, including to attack should there be need. He will watch over you when I cannot be with you. Did you hire a bodyguard?"

"Justine is working on that for me. I know a woman who runs an international agency. I met her several years ago and was impressed. She's an American, but all of her people are skilled and speak several languages. I'm certain whomever she sends will be fine." She allowed the dog his own inspection, knowing scent was important in the animal world. "So you are called Celt. I'm Antonietta. I've never had a pet in my life, so please bear with me. I'll do my best to learn quickly."

"He is not a pet," Byron corrected. "He will provide protection and companionship, but he chooses freely who he wishes to stay with. You can connect with me, so it is possible you can connect with him. The brain patterns are different, but if you practice, you can pick up his signals. It is all electrical currents."

"I never thought of how it worked or that telepathy could be used with animals. Can you pick up his feelings?"

"Of course. He picks up ours. An animal will become upset if a child cries or its companion is distressed or in danger. You will see."

"*Grazie*, Byron, this is a wonderful surprise." For a moment she hugged the animal, trying to remember the last time she had been given a gift. Her cousins thought she could have anything she wanted, so they never bothered. "You'll have to tell me how to exercise him properly."

"I think Margurite will like him," Byron said. "She has a natural affinity for animals. I have noticed she can draw wild creatures to her."

"Can she?" Antonietta was astonished. "No one has ever said a word to me, not even Justine, and she's my eyes here at the palazzo." With one hand resting on the dog's head, she tilted her chin at Byron. "What did you mean, when you were carrying me home from the cliffs, that there was a way I could see through you? You do incredible things. Is there a way you can make me see?"

Byron let out his breath slowly. His own hand found the

dog's silky fur. "That question is difficult, Antonietta. It is wrong to tell an untruth to one's lifemate. Yes, I can aid you to see through my eyes, but it wouldn't be permanent. You would see what I see through our mind link. As long as I was with you, sharing my eyes, you could see. Anything beyond that is a different matter and one I do not have all the answers for at this time."

For a moment his wording threw her off. She'd never heard the words *lifemate*, but the idea of seeing was far too intriguing to change the subject. "I'd actually see? I would see little Margurite? My grandfather? The cousins? You? I could see myself in a mirror?"

"Yes, but you would be disoriented. Your body isn't used to signals from your eyes and would become confused. It would be better to start with something small while you are staying perfectly still. Moving would probably increase your discomfort." He wanted to gather her in his arms and hold her tight while he offered her an explanation. He could feel her confusion. It amazed him how much it bothered him when she was distressed.

Antonietta took a deep breath. "I'm going to settle Celt in my room and introduce him to the family when things calm down." She turned his words over and over in her mind, trying to make sense of them. Trying to puzzle out what he wasn't revealing to her. Trying to imagine being able to see, even if it was through his eyes.

She was surprised when the dog moved instantly to her side as she began to walk. It paced easily, not getting in her way yet remaining close to her.

"If he swerves in front of you, he wants you to stop, and there will be a reason," Byron said. "It would be good for you to try to connect, as he can also be your eyes."

"I don't like relying on anything if I can help it," Antonietta said. "It makes me more dependent."

"You rely on Justine." He kept his voice carefully neutral. "Celt is just a different tool as well as a companion. You might find he gives you even more freedom and independence. In any case, with him here, I will feel more at ease during the hours I am not with you. He needs rest now, but you will find, if he does bond with you, he will need to be with you most of the time for companionship."

Antonietta hugged the dog again. "Don't worry, Byron, I'll cherish every moment with him."

They went up the staircase and down the long hall to her rooms. After a brief inspection of the suite of rooms, Celt settled in as if it had always been his home. Antonietta was all too aware that Byron had closed the door to her quarters, leaving them alone. "It bothers you that I don't ask you questions about your life, doesn't it?"

"Why do you accept my differences so easily, Antonietta?" Byron asked curiously. "If I pushed beyond the barrier in your mind, I would be able to read your thoughts as lifemates do with one another, but I am trying to be considerate and wait until you wish to share your thoughts with me. If you do not talk to me, I have no way of knowing what you are thinking." He spared a thought for human males who had no way of reading their women's minds.

Antonietta rubbed the dog's silky ears. "Do you know the history of the Scarlettis and the palazzo? Did you know that this entire building is riddled with secret passageways? The passageways guard Scarletti treasures as well as our secrets. I want to show you something." She leaned down to hug the dog again. "Stay here, be warm."

"You are not going into the passageway, are you, Antonietta? I heard enough to know that those passageways are dangerous. I understand lethal traps are built into the walls and floors."

She slipped her hand along the bottom of the wall until she located the mechanism to open the hidden door leading to the narrow passageway.

"The secret passageway is more than a means of escape to the sea," Antonietta said. "It has been used by our family for generations to store valuable antiquities that conquerors, governments, or even the church might covet."

"With all the traps in here, are you not afraid you might take a misstep and be killed?" Byron didn't like the idea of Antonietta moving with her usual confidence through the darkened hallways, knowing sharpened blades were hidden for the unwary.

Antonietta laughed softly. "The blades were removed many years ago, just for that reason. We no longer needed to escape into the sea when invaders were upon us, so for the safety of unwary family members, the traps were dismantled." She took his hand and smiled up at him. "It is quite safe. Come with me. I'm at home in the dark, and I won't let anything happen to you. There's something in here I discovered some time ago. To me it was worth more than all the golden treasures and artwork stored in the hidden rooms."

"You are certain the traps have been dismantled?"

"Yes. Even the Scarlettis had to come into the modern age." We even installed electricity here in the passageway. We needed it for the vaults as well as lighting. Her laughter was soft and inviting. How could anyone resist her laughter, least of all he?

Byron took her hand and followed her into the dark passageway. She didn't turn on the lights in the hidden labyrinth of hallways. She didn't need a light, and it said something about how well she knew him that she didn't bother with one for him.

"The night my parents died, I knew something was wrong. I woke up and could barely breathe. I called to them, but they didn't hear me. I ran up onto the deck. I could hear the sound of the clock ticking. Later, when I told Nonno, he said it was my imagination. But it wasn't. I knew there was a bomb on the boat. I jumped into the sea as it went off."

The door swung closed behind them, locking them in the narrow passageway. It was pitch black. No light seeped its way into the maze of halls. It was so narrow, Byron's shoulders nearly touched on either side. "It is possible you heard it and felt it, Antonietta. Many people have built-in alarms and even a kind of radar."

"For years I blamed myself. I left them there. They didn't come up on the deck when I yelled to them there was danger. I don't know why, but they didn't come." She led him through two sharp turns, steered him away from the wider of two passages. "That was the first time I ever felt the beast."

Byron felt her fingers tighten involuntarily around his. He immediately pulled her close against his body. "You were a child, Antonietta, five years only. You barely escaped death yourself. As it was, you must have hesitated long enough to get caught in the blast."

She ran her hand over his chest in a stroking caress, and

her fingers were trembling. "I know that . . . now. Children tend to blame themselves. I turned back when I saw they hadn't come up on deck, and I screamed for them to hurry." For a moment she rested her head against his chest. "I was too small to climb up on the railing to get over the side, but I felt a power moving inside of me. It was growing and spreading. The night was so dark, there was no moon, and it was black. The sea was black. All of a sudden, I felt something moving under my skin, almost as if it were alive, and I itched terribly. And then I could see everything. Not like my normal sight—in a different way—but the night was suddenly clear. I heard my mother whisper to my father. She'd be right back, she was going to check on me. They thought I had a nightmare. But it was already too late. I leapt up on the railing. One single jump. It was so easy. And then the world went white, and then red and orange, and then black for me."

Byron could feel the deep sorrow in her. It didn't matter that the events had taken place so many years earlier, they were as fresh in her mind as the day they happened. He held her tightly, buried his face in the fragrance of her silky hair. "I am so grateful you survived, Antonietta. I am sorry for the loss of your parents. You must have loved them very much." He reached to breach that ever-present barrier in her mind. Wanting her memories. Wanting to know what the power inside of her had been. Where it had come from.

"They were wonderful. You rarely saw one without the other. They were so close. They always seemed to have secrets. Come on, I want to show you this." She stepped away from him to tug at his hand. "I've never told anyone what really happened that night. I knew they would think I was crazy. I was born with the Scarletti ability to heal. And several of us are telepathic, although the ability is limited. I've never been able to communicate so clearly with anyone as I can with you." She stopped in the middle of the long passageway and ran her palm along the top of the wall. "When I discovered this room, it was covered in cobwebs, I don't think anyone had been here for years."

Byron reached up to find her hand with his, to slide his fingers into the centuries-old depression to find the hidden mechanism for revealing the chamber. As the door opened, a light glowed from within, automatically coming on. At the same time a musty, stale air greeted them. Byron turned her away from it, shielding her with his larger frame while he blew into the room, at the same time creating a small wind with his arms. He waited until he was certain it was safe to breathe before he moved out of Antonietta's way.

"How did you do that? I can do a few things, but I can't carry two adults across the cliffs and down that narrow, slippery trail to the palazzo. I swear our feet never touched the ground, and you were moving so fast the wind blew in our faces. I can draw on the strength of the beast, and sometimes, I can see images of heat, much like an infrared I suppose, but I can't do the things you do. Like I saw the other night when it scared me. It wasn't me seeing, but something else."

She stepped into the small room. Byron followed her. It was no more than the size of a walk-in closet, long and narrow. And the walls were carved from floor to ceiling with a mixture of symbols, pictures, and ancient language.

"This is the history of my family," Antonietta said. "Our heritage, what we are. And after Nonno showed me this room, I wasn't afraid of myself anymore." She tilted her head toward him. "And I would never be afraid of you." She waved toward the wall. "I give you the cat you were looking for last night. The Scarletti cats."

Byron stepped closer to the wall, ran the pads of his fingers over the intricate carvings in the same way she had "read" the images. There were pictures of jaguars, men and women half jaguar, half human, caught for all time in transition. The earlier carvings were crude but detailed. The later drawings quite beautiful as if great care had been taken in creating them. "This is amazing, Antonietta. Has anyone else seen this?"

"No, I felt it was better to keep it to myself."

Byron had to agree with her. The contents of the room would be very damaging to the Scarlettis and their position in society. But the carefully kept account of the Scarletti history was important to his people. His fingers flew over the wall, reading as quickly as he was able. "So this is the reason you do not fear my differences, and you accept them so easily."

"I knew immediately you had to be one of the males, and

your bloodline must be stronger even than mine." She took a deep breath and let it out. "I know you won't stay, Byron, and that's okay. It really is. I have no wish to be married. I'm quite content with my life the way it is. I've never considered a permanent relationship with a man. Taking a lover is a different thing altogether. For as long as you want to stay, I think it will work out perfectly for the both of us."

He turned slowly, rested one hip against the carved wall, and folded his arms across his chest. There was a long silence. "So you will not mind when I leave you?"

Antonietta heard the soft underlying growl in his voice, the snap of his teeth. A shiver went through her, and for the first time unease crept into her mind. Byron seemed an easygoing, courteous gentleman, with old-fashioned, courtly ways. She remembered the way her assailant had been flung backward, the distinct sound of bone snapping. How carelessly the body was thrown away from them. Byron had never even checked to see if the man still lived, he had known he was dead.

"Well, obviously, I've read this many times. I understand perfectly the need for the male of this species to wander. I'm telling you I accept the inevitable and don't want you to feel bad about it." Even as she spoke, she took a small step backward, her hand going protectively to her throat. Her pulse beat frantically as if calling to him. The spot where he had left his mark the night before throbbed and burned.

"There is an inevitable, but I doubt it is what you envision." He reached out casually, almost lazily, and circled the nape of her neck with his palm, drawing her toward him. She went reluctantly, taking one small step at his urging, then another until she could feel the heat of his body right through the thin barrier of her clothing.

Both hands found his chest. "Why are you angry?"

He was smoldering with anger, with the thought that she was certain he would leave her. That he would *want* to leave her. That she seemed totally accepting, even grateful that he would leave her. Byron made an effort to tamp down the seething cauldron of emotions. That way lay disaster. "What it says on this wall is that a group of women and children arrived, seeking sanctuary. There were a few males, old mostly, or very young, but the women had no men to protect them. They wanted permission to live on Scarletti land, under the protection of the Scarletti family. They were foreigners, come from a distant land with strange ways. It is said these women had tremendous psychic abilities. They were telepaths. Healers. And all of them were shape-shifters."

Antonietta nodded. He wasn't holding her in place, his fingers were very light, almost gentle around her neck, but she still felt the tension vibrating in the air between them. "The picture clearly shows a large cat of some kind."

"The Jaguar," he supplied. "I have heard of this species. They are all but extinct. The males refused to stay with the females, and eventually the females took on human husbands. The bloodline thinned over the centuries."

She nodded her head in agreement. "I feel the cat inside of me at times. Warning me. I have an acute sense of smell. I'm blind, yet at times when the wildness inside of me is growing, I see in colors of red and yellow and white. Heat images. I thought when you smelled the cat last night perhaps one of my cousins is the same, and I'm not such a freak. It's true, Byron. This is the reason the Scarlettis made a bargain with the women in the village. They wanted the gift of the Jaguar people for their own. Some of the Scarletti men intermarried with those women, and some have the blood strong and some don't. I read the wall carefully. You are so correct about the men leaving. The women were willing to stay with humans because their males never stayed. They got them pregnant, and they left, even during times of war and hunger and plague. So the women turned to our race for companionship and love and a family."

"As they did in other places as well," Byron said.

"In the old days, women had few rights and little protection, but in the world today, we're quite capable of caring for our children and providing for them. I have a good life, and I never expected to meet someone I was so attracted to. Honestly, Byron, I'm just saying I didn't expect nor want a lover for more than a short period of time."

His breath escaped in a long, slow hiss of annoyance. "Unfortunately, that is not what I expect or want, Antonietta. I am not Jaguar. My people do not leave one another for reasons of convenience or wanderlust. We mate for life. For eternity. I do not want less, nor will I accept less. You have much to learn of who and what I am." His dark gaze roamed possessively over her face.

She could feel the impact, the intensity, as his gaze burned over her. She was immediately reminded of the suffocating darkness she lived in. Alone in the close confines of the room, it was too late to remember she knew very little of this man standing so close to her. She knew nothing of his family or his heritage or even his heart. He was always alone and very quiet, very polite, but he could be shockingly violent in an instant if need be.

"Who are you, Byron?" Her voice came out a husky whisper of fear when she needed her confidence most. "Tell me who you are then. Tell me what you are. If not Jaguar, like me, what are you then?" She held her breath, pressed her hand to her somersaulting stomach.

Byron's thumb tipped her chin up. She felt his breath on her face. Warm. Inviting. His lips skimmed the corner of her mouth. Velvet soft. So persuasive her heart leapt. "I am your lifemate. Keeper of your heart as you are the keeper of mine." The words were whispered against her eyes. His lips trailed down her face to find her mouth again. Soft. Insistent. Feather light, yet with all the power to rob her of breath. Of speech. Of sanity. Her brain refused to think of anything other than wanting him. Having him for her own.

His words sounded foreign and even formal, but it still didn't stop her from turning her mouth up to his. Of wanting him with every cell in her body. Byron. She had dreamt of him for so many lonely nights. Erotic, passionate dreams of wild sex and heights of pleasure she didn't believe really existed. His lips crushed hers, and he was devouring her, his mouth hot and male and exciting there in the dark of the hidden room where the bizarre secrets of her ancestors decorated the wall.

They simply melted together, two halves of the same whole. There was fire and electricity. There was a curious rippling of the earth beneath their feet. He pulled her closer, fit her body tightly against his, imprinting his every muscle on her soft flesh. He knew how she would feel, all soft curves and mesmerizing heat. The flood of passion welling up in her to meet his darkest cravings. Byron had known almost from the moment he had heard the first exquisite note of her music.

Antonietta circled his neck with her arms. Byron took her into a world of hunger and passion and light. Where her music came from. Her deepest joys and sorrows and erotic dreams. Her every want. She couldn't help wanting to be closer, wanting to feel the incredible heat of his skin. She slipped her hands beneath his shirt to feel his defined muscles. She ached with wanting him, her body already turning liquid and needy.

"Byron," she whispered his name, the voice of a siren. An invitation to paradise.

His teeth nipped her full lower lip. "Do you want me to make love to you, Antonietta? That would be so simple for you. No attachment. No love between us to get in the way." His hand shaped her breast, his thumb teasing her nipple into a hard peak. He bent his head to the temptation right through the thin fabric of her blouse. Her breasts were luxuriously soft and full. She had a woman's curving body and was generously endowed. His mouth closed over the soft, luscious mound, hot and moist and suckling strongly so that Antonietta arched back and caught his hair in her hands to drag him closer to her.

Her knees went weak, and she cried out, afraid she would have an orgasm right there, just from his mouth on her breast. His tongue licked along the valley between her breasts up toward her throat. "Is this what you want? Just a physical relationship?" He lifted his head, and she felt his eyes burning like lasers. "This is good enough for you?"

Antonietta's fingers bunched in his hair, nearly desperate to pull him back to her. There was no reason to feel guilty, but she did. "It has always been good enough in the past," she said defiantly, and then was instantly ashamed that he had managed to rattle her when it was none of his business what she did or even what she preferred.

Byron straightened slowly, his hands slowly releasing her. His body withdrew from hers, leaving her feeling cold and alone and bereft. "It is not good enough for me."

Antonietta pushed an unsteady hand through her hair deliberately stepping into the passageway to give herself space.

"You can't possibly want a long-term, *permanent* relationship with me. You don't even know me."

"That is not precisely true, Antonietta. There is very little about you I do not know. I took the time, sitting quietly in your home, listening to you. Hearing the music you play, watching you with your family. I know you far better than you think. You have not taken the time to get to know me. You thought you could have me for a lover, and your perfect world would remain intact. You wouldn't have to do anything different at all, but in truth, there is always change and consequences."

She didn't like seeing herself through his eyes. He made her feel shallow and self-centered. "There is nothing wrong with a woman being practical, Byron. Men take lovers and walk away all the time. They've been doing it for centuries. I'm practical, not unemotional. I have a family depending on me, I have a full-time career. Can't you see that I'm making sense? You're not in love with me." She dared him to lie to her and say he was.

He paced away from her, returned to stand over her. She felt his shadow even in the darkened passageway. Felt his presence, not the man she was so comfortable with, not the man she had come to think of as sweet and courtly, but a dangerous predator stalking her in the narrow confines of the Scarletti passageway. She had the impression of lips drawn back in a silent snarl and fangs exposed. "How would you know what I feel or do not feel?" His voice was so low it could barely be heard, yet there was a note in it that increased her fear even more.

Antonietta put out her hand. A test. Byron instantly caught her hand, drew her palm to the warmth of his chest. She could feel his heart beating. Steady. Strong. A perfect rhythm, and her own heart seemed to want to follow. "I didn't mean to hurt you." She stepped closer to him. "I did, didn't I? I hurt you by saying I didn't want a permanent relationship with you. I didn't mean it the way it came out." Why had she been so afraid? How could she ever think that Byron, with his impeccable manners, would be anything but generous and courteous? She was becoming fanciful after her misadventure in the night.

"No man wants to be told he will be discarded gladly,"

Byron said. "It is a bit hard on the ego." He brought her fingers to his mouth.

Antonietta expected a brief kiss. His mouth closed over her finger. And it was hot and moist and everything it had been when he had been lavishing attention on her breast. She thought she might fall down, simply melt into a puddle on the floor. "I think my hormones are in overdrive, Byron." She had no other defense besides humor. "If you keep that up, I might have to consider ripping your shirt right off of you."

"I do not think that is designed to stop me, Antonietta." There was a hint of laughter in his voice. His teeth nibbled at her finger, scraped along the pad of her thumb. "How did you discover this room? You do not come into the passageway that often, do you?"

His tone sounded mildly curious, yet she had the impression he was waiting for her answer. That his tone was quite at odds with his emotions. "Most of my life I could manage to read people, Byron. I've always thought it was because I was blind, and I had to rely on other senses to get by. You're very difficult, because you don't say very much and I can't rely on your voice to give away your emotions." She reached up to touch his face, gently mapping his expression with her fingertips.

"I have never been blind, Antonietta, although for a long time I was color-blind. I saw the world in shades of gray and white and charcoal. It is a condition in the males of my people. Most lose the ability to see in color when they come into full power, but I took much longer."

Byron seemed so sad, suddenly she pressed closer to him. "What is it? What are you thinking of?"

"A time long ago when I had a childhood friend. More than a friend. In my world, our siblings can be quite a bit older. My friend was my family. We were never far apart from one another, and he made life bearable for me. I worked with jewelry, and Jacques would try his hand at it." His mouth curved at the memory of Jacques's antics. Byron was a gem-caller, able to sing the stones of the Earth into revealing themselves, and Jacques often accompanied him into the deepest caves. "My friend disappeared for several years and was presumed dead. My life was hell after that. I felt alone, and maybe I was even angry with him for dying and leaving me behind. I felt lost, without an anchor. And one day I saw a woman. I could see her in color. I knew she had red hair and green eyes. When that happens, the male of our species knows she is the one woman. But I could not see anyone or anything else in color, which did not make sense if she were my lifemate, as colors are fully restored to us through our lifemate. I should have known better, should have taken the time to think things through, but I was not so patient back then."

The sadness weighed so heavily on him, it seemed a burden, a great sorrow. Antonietta felt it in her heart, in her mind, but she remained silent, hoping he would continue. She had a feeling he had never told the story to anyone else.

Byron turned his head to kiss her fingertips. "Later, I realized my friend Jacques and I were so close I was picking up visions from his head. He had been tortured, and he was half mad. He did not remember any of us, so it did not occur to me, at the time that I was still connected to him, still seeing through his eyes as we had often done, sharing information on our personal path. But by the time I figured out what was happening, it was too late; I had ruined our friendship and instilled a deep distrust of me in him. He needed me, and I let him down. I have regretted those rash days bitterly."

"How sad, Byron. I hope your friend is better now. And if he was such a good friend, I'm certain as he heals, he'll forgive anything you might have done."

"The connection between us is still there, should either of us decide to use it, but I no longer saw in colors. My life returned to grays and shadows. Until I met you."

The way he said it, starkly, honestly, tugged at her heartstrings. *Until I met you.* It had to be his voice that affected her so completely. "What changed?" There seemed to be a lump in her throat. Antonietta gave herself a stern warning. He was a man, just like other men, one who would come and go just as they all did. It mattered little what sweet words he came up with, in the long run, the prenuptial agreement always told what they were after. And it was never Antonietta, the woman.

"My entire life," he said simply.

And there in the absolute darkness, she wanted to believe

him. "Kiss me, Byron. Just kiss me again." Her arms slid around his neck, and she pressed her body close to his. An offering. A hunger. A need. She might not want him to be special, might not want to believe he was different from all the others to her, but she needed him to kiss her. And she had never needed anyone.

He murmured something in a language she had never heard before and bent his head to hers. His lips feathered over her face, along her cheekbones, a soft assault on her senses. There was tremendous strength in his hands as he pulled her even closer, fitting her body into the cradle of his hips. His mouth teased hers. His teeth tugged at her bottom lip, a sweet temptation that left her helpless to resist had she wanted.

Antonietta moved restlessly, a deliberate enticement. When he was with her, when he was near, she had a difficult time thinking of anyone else. Anything else. She craved him in the way an addict might a drug. "A compulsion," she murmured. "That's what you are. A sorcerer, and you've cast a spell on me."

"And here I thought it was the other way around." He whispered the words against her lips.

Before she could answer, his mouth took possession of hers, and the world turned upside down. It didn't matter that there was no light, colors burst behind her eyes and exploded like fireworks in her mind. Beneath her feet the earth rippled so that she clung to him. She lost all ability to breathe, yet he was the very air for her. Antonietta clung to him, unprepared for the way her body simply went soft and pliant and needy. "This has never happened before."

He kissed her again. Thoroughly. Hungrily. As if she were the only woman in the world, and he *had* to kiss her. Needed to kiss her. And then, abruptly, he lifted his head. His eyes glittered a fiery red above her head and for just a moment fangs gleamed white in the stark black of the passageway. "There is someone coming this way," he said. His tone was free of all menace, but she caught a brief glimpse of the inherent violence in him. A beast roared for release, struggled for supremacy. His calm demeanor never wavered, but she felt it just as if it were in her.

She felt him reaching out with all his senses, inhaling

deeply as if he could scent an enemy. "No one comes in here, Byron," she whispered. "We store great treasures, artwork, and jewels. The rooms are designed to keep them in the precise temperatures needed to preserve them. Not even family comes in here without first getting permission from Nonno or from me."

He placed his lips against her ear. "Someone is in the passageway and moving stealthily, not with confidence. I doubt they have permission." He saw the glimmer of a light moving toward them. "They are nearing us. I can hide us from his sight, but the passage is too narrow for him not to bump into you. We will have to go into your history room and close the door."

Byron felt her swift intake of breath in reaction to his words. The involuntary clenching of her fingers into a fist in the fabric of his shirt. His arm tightened around her. "You will be safe with me. I know the space is small, but I can get out, should something go wrong with the mechanism."

There was complete confidence in his voice. Antonietta could not tell him of a world of suffocating darkness. Of waking up choking, strangling, her throat closed, fighting desperately for air. Her heart pounded with alarming force. She nodded wordlessly, not trusting her voice. She abhorred the mind-numbing fear that inevitably caught hold of her when she was on unfamiliar ground.

Byron drew her into the small confines of the little room and nudged the door until it swung shut, sealing them in. He dragged her close beneath the protection of his shoulder. With the door closed, the light was gone, hiding the Scarletti secrets as it had for centuries. Byron ran his fingertips along the wall. The carvings were smooth and precise, a work of art, even as it was a kind of diary of each generation. He caressed the figure of a shape-shifter, first in human, then half and half, and then fully in cat form. The Jaguar. A sad ending to a species. The blood was so diluted it was doubtful if more than a handful remained with full abilities. So many species gone or nearly gone from the earth.

Antonietta's fingers found him, tracing over the same beautifully drawn figure. *If you are not, Jaguar, what are you, Byron?* Instinctively she used the more intimate form of communication. Somewhere on the other side of the wall someone skulked about the passageway with a hidden agenda of their own.

I am of the earth. My people have been in existence since the beginning of time, in one form or another.

Then you do shift shape! You can, can't you? She was very excited.

His breath was warm on her face. His lips touched her cheekbone. *If I were to answer yes, would it in any way influence you to consider adding me to the Scarletti gene pool?* He was listening to the furtive footsteps as they moved past their hiding place.

That's not funny. But laughter bubbled up anyway. And joy. It was true. She wasn't losing her mind as she often imagined when the beast rose up strong within her, roaring to be set free. *I'm too old to even consider having a baby.* She said the last to sober up. She was too old to consider a permanent relationship, even if the man intrigued her and made her feel beautiful and young and filled with happiness. It was infatuation, physical attraction, a crush that would soon pass. It had to pass soon.

His palm slid down the length of her hair, weighed the heavy braid in his hand. *You do not know what old is, Antonietta.*

There was a wealth of amusement in his voice. *I would like to find out who is out there. He is male, and a member of your family. Normally I can easily scan human thoughts, but the Jaguar influence is prevalent in this area. He feels like Paul, but I cannot scan many of the people here as easily as most others. If I press, he will feel my presence. But I can follow him and see what he is up to.*

Antonietta bit down hard on her knuckle to keep a protest from escaping. She had come into the maze of tunnels hundreds of times. It would be silly to be afraid of being alone. She could easily find her way back to her room once out of the history room. Byron would be the one in danger of being caught in the intricate labyrinth that ran through the many levels of the Scarletti palazzo.

Scan them? You read thoughts? I thought it was only me, that we just had some form of telepathy together. You can read everyone?

And you do not? In the board meetings your grandfather

insists on dragging you to, do you not hear what the others are thinking? Before she could answer, he patted her hand. *I will return in a moment.*

Antonietta opened her mouth. Whether she was going to agree or protest, she wasn't certain, but he simply disappeared. His body had been warm and solid, and then it was gone. They hadn't shifted position to open the wall entrance. She put out her hands, carefully explored all four walls. He had simply vanished. Silently. Completely.

She pressed her hand against her open mouth and leaned against her ancestor's wall of records, shocked. *What are you?* She ran her fingers over the wall, searching every word, every symbol, and every picture in the hopes of finding another shape her people were capable of shifting into. There was nothing to indicate any of them could simply disappear. She believed in shifting shapes, but completely disappearing was an altogether different proposition. Why did Byron's ability to vanish make her so uneasy when finding her family's history had been such a relief?

7

Antonietta *nearly had* a heart attack when Byron's body was suddenly crowding hers in the small confines of the room. She flattened herself against the wall as his much harder frame pressed against hers, but her fingertips went to his face, reading his expression, mapping his familiar face. As often as she did it, he never flinched away, never seemed to mind. "Byron." She breathed his name aloud, thankful he was back, wanting to know his every secret.

Did I startle you? He kissed the corner of her mouth, left a trail of flames down the side of her neck in apology. *It is Paul.*

Antonietta went still. "Paul." She said her cousin's name aloud. "He never goes inside the passageway. He's never even looked at a map. He doesn't like confined spaces. His father used to lock him in a closet when he was angry with him. Which seemed to be all the time. Are you certain? What would make him chance coming in here?" Her fingers were already searching out the hidden mechanism to open the wall. "He's bound to get lost in here. Unless you have the map and the key to the map, you could be lost for days."

"It might do him good," Byron said grimly. "He is up to no good."

"You don't know that." The door slid open without a sound, telling Byron that Antonietta came to the room often enough to keep the mechanisms running smoothly. She had that faint haughty note in her voice that always made him smile. He followed her into the passage. "Which way did he go?"

"To the left." He placed his lips close to her ear. "What is to the left."

"The vaults. How would he know that? Only Nonno and I know the exact location of the vaults. He can't be going there." To her annoyance, she didn't sound certain.

"Perhaps he had help. When you come in here to catalogue, do you have a pair of eyes? I would venture to say Justine knows exactly how to get to the vault room."

"She wouldn't—"

"She is in love with him." Byron paced along behind her in the narrow confines of the tunnel. His breath was on the nape of her neck. His body heat warmed her. "What would you do for the man you loved, Antonietta? Would you betray your family? Your friends? Would you do anything for him?"

"Any man I loved would not want me to betray my family and friends." She lifted her chin as she moved confidently through the twists and turns. "If he did, he wouldn't be worth loving, now would he?"

"How do you know where you are going?"

"I count. I memorize everything."

"You are amazing." There was sincere admiration in his words, in his tone.

The genuine compliment made her insides glow. No one said things like that to her. No one else ever gave her personal compliments. Not even her grandfather. Her talent as a musician and composer was taken for granted. Don Giovanni simply shrugged and said with all the lessons she'd been given, she better be considered one of the best in the world. A Scarletti could never be second.

Byron's hand simply rested on the small of her back, but it generated so much heat, so much desire, she felt her skin melting beneath this touch. The physical awareness was so great she had trouble concentrating. Antonietta reveled in the intensity of her craving for him. It had never happened to her before, and at thirty-seven, she never thought it would. She was determined to enjoy every moment with him if she could, as long as she had him, even here, in the dark passageways of the Scarletti palazzo with her idiot cousin sneaking to the vaults.

Antonietta could feel the pressurized air flowing through an open door. She instinctively slowed down, keeping her footfalls soft on the cool tile. It was only then that she realized that, although she was very aware of Byron, she couldn't hear him. She could feel his hand melting through her back, at times his breath on her skin, but he moved so silently, she would never have known he was there without her heightened senses.

Her heart was pounding overloud in alarm. In regret. Not so much at what her cousin was doing but the fact that Justine had to have helped him. Her Justine. Antonietta's eyes and ears in the palazzo. In the business world. In her profession. She trusted Justine implicitly. She had to. The door opened to the vault room tore apart her heart, shaking her hard-won confidence.

Byron's heart was breaking for her. His Antonietta, who loved and trusted her cousins and Justine. She had made them her world, and yet they thought nothing of what it cost her. Anger swirled inside his gut, a hot, roiling emotion that thickened the air in the passageway, making it difficult to breathe. The tension magnified until raw energy ran through the tunnels, a forerunner of immense danger.

Looking over Antonietta's shoulder into the vault room, Byron could see Paul examining several gold artifacts. Several times, he picked up an intricately detailed ship made of gold and put it back down. It was large, and he couldn't find a way to hide it under his shirt. *He is helping himself to the Scarletti treasures. At the moment he cannot choose between a golden ship or a necklace of rubies and diamonds.* Even from the distance, Byron recognized the glittering piece. He had crafted the necklace with great care, his hands fashioning the gold into the intricate setting for the beautiful gems. It had been a lifetime ago. And he thought of his lifemate while he worked, making it with infinite care, knowing he was making it for the bride of someone considered important in the political world. It fascinated and intrigued him that a Scarletti bride had worn his creation. A soft hiss of anger was trapped in his throat as he watched Paul's greedy hand grasping the necklace to him.

Show me.

He hesitated but shared the images reluctantly.

Antonietta made a single sound. A soft cry of despair. She remembered that necklace, one of the few things she did remember from her days of sight. She had loved it, been fascinated by it, and the thought of her cousin stealing it, taking its elegance and fire out of the family, was horrifying. That small sound of heart-wrenching despair called to the demon already roaring for release buried within Byron.

Startled, shocked, Paul swung around, his face twisted with fear and purpose. There was only one heartbeat of time to see the shiny metal object clasped in Paul's hand as he turned. Time slowed, tunneled, as Byron dissolved into molecules, to materialize once again in between Paul and Antonietta.

The blow to Byron's chest was so hard it knocked him backward, off his feet, slamming his body into hers, driving them both against the opposite wall. In the small confines of the passageway, the explosion was deafening. The bullet tore its way through his body and out his back, slamming into Antonietta's shoulder. As he fell on top of Antonietta, his body protecting hers, he tried to focus on Paul, focus on his throat to cut off all air. He could not leave Antonietta, helpless and vulnerable, alone with her treacherous cousin.

Paul coughed, staggered, nearly went to his knees. The gun in his limp fingers wavered alarmingly. Byron's vision blurred. He was losing too much blood too fast. Without shutting down his system, he would be unable to recover. Animal instinct turned his head to see Celt racing toward them.

The borzoi had sensed trouble and managed to nose open the hidden door. A silent hunter, the animal ran full out, his long legs covering ground like a well-oiled running machine. The eyes were fixed and focused on prey. It mattered little that it was human. Celt leapt over Byron and Antonietta, going straight for Paul, teeth slashing at the arm holding the gun. Paul screamed in pain and dropped the weapon.

"Antonietta! I didn't know it was you!" Paul yelled, struggling to hold off the dog. Already his arms were a mass of cuts from the slashing teeth. "Call him off, call off the dog!"

"Celt!" Antonietta used her most authoritative voice. She could see nothing. Byron's motionless body covered hers, pinning her to the floor. Her back hurt as well as the front of her shoulder. "Stay, boy. Paul, if you make one move toward me or Byron, I'm letting him loose, and I won't call him off." She had no idea what had happened, but she smelled blood. Her sensitive fingertips found liquid, warm and sticky. Pools of it.

"It was an accident. I didn't know it was you. The gun just went off by itself. You startled me." Paul realized he was babbling and started toward his cousin.

The borzoi stood between them, head down, eyes alert, still in hunting mode. Paul stopped at once. "He won't let me get to you, and Byron's bleeding all over the floor. *Dio*, Antonietta, I think I've killed him."

"You shot him?" Antonietta fought down hysteria and panic. "Get over here and move him off of me. Stop feeling sorry for yourself and help me save him."

"The dog—"

"Is going to tear you apart if you don't do exactly what I say! Now come here and move him. Be very careful, Paul. If he dies, you're going to spend the rest of your life in prison. I won't even help with your defense!"

"I'm telling you, Antonietta . . ." Paul carefully skirted around the dog. "I didn't shoot anyone on purpose. I didn't know what was down here, so I brought protection with me. I never even came in the tunnels when I was a child."

Antonietta felt Byron's body shift, move off of her, allowing her to crawl out from beneath him. "You were an idiot to bring a gun with you. Where in the world did you get a gun, anyway? Why would you even have one?" She was frantically trying to find the wound, searching for a pulse.

Paul moaned loudly. "He's dead, Antonietta, there's no pulse."

She shoved her cousin hard. "Get away from him! He's *not* dead. I won't let him be dead. *Byron!* Don't you dare leave me alone. Come back! Damn you, Paul, how could you do this?"

She couldn't find a pulse either, and for a moment her world stopped. There was no air to breathe. Her vocal cords wouldn't work. There was nothing. Emptiness. A black void where there had been life and laughter and her music. She had nothing.

The struggle started in her mind. A voice whispering to her from far away. Soothing her. Telling her it wasn't so. *I must see him.* The words were the first she understood. *Look at him. I must see him.* She had never heard the voice, but it was low and compelling and insistent on obedience. He spoke in her language but with a definite accent, so velvet soft he seemed to purr.

Antonietta took a breath, let it out slowly, her hands gripping Byron as if she could hold him to her. She forced herself to follow the path of that faraway voice. She wouldn't waste time on fearing it. She feared that the meaning of her entire life was spilling blood on the tiles there in passageway. Nothing mattered to her but to save Byron. *I am blind. I cannot show you what I see.* The borzoi pushed his nose against her face as if to remind her he was there.

A dog is with you? This dog was Byron's dog? I have it now. Yes, the wound is bad. He is not dead but has shut down his system to conserve blood. He will need special care. Do you have help?

My cousin. Paul is the one who shot Byron.

There was a moment of silence and Celt shifted his body, his dark eyes focusing on Paul. "I don't like the way that dog keeps looking at me," her cousin said. "I think it wants to tear my throat out."

"I should let him," Antonietta snapped, furious that Paul would want sympathy.

Are you near soil of any kind? Rich soil? You will need to pack the wound with it. The bullet exited and tore a hole through his back. Your shoulder is injured as well.

"I'm going for help, Antonietta. We'll need the doctor," Paul said decisively. "I think you were shot, too."

She didn't notice, she concentrated on the voice. *Tell me what to do.* She had to believe that distant voice. *Who are you?*

Jacques. Byron has family in the area. If you can get him out of there into the open, they will come and care for him.

I want to care for him. But Antonietta was already on her feet, tugging at Byron's dead weight, trying to drag him down the tunnel. The dog caught at Byron's jacket, adding his strength to hers.

"What the hell are you doing?" Paul demanded. "He's dead, Antonietta. We have to get you medical attention."

"Just help," she snapped. "Don't say anything, or I may pick up that gun and shoot you myself! I can't believe you brought that thing into my home."

"I have people after me," Paul admitted, reaching down to help pull Byron along the floor. "I got into some trouble with some people I owe money to. They aren't the kind of men you want to meet up with without a gun."

"I thought you quit gambling, Paul."

"Aren't we going the wrong way? We're going downhill, toward the cove."

"That's right."

"You aren't going to just dump the body, are you, Antonietta? I mean, *grazie,* but we have to inform the authorities. I could have killed you, too. We have to give them the body, well, we *should* give them the body, but if it was found in the sea, or never found—"

"He isn't dead," she said between her teeth. "Shut up and concentrate. We have to get him outside."

"You aren't making sense, Antonietta." But Paul continued to help pull the body down through the maze of tunnels until he could smell the sea.

It took hard work, but between Antonietta, Paul, and the borzoi, they managed to get Byron outside. The rain was falling steadily, sheets of it, so that they were instantly soaked through. The wind whipped at them.

"Find me soil, Paul, rich soil, not sandy sod. I want good soil."

Paul muttered and shook his head, but he did as his cousin wished, taking off his shirt to heap the soil from the beds the gardener had planted just above the cove. He was well aware Antonietta had remarkable powers as a healer, but even she couldn't bring back the dead. He rushed back to her side and knelt to watch as she packed the wounds, front and back, with the soil. "If you did manage to bring him back, he'd just die again with gangrene."

"That's not funny." Antonietta wanted the reassurance of the voice again. *We're outside, near the cove. I've packed the wounds with soil, but he isn't responding.*

Call to him. He will hear you.

Antonietta didn't hesitate. Her insides were churning, and she wanted to scream and scream. To let the wind carry her horror and the fear held so tightly in check out over the sea and away from her. She never wanted to feel so afraid, so empty and dead again. She leaned close, sheltering his face from the rain. *Byron. Byron, open your eyes.* Her hand trembled as she stroked back his hair in a small caress. *Don't leave me now that I've just found you. Wake up before I begin to weep and scream and plead like a ninny. I'm really afraid, and I need you.*

Byron became aware of many voices. At first he couldn't sort them out. There was chanting in the ancient tongue. Antonietta, summoning him imperiously back to her. Someone was yelling his name. He identified his sister Eleanor's voice. She sounded close to him, yet he knew she was far away. A man's voice called to him calmly yet with command. Jacques. Byron was certain he was hallucinating. He hadn't spoken telepathically with Jacques in years. "Maybe I really am dying." He muttered the words aloud to test his voice.

"No you're not! I refuse to allow it," Antonietta replied firmly. The relief was so tremendous she felt ill.

Pain spread through him, and before he was fully aware, through her, so that she gasped and caught at him. "You need a doctor desperately. You've lost so much blood, Byron. You appeared dead, I couldn't even find a pulse."

"No, I do not need a doctor, but I would not mind strangling your cousin. Was he trying to kill you or me or both of us?" Byron's black eyes had already found Paul kneeling beside Antonietta. Paul was very pale. He shook his head in denial. Byron noted Celt had positioned his body for a full-out attack should one be necessary. The dog was in alert mode, watching Paul's every move. Byron's dark gaze went back to Antonietta's white face. There were dark circles under her eyes and blood all over her. It took a minute before he realized not all the blood was his.

"Antonietta, you are injured." Byron made an effort to rise despite the weakness sweeping through him. The world tilted alarmingly, and blood gushed from his abdomen. His fingers found the gash in her shoulder, lingered there.

Strangely, at his touch, the pain in her shoulder lessened. She pressed him back. "It's nothing, lie still. Your friend Jacques told me your family was close. He said they would come for you."

"I had no idea any of my people were near. Go into the house. Keep Celt with you at all times. I will come as soon as I am able. Go now, Antonietta, or you will catch a chill. Your shoulder needs attention."

"I'm not leaving you alone."

Byron waved his hand to still all speech. His concentration couldn't be broken when his reserves were nearly gone. The rain fell steadily. The waves crashed and boomed endlessly. Paul knelt motionless, unable to move or speak. Celt stood over the man, eyes burning alertly. Byron reached for Antonietta. No one else mattered. Nothing else mattered. Not even his broken, torn body. He caught her to him, drew her down, his mouth finding her torn wound. He didn't have the energy to leave his body and enter hers, but he took his time, using precious minutes to heal her shoulder.

Byron fell back, exhausted, watching the blood soak into the ground from a distance. He hurt, the pain intensified by his movements, but it didn't concern him as much as watching Antonietta come out from under his enthrallment, seeing her move much more easily, seeing the white lines of pain etched into her face ease.

Paul pressed forward, jerky now that his body was once again his own. He blinked several times, trying to remember what he had been doing. He only saw Byron's nearly translucent face turned up to the rain. If a smear of blood had been on his mouth, it was gone now, washed away by the rain. "I'm sorry I shot you, Byron. The gun just went off."

"And if Byron hadn't jumped in front of me, you would have shot me," Antonietta said, glaring at her cousin.

"Nonno is going to throw me out," Paul said.

"I'm going to throw you out," Antonietta countered, furious with him. *Does he really think an apology is sufficient?*

She was shaking, and she preferred to think it was from anger and outrage rather than fear.

Byron took her hand, brought her fingers to his mouth. *Probably, but he will find out differently. Please do as I ask and go in. Someone is coming for me.*

Celt stiffened, his head going up alertly. Dark clouds swarmed across the sky, shadowing even the rain so that it went from silver to black. Plumes of white water swirled madly, rising in several towers toward the veiled moon. A bird of prey with a hooked beak and razor-sharp curved talons flew overhead and circled the small group in the cove. The wind rose to a howl. Faintly, far off, the sound of animals answering could be heard.

The rain slashed at them, whipped into a frenzy by the sudden fury of the storm. The large owl landed on a tree above the path leading to the cove several yards from them. The heavens opened up and poured the rain down, a solid sheet, blocking sight of the bird. When it cleared, a man walked down the path toward them. He was enveloped in an old-fashioned, long, black cape. The folds swirled about his legs and body, and the hood hid his face. Rather than walk, he gave the impression of gliding, his feet not quite touching the ground. He halted a short distance from them, his outline vague and insubstantial in the silvery rain.

Byron struggled to a sitting position, holding out his hand toward the stranger in warning. He tugged at Antonietta's wrist. "Go, now, take Paul and get him inside the tunnel. He is not safe out here. Do as I say quickly." He issued the command, nothing less, burying a push in his tone to force compliance.

There was something so compelling in Byron's voice that Antonietta took Paul's arm without protest and hastened back into the Scarletti passageway. Celt stayed a moment longer to study the motionless figure in the distance, but he loped after Antonietta, disappearing into the dark caverns.

The two men stared at one another in silence. Byron pushed himself up with an unsteady hand. Blood ran into the sand and dirt beneath him, staining the ground a reddish pink. He managed to get his feet under him.

"Do not be foolish and waste your energy." The voice

rippled with power. It was quiet, almost soft, yet carried the force of nature.

Byron studied the man approaching him, gathering his strength as he did so. Lightning flashed across the sky, lit up the ground to reveal the small river of blood. "I do not recognize you. Have we met before?" Byron knew he had never before met the ageless stranger. The eyes were shimmering fire, the face etched with hardship.

"Your kin was not close enough to reach you in time." The voice was very quiet, a pure, velvet tone. "I offer my blood freely that you may live."

Byron knew even the most evil and cunning of vampires could appear noble and virtuous. They were master deceivers. Without taking his eyes from the stranger, Byron nodded slowly, even as he sought Jacques. *Do you know this one?* It had been years since he reached down that familiar path to his childhood friend. He felt awkward and stiff, but it was necessary. His enormous strength had run out onto the ground, leaving him swaying and weak. And there was Antonietta to protect. He would live to defeat any vampire to protect her.

He must be one of the ancients sent out by my father. I do not recognize him, nor has he yet sworn allegiance to our prince. It was discovered ancients were sent out across the seas to protect where they could. The call has gone out to bring them home. Jacques was guarded in his reply. *Do not lose consciousness. Focus on him.*

Byron burst out laughing. "Does one have control over losing consciousness? What do you think?"

The stranger was on him, a tall man with old eyes and a faint, humorless smile. "My guess would be that you should remain alert so your friend, watching me so closely, may continue to guard you properly. I am called Dominic." He bowed low, an Old World, courtly gesture of respect. "I have been long from our homeland. You are one of the first of our kind I have seen in a long time."

"I am Byron. I thank you for your assistance," Byron returned formally. "I would greet you in the proper way of the warrior, but I am afraid I would fall down." A faint smile took some of the pain from his face.

"It is not necessary. We are brethren. It is enough." Very

casually, Dominic tore at his wrist with his teeth, opening a gaping wound that he pressed to Byron's mouth. "I am on my way to see our prince and to see for myself if it is true that his lifemate was human."

The blood poured into Byron's starving cells, ancient blood, pure and strong. Byron tried not to be greedy when his strength was all but gone and the sudden infusion of ancient blood hit with the force of a freight train. The rush was heady and overwhelming.

"The borzoi guards your lifemate well. He would have attacked me, had I made a wrong move, yet he recognized what manner of creature I am. I had forgotten their loyalty and heart. I thank you for providing the memory."

Byron sank down onto the earth, felt the soil reaching for him. Comforting him. Very politely he closed the wound on Dominic's wrist. "You have hunted long."

"Too long. I have grown weary and wish to sleep, but I must bring news to our prince. There is something evil sweeping the land. It is subtle. So subtle I cannot find the source of it, and I have looked. But it threatens our prince and our people. It threatens our very existence and way of life. I must warn him and then continue in my hunt for my lost kin."

Byron felt the blood moving through him. It had been so long since one of his own kind had shared blood with him that he had nearly forgotten the heady rush. "Lost kin? Is the prince aware one of our people is missing?"

Dominic leaned down, gathered Byron into his arms as if the full-grown man were no more than a child. "My sister was an apprentice to a great wizard. She had amazing skills, and under his tutelage she became adept at many things now lost to our kind." Dominic shifted shape, still holding Byron securely, sweeping through the sky under cover of the storm.

The words triggered a distant memory, a fairy tale told of magicians and wizards among their kind teaching safeguards and spells to their people. Byron closed his eyes, allowing weariness to sweep through him. He reached to connect with his other half. His soul. *Antonietta? Are you well? Did they see to your wound?*

Byron? I left you alone. I can't remember what happened. Why would I leave you alone? There were tears in Antonietta's voice. She sounded forlorn, agitated. Not at all like his confident lifemate. *How could I have done such a terrible thing? For my cousin? To save my cousin? I can't think why I would have left you.*

Be calm, cara mia, *I am fine. I asked you to leave me so my people would heal me in our way. It would have been too complicated to allow a doctor to see to my wounds. They would have insisted on calling the authorities. This is best.*

No! It isn't best! I knew there was danger, I felt it all around us. It was storming and cold, and you lost so much blood. Tasha screamed when she saw me. I was covered in your blood. I should have stayed with you to protect you. To heal you. I have skills.

Byron smiled. Even a Scarletti with her unusual legacy did not have sufficient skills. He sent her waves of warmth, of love. *I shall be with you tomorrow night. Keep Celt close to you at all times. You will not be able to reach me until sunset tomorrow, so do not panic if you reach for me and I am not there.*

I need to touch you. To know you're really alive.

Their connection was already fading. Antonietta tried desperately to hold on to the link between them. Byron drifted in and out of consciousness as Dominic took him to a series of caves deep beneath the earth.

"We will rest here this night." Dominic opened the earth, cutting into a section of rich soil before lowering Byron into the cool, welcoming ground.

"Tell me of your kin. How is it she is lost to you?" Byron roused himself enough to seek the companionship of his kind.

"I am a hunter of the vampire. I was born a hunter."

"Where I was not."

Dominic shrugged his shoulders. "One who hunts when it is not their heritage is a warrior to respect. It is all I have known, even in my fledgling days. Those were dark times, long before the wars that destroyed most of our people. My sister learned much, and even Prince Vlad consulted her. Some say she knew too much. Some say she turned on her people, wanting to rule, believing it was her right."

"You are of the Dragonseeker blood." Byron leaned his head against the soft soil and looked up at the man who had shared his lifeblood. "When I was a fledgling, I used to go to the house where you once must have dwelled. The carvings, the artwork was so beautiful. I wanted to be able to create such wonders. That was a long time ago."

"The old house still stands? It would be a miracle to see it again."

"Out of respect for your lineage," Byron said. "Nothing has ever been touched, only to preserve it for you or any of your kin should they remain."

"My sister was loyal to Prince Vlad and our people. No Dragonseeker has ever betrayed our people. Not one ever turned vampire. I cannot rest until I find who took my sister from us and clear our name."

"I have never heard it whispered the Dragonseeker blood was tainted," Byron objected. He watched as Dominic swept his hand around the cave so tiny pinpoints of light leapt to life. The stranger took powder from a small container and blew it across the cavern. The scent was aromatic and soothing.

"I am grateful that in my absence, such a thing was never suggested." Dominic knelt beside Byron and began to gather handfuls of the earth. He mixed the soil with a second powder and his own saliva. "You will need more blood before you go to ground. The wound is quite extensive and did much damage to your internal organs. How is it you have hunted the undead, yet that human male was able to harm you?"

If there was a reprimand in Dominic's voice, Byron couldn't detect it, only mild interest in how a human managed to injure a Carpathian hunter. "Perhaps I am a better craftsmen than hunter."

"I have noticed several of the people in this place have strange barriers. It is better to take your lifemate and leave this place. Take her to our homeland. She will eventually get used to it and get over being annoyed with you." Dominic helped Byron to lean forward so he could pack the material tightly into the gaping back wound. "A craftsman who turned hunter to aid his people is always welcome at a warrior's campfire. Craftsmen are meticulous and methodical. It is an honor to meet one such as you." Dominic's hands were gentle as he helped Byron to lie back down.

"The prince found his lifemate some time ago," Byron volunteered the news. "It seems that some human women possess psychic abilities, and those women can be successfully converted without fear of madness."

"I have heard this rumor. How can this be?"

"I believe it is possible that the women we are finding with psychic powers are descendents of the Jaguar race."

Dominic once again mixed the rich soil with his powder and saliva to pack into Byron's chest. "I had not thought that any remained unless deep within the jungle."

"Not true Jaguar, but of their blood. It would explain why the women are compatible with our race. The Jaguar are shape-shifters, and they had many gifts, as our people had." Byron closed his eyes. "Do you leave tomorrow?"

"At sunset. I have not found the undead dwelling in this region," Dominic answered. "I will continue my travel as soon as I rise. You will heal in the ground and be safe for several risings."

"I must be able to wake tomorrow evening. Antonietta will grieve. I do not want her to suffer."

"You will not be at full strength, but I will make certain you wake."

Byron's attention was caught and held by the piercing gaze. "You have green eyes." Not just green but glittering, metallic green. Eerie. Eyes that saw through to the soul. "I should have remembered, it is the Dragonseeker's legacy. Eyes of the seers."

"I am weary now, Byron, I do not see what should be seen. Once I find the answers I seek, I will follow my kinsmen into the next life."

"Or find your lifemate. I did not think it possible, yet there is no doubt that Antonietta is my other half."

"My lineage is all but gone. Rhiannon and I were the last of our line. I doubt if either of us would have been so lucky." Dominic stood, looming over the deep cut in the earth. "Sleep now, and wake fully healed. I will give your regards to our prince and give him the news that another woman will join our ranks soon. That alone is cause for celebration."

"I thank you for your courtesy and for my life."

Dominic bowed low in the way of the Carpathians. "You

must sleep now and allow me to attempt to heal these massive wounds."

Byron could hear the voices again, many of them, male and female, chanting the healing ritual in his head. *Sleep, old friend, we are with you, and we will watch over you while our brother heals your body.* That single voice of friendship took him back in time, when he ran free with the wolves, sat in the tallest trees, and was simply a boy playing with a friend. He allowed himself to drift off, the soothing voices distant. And one feminine voice whispering, *Come back to me.*

8

Antonietta sat at the piano, her hands curved over the keys. Music welled up inside of her. Poignant. Frightened. A clash of emotions. Her fingers brought beauty and poetry to the chaos, blending notes until the music swelled in volume, unable to be contained in the room with its perfect acoustics. She was blatantly calling to her lover to end her mourning. The music moaned and wept, pleaded and begged. Became soft and lilting as a siren. A melody of enticement.

The doors to her rooms were locked as they had been all day. She would see no one. Not even Don Giovanni could persuade her to open her doors. The seconds had ticked by, as loud as heartbeats. Long. Lasting minutes, hours, days. She couldn't bear to go on without him. Byron. Her dark poet. She had lost him before she had a chance to know him, and the agony was beyond her comprehension.

Grief ravaged her. Ate at her. Blocked out her anger at her cousin. At her family. At Justine. She refused comfort from them all. Only Celt was allowed to remain with her as she wept and threw things in a way very unlike Antonietta. She cried a storm of tears, raged at the heavens that they would allow her cousin access to a gun. Through it all, the dog paced at her side, guided her around the missiles she had thrown, and thrust his head lovingly against her in consolation and camaraderie.

The music shifted into melancholy, the notes taking flight, spilling out into the great halls so the entire household was silent with grief. Even the children spoke in whispers, and Marita shushed them. A pall hung over the palazzo. Antonietta, their lifeblood, their mainstay, the one person constant in their lives, was devastated as she had never been before. Over a man. Worse, over a man they feared. The symphony played on endlessly, an outpouring of tears and anguish, until even the servants were weeping.

Outside, beyond the multitude of colors in the priceless stained glass windows, the storm had long since passed over, yet clouds rolled across the sky, darkening the moon and blotting the stars so that the gargoyles and winged creatures sitting atop the eaves and battlements were shadowed and dark.

Antonietta felt the music rising in her, the relentless, merciless emotions, a volcano erupting endlessly. She was driven to play, unable to stop. And then she felt the weight of his hands on her shoulders. The warmth of his breath on the nape of her neck. The touch of his lips in her hair. Her fingers stilled on the piano keys. There was abrupt silence after the intensity and power of the music. The palazzo hushed instantly, an eerie shock after the hours of passionate sound.

Antonietta sat on the gleaming piano bench without moving, without daring to believe he was there with her, that he had come to her after all the long hours of stark fear and grief. Her heart seemed to cease beating in her chest, her world narrowed to his hands. The heat of his skin. The warmth of his breath. The beating of his heart. Her heart stuttered, found the rhythm of his. Beat in perfect synchronization. She whirled around, her arms going around his neck, her cry muffled by his mouth melding with hers.

Byron tasted her tears, tasted love and acceptance. His lips traveled over her face, her eyes, memorized her high cheekbones, the small dimple, returned to capture her mouth. There was heat and fire and need. The earth shifted out from under them. Her hands tugged at his shirt, desperate to inspect his body, to see with her fingertips. It was almost more than she could bear to wait. She nearly ripped the material covering his skin even as she kissed him back, ravaging his mouth, telling him without words what she needed.

Byron shrugged his shoulders, and the shirt fell away, exposing his chest to Antonietta's inspection. She couldn't stop kissing him. Over and over, frantic, long, drugging kisses. Her fingertips inspected every inch of his chest, every defined muscle, his rib cage, his narrow waist. She found the scar, still raw but nearly healed, and she gasped with alarm into the heat of his mouth.

He nearly killed you. I thought you were dead. She couldn't speak aloud, her mouth traveled over his jaw, down his throat to his chest.

I told you I would live. I am sorry you were so frightened. He closed his eyes, threw his head back, his fists bunching in her hair as she tugged at his pants, desperate to take them off of him.

I need to touch you, every inch of you, and know you're alive and here with me. I never want to feel like that again! Her tongue tasted him. Textures and feel and taste were all important to her and in the aroused state she was in, a mixture of sexual hunger and intense emotion, Antonietta wanted to touch and explore and savor him.

Your shoulder? His hands left her hair to push her robe from her arms. It floated to the floor, a soft pile of lace. The spaghetti straps of her gown were minute, yet he pushed them off her arms as well so that the gown slithered to the floor.

Antonietta barely noticed, as she dragged his clothes from his body. She rubbed her face over his chest, his abdomen. He tore the tie from her long hair so that it spilled, unbound, around them, silky and teasing her flesh.

"Antonietta." He whispered her name in a husky blend of hunger and need as his own inspection began. The wound on her shoulder was nearly healed, although she was bruised, but the bullet had been spent from tearing through his body. It had lodged in the hollow of her shoulder, a shallow penetration, and Byron had removed it when he attempted to heal her. There was little damage to the muscle, but he leaned down to lap at the bruise.

It's nothing. Nothing at all. I have no idea how you man-

aged to get around me in the narrow confines of the passageway, but you saved my life. She was moving her hands with loving patience over the ridges of his hips, his buttocks, moving them around to the hard column of his thighs.

"You are distracting me." He barely managed to get the words out. It was too late anyway. Her hands cradled the thick length of him, her fingertips memorizing the feel and shape of his heavy erection with maddening slowness. Flames danced over him. Her fingers were strong and sure, not tentative in the least. She knew exactly what she wanted, and she did it, tracing every inch of him, her fingertips dancing and playing with the same expertise she used on the piano.

The breath slammed out of his lungs. His body tensed, went taut, every muscle contracting in reaction to the caressing stroke of her hands.

I need this, Byron. I need to know every inch of you. You can have later, but give me this. She didn't wait for an answer. Her teeth nipped his belly, her tongue tasted his skin. She blew warm air over his erection, was pleased when he hardened even more.

He made a single sound, somewhere between torment and ecstasy, when her mouth closed over him, hot and moist and suckling strongly. "Antonietta." His voice was husky, his breath slamming out of his lungs. "*Dio,* woman, I cannot believe you." His fingers found her hair, held her to him while his hips found a gentle rhythm he could barely endure. It was sweet torment. Fire burned in his belly and spread through his body until flames were consuming him, and the roaring in his ears joined with the roaring of the inner beast, insisting on his rights.

The need to claim his mate rose sharply, more intense than any sexual appetite. He felt his incisors lengthening, and he turned his head away from the temptation of her soft skin, vulnerable and exposed to him. Flames licked at him, devouring every good intention. "Antonietta, you are in danger." He gasped the warning out, tugged at her hair to raise her head, to acknowledge she had some modicum of self-preservation. He couldn't save her alone. He had waited and needed and longed for her for far too long. She had nearly been killed in front of him, not once but twice. He was at odds with his own nature in trying to court her in the human manner.

Antonietta lifted her head. She looked a sexy siren, a wild, uninhibited temptress, with her long coils of hair cascading around her like a living cloak and her dark, haunted eyes, heavily fringed with long lashes. "Never from you."

A low warning growl rumbled. He kept his face averted. "I am trying to protect you."

"I don't want protection, Byron. I don't need it. I'm a grown woman, and I take responsibility for myself. I know what I want, and I want you. I want you to make love to me." Her fingers never stopped moving, caressing, playing. She kissed his belly, his chest, leaned into him to nibble on his chin.

Byron could feel her there, pressed tightly against him, into him, her body soft and pliant, a willing offering. Her blood called to him, hot and sweet and addicting, a potion made just for him. *Antonietta. Lifemate. You are mine. I have searched an eternity for you.* "I will not go quietly away into the night. Do not think I will, Antonietta. I am not Jaguar. There will not be an easy way to rid yourself of my presence should you decide you are bored."

Her arms circled his neck. She fit her body close into the cradle of his hips. "Now you are trying to scare me by sounding like a stalker. Just make love to me. Does it matter that we may have to talk about our future later?"

She smelled so good. Clean and fresh and tempting. Her head was back, her throat alluring. Byron buried his face against her neck. Against temptation. His tongue found her pulse. Felt the beat. The rhythm went through his body so that he shuddered with the pleasure of it. With the hunger of it. His need was so intense he burned throughout every cell in his body. Teeth teased her skin over her throbbing pulse point. He inhaled her scent. "It matters that you know I tried to court you in the way of your people." He closed his eyes, aching with need.

"I think you did an admirable job." She rubbed her body against his, much like a cat, skin to skin.

His mouth moved over her neck, left a trail of fire, of flames. His teeth scraped gently back and forth, his arms tightened possessively. His body was alive against hers, hard and thick with life and energy and hunger. Matching the hunger sizzling in his veins. His mouth moved, once, twice. Mesmerizing her.

Antonietta's entire body clenched in reaction. Heat spread, built like a wildfire. A firestorm of need and far more emotion than she wanted to admit. There was white-hot pain, instantly giving way to erotic pleasure flooding her body, heart, mind, and soul. He lifted her as if she weighed no more than a feather, as if she were his entire world. She felt like she floated across the room, a dream of passion such as she'd never known.

He murmured to her, the caress of his tongue stealing the ache from her neck as he laid her on the bed, his body blanketing hers. His mouth drifted over her face, her eyes, settled on her mouth. *How could you think I would not love you?* His teeth teased her chin, feathered down her throat to blaze a path of fire to the swell of her breast.

Antonietta cried out, arched into him, craving more. She cradled his head to her while her body rippled in response, tightening in exquisite need. Hunger built, swamping her with its strength, until she was frantic for him to be inside her, frantic for some semblance of relief. "Byron, don't wait." She tried tugging him to her, trying to drag him over her, her hips urging him into her. Byron was patient, taking his time, his hands leisurely exploring her body, memorizing every detail, imprinting her body on his mind for all time.

Antonietta closed her eyes, the pleasure so intense it bordered on pain, as his mouth moved over her belly, lower to explore the triangle of curls. She felt frantic to have him. To feel him deep inside of her. The need was so strong, so intense, her entire body shook. Everywhere he touched her, kissed her, she ached and burned for more.

His hands parted her thighs. She waited, holding her breath, and then the air exploded from her lungs as he tasted her, as he stroked and caressed and brought her body to full life. His name came out in a sobbing plea for mercy. Antonietta had never wanted anyone more. Byron. Only he could complete her. Her fingers found the silk sheets, bunched there, as waves of ecstasy swept over her, through her. She transferred her hold to his hair because she couldn't, *wouldn't* burn alone.

Byron lifted his head, slid over the top of her, his hips settling lovingly into the cradle of hers, a coming home. She was wet and hot and slick, so tight he gasped with joy as he entered her. One slow inch at a time.

His entire body shuddered with pleasure. He caught her hips in his hands, surged forward to bury himself deep inside of her. A safe haven. His world was changed forever. He no longer walked the earth utterly alone. He would never be alone again. Antonietta changed his world. Brought him light in his unrelenting darkness. He tilted her hips, wanting more, wanting her to take all of him.

Antonietta's body rippled with life, an earthquake that went on and on until she thought she might die of ecstasy. Nothing had prepared her for the strength and intensity of her orgasms with Byron. She hadn't expected such a gift. No previous experience had even come close. She actually sobbed, her senses so heightened, her body so sensitized, his every movement sent whips of dazzling pleasure sizzling through her.

Her world narrowed to one man, one being, his body moving in perfect rhythm with hers. Blood sang in her veins, her pulse pounded in her ears. Music rose in a crescendo as he threw back his head, his body driving deep into hers, long, hard surges meant to weld them together. Two halves of the same whole. Antonietta thought she screamed with the intensity of it, with the dark endless joy sweeping through her. Byron's voice blended with hers, or maybe it was only in her mind, she honestly couldn't tell. There was only the heat and fire and blessed melting together until they were exhausted, two puddles lying in ecstasy on the sheets.

His body shuddering with pleasure, Byron put his lips against her ear and whispered a command. His fingernail lengthened, razor-sharp, and slowly opened a wound on his chest. He pressed her mouth to his skin. The first touch of her lips had him gasping, whips of lightning dancing in his bloodstream. He heard the words beating in his mind. His heart. His soul. Clamoring to be said aloud. The beast lifted its head, unsheathed its claws, and roared loudly for its mate. Ti amo. *If I have been remiss in telling you,* ti amo, *Antonietta.* He took a deep, calming breath for both of them, holding on to his control while he fought down madness. "I claim you as my lifemate. I belong to you. I offer my life for you. I give you my protection, my allegiance, my heart, my soul, and my body. I take into keeping the same that is yours. Your life, happiness, and welfare will be placed above my own. You are my lifemate, bound to me for all eternity and always in my care."

He could feel the ties binding them, millions of threads tying them together for all eternity. Everything inside him shifted and settled. Peace stole into his heart and mind. He gently stopped her from taking more of his lifeblood than necessary for a true exchange. He woke her from the enthrallment with a long, drugging kiss, taking the haze from her mind, pouring the intensity of his emotions into the kiss.

Antonietta wrapped her arms around Byron's neck, giving him back kiss for kiss, reveling in the thickness of his body buried deep inside of her. "I've never felt like this in my life. Never." For one moment there was a peculiar taste in her mouth, not unpleasant, but unfamiliar, but then it was gone, and fire sizzled hot and out of control.

"You sound so astonished." Byron nuzzled her throat. "You obviously had little expectations."

She laughed, and there was real joy in her voice. "I had *great* expectations, and you lived up to every one of them." She wanted to hold him forever. Her hands smoothed his hair, found his back, moved to inspect his chest. "Roll over. I want to check your stomach. I still can't believe you're alive. I was so certain you were dead. I reached for you, over and over, but I couldn't connect."

Reluctantly, Byron eased out of her, separating them. At once he felt bereft. "I think I will have to make love to you again, Antonietta."

Her fingertips found the wound in his chest. "You should be dead."

"Yes. My kinsman saved my life by giving me his blood. Where is Paul? Has he been questioned?"

She pressed her lips to the wound. "Not by me. I couldn't bear to talk to any of them. I didn't want to hear his excuses." She shivered suddenly. "I didn't realize that it was cold in here. I didn't even notice, you should have told me."

"I rarely get cold. I will start the fire, and we can sit in front of it." He stood up in one smooth motion and tugged at her hand.

"I don't have any clothes on. I can't just walk around naked." The thought of him staring at her body alarmed her. For once she wished she really knew what she looked like.

"Of course you can. You do not need clothes," he said softly. "I prefer to look at your body. It is beautiful. A woman is such a miracle of soft curves. And it gives me the opportunity to touch you when I have the need." His palm skimmed over the swell of her breasts, over the small mound of her belly, and nestled for a fiery moment in her dark curls. His finger slid into her, teased and caressed until, wet and hot, she pushed back with her hips, riding his hand with a gasp of shocked surprise. "I love this about you, you heat up for me so fast."

She gasped as an orgasm rippled through her. "I've always enjoyed sex, but I had no idea it could be like this. I really didn't. It's frightening how good it feels. Frightening and addicting."

"Good," he said with evident satisfaction.

"I can't just stand here naked while you stare at me. It's cold in here." Her body was tingling, throbbing with life and pleasure.

Byron brought his fingers to his mouth. "You taste good. Did you know that? I'll start the fire. The chairs are comfortable, and we can stretch out while we talk. I would like to hear how Don Giovanni took the news that Paul not only shot me, but you, too." He waved his hand toward the large fireplace, and it leapt to life, flames crackling around the logs. "Surely your grandfather was informed. You were injured. They must have brought in the doctor to treat you properly."

"I didn't need to be treated. The bullet was already out of my shoulder, and it was nearly completely closed. You did that, didn't you?"

He touched her shoulder, the lightest of touches. "I would never leave you in pain. I knew it would take time to return, but I thought your family would insist on a human doctor to make certain."

Antonietta was certain he hadn't moved, hadn't stooped over to start the fire, yet almost as the words left his mouth, she felt the warmth of the flames. She could smell a wonderful, aromatic fragrance. "What is that?"

"Candles. My people believe in the benefits of aromatherapy. Both of us could use healing and more energy." His fingers skimmed her bare shoulder a second time, traced the wound there lightly, lingered with a soothing touch. "Your cousin is very lucky to be alive." He wanted to rip Paul's throat out for even coming close to endangering Antonietta.

"My cousin is an idiot. I have no idea what I'm going to do with him."

"Is it possible to read the mind of your family in the same way you eavesdrop in the boardroom? Perhaps next time, we should probe to see what he is going to do next."

"I don't eavesdrop," she denied. "I listen, there's a difference. Read the minds of my family? My cousins? Why would I want to do that? I know what they think about, and its scary just contemplating it, let alone actually hearing it." The smile faded from her face. "I believe in privacy, Byron. I wouldn't want to spy on my family's private thoughts."

"Let me get this straight, Antonietta." Byron sat in the deep-cushioned chair and leaned comfortably against the high back. "It's perfectly okay to eavesdrop on business conversations using your acute hearing, a gift most humans do not have, by the way, but it is not okay to eavesdrop on family." There was something frightening in his voice, so much so that a shiver went down her spine. She knew she would never be in danger from him, but at times, he seemed more a wild animal, untamed and prowling and capable of great violence.

Antonietta took the chair facing his. The warmth of the fire reached her and took away the chill of the aftermath of fear. "When you put it like that, I'll admit it doesn't sound right, but business is what keeps our family and our lands. Nonno is having a much more difficult time remembering details. I've had to stop him several times from signing something that would have cost us an enormous amount of money. Fortunately, we have great lawyers, and Justine reads everything to me so we have a net, but without me listening in, we could have problems." Her sigh was loud in the quiet of the room. The rain outside fell softly on the French doors, matching her melancholy mood. "I had hoped that Paul would take an interest in the company."

There was something very sexy about sitting naked in front of the fireplace. She could feel his gaze, hot and intent and entirely focused on her.

"I would worry that perhaps he *has* taken an interest in the company. The gun was aimed at you."

"It was an accident. I know it was. Paul has admitted he made terrible mistakes. He owes money to people who he says will get rough if he can't pay them back. He bought a gun but didn't really know how to use it. I spoke with Justine—"

Byron nodded. "Ah, yes, the loyal and trustworthy Justine."

Antonietta frowned at him. "These people are my family, Byron. I know you've been wonderful about not going to the authorities and reporting Paul. You have no idea how much I appreciate it. He would go to prison, and we both know he wouldn't stand a chance there." Without conscious thought, she leaned her head back, the action jutting her generous breasts toward him. "You should have seen him when we were young. I wish you could have known him. He has a brilliant mind, and he was so wonderful as a boy. His father stripped him of all self-confidence and the will to even try. Adults certainly have a way of ruining children."

For the first time Byron laughed. "That is the truth. My sister took in a boy a few years ago. He is proving quite a handful. Eleanor, of course, thinks he is an angel and indulges his every whim." He couldn't resist the silent invitation, his hand cupping the weight of one breast in his hand, his thumb caressing the tempting peak.

"You have a sister?" She was surprised. He never talked of his past or his future. And he never talked of his family. "That man the other night, Jacques, said you had family in the area." Her entire body was hypersensitive. She never wanted him to stop. She needed his touch, the way he always seemed to *have* to touch her. It was addicting.

"Did you think my parents found me under a rock? I have in-laws as well." Reluctantly, Byron let her go, leaned back, stretched his legs toward the fire, and watched the way the flickering light played over her face and body. "You have beautiful skin." The words slipped out before he could stop them. Personal observations made Antonietta uncomfortable.

She was startled by the honesty in his voice. It was impossible to keep pleasure from rising. *"Grazie.* It's nice to know that."

He reached out and took her hand. "Eleanor lost several children, and it was very hard on her. She had one son and managed to raise him into a reasonably decent man. You would like him. Vlad, Eleanor's lifemate, took him firmly in hand when Eleanor would get too carried away with spoiling him."

"Why don't you use the term husband? You always say lifemate."

"In my language, in my people's world, we refer to our other half as lifemate. Unlike the Jaguar, we mate for life and beyond. Not for momentary pleasure. We consider the art of making love and keeping our mate happy to be a lifelong commitment."

There was something very wicked in his voice, almost a challenge. She had the feeling he was smiling. Antonietta decided discretion was the better part of valor. "So you have a nephew, too." She was all too aware of his fingers stroking her skin. His thumb slid over her inner wrist. She had no idea how sensitive a wrist could be. Her insides instantly melted.

"Yes, Eleanor managed to carry a son. Benjamin. Benj was—is—a miracle to all of us. He is shaping up quite nicely, and we are all very proud of him. My family is of the crafts. Benj prefers to work with gemstones just as I always have. I would love to take you to the caves where you could pick a gem from the walls of the cavern." There was a note of longing in his voice.

"I would love to go to a cave with you. Do you still make jewelry?"

"I have plans to begin again, now that I have found you. Looking at you sitting there with your hair spilling around you and the firelight dancing over your breasts, you inspire me. I would make a necklace of fire and ice to lay around your throat."

His tone created a very real sensation of cool gems on her skin, so much so that she reached to touch her throat, expecting to find a necklace of gold, diamonds, and rubies. "I would love to have something you designed."

"I will make you something beautiful to go with your skin and hair. It would be such a pleasure for me."

"Your nephew makes jewelry?" Antonietta loved feeling his eyes on her. She didn't need sight to know he was watching her. She was past embarrassment. She wanted his gaze on her. She wanted him to feel ravenous hunger for her. She was feeling it for him. It was even becoming difficult to keep her mind on the conversation. She was too busy thinking of straddling him right there in the chair in front of the fireplace.

"My understanding is he has begun to work as an apprentice. I have not seen him in some time. But Eleanor also has young Josef, and he is another story altogether. His birth mother was quite old when she had him, and she died within an hour of his birth. Eleanor and Vlad immediately offered to take him. Deidre, Vlad's sister, and her lifemate, Tienn, were chosen at first to watch over him, but Deidre lost so many children Tienn was afraid it would prove to be too much if the baby did not survive. It is very hard on the parents when they lose so many children. Many of our children do not survive beyond the first few months."

"I couldn't imagine losing Margurite and she isn't even my child," Antonietta said. "How sad for your sister and sister-in-law. So many people have children who really don't want them, and yet so many want them that can't have them."

"What about you? Do you want children?"

She shrugged. "There was a time I dreamt of having children. I think most women do, Byron, but I had responsibilities, and my career was taking off. I didn't find a man who appealed to me as a lifetime partner and, although I considered raising a child on my own, I decided it would be cheating the child. I often go on tours, I'm in demand when one of my operas is chosen, and I am always involved in my family's business. It leaves little time for a child."

"I see."

For some reason Antonietta immediately felt defensive. It was a silly reaction, when his words held no inflection whatsoever, but she had the feeling he was misinterpreting things she said. Over the years, she had learned to live without sight, judging reactions by voices and even tension in the air, but she couldn't do that with Byron, and it made her feel vulnerable and off balance. She pulled her hand out of his, aware he could feel her pulse jumping in her wrist. "Do you? That would be a miracle, when few people have a clue what my life has been like."

"But then I am not most people, am I?" There was the merest trace of mocking amusement in his voice.

"No, you're not," she agreed. "You are someone very special. If you are not Jaguar and you are not quite human, what are you? What exactly? And don't just put me off with some strange answer that doesn't make sense."

"I am Carpathian, of the mountains in that region. My people are as old as time and we are of the earth. You have your legends of vampires and werewolves and jaguars, and we belong to that realm." He answered honestly in the way of lifemates. His gaze didn't leave her face, judging her expression there in the darkness.

"I know you're different, Byron. It's funny, I can accept the thought of Jaguars so easily, but a werewolf or vampire seems preposterous." She laughed softly at herself. "Why would that be? Why would my mind so easily accept one as reality but refuse to give the possibility of credence to the other?"

"A Carpathian is neither werewolf nor vampire. We are a species of people near extinction and fighting for our place in the world."

She turned his words over carefully in her mind, examining them for signs of a hidden meaning. "Are you like either of those species? You must be a shape-shifter just as a Jaguar is. I've done a tremendous amount of research on the legends and mythology of the Jaguar people. Can you shift your shape? I can't. I feel it reaching for me, and I know its somewhere inside of me, but on command, I can't really do it. I have summoned the power of the creature but never really managed to bring the power out all the way."

"Yes, I can shift."

She hadn't really expected him to admit it. The idea was exhilarating and frightening at the same time. She took a deep breath. "Can you fly?"

"Yes. You know I can. I didn't erase your memory of it."

She was in the dark, where she had grown most comfortable, and she waited there for several heartbeats in silence to give her mind time to assimilate what he was telling her. Flying. Her heart soared at the idea of it, even when her human mind set limitations. "That would be such an enormous gift." Her lashes lifted. She couldn't see him, but she looked directly at him. "For a gift so wonderful, there must be a terrible price."

Byron looked at her and wanted to laugh. She was sitting across from him. His lifemate. Her bare skin gleaming in the firelight. His world of color dancing in front of his eyes. His emotions so raw and intense he could barely control them. What price had he paid? Centuries of a bleak existence. A world of gray and despair. The relentless whisper of evil calling to him. The endless minutes and hours and days and years of being truly alone. Her very existence had wiped it all away in a moment.

"I live, Antonietta. I have a way of life, and I live it. It is neither good nor bad to me to be the way I am. I simply am. I accept who I am, and I am proud of my people. We have honor and loyalty and many other traits of strength, but we also have weaknesses just as any race. I cannot walk in the sun. It would harm me. That is why I cannot be with you to guard you through certain hours of the day." His voice was very matter-of-fact. "I see beauty in the night, it is my world, my existence, and I love it. I want to share my world with you so you are never afraid in it. So you see its beauty for yourself and not just for me."

Antonietta didn't know if it was what he said to her or how he said it, but she melted inside. Craved him. Wanted to wrap herself up inside of him, deep in his heart and soul. And she wanted to see his world and experience it. His voice nearly purred when he called the night beautiful. She lived in darkness, and she wanted to see it that way.

Antonietta couldn't resist the temptation any longer. She simply stood and took the few steps to stand in front of him. Byron didn't disappoint her. He reached for her just as she imagined he would, his hand sliding up her thigh, caressing the inside of her leg with graceful, expert fingers. Her body responded instantly with a heated liquid welcome, an eager anticipation of the sheer magic waiting for her.

His hands urged her closer, and she went, standing between his legs while his palm found her wet channel, pressing heavily in exploration. Flashes of light burst behind her eyes, a show of brilliant color, while her body pulsed with pleasure. His finger slipped inside, and her muscles clenched around him.

"When I'm with you, Byron, you make me feel like I can fly with you." She had to catch his head for balance when her legs threatened to give out. Her hips pushed against his hand, wanting more, wanting him.

Impatient, she simply moved forward, straddling his thighs so that he had no choice but to remove his hand and allow her what she most needed. Her hunger was rising rapidly, almost ravenous, an insatiable appetite that could only be appeased momentarily. She settled her body over his. He was thick and hard and pierced her sheath slowly, filling her, stretching her, until the tight friction was incredible and perfect and everything she wanted.

Her breasts brushed his chest, her hair fell in wild abandon as she began to move with her dancing rhythm, with all the volcanic passion inside of her, waiting for him, waiting for Byron. She rode him hard and fast, slow and leisurely, giving them both exquisite pleasure. She heard sounds. The wind. The beat of her heart. Whispers somewhere far off. She felt everything. The texture of his skin, the shape of his bones, the definition of his muscles, and the endless rush of an orgasm that rocked their world in complete harmony.

9

"I *think your* family is getting restless," Byron said, possessively wrapping his arms around her. He could hear them, the continual whispers. Her cousins wanted someone to check on Antonietta but were afraid to approach her.

She snuggled against his chest. "It's very strange, but I can hear everything they say as if I were in the same room with them. My hearing has always been very good. I thought it was a result of my being blind or perhaps being a descendent of the Jaguar people." There was a hint of a question in her tone.

"I want to take some time to really read the history of the Jaguar people. I think it is very pertinent to my people. I have all kinds of questions for you, but I guess they can wait. I have had you to myself for some time, and I cannot blame the others for growing so restless." He leaned down, brushed silken strands of hair from her face. Bent even lower to feather kisses along her chin and down her throat to the inviting swell of her breast.

Antonietta closed her eyes as ripples of pleasure assaulted her from the inside out. She loved every moment with him.

Nothing in her life had prepared her for the way he made her feel. She could listen to the sound of his voice forever. And she reveled in his touch. "My hearing is getting better." Now there was amusement in her voice.

"It is a good thing. Someone is approaching your door. I would not want you to be caught unawares in such a compromising position." His mouth closed over her breast, and the heat and fire exploded through her body.

The knock on her door was soft. "Antonietta. Please let me in. We have to talk. You must allow me to explain. Surely our friendship over the years earns me that much."

Antonietta stiffened at the sound of Justine's pleading voice. Byron lifted his head alertly, leaned over to kiss her gently. "They are going to insist on seeing you."

"Antonietta, please. You must let me explain. Paul is devastated over this. Your entire family is in distress. Please open the door."

Antonietta winced when Justine said her cousin's name, a physical blow to the pit of her stomach, making her feel ill. "I don't want to see any of them. I don't know what I'm feeling toward them right now," she whispered and buried her face in his neck, waiting for Justine to go away.

"She hurt you. She hurt you more than Paul did." Byron stroked back the mass of silken hair from her face.

"Paul's weak. He indulges his self-pity, and I've come to expect that of him. But Justine is strong, a leader, and she's always been my most trusted confidante. She took something important from me that I'll never be able to regain. The worst of it is, she doesn't even realize it. What she meant to me is not what I was to her." Antonietta listened to the retreating footsteps. "In all honesty, I don't know what I'm going to say to her. When I think about it, I end up crying. Don't you hate emotions? They just mess everything up."

Byron feathered kisses in her hair. "You have always had emotions. I was without them for some time. I prefer to feel sentiment, any sensation, even if it is in excess."

"Even betrayal? Even pain?"

"At least you are capable of loving enough to feel love and betrayal. In any case, I believe Justine will come to regret her actions, and she understands what she lost between you.

How could she not?" He lifted her chin to kiss her mouth lightly. "They are whispering together."

"How is it we can hear them, Byron? They're downstairs. In the conservatory, I think. Why would we be able to hear them? And why don't they all go to bed and leave me alone?"

"Because, *cara,* you are important to them, and they love you. They are only showing their concern."

"Well, I wish, just for this one night, they would leave us alone."

The second set of footsteps, this time undeniably determined, was coming up the stairs. They listened as the door was approached. This time the knock was authoritative. "Antonietta. *Cara mia,* you must open the door for me at once, or I'll use the master key I've collected from Helena and open it. I mean it. I must see that you're all right. You don't have to talk to me, but you must allow me into your room. You're scaring Nonno and the children." Tasha was very firm.

"She'll open the door, too. Tasha would never bluff. I haven't a stitch on and the room is . . . Well, it's obvious what we've been doing." Antonietta panicked.

Byron waved a hand toward the bathroom. At once there was the sound of running water coming from Antonietta's private bath. The heady scent of their lovemaking dissipated, to be replaced by the fragrance of her favorite bath salt. Byron bent his head, took his time kissing her thoroughly. "You take a nice, refreshing bath. I know you have been secretly longing for one. I will let Tasha in and keep her occupied until you feel up to facing her."

Antonietta slipped from his lap. "Well, please put your clothes on. I don't want her suddenly thinking you're so hot she has to have you. *Grazie.* You amaze me how thoughtful you are." It was a measure of how upset she was with her family that she allowed him to handle the details, that she would allow him to meet with her cousin alone while she bathed in the adjoining room.

Byron waited until Antonietta had closed the door to the bath before sauntering over to the door. Another wave of his hand made the bed and clothed him in the way of his people.

He pulled open the door just as Tasha thrust the key in the lock.

Tasha screamed, a cry of shock and horror. Her hand flew to her mouth, her eyes widening. "We all thought you were dead." Her voice came out a whisper. "Thank the good *Dio* Paul didn't kill you."

Byron stepped back courteously to allow her entry. Celt inspected their visitor and turned to follow his mistress into the large bathroom, making it clear he was on the alert. The closed door didn't present a problem, the borzoi merely turned the knob with his strong jaws and disappeared into the steam.

"Antonietta is taking a bath. I think it will help to calm her and make it easier for her to talk with her family," Byron volunteered. He followed the borzoi across the room, pulling the door closed to allow Antonietta complete privacy. He was hoping it would give Tasha time to recover. She was so pale he was afraid he might have to deal with an old-fashioned swoon.

"I had no idea you were here, or I wouldn't have interrupted." She glanced at him from under long lashes. There was a mixture of weariness and relief in her dark eyes. "Antonietta was devastated over what happened, you know, and she blamed herself for leaving you when you were so injured. Paul doesn't remember why they left either."

She sighed and paced away from him, putting distance between them to help recover from the shock. Tasha always found Byron's presence unsettling, and up close, in her cousin's bedroom, she found he seemed more powerful than ever. Tasha cleared her throat nervously. "I know I haven't been very welcoming to you, but it is more than obvious Antonietta cares for you, and if you don't mind, I'd like to start over."

Byron regarded her with a raised eyebrow. Her words had been forced out, and there was a small underlying spurt of distaste he caught in her tone. "Why the turnaround? You do not need to pretend with me in order to save Paul from prison. The incident will not be reported to the authorities. You have your cousin to thank for that."

A small smile tugged unexpectedly at the corners of

Tasha's mouth. "You don't think much of any of us, do you?"

Byron didn't answer her but crossed the room to the stained glass window. "Why do you dislike me so much, Tasha?"

She laughed softly, but there was little humor in her tone. "Because you are the first real threat to ever come to us."

He swung around, frowning at her, his dark eyes puzzled. "I am not a threat to you. You are Antonietta's cousin. Unless you sought to harm her in some way, I would do my utmost to protect you. Why would you think me a threat?"

She turned her head away from him quickly but not before he caught the sheen of tears shimmering in her eyes. "That's so like you." She waved a dismissing hand.

"Tell me." This time his voice was low and compelling. If she didn't cooperate with a slight push, he had no problems pushing past the natural barriers in her mind to find her thoughts. As far as he was concerned, Antonietta's family deserved little consideration.

"Look at me, Byron. You've never looked at me. I'm beautiful, my body is absolutely perfect." There was bitterness in her voice. "That's all anyone sees when they look at me. They never look past it to see me. And if they did, I'm not talented like Antonietta or brainy like Paul. I can't have children like Marita. The moment Christopher finds out I'm barren, he'll get rid of me or take a mistress to have his child. Even if he didn't, the moment my looks go, and they will eventually, he will abandon me. Nonno barely tolerates me, and Paul is too busy feeling sorry for himself. Franco doesn't notice me because, why bother? I can't talk about stocks and the business to him." She picked up her cousin's perfume bottle and inhaled the fragrance. "I only matter to Antonietta. She can't see the way I look, and she loves me for myself. Unconditionally. I never even had that from my parents. Of course you're a threat to me. She's actually interested in you. Really interested, not some passing whim."

Tasha did turn to face him then. "I can see you're a dangerous man, anyone can see it. It's all over you, yet I know you'd never hurt her. But you'd take her away from us. Is it any wonder I fight for my own survival? Without her, I have no one." There was no self-pity in her voice, only stark truth.

"I think you are selling yourself short, Tasha. It is true that I have not seen you as a person other than Antonietta's cousin. I have been rather obsessed with Antonietta since the first moment I laid eyes on her. I knew immediately she was born for me, my other half." He smiled at her, a genuine smile. "Please forgive me for not taking the time to know you. Antonietta is my world, and that means anyone in her world is in mine also. I have no intention of doing anything that would make her unhappy, and you are very important to her."

"You do have a certain charm, I can see why she might have fallen hard." Tasha made an effort to smile at him, in spite of her feelings.

"And you have many admirable traits you do not seem to regard as assets. You are wonderful with the children. They prefer you to their own mother."

"I haven't quite figured out Marita yet," Tasha admitted. "I think about her a lot and wonder why she isn't happy. If I had the children and a devoted husband, I wouldn't need anything else."

"Not even money?" His eyebrow shot up.

"I've always had money, it's just been a part of my life. I don't know how not to have it, but it's never made me happy," Tasha conceded.

"So your greatest wish is not to have more money?" There was a certain soft note to his voice. A mesmerizing, pure tone.

Tasha tilted her head toward him, her eyes suddenly dreamy. "My greatest wish is to have a child. I want a baby to hold in my arms. Just to love. I would have made a good mother. I would have liked the chance."

"I have missed much by my ignorance, Tasha. You are a special woman."

Tasha flashed a tentative smile. "Just for that, I suppose I could call a truce between us."

"I would very much appreciate that."

"*Grazie,* for saying I am important to Antonietta." She looked around the room. "How in the world did you manage to get in here without any of us seeing you? I think that's one of the reasons everyone is a little afraid of you. No one ever sees you come and go."

He grinned at her. "Like the proverbial ghost."

Tasha took a deep breath. "Do you really think Paul was trying to kill Antonietta? Do you think he's capable of murdering her and Nonno because of a gambling debt?" Her questions came out in a little rush.

Byron hesitated, weighing his words carefully. "People do things they would not ordinarily do when they are very afraid. It is possible someone has threatened his life and he is desperate. I would hope not, but you know him better than anyone. What do you think?"

"I think I wish we were discussing Marita, not my brother. That one is so hungry for money and social position. She can't even see what she has, she's so greedy for more."

It was a typical Tasha comment, one Byron would have expected of her, but he felt he knew her a little better, and she simply said things for effect, not necessarily because she thought they were so. It was either a habit or a protection. Byron couldn't decide which, and it didn't matter.

Tasha sighed. "Paul used to have the sweetest heart. I hardly recognize him anymore. He takes advantage of everyone." She looked down at her hands. "If you had known him before, you could never have considered that he would try to harm Antonietta."

"Yet you are considering the possibility that Paul might choose to harm her now. Tell me this: If something happened to your grandfather, who inherits?"

"The bulk of his fortune would go to Antonietta. For all I know, it could already be in her name, but the rest of us would receive several million each."

"Several million each? That much? All of you?"

"Yes, of course. I don't know exactly what Nonno's worth, but it's massive. He's quite wealthy. All of us will receive enough for a lifetime, even an excessive one."

"So everyone would benefit financially if Don Giovanni died? And if something were to happen to Antonietta? Is there a will?"

"Of course. A Scarletti doesn't turn around without a will." Tasha looked uncomfortable. "I don't really know who would inherit, but it is possible most of it would come to me."

"I see."

Two bright spots of color stained Tasha's cheeks. Her enormous eyes flashed fire at him. "How dare you! What are you implying? Are you accusing me now?"

He raised his hand to calm her volatile nature. "I was merely gathering facts. I have no idea who would want to harm your cousin, but I doubt very much if you would do such a thing for money." *Jealousy maybe. But not money.* Byron thought it prudent to keep his thoughts to himself.

"What is going on out here?" Antonietta swept out of her private bath, fragrant and alluring.

Bryon's breath caught in his lungs. Everything about Antonietta glowed from the inside out. He took her hand, brought her fingertips to his mouth. "Tasha and I are getting to know one another. We have, for your sake, decided to call a truce."

Tasha went right past Byron and gathered her cousin to her. "I was worried about you, Toni."

"I was worried about me, too," Antonietta admitted. "I honestly felt if Byron was gone, I couldn't continue." She hugged Tasha back, feeling the trembling in her cousin's body.

"You are far too sensitive, Antonietta. I should have taken precautions," Byron said. "Another Scarletti gift." The first blood exchange had bound them dangerously close. If one had nearly made her mad with grief, what repercussions would the second exchange bring? He frowned, suddenly worried.

"Byron is obviously alive and well," Tasha pointed out. "You can't make yourself sick with grief like this again, Toni. And poor Nonno is beside himself. You must go to him, or he'll never go to bed."

"I will, Tasha. Until I knew Bryon was safe and out of danger, I couldn't bear to look upon anyone. And I need to check on Margurite, too. Is she happier now that she is home? Is she better tonight, Tasha? In less pain?"

"She's very restless. Marita has been harping on her that Scarlettis do not cry, that we don't make a fuss, that she should take the time confined as she is to study and fill her mind with great things. What do you suppose is wrong with that woman?" Tasha was clearly exasperated. "I've spent several hours reading to Margurite and playing games, but

Marita won't even allow television. She wants Margurite to read. Franco can't even dissuade her, and he tried, I heard them argue. If you would look at her again and see if you can speed her healing, it would be wonderful."

Byron was intrigued with the way they took the Scarletti gifts for granted. It was a natural part of their lives, just as his gifts were. They were comfortable with the use of them.

"Byron has some ability in the area of healing. He's the one who attended my shoulder, even when he was in such danger," Antonietta said. "Maybe between the two of us, we can speed her recovery. As for Marita, she seems to be obsessed with Margurite becoming a great scholar and is forgetting to allow her to be a child. She was never like this before."

"That's true," Tasha agreed. She sighed. "Honestly, Antonietta, everything seems to be falling apart all of a sudden. Tonight, I asked Helena to have a tray brought for Nonno, and he seemed reluctant to eat the food. He was muttering to himself, and I swear, he said I was trying to poison him. He denied it when I confronted him, but I swear that's what he said, and he didn't touch the food. The crazy part is, Paul did the exact same thing. I took the tray up to his room myself, and he threw it against the wall and said I was trying to poison him." She waved her arms. "I don't know how you put up with them all. Two minutes later, he was acting like I dropped the tray."

"Why would you take the food personally to your grandfather and cousin?" Byron demanded. "You have never done such a thing in your life."

Tasha glared at him. "I was trying to take Antonietta's place. Nonno was so upset, and he hadn't eaten all day, so I insisted on a food tray for him."

"Where is the food? Was it taken to the kitchen?" Byron nearly growled the question. Antonietta turned her head sharply toward him in inquiry.

Tasha shrugged. "How would I know? I certainly didn't clean either mess myself, I had Helena handle it. I doubt if they kept the food. It must have gone in the garbage can." She lifted her eyebrow. "Surely you're not hungry. And if you are, please don't eat from the trash. We do have decent food elsewhere."

"Your truces do not last long, do they Tasha?"

"Not when you behave like a moron." She looked down her nose at him. "I often do good deeds around the palazzo. Why wouldn't I?"

Antonietta decided to intervene. "What of Enrico? Has there been any word on our missing chef?" She casually tucked her hand into Byron's arm to hold him to her side. The moment he had heard of Don Giovanni's and Paul's strange behavior, she sensed he knew what their actions meant. *Tell me.*

Let me go to the kitchen and do a little investigating first. You think the food had poison in it, don't you? How could either of them possibly know such a thing?

"Enrico is still missing. The wonderful captain was here, but of course we couldn't allow him to know what had transpired, so we entertained him briefly, allowed him to search Enrico's room again, and he left." There was regret in Tasha's voice. "He's quite nice, Antonietta. And he loves the opera. I told him that for your next performance, I would try to get him good seats, and he said only if I attended with him."

"Did you keep him away from Paul?"

"Paul wouldn't come out of his room except to speak with Don Giovanni. He wouldn't see Franco or me, but Justine was in and out several times. I wasn't about to allow the captain near him. Paul was so upset, I was afraid he'd turn himself in." Tasha glanced warily at Byron. "You aren't really going to go to the authorities, are you?"

"No, Tasha, I have no intentions of turning your brother in."

"*Grazie*, you are a good man to be so kind."

"Do not mistake my intentions for kindness." There was a distinct bite to Byron's voice, and for a moment his teeth gleamed white like that of a wolf. A fierce flame burned in the depths of his eyes, giving his pupils the illusion of a fiery red.

Tasha gasped and stepped away from him, her hand going to her throat protectively. She blinked the illusion away, feeling foolish when there were only Byron's familiar dark eyes glinting at her. Watching her. Without blinking. Much like that of a predator. She shivered, afraid all over again.

Beside Antonietta, Celt lowered his head, his eyes focusing on Byron, his hair up. The ever-present supreme hunter.

Antonietta put her hand on Tasha's shoulder. "What is it? And don't say 'Nothing.'" Gently she touched the dog's head in a gesture meant to soothe. "Celt senses something. A wild animal perhaps." *Do you smell the cat, Byron?*

Tasha hesitated. "I'm being silly. For a moment Byron frightened me. He reminded me of a . . ." She trailed off. She could hardly say wolf.

Byron bowed from the waist. "I did not mean to alarm you, Tasha. I just do not want you to get the wrong impression. Paul nearly killed Antonietta. If he is the one behind the attacks, he will not get away with it. I will see to it personally. And if he proves to be innocent and someone else has targeted her, I will find them." *Celt smells the shapeshifter in me. Do not worry. There is no danger near us.*

Byron wasn't bragging, Tasha decided, he wasn't even threatening. He meant every word and uttered each with absolute conviction. The thought set her heart pounding. There was retribution buried in his tone.

"I will go down to the kitchen to investigate and then meet the two of you in Margurite's room." *Celt, forgive me, my friend, the wolf comes out in me at the thought of Antonietta in danger.* Byron placed his palm in front of the dog's nose, allowing him to catch the mixed scent.

The dog's alert posture changed immediately, the tension draining from the animal, although he stayed protectively close to Antonietta. She stroked the dog's head with caressing fingers. "Celt is already such a part of my life, I can't imagine what I did without him," Antonietta said.

"He's so devoted to you," Tasha observed, "but he's so big and sort of scary. We've never had a dog in the palazzo. Margurite will love him. Is he good with children?"

"Celt loves children. A borzoi is a great family addition. A companion and protector. Believe me, the children will come to love him," Byron assured her. He reached out to scratch Celt's ears. His hand brushed Antonietta's. Instantly, electricity sizzled and arced between them. The sexual tension in the room was shattering.

Antonietta rubbed her body along his, a contented cat, stretching leisurely. Byron bent his head to hers. Heat raced over Antonietta's skin, spread through her body instantly.

She wrapped her arms around Byron's neck, her mouth melding to his. The world was gone in an instant. There was only heat and fire and the feel of his hard, masculine frame pressed so tightly to hers.

Tasha's gaze narrowed in disgust, bored into their backs. She made a soft hissing noise of distaste. Byron swung Antonietta around, moving her toward the stained glass window even as he seemed to be devouring her, feeding on her mouth with voracious hunger. Tasha blinked, and the couple was difficult to see. The moonlight hit the glass in some way that spread a hazy veil around Antonietta and Byron. Tasha curled her hand into a fist, her fingernails driving into her palm.

She felt his eyes on her. Dark. Brooding. Filled with speculation. Engulfed in Byron's arms, Antonietta couldn't be seen, but his head went up alertly as if sensing danger. The hair on the back of her neck actually stood up in response to the intensity of his gaze. Tasha shivered and hurried to the door.

"Are you coming, Toni? It's so late, Nonno should already be in bed."

"Of course I'm coming." There was a multitude of shared secrets in Antonietta's voice. She kissed Byron again. "I won't be long."

"Keep Celt with you." It came out a command. Byron buried enough of a compulsion in his voice that Antonietta didn't hesitate, even though she frowned. Antonietta was clearly used to going her own way and making her own decisions, and very few people attempted to tell her what to do.

"Toni!" Tasha said sharply.

Antonietta touched fingertips with Byron, the merest brush, signaling camaraderie. She knew very well that Tasha, in spite of her truce, was displaying her disapproval. *She's temperamental.*

She is mental.

Antonietta burst out laughing. Tasha glared at Byron, suspecting the two of whispering together, or worse, of being amused by her jealousy. She reached out to grab her cousin's wrist with every intention of yanking her out of the room. Somehow the dog was there, inserting its body almost casually. The dark eyes looked quite innocent.

"I feel like kicking you," Tasha said, closing the door to

Antonietta's bedroom with a louder than necessary thud. She hoped she shut it on Byron's nose.

"Why would you want to kick me?" Antonietta asked as she followed Tasha into the wide hall.

"Not you, the idiot dog and that man you are climbing all over. What kind of a display is that, Toni? You have a certain position to uphold. You shouldn't be making a fool of yourself over a man."

The whip of contempt in Tasha's voice made Antonietta wince. "I was in my own private quarters, so I don't see how I could have been making too much of a fool of myself."

"You're acting like a lovesick teenager. It's embarrassing. And that dog is annoying. He's too big and gets in the way all the time. Why would you want a dog underfoot? I don't know what Byron was thinking giving him to you. If Marita finds out he's dangerous, there will be hell to pay."

"Why would you think he's dangerous?" Antonietta allowed her exasperation to show. "You may not like Byron, Tasha, and that's okay with me, but don't you make trouble for Celt just out of spite."

"I'm *never* spiteful." Tasha's feet beat out a rhythm of annoyance. "Five minutes with a man, and you're turning on your own family. I hope you realize you're totally infatuated. It's sickening to watch you make an utter fool of yourself, but by all means, don't listen to my advice."

"I haven't heard any advice," Antonietta said, "just sour grapes."

Unexpectedly, Tasha laughed. "That's so true. I'm so jealous I could tear out that man's eyes. I want to be involved in a love affair. In a drama. In *something*. Someone tries to murder you, Paul even shoots you. You spend an entire day in mourning. It was so perfect, the palazzo silent and all of us caught up in your grief. And then I come up to find a man in your bedroom and you positively glowing. It's enough to make me throw myself from the battlements in absolute envy. Well," she hedged, "the lower balcony."

"He's so wonderful," Antonietta said. She found it easy to walk with Celt beside her, his body posture guiding her far better than even Justine had managed.

"I'm sure you think so. He still frightens me, Toni, and I don't know why. Paul said he saved your life at the risk of his own, yet I'm still afraid of him. There's something about him that isn't right."

"Everything about him is right for me." Antonietta went down the long, sweeping staircase with total confidence. Sometimes she felt Celt shared his eyes with her. She saw nothing, yet she knew exactly where to step as if he were guiding her through imaging in her mind.

Tasha placed a hand on Antonietta's arm to stop her before she turned toward Don Giovanni's rooms. "Why was Paul in the passageway? And why would he have a gun? Did he tell you?"

"He owes money to some dangerous people. He said he purchased the gun for protection. And he was in the passageway to steal the Scarletti treasures and pawn them to pay his debts."

Tasha shook her head sadly. "I thought he quit gambling. He promised us. He didn't tell me he needed money. Did he go to you? Or Don Giovanni? Why would he make a decision to steal from the family?" She sank down abruptly on the bottom stairs. "I'm sorry, Toni. I didn't know. I thought he would come to me if he were in trouble. I'm so ashamed."

Antonietta heard her weeping softly. She laid a comforting hand on her cousin's shoulder. "You aren't responsible for Paul, Tasha. He's a grown man, and he makes his own decisions. He'll have to face up to this. He nearly killed both Byron and me. Hopefully, he'll think about that and get help before it's too late."

Tasha lifted her head, swiping at the tears, careful of her makeup. "You have to tell Nonno the truth."

Antonietta sighed. "I suppose so, but I'm not looking forward to it." *Where are you?* She needed comfort. A battle with her grandfather over Paul's fate was more than she wanted to deal with. She had a mad desire to dash back up the stairs and lock herself in her bedroom, keeping Byron a prisoner there.

I am raiding your kitchen, looking for clues. I think my detective skills need work.

Antonietta wrapped his laughter around her like an invisible shield.

I like the idea of being your prisoner, by the way. Especially if the door were locked, and your family stayed away for a very long while. There are traces of the same substance

*I found in you, your grandfather, and Paul in the remains of
the food in the rubbish.*

Antonietta's smile faded. If she believed Byron, someone
in her own home was trying to kill all three of them. *There's
no mistake? You're certain?*

Cara mia, *I would never alarm you without cause.* He sent
her waves of warmth and reassurance. *Go to your grandfather. He is distressed and needs to sleep. You can talk to him
about Paul later.*

"I'm going in to Nonno, Tasha. Would you like to come
with me?"

"I think I'll just sit here awhile and feel very sorry for
myself, and then we can meet in Margurite's room. I promised her I'd sleep in her room tonight."

"You hate that, Tasha. You've always hated not being in
your own bed at night. Margurite is old enough to sleep in
her room alone."

"I know she is. She just looks so fragile. The house has
so many noises, and with the break-in and all the commotion
of you being shot, she's afraid. It won't hurt me to stay in
her room one night."

"Unless Marita catches you," Antonietta warned.

Tasha made a rude noise. "The day I can't handle Marita
is the day I deny being a Scarletti."

"Give me a few minutes with Grandfather, and I'll meet
you." Antonietta stood beside her cousin while the silence of
the palazzo pressed in on them. "While you're thinking about
things, please do decide you're going to make an effort with
Byron. He's going to stay."

Tasha sucked in her breath sharply. "Surely you wouldn't
contemplate marriage? Permanency? He's a toy. A plaything.
You know he could never be more to you. There's too much
involved."

"You mean money."

"Not just the money." She waved her hands to encompass
the palazzo. "All of it. All of us."

Antonietta didn't answer. She sensed Byron's stillness. The
waiting. "I so appreciate your understanding, Cousin." She
wouldn't give either of them the satisfaction. She went in to
comfort her grandfather. It was easy enough when she knew
Byron was waiting to share the rest of the long night with her.

10

Byron woke deep beneath the ground with the sound of Antonietta's voice calling to him. With the sound of her music summoning him. He lay there in his bed of rich soil, listening to the rhythm of his heart matching the beat of hers, of her music. The earth around him hummed with life, the sounds of insects and the trickle of water, all adding to the melody she was creating just for him.

Why won't you answer me?

His heart leapt at the little catch in her voice. *I am here with you.*

Here is not where you were when I went to sleep. You left me alone. I woke up and you were gone. It did not occur to me you would have sex with me and get up and leave.

He lay in the warm arms of the earth, listening to the nuances of her voice, paying particular attention to the shadows lurking in her mind. Peace swept over him. Antonietta was bound to him. Belonged with him. She had ideas that didn't quite match his own, but the ties between them were already formed and pulling tighter with each connection. It was fortunate she awakened as he did. By binding them, her discomfort level, if unable to reach him, would have soared.

His teeth gleamed white at the little bite in her voice. *Sex? You may have had sex with me, but I was making love to you with every breath in my body. You are the one who wants no emotion between us.* He stretched, knowing she would feel his leisurely, tranquil movement. *I told you separation could be difficult. Are you feeling the effects?*

There was a small silence. *Difficult? I didn't use that word. I didn't even think it. You can choose to sleep anywhere you like.* Antonietta sounded regal, haughty, very much a Scarletti. And humming with anger.

Byron's smile widened. The soil fell away from him, allowing him to float free, clean his body, and dress in immaculate clothing. *You are very accepting of our differences. Grazie, Antonietta, for your understanding.*

Again he felt her pull back, a silent withdrawal while she attempted to regroup. *What differences? You didn't mention differences when we went to bed last night. I've slept the day away and thought I'd wake up with you beside me. I hoped I'd wake up with you beside me. Do you grow horns in your sleep? Is that why you left, so I wouldn't see that you are not human?*

It was that tiny spurt of humor that melted his heart. *I have never looked, but the possibilities are endless.*

You aren't married, are you?

Ouch. What a thing to ask me. I am your lifemate. I cannot be with another woman. I am afraid you are permanently stuck with me. Horns and all. He reached for her in his mind, holding her to him. *I would much prefer to wake with you in my arms. I can bring you to my home this evening, and you can share my bed here.*

She sensed a hidden trap. He could feel her moving through his mind, touching his thoughts. It took her a few moments before she realized what she was doing and how easy it was. She grew even quieter, withdrawing farther from him.

Well? He prompted her, mocking male amusement brushing at her teasingly.

You're so charming, I guess I can't resist you. Deliberately she sighed. *I should, but I don't think I can. I prefer to sleep in my own bed and have you here with me. Take your time*

*coming up with a good reason for slinking off like a hound
dog in the middle of the night, or day, or whenever you left.
But make it good and somewhat believable.*

Byron laughed. He began to move, floating upward, finding the chimney and slowly, without effort, drifting steadily
toward the night sky. *You want to stay in your own home
where you feel you have the power. Do not think I do not
understand that is what you are doing.*

Antonietta gasped. *You're flying. I feel it with you. You're
flying through the air, aren't you? I want to do that.*

*I am floating, gliding really. It is a pleasant sensation. Not
nearly as pleasant as sharing your bed.*

Pretty words aren't going to get you out of trouble.

Sure they are. He was openly laughing, happy.

*Are you on your way back to me? If so, you can take me
flying tonight for your punishment for leaving me all alone
in this great big bed.*

You are still lying in those silk sheets without a stitch on.
The thought of her warm and soft and waiting there for him
left him breathless. Just that she would want him with her.
Just that she was thinking of him. *Do you, Antonietta? Do
you think of me? Dream of me?*

*Always. I have since the moment you came into our lives.
You humble me. I will be there soon.*

Byron shot into the sky, wings spreading wide as he took
the form of an owl, circled over the sea, enjoying the
way the moon spilled light on the choppy surface. He needed
to feed. He was not completely healed, as he couldn't afford
to spend time in the healing earth when Antonietta was in
danger. Even with Celt guarding her, Byron was uneasy separated from her.

She didn't have a clue what he was or what he intended.
He was now used to the strange barriers in her mind and
could easily maneuver around them. Antonietta wanted him,
even accepted him, but she didn't think in terms of a future.
Not ever. It didn't enter into her realm of possibilities.

Spotting prey, Byron circled lower, a silent drop, eyes
fixed on his quarry. As he settled to earth and reached for
the man staring up at him with such shock, he smiled. Antonietta had a few surprises in store for her. Someone needed
to shake up her tidy little world.

He drank deeply, allowing the rush to hit him, allowed himself the feel, just for a moment, of absolute power. It would be easy to give in to the whispers calling to him if it weren't for her presence. Antonietta would call him back as she had unknowingly with her music in the past. He wasn't as near to the edge as most of the hunters. Byron rarely had to kill, yet the pull to feel absolute power was strong, even with knowing right from wrong.

You're feeling very sad.

Her voice startled him. He nearly dropped his prey. Antonietta sounded so close to him. So concerned. Quite gently, he closed the small, telltale pinpricks and eased the man to the ground.

A few moments ago you were so happy. What's wrong, Byron? I can come to you if you can't get here. Tell me where to meet you.

Her voice, soft with concern, turned him inside out. *I am coming to you. I was just thinking of my kinsmen, some sadly lost to us.*

Hurry. I'm waiting to see you.

He took to the sky again, moving quickly toward the Scarletti palazzo. The rounded turrets drilled through the wisps of fog and clouds, a massive castle of stone and secrets. A ripple of awareness touched him. Another of his kind shared the skies with him. Female. Familiar. The owl came winging out from around the tower and rushed him, feathers nearly iridescent. *Eleanor!* His sister, gone from him many years.

Byron dropped down into the middle of the maze, signaling to his sister to do the same. He caught her in his arms, even as she shimmered into substance, dragging her close and burying his face against her neck. "How is that you have come to this place? I cannot believe that you are here, Eleanor. Let me look at you." He held her at arm's length, then pulled her close again. "I have not seen you for so long."

Eleanor hugged him back hard. "It has been too long, brother. You look so good, so strong and fit. I was so frightened for you. We were still too many miles away from you when we felt you go down. I collapsed. Poor Vlad had to attend me. I wanted him to leave me and go to you, but he said he would not make it before the sun rose. I am so grateful another of our kind was close. I did not recognize him when you showed us your mind. Who was he?"

"I will admit I was grateful also. He was an ancient, with powerful healing blood. Dominic of the Dragonseekers."

Eleanor drew back from him. "A Dragonseeker?" Her hand went to her throat in a purely defensive gesture. "I have not heard that name said in a long, long while. It brings back the memory of the ancient wars."

"That is all a fairy tale, Eleanor," Byron pointed out. "Much like the human stories of werewolves and vampires. No one has it right. They make it up as they go along. Maybe one or two people really saw a werewolf or a vampire, and they allowed their imagination to take flight, and the result is the silly stories they have now. I think much the same thing happened with our people and the stories of the wizards."

"I wish it were true, Byron, but the wizards were very real. Our races were close at one time, worked together for the good of the planet. The wizards were powerful and great seers. They studied magic and the things of the earth, much as we did. Many of our safeguards for protection came through their knowledge. Many of our people studied with them. Unfortunately, power can corrupt." She smoothed back her brother's hair. Touched his chest to assure herself he was alive and well. "I do not recall that Dominic had much to do with the wizards, but his sister did. She was incredibly talented. . . ." Eleanor's voice trailed off, and she stepped back to study him with her dark eyes. "You look fit, completely healed, and it is a miracle. You look quite different. More powerful maybe, yet happy."

"I have found her, Eleanor. At long last, I have found my lifemate. She is here, at this palazzo, the concert pianist, Antonietta Scarletti. She is an amazing woman."

Eleanor flung her arms around her brother's neck again. "I am so happy for you. You must introduce us. Have you claimed her? Have you told our prince? When are you taking her home?"

There was a small silence while Byron hugged Eleanor a second time, grateful he could feel the flood of love for her. Grateful he could look at her and *feel*. Antonietta had given him that gift. A priceless gift of emotions and vivid colors.

"Byron?" Eleanor looked at him with all-too-knowing

eyes. "You have not converted her." She made it a statement, almost an accusation. "We need every woman. You know we need women desperately. And you have suffered for so long. Surely your lifemate wants to be with you."

Byron smiled, a wolfish smile, more a baring of his teeth. "She has the strange idea that we will spend time together, and then she will send me on my way."

Eleanor studied his face. Her brother had an edge to him that had not been there before. "What are you up to?"

"Antonietta has to find her own way to me. She has lived a certain life, ruler in the palazzo, her family dependent on her. She also is safe there. It matters little in the palazzo that she is blind. Her life is set on a path, and she intends to follow it. She does not yet realize that her path is intertwined with mine. But she will."

"How long will you wait?"

"For what? Antonietta is bound to me. She is in my care. I have made provisions for her safety, and I will find who threatens her. She is mine, in heart and soul. She just needs to come to terms with who she will be when she embraces her choice."

"Of course you will return with her to our homeland." Eleanor made it a statement.

Byron smiled at her. "It is good to see you. Where is Vlad? Surely your lifemate did not allow you to travel unprotected?"

"I am not without my own protections," Eleanor reminded. "Vlad is here, and we have Josef with us. He wanted to visit other countries and see something of the world. We thought it best that we travel with him."

Byron couldn't stop the small step away from her as the horror of her words penetrated. "Josef?" The name came out a croak. "You have not brought that horrid child with you. Not here? Near the palazzo?"

"Byron, he is your nephew." Eleanor sank onto the curved marble bench seat and glared up at her brother. "What a horrible reaction."

Byron shook his head. "Benj is my nephew. I will be more than happy to claim him, but Josef is an altogether different matter. There is no blood between us."

"He is my son. I took him when Lucia died in childbirth.

I love him no less than Benj. I know he can be difficult—"

"Difficult! The boy is a menace. Lucia had no business having another child. She was so old, an ancient spending most of her days in the ground and hiding from the changes around her. She had no intention of living in a modern world. What was she thinking to try such a thing?"

"She was thinking of the preservation of our people. Byron, you are being overly harsh, and it is so unlike you."

"I am not being harsh, Eleanor, only truthful. The boy has done nothing but get in trouble almost since his first step."

"He was *orphaned,* Byron. He lost his parents the very day he was born."

"Most of us lost someone, Eleanor, and he didn't even know Lucia and Rodaniver. You and Vlad have been his parents, and no one could have loved him more. Lucia and Rodaniver lived in the past; they would have made that boy's life hell had they lived, and you know it. Now he just makes our lives hell."

"Byron!" Eleanor twisted her fingers together. "He needs love and understanding. You should make an effort with him. Guide him on the right path."

"Why do I get the feeling there is more to this visit than luck? You did not just happen to come to Italy, did you?" His black eyes began to smolder.

Eleanor looked away from him. "Despite what you say, Josef is your nephew, and I think you should take an interest in him. He wants to paint. Italy is a wonderful country to paint in. Benj was too busy and could not escort Josef. He still needs looking after, and since you're here . . ."

"No! Emphatically no! I cannot possibly take care of a child. And I don't want him anywhere near the palazzo." Byron shuddered visibly. "He wears his pants ten sizes too big. In fact, when you took him to see Mikhail, he stood right there in front of our prince and his lifemate, wearing baggy pants, a ring in his lip, nose, and eyebrow." He shook his head. "I do not want to know where else he had one, but every time he opened his mouth, I saw something hideous attached to his tongue. And even worse, he wanted to perform for them, and you let him."

"He was only a young boy, Byron, and it meant so much to him."

"I prefer Mozart and Chopin, opera and even the blues, but not rap. What was that horrible song he made up? I still hear it in my nightmares. I believe he spat a lot and made strange sounds before he graced us with the lyrics." Byron showed his gleaming white teeth, his incisors slightly prominent as if he could take a bite out of his nephew. "It was so shocking, I cannot, nor ever will forget the lyrics. In case you have forgotten, they went like this: *'I'm the man, / The man you can't see, / An invisible man, you ought to fear me, / Fangs and cat's eyes, / Your blood on my hands, / I come out at night when the moon rises high, / I'm a blood-sucking fiend, a most fearsome sight.'* I particularly enjoyed watching the prince's face when he sang the blood-sucking fiend part and the refrain of *'I want to suck your blood, blood, blood.'* " Byron found he wanted to laugh at the memory, as he couldn't those many years ago. "The only good thing that came out of that was it made Jacques laugh. I had not seen him laugh in years. It was the only reason I forgave Josef for such an obvious attempt to draw attention to himself."

"But Byron, he has such talent. Even then, and he was only a child, he was creative." There was a small silence. Eleanor was exasperated with him. "He was only fifteen, and at that awful age. He is much older now."

"Do not give me that, sister dear. I heard he had taken to wearing all black, including a swirling black cape, and lying on graves in the cemetery with a group of his human friends. I heard he had so many rings in his bottom lip no one could look at him for fear of laughing."

"That is so unfair. Oh for heaven's sake, all the children try things out. He was going through his Goth period, at least that's what Vlad called it. That was years ago; he was only seventeen. You know by our standards, he is still a mere fledgling. He is your nephew, Byron, and he wants to visit other countries. It would not hurt you to show an interest in him. He needs attention."

"I do not care if he is a mere fledgling. The prince's daughter was forced to take her lifemate as a mere fledgling, and she rose to the occasion."

Eleanor made a rude sound. "And you know *exactly* what I thought of that. How dare the prince sacrifice his own daughter's childhood? It was an abomination. They deliberately tried to age her by sending her out on her own with only hidden guards to watch over her. She deserved a childhood. Mikhail has been around humans for so long, and Raven *was* human, so they they have forgotten our children are young for a much longer time. Fifty years, and they still do not have full power."

"We would have lost Gregori, our greatest healer, and ultimately, Savannah. You know that, Eleanor. All of you women were up in arms, but in truth, the prince had no choice in the matter."

"No child can learn what they need in that short of time. She was lucky to be able to shape-shift or even protect herself. I can forgive Raven. She was born human and thinks in terms of human aging. But Mikhail was desperate to save his second-in-command. No female ever had the males brought in while she was a mere child. Mikhail arbitrarily decided to introduce the practice of bringing in the males when they reached the age of eighteen in the hopes of finding lifemates. His daughter just happened to be the first. Two hundred was the coming of age, not a baby of eighteen. It was appalling. It was no wonder Savannah panicked and fled the country. I know her father sent protection, as did Gregori but, in truth, they allowed her to be on her own to help age her. I do not know a single woman who did not protest such an abomination. It is no wonder our race is dying out when our prince does not treasure his own child above his friend."

Byron sighed. "Mikhail is hardly responsible for the extinction of our race." It was a long-standing argument he hoped Eleanor had gotten over. "Next you will be accusing him of being responsible for the inability to feed our children naturally."

Eleanor had the grace to look slightly ashamed. "I have no idea why we can no longer produce the perfect food for our children. All of us have discussed it at great length, and Shea has done much research." There were tears in her voice. She wept for her people, for the mothers and babies who had lost so much.

Byron put a hand on his sister's shoulder. "I did not mean to make you feel such sorrow, Eleanor. Our males certainly do not blame our women for such a tragedy." He kissed the top of her head in silent apology. "What happens to one of us happens to all. Every child saved, however we can manage to save them, every lifemate found, every male saved, even at the expense of a childhood, is a step forward for our people. Savannah was far too young. We all know that, but she rose to the occasion. Perhaps it was her bloodline, perhaps she is simply an extraordinary woman, but Gregori will care for her and protect her and aid her in learning the things she must learn."

Eleanor rubbed her forehead. "I know he will, and I know he is needed. It is just that our children have suffered so much already. So many die. Such a simple thing, feeding and caring for a child, yet we, of the earth, cannot do this simple service for our children. We cannot afford to take anything more away from them. If they need a full fifty years to mature enough to allow them on their own, so be it. What is that to give to a child?"

"You are right, of course, Eleanor. I have every belief that Shea and Gregori will find an answer that will allow our women to once again carry our children without the loss of so many. And with that, you will be able to feed them with your own bodies as you were meant to do."

She took his hand. "You remember that Celeste and Eric had a son when we had Benjamin, and he did not survive? They have tried again, and the child was lost to them. She is very distressed, and Eric has taken her away to try to help her get over the loss. I know what it is like to watch a child die, to have a hole in my heart that will never go away. It is painful to see my friends suffering so. Vlad's sister Diedre spends more and more time in the ground. I fear we will lose them if she becomes pregnant and does not succeed again. Tienn has refused to try again, afraid, as I am, that she would choose to meet the dawn." She put her hand on his face, needing the contact with him. "I am so grateful that you have found your life mate. Cherish her. Live for her. And hopefully she will live for you, and that will be enough."

"There is hope, Eleanor," he said softly.

"Is there? I wish that were true. Perhaps if we had the wisdom of the wizards or their power, we would find a way, but the war between our peoples destroyed all ties. If any remain, their hatred runs deep, and they would wish the destruction of our race."

The wind rushed through the trees so they swayed and danced. The bushes in the maze shivered with awareness. Eleanor waved a dismissing hand. "I did not mean to be melancholy. I am filled with joy for you. It is good that we are together as a family again, you with your new lifemate. Josef will love to meet her. Give him a chance, Byron, and you will see what a wonderful boy he really is."

Byron sighed. "I'm doing my best to make a good impression on Antonietta. The last thing I want to do is have her see Josef dressed in his whirling black cape and baggy pants, singing rap."

"He was a child, that was a long time ago. All children try things. She will find him endearing and charming."

"Charming?" Byron made a face at her. "As I recall, he went from lying in cemeteries to slamming into other people in a pit during concerts where singers tried biting the heads off living creatures. Really, Eleanor, the boy needs discipline. I do not intend to be the one to deal with his problems. Certainly not now. I would cuff the boy a few times on his ears in the hopes he would behave like a rational being."

Eleanor sighed heavily. "Byron, he is no longer such a handful, and you are still thinking in human terms. You have been away so long."

"Am I? What about the makeup? He was definitely wearing makeup and dyeing his hair all sorts of colors. I do not see how that was keeping a low profile and blending in with society."

"Who told you that? I cannot believe someone told you. The old gossips. That was his androgynous period. And he was blending in with his own age group. All children have to find themselves, Byron." Eleanor was outraged on her son's behalf.

Byron's long-suffering brother-in-law Vlad had told him in great frustration, but Byron believed discretion was the better part of valor. He didn't want Eleanor angry with her life mate. Byron forced a cajoling smile. "The point is, at this time, I am trying to court my lifemate, and I have no time to monitor a fledgling."

"We must meet her," Eleanor leapt on that. "I cannot wait to see her."

Byron took both of his sister's hands in his and drew her

to her feet. "You know I want to introduce you and Vlad to Antonietta, but the thought of Josef going anywhere near her or her family is frightening."

"You face vampires, Byron. You can face your nephew."

Byron sighed. There was no way to win, and he knew it. It didn't matter that he was a vampire hunter or a Carpathian male in full power. Eleanor was his sister, and like most Carpathian women, she was going to get her way. He might as well save himself the argument. "I will be happy to introduce all of you to Antonietta, but you must give me a period of time to adjust to having Josef around. He is not to do anything foolish."

"Of course he will not." Eleanor broke into another large smile. "Have you fed this night?"

"Yes, I am going to her. I will tell her that my family has arrived, and she will certainly invite you to her home. There is much going on. Someone is trying to kill both her and her grandfather."

Eleanor hissed, a long, slow sound of disapproval, her dark eyes flashing dangerously. "Take her and leave this place immediately, Byron. What are you thinking?"

He burst out laughing. "You are such a contradiction, Eleanor. Savannah's rights were stepped on, and you are up in arms, but my lifemate has no say in what she does or where she goes."

"If anything happens to her, it happens to you," Eleanor pointed out.

"Is that not the same with Gregori and Savannah?"

She bared her teeth at him. "Gregori is not my little brother. Go to your lifemate before I box your ears for your impertinence."

"Save your ear-boxing for that nephew of mine." He leaned down and kissed the tip of her nose. "Do you have a place you are staying?"

"We rented a villa. Josef wanted to experience the 'flavor of life,' as he puts it. Vlad found one we could use and still be safe. You are more than welcome to stay with us. Josef would be thrilled. He already has his paints set up on the balcony, and he looks stylish in his beret. What of you? Where are you staying?"

"Below the earth."

"You must seem a respectable human, Byron. I will see to it that we find you a place of your own. Do not worry, I will find something very suitable so you will be able to take your lifemate to a safe residence."

"*Grazie*, I did not think of that. Let me know the location when you find one. I will send word to you after I have talked with Antonietta. I have seen no evidence of vampires in the area, but that does not mean they are not among us. Be careful, Eleanor."

"You, too. It is so good to see you." Reluctantly, she allowed his hand to slip from hers. "Do not delay too long in taking your lifemate to our world, Byron. You belong in our homeland, you know. You always have. You were the one who imposed a sentence on yourself, leaving our people, fighting the vampires when you are a true, gifted artisan."

"I long to feel the gold and silver in my hands, to find the perfect gemstones in the sacred caverns." Byron smiled at her, shadows in his eyes. "There are times I find myself fashioning jewels in my mind when I should be doing much more important things. Now that I have found Antonietta, I long to make her something beautiful."

"Every craftsman is highly prized by our people, Byron," Eleanor reminded. "Especially a master at finding the gemstones."

"It is a world like no other. No one can understand such a thing unless they are born to the craft. Emotions bring back needs I wish I did not have."

"Your craft will always need you, Byron. You are a master such as our people have not seen in centuries. The prince has often commented to me that only you could design the perfect gift for Raven. He will not ask another."

"He is so certain I will return?"

"All hope it is so."

"Few brothers were luckier than I in having such a sister. I will see you later." Byron's solid form dissolved into droplets, and he streamed away from the labyrinth and toward the massive palazzo.

He circled above the towers and turrets, slipped through the sculptures of winged gargoyles, and dropped toward the second story and a window nearly always left open a few inches. Far below him he caught a glimpse of movement on a narrow, twisting path leading up the mountain, away from the palazzo and away from the city. Ordinarily, he might not have paid attention, but there was something furtive about the way Franco Scarletti's wife, Marita, was moving along the path. She was deliberately keeping to the tree line, rather than walking along the open trail. He could see she didn't want anyone from the palazzo to spot her.

Byron circled back, floating almost lazily in the clouds. He kept the woman in his sight as she slipped in and out of the trees. He could see her head continually turning left and right, eyes shifting restlessly, her body hunched. She was carrying a small package, plain brown wrapper tied with a single string. She took the more difficult climb winding steadily away from the city and the cliffs, moving inland, moving ever upward.

Byron caught the scent of the cat. The smell was wild and pungent and evil. At once his lazy facade disappeared entirely, and he was on the alert, streaking through the skies toward the groves of trees near the top of the mountain. Lines and lines of trees dotted the hillside. He swirled around the trunks. The odor was strong in the grove. A large cat had spent some time rubbing against the bark, stretching out in the branches. The wind shifted, whispering to Byron. Bringing with it the scent of freshly spilled blood. The coppery scent permeated the air, rose on the wind.

Marita screamed. The sound sent birds scattering from night perches into the air so that for a moment the flutter of wings was loud. Bats wheeled and dipped, performing their acrobatics. Byron moved with them, taking their shape to blend in, hunting for the cat. Knowing it was aware of him. Knowing it was hunting, too.

Marita's scream was cut off abruptly, forcing Byron to turn away from the search to ensure she was not being attacked. She lay crumpled on the ground. The leaves on the trees were smeared with a black, shiny substance. It dripped from the leaves to the ground just beside Marita's still body.

Byron dropped to earth, taking care to be light and airy, not wanting to leave prints behind. The torn, bloody body of a man hung in the fork of the tree branch much like cached meat. The moon revealed the trunk, black with blood. Marita lay at the bottom of the tree. Byron bent over her to check to see if she were injured. She appeared to be breathing without difficulty. The package had fallen from her limp hand, so he pushed it into his coat pocket without a single qualm.

The last thing he wanted to do was pack the woman down the mountain in the way of humans and waste time with hysterics. Marita was capable of sending the entire palazzo and the nearby city into a full-blown panic. Byron examined the victim. He appeared to be in his late thirties. He had seen it coming, died hard, been torn open by a wild animal, and partially devoured. The death had been only an hour or so earlier. Marita had stepped in a puddle of blood, slipped, and fallen into another puddle. Apparently, the fright had been too much for her.

The cat had been close, very close, and had sensed a predator coming near. It was gone, out of the area. He might have been able to track the jaguar, but he couldn't leave Marita to wake up in the midst of all the blood. With a little sigh he plucked her out of the mess and started down the mountain with her.

Almost at once Marita began to stir, moaning in fear and abject misery. Byron hastily put her on the ground, stepped back to give her room, and stood waiting. She thrashed for a moment, sat up straight, looked down at her bloodstained clothing, and screamed shrilly. Byron waited, but she didn't stop. Her eyes rolled back in her head, and she began to slump again.

"Marita." He said her name sharply, burying a compulsion. "You are safe here with me. Nothing can harm you."

She blinked rapidly, her hands fluttering wildly. "Did you see it? The body? It was horrible." She shuddered. "Utterly horrible."

"Allow me to escort you home, and we can inform the authorities." He held out his hand to her to help her up.

Marita obeyed the compulsion in his voice, placing her hand in his.

"What are you doing up here, so far from the palazzo, so late at night?" His tone was beautiful, a pure cadence that soothed her into a trusting state.

She frowned, squirmed in resistance, yet couldn't prevent the admission. "I was meeting someone. A man."

"A lover?"

"Yes. No. *Dio,* you must not tell. You must not tell." She fell into a storm of weeping, her cries reaching to the heavens. She clutched at her heart, the tears making it impossible to see so that she sat down again and covered her face.

Exasperated, Byron blurred her mind and simply lifted her, moving through the air to cover the long distance to the palazzo. He'd had enough of the screaming, weeping woman. He wanted Antonietta. To see her face, touch her, and know she was waiting for him, every bit as eager to see him as he was to see her.

11

Byron *deliberately took* Marita to the front entrance of the palazzo with its double doors and marbled stairway. So late at night, the doors were securely locked. He used the knocker ruthlessly. Holding her upright, he whispered the command to awaken her, making certain to plant the memory of a long, fast trek through the mountain path in her mind.

Helena opened the door. She took one look at Marita covered in blood and shrieked loudly. Two servant girls, gathering wraps for the evening to go home took up the cries until the palazzo was ringing all the way to the vaulted ceilings. Marita burst into tears again, wailing to the dead and everyone else in hearing distance. She clung to Byron like glue, holding him prisoner in the midst of drama.

Antonietta. Lifemate. Rescue me. I cannot take these women and their histrionics another moment. Where are you?

She was as calm as ever. *Where were you when I woke to find my bed empty?*

Byron sighed. The household erupted into total pandemonium. Helena drew Marita into the entryway, speaking so rapidly he could barely understand her. For a brief moment he was free. Marita collapsed again on the floor. He did the gentlemanly thing and caught her before she hit her head on the cool marble. *I could use a little sympathy.*

What happened?

Marita found a dead body up in the grove.

A dead body? How awful. No wonder she's carrying on like that.

He had been dead for some time. It is not necessary for her to carry on. She did not see his throat ripped out.

His throat was ripped out? Poor Marita, no wonder she is so upset.

Upset is not the word I would have chosen. And what of me? I am a sensitive man, but you have no sympathy for my nerves when she is screaming so.

Sensitive? You with the dead body and no reaction?

Antonietta. A gentle reprimand when she was having so much fun at his expense.

Was it Enrico? He is still missing.

Bryon paused before answering. Antoinetta was beginning to sound horrified. He didn't need her joining the other women with their hysteria and shrieking cries.

I do not get hysterical. A heartbeat. Two. *Ever.*

She was closer. The entryway was crowded with women talking, crying, and screaming. Byron thought he might break into a sweat if he wasn't rescued soon. Marita leaned heavily against him, clinging with hands that were trembling. *Antonietta, move it! I know you are coming as slowly as possible.*

Franco rushed into the entryway, caught sight of his wife covered in blood and sagging against Byron's restraining hands as he held her up. Franco didn't even pause. He charged Byron, flailing at him with fists, nearly hitting Marita in the head when she bobbed in his way, trying frantically to grab him.

"Enough." Byron uttered the command between clenched teeth. His voice was ultralow, but the power and force of it swept through the room, could be felt all the way to the highest reaches. Vases rocked. Pictures on the wall shuddered and went still.

There was instant silence. No one moved or spoke. A wind swirled through the room, a rising howl of protest. Antonietta swept into the entryway, Celt close to her side. "Byron, do shut the door. The air's so cold, and poor Marita is in shock. Helena, quickly, see to it that Marita's bath is run. Franco, take her upstairs at once while I inform the authorities of the terrible tragedy in our grove."

The world narrowed and curved until his vision tunneled and the room was gone. The women disappeared. Franco was gone. There was only Antonietta coming toward him. Byron couldn't help staring at her. Her voice had always carried confidence, but now her tone was even more compelling. She seemed to glow. His Carpathian blood in her body was already enhancing her natural beauty. She carried authority like a mantle, dignified and unafraid while chaos reigned around her. She left him soft inside. Happy. At peace. Whole.

Her family responded to her voice. Marita collapsed in her husband's arms. Paul and Justine arrived together, breathless and wide-eyed. Tasha hovered near the archway, regarding Byron with suspicion.

"He saved me." Marita buried her face against Franco's chest. "I can't bear to have this man's blood on me. It was horrible."

Franco looked up at Byron. *"Grazie.* I owe you."

Byron walked straight, purposefully, to Antonietta. In front of her entire family he pulled her into his arms, held her close to him until their hearts picked up the same rhythm. There was pure possession in his posture, a clear signal to the others that he was with Antonietta to stay. She responded immediately, wrapping her arms around him and turning her face up for his kiss.

He bent his head to hers. Her lips were warm and soft and welcoming. Her mouth was hot and moist and exotic. For a moment everything and everybody receded to a distant place. Antonietta tasted of honey and spice. Of love and laughter.

"Funny how he always shows up right when one of us is in danger," Tasha muttered loud enough for everyone to hear. She glared at Byron.

Byron lifted his head to look at her, his black eyes burning red, his fangs exposed when he smiled. He had enough of Cousin Tasha and her ugly games with Antonietta. If she wanted to play with no rules, he was more than willing. She often made Antonietta's life very uncomfortable. It wouldn't hurt the woman to have a taste of her own medicine.

Tasha gasped and stepped back, crossing herself. When she blinked, Byron's smile was normal, his face handsome. The red flames flickering in the depths of his eyes were merely a reflection of the many burning candles scattered around the entryway.

Tasha shivered, but she deliberately walked straight to her cousin's side, her huge, dark eyes angry. "How did you happen to come upon Marita and a dead body, Byron?" There was a challenge in her voice.

"Thank the good *Dio* you found her, Byron," Antonietta said. She touched Tasha briefly. "You must call the authorities at once. Say there has been a dreadful accident in the grove. Ask the good captain to come. Tell him our people are already used to his presence, and with everyone so nervous, I would appreciate it if he were to come personally." *I sense her uneasiness. What are you doing to her?*

What am I doing to her? She practically accused me of assaulting Marita.

Antonietta made a small gesture of acceptance. *That is just her way, to strike out when she is upset or afraid.*

Byron set his teeth. *Cousin Tasha needs manners.*

Tasha nearly leapt for the phone, forgetting her determination to save Antonietta from her own folly in the hopes of seeing the handsome captain. "Of course, Antonietta."

"Paul, go to Nonno and let him know what is happening. I don't want him any more upset than necessary."

Franco led a sobbing Marita away, with Helena clucking soothing nonsense and promising a bath immediately.

That was it, Byron decided. Antonietta was blind, yet she knew who was in the room, and she took instant command. She was incredible. His heart was beating loud, and he calmed it. Pride for her. It both amused him and alarmed him that he could read her thoughts of confusion in her relationship with him. She believed they would have a short-term affair, he would go on his way, and she would continue her life. She was slowly coming to the realization that she didn't want him to go, but she still expected it. Neither of them had a choice, but she had no way of knowing it, and he had no intention of compounding her resistance by enlightening her.

Antonietta moved closer to him, fitting her body into his,

resting on his strength in the midst of the hysterics. She rubbed her face along his chest, went ramrod stiff, and stepped away from him. *You've been with another woman.* The accusation was a statement of fact, the words shimmering in his mind, orange red with flames. It was another betrayal, and it shattered her. He could feel the waves of anger mixed with a ferocious grief.

There will never be another woman. Never. Not for me. He used his purest tone, one unable to utter an untruth.

"Antonietta," Justine said. "We have to talk, all of us. Paul, you, even Bryon and me. We can't let this continue."

Antonietta lifted her chin, her body slightly swaying toward Byron's as if for protection or comfort. The small, telltale gesture turned his insides to mush. Byron put his arm around her and gathered her beneath the protection of his broad shoulder, sheltering her from the pain of Justine and Paul's treachery. He could feel Antonietta wanting to believe him, struggling against the purity of his tone and her own senses.

"This is hardly the time for me to try to make sense of what you did, Justine. I am too angry and hurt to listen to either of you. As for Paul shooting us, I still have no idea what to do. I suggest he stay out of the way of the authorities when they arrive." There was that faint haughty note in her voice that Byron was beginning to recognize as more of a defense than an offense.

I still can smell her on you.

He bent and kissed the tip of her nose. *My sister has arrived from my homeland. She has taken a villa with her lifemate and son near the city overlooking the sea. I believe we discussed Josef and his peculiarities. He wishes to paint, so they are allowing him the opportunity.*

The suspicion in her mind cleared at once. Antonietta flung her arms around his neck. *I'm sorry. I don't know why I doubted you.*

Betrayal is a way of life in your family, Antonietta. It is not in mine. I say that only to reassure you. It is a natural conclusion when you wake alone, and I return with the scent of another woman on me.

Justine planted her body firmly in front of Antonietta even as Paul hurried off to his grandfather's room, carefully avoiding Byron's gaze. "Antonietta. I made a terrible mistake, but you can't just throw away thirteen years of friendship. You know you're my family. My only family. This is painful."

Byron's hand came up to massage the sudden tension from the nape of Antonietta's neck. His fingers were gentle, his mind soothing so that she was able to keep from shaking with anger and hurt.

Antonietta was silent a moment. "I'm glad it's painful for you, Justine. It should be. It's painful for me to know you would betray everything we had simply because you're sleeping with my cousin. I can't imagine the man I am with asking me to do such a thing, and if he did, I can't imagine complying or staying with him. Paul uses people. He's very good at it, but then you knew that going into the affair."

Justine turned a dull red, her eyes avoiding Byron. Her lips quivered for a moment, but then her chin went up, and she turned abruptly on her heel and swept away. Byron watched her go, noted that her back was ramrod stiff and her hands were clenched into tight fists.

"What are you going to do about her?" Byron asked. His hand moved from her nape to the small of her back, continuing the soothing massage.

"I have no idea. I should fire her, tell her to pack her bags and go, but I don't know if that's hurt talking or good business sense. Justine is just as entitled as everyone else to her mistakes."

Treachery. The word hissed through his mind, a clear, scorching burn that left black smoke and a bad taste behind. Byron liked none of it, but Antonietta's sense of loyalty and responsibility to her family and friends was enormous. He tried hard to understand why she loved them so much. Why it was so important to her to help them. He wanted to see the things in her family she saw. He wanted to care for them as she did. Don Giovanni had earned his respect and loyalty. He doubted the others ever could, but he was determined to give them every chance.

"I wish you could grow to love my family, Byron," Antonietta said.

He could share her mind and view them the way she did, but Byron wanted nothing to inhibit his senses when it came to her family. "We will work it out."

"Is your sister really here, Byron?" Antonietta didn't want to think about either Paul or Justine.

"Yes, she is really here. Do not sound so happy about it. She has brought young Josef, and that alone is enough to have us all running for cover. If you think you have strange relatives, you have not met Josef."

"They must come for dinner," she said. "Tomorrow night. You'll invite them, won't you?" She rubbed her face along his shoulder much like a cat. "That way I can meet the infamous Josef. I'm really looking forward to it."

He groaned deliberately to make her laugh. "You just want to make me squirm."

"Well, there's that, too."

"Do you think it will help Tasha to remember I was not found under a rock?" There was wealth of amusement in his voice.

She tipped her head back as if she could see him through her dark glasses. "You honestly don't care whether she likes you or not, do you?"

"Not particularly. I have never cared one way or the other. Does it change who or what I am? My honor demands a certain code of behavior. I cannot change it for someone else."

"Can you really read minds? Literally? I have ideas, like a thought or image in my head, and I know I'm picking it up from someone else, but I can't read minds," Antonietta admitted in a burst of confidence when she was normally very discreet about her unusual gifts.

He laced his fingers through hers and brought her hand up to his mouth, nibbling on her fingers. "Sit down with me a moment in the solarium. After all the screaming, I could use peace before the captain arrives."

She went with him, intrigued by the idea he might be able to read other minds. They were connected, she accepted that, but it seemed different that he might be able to hear the thoughts of others. "Is that what you do," she asked curiously, "do you hear their thoughts?"

"I have the ability to scan minds." He held the door courteously, eager to be alone with her. He *needed* to be alone with her. "It is not so easy in this particular region or with your family as with most. You have built-in barriers, some more than others. I suspect it is due to your bloodlines. Marita is easy enough. I picked up the image of a man. She was obviously on her way to meet him."

"That can't be," Antonietta denied again. "I'm telling you, Byron, she *loves* Franco, almost to the point of obsession. She would never do anything to lose him. She loves being a Scarletti as much as she adores Franco. She would never have an affair. Is that what you're implying? I will never believe it of her."

"And why is amour the only reason for a woman to meet a man clandestinely?"

Antonietta allowed him to seat her in the deep, comfortable chair facing the waterfall. She loved the chair not for its comfort but because she could feel the spray of droplets on her face. "You're right; of course it had nothing to do with an affair. It could have been any number of reasons."

"She was meeting a man, Antonietta, and she was going to deliver a package to him. For all I know, it was the gentleman found with his throat torn out."

Antonietta shivered. Byron sounded so matter-of-fact, even when discussing infidelity or brutal death. His fingers on her nape were soothing, gentle, tender even. "I highly doubt Marita was going to meet a man for any purpose. What package? You never said a word about a package." Celt pushed his nose into her palm, and Antonietta obediently scratched his silky ears.

"In all the excitement, Marita forgot she was carrying a package, but I am willing to bet she will remember when her head clears of fear and distaste. She did not want anyone to see. That was very important to her."

"I don't like this. I feel in the middle of a great conspiracy. I have no idea what's going on around me, or even why."

"I just happened to pick up the package when Marita swooned."

"She swooned? She is very good at that. Tasha is jealous and wants to be able to drop gracefully to the floor at a moment's notice. I doubt if anything is capable of making me swoon."

He leaned into her, kissed her hard, possessively. "I can make you swoon if you wish it."

She loved the way he sounded. Mischievous. Laughter in

his mind. In his heart. He had a way of making her world right again. "I seriously doubt it."

"I will take that as a challenge."

"Did you open the package?" She had to ignore him. It was the only sensible thing to do when little flames licked over her skin at the heat in his voice.

"I waited for you." He pulled the brown wrapper from inside his coat and turned it over so that the paper rustled with invitation. "Would you like me to open it?"

"Have you looked into Paul's mind, Byron?" Her voice was suddenly tight. She caught at him. "Did he try to kill me? I love Paul. I'm not certain I can bear his wanting to murder me. Or worse. If he wanted to harm Nonno."

For a moment, a black violence swirled in his belly, a reaction to her pain. His hand caught her chin. "I would take you away from this place and these people. We would love and live and never look back if you simply said the word to me."

She heard the words in her head. Felt them in her soul. Byron was magical to her. If she was asked to explain it, she couldn't, but she longed to be with him. Not for a few stolen moments but always. In his arms. Listening to his voice. Laughing at his antics. His sense of humor appealed to her. *He* appealed to her on every level.

"This is my home." There was a trace of regret in her voice. "I love my family. I worked hard for my career. Would you be happy here, with me?"

His gut lurched. The doubt in her tone had him tossing the package aside and pulling her right out of the chair and into his arms. "I can be happy anywhere, Antonietta, as long as I am with you." He pulled her to her feet, into his arms.

"I don't know what you are, do I?"

"Does it matter? Will you love me anyway? Can you? Does it matter that I am not Jaguar? Or human? Can you share my mind and know I am of the earth, a Carpathian male, with honor and integrity? Can you not see what I stand for?" His fingertips brushed her face, down her arms to slide up inside her white lace blouse. Her skin was warm and inviting. A lush temptation far too exotic for him to ignore. He cupped her breast, took the weight in his palm, his thumb sliding in a caress over her nipple. *Celt, a little privacy would be nice.*

The borzoi shifted positions, padding a few feet away and dropping down to curl up, no doubt thinking him crazy.

"Can anyone see us?" Antonietta's knees were already weak with desire. Her body flooded with hot need. How could she possibly want him, no *need* him, so quickly? So completely? It was actually frightening to think she could be so out of control at a mere touch. So out of character for someone who thought through her every move and planned everything down to the smallest detail.

"Does it matter?" He demanded, "Tell me, Antonietta, will you want me if I am not what you expected?"

She pushed her breast deeper into his palm, savoring the way her entire body responded to the friction. Behind her dark glasses, her lashes drifted down. "You aren't at all what I expected. This terrible hunger I have for you isn't at all what I expected. You make me feel desperate."

"I am feeling a bit desperate myself."

"You're distracting me from the package."

"We would not want to forget the package." He leaned down to brush a kiss on the top of her head. His fingers massaged her body. "I cannot take my hands off of you. I am trying. But it is not working."

Antonietta found it fascinating the way her body tightened and clenched in reaction to the stroking caress of his fingers. She wanted him right there. Right at that moment, in the solarium with its glass walls and hanging plants. With the waterfall in the background and her body wrapped around his.

"You are not helping," he said, confirming he could easily read her mind.

"Someone could see us, Byron, walk right in, couldn't they?" The package was beginning to be a distant memory. She should have been embarrassed that he could read her mind, read her every erotic thought, but she was grateful. She wanted him to take her, wanted to feel his body plunging deep and hard inside of hers.

He replaced his hand with his mouth. Antonietta cried out with the wave of sensations swamping her. Her arms circled his head to cradle him to her breast. Ravenous hunger rose to swamp her. Her legs shook.

"Byron? What's happening to me? I'm not like this." She was always cool and confident and in control in her dealings with lovers. She was never a flame burning with the raw force of a firestorm. Uncaring where she was. Whether someone might see her. She was a private person. Sex was never intense and *hungry*. The most important thing in the world to her at that precise moment was ripping away Byron's clothes.

He took her glasses from her nose and set them aside. "No one can see us, Antonietta. It is impossible. Even if there was someone in the room with us, I could shield us from view." His voice was husky. He drew her shirt over her head and let out his breath at the sight of her breasts. His senses were heightened by her needs. He could feel her through their mind link, the terrible pressure building and building deep inside of her. The heat. The shimmering fire.

Antonietta shuddered. "What are you doing to me? I can feel you in my head, feel what you're feeling." There was a dangerous edge to his hunger. To his need. His body was heavy and full and thick, pressing tightly against her. And he was without clothing. Her hands found his broad back, traced the muscles there. Her neck throbbed and burned. A spot over her left breast throbbed and burned. In her deepest core, small miniexplosions seemed to be going off, rocking her, making her weak.

Byron dragged her slacks down, stripping away her lace panties. "Keep your arms around my neck. Hold on, Antonietta. Hold tight."

She wanted to protest. She should have protested if she had an ounce of decency. Instead, she wrapped her arms securely around his neck and held on tight. He lifted her. Easily. As if she had no weight to her at all. "This is crazy. And too fast. How can I want you like this?" And she was much too heavy for acrobatic lovemaking.

"Wrap your legs around my waist."

The catch in his voice destroyed her. She obeyed him, her body open and vulnerable to the invasion of his. Antonietta cried out as he pressed against her very core. Wave after wave of sensation rocked her. Rocked him. She could feel herself through his mind. Hot. Wet. Slick. A velvet fist wrapping tightly around him as he entered her. She thought she might have screamed with the sheer ecstasy of it. But it might have been him, calling her in her mind. Pleasure shimmered around her, over her, and through her. Through him. He moved, his hips surging into her hard. Deep. She rose up, using her strength, slid down the length of him with exquisite slowness, paying particular attention to how she made him feel.

The breath slammed out of his lungs and he burned for her. Antonietta accepted her own power with a very feminine smirk and took the initiative. She began to ride him, using his mind to guide her, searching for the perfect move, her muscles milking and gripping strongly. It was heaven. Paradise. She didn't want to ever stop.

His hands massaged her buttocks in time to the wild ride, driving the passion up another notch, while flames licked from their toes to the top of their heads. Breath mingled, air disappeared, lungs burned. Nothing mattered but the waves of pleasure washing over them. The pressure continued to build. She could feel it like a gathering volcano in him. He could feel it like a racing storm in her.

Antonietta suddenly tightened her arms around his neck, leaned into him, her teeth finding his shoulder as he plunged deep, dragging her hips downward to meet his body. Flames crackled and sizzled. Colors burst behind her eyes. Or maybe it was his eyes. It didn't matter. His mind was solidly in hers, his body sharing hers. The earth around them rocked, rippled with life, exploded into a thousand pinpoints of light.

Antonietta lay on his shoulder, unmoving, uncertain she could move. Wondering why they both weren't a puddle of water on the floor. The most energy she could summon was to touch her tongue to the bite mark on Byron's shoulder. She could feel the tiny indentation with her tongue. "I bit you."

"You do not sound sorry."

"I think it was in retaliation. I'm fairly certain you bit my neck the first time we made love."

His rumbling laughter caused an electrical vibration to sizzle through her body. Just that fast, it brought another orgasm. She rode it out, savoring every shudder. "I could just stay here forever."

"I would not mind," he agreed companionably, "but we have company."

The door to the solarium rattled, stuck for a moment, then fresh air circulated through the room, taking the combined scent of their lovemaking and dispersing it immediately. Misters on timers began a soft spray of the plants.

"Where are you?" Tasha demanded. "I swear they came in here," she said to the captain. "Antonietta? Byron? Diego is here. You don't mind me calling you Diego, do you?" Her voice was sultry with heat.

Byron lowered Antonietta carefully to the ground, holding her until her legs stopped shaking enough to take her weight.

"There's her dog." Tasha spotted Celt. "Antonietta hasn't gone anywhere without that dog since she got him a few days ago. She's in here somewhere. She loves the exotic plants. Over this way."

Antonietta stiffened, buried her face on Byron's shoulder. She was completely naked and only a large leafy plant separated her cousin and the policeman from her. Byron's large hands cupped her buttocks, pressed her tightly to him. *They cannot see us here. Have no fear of discovery.* He reluctantly let her go to drag her shirt over her head and settle her dark glasses back on her nose.

Antonietta stood in silence and darkness while he retrieved her slacks. She jumped when his hand slipped between her legs, his finger pushing inside of her. *I want to be alone with you,* cara mia. *I hate that we can never be alone.* His finger stroked deep. Her highly sensitized feminine muscles convulsed around him. She clung to him while her body went up in flames again.

Byron's hair brushed her face as he leaned close to help her into her slacks. *You are my lifemate, always in my care.* He was fully clothed.

I don't think I can breathe. Carry me upstairs. Let's run away together.

His mouth settled over hers, a long, leisurely kiss.

"What in the world is this?" Tasha picked up the package lying in the middle of the floor. There was a smear of blood on the brown wrapper.

I fear it is too late, my love. Byron moved them so that they appeared together, walking around a giant potted palm, hands linked. *Tasha found the package, and we need to know what is inside of it. We must reveal ourselves.*

Antonietta tried to appear calm and cool and not at all as if she'd been having wild sex only moments earlier. Laughter was bubbling up, a very unlike Antonietta characteristic. She hardly recognized herself anymore.

"*Grazie*, Tasha." Byron took the package right out of her hands and gave it to Antonietta. "I was not certain where we left that. Good evening, Captain Vantilla." Byron bowed low at the waist.

"Signor Justicano, its good you were there to rescue Signora Scarletti."

Tasha made a sound of annoyance. "Diego, didn't you listen to a single word I said? What were you doing wandering the grove so late at night, Byron?"

"Tasha, you go too far," Antonietta said quietly. "I want you to stop. There is more at stake here than your petty jealousies."

Tasha's breath hissed out. "Call it what you will. That man is dangerous, and I refuse to allow you get involved with him."

Byron studied her scarlet face. She was humiliated in front of the captain, yet she persisted in spite of Antonietta's warning. It seemed at odds with her sense of self-preservation. *Could she really be afraid for you?*

You're the one who reads minds.

She would know. If I push beyond her barriers, she would know I was there. I am uncertain if I could fog her memory enough to make it worthwhile.

Who knows why Tasha does and says the things she does? Antonietta sounded weary enough that Byron swept his arm around her and dragged her to him, giving her shelter against the steady rhythm of his heart.

"You do not seemed surprised, Captain," Byron said. "Is this the first kill? You must tell us what you know."

The captain pushed his hand through his hair, a clear sign of agitation. "This is not the first person killed in this way."

"Do you mean to say you've known of this creature, and you didn't warn everyone?" Antonietta was outraged.

"It has been in the newspapers, signorina. We brought in the best trackers we could find. The cat has not been found."

"In the meantime, my cousin's wife could have been killed. That's completely unacceptable." There was a soft whip in Antonietta's voice. "I have employees who walk from the city to my home daily. I don't want to lose any of them to such a hideous fate as a wild animal killing them."

"It doesn't bear thinking about," Tasha contributed with a shudder. "Marita had blood all over her. No wonder she collapsed."

"No one should be walking around alone at night." The captain pinned Tasha with a steely eye. "There is no reason to be in the grove until this animal is found. I believe the gentleman we found is most certainly one of your groundskeepers. Signor Franco Scarletti identified him."

"Oh, no." Antonietta's fingers curled around Byron's, hung on tight. "One of ours? We must hire security to escort our people back to their houses until this creature is caught."

"And this has been going on for some time?" Byron prompted, his voice a compulsion for truth.

"Unfortunately, yes. In other areas for some time. Our first discovery was a young woman's body by the sea with her throat torn out. We have plaster of the paw prints. It was identified as a jaguar, a rather large one. The general belief at the time was that someone had one of these cats as a pet, and it either escaped or, like so many others when the laws went into effect against exotic pets, it was dumped in the middle of the night."

Tasha sank into a chair. "Our grounds are extensive, the wildest country around, and little Vincente and Margurite play all the time in the maze. They were in such danger, and we never knew."

Diego put a comforting hand on her shoulder. "I have three children at home. *Madre mia* takes care of them, and she is old and frail. I've given orders that they remain indoors, but the two oldest get away from her. I worry myself. I do know how you feel. The killings have been far between in a range of well over a hundred miles. We didn't put it together until several months ago."

"When did this start around here, Diego?" Tasha asked.

"The first body was found in our area nearly two years

ago. We searched, of course, but nothing was found. There were two bodies found prior to that one, but it was thought they were dead and wild animals got to them. It took us awhile to put it together that one cat might be actually preying on humans."

"And what does your wife say to this? Why does she not stay with your children?" Tasha asked.

The question was unexpected, and Diego answered truthfully before he could stop himself. "My wife did not want our children or a policeman for a spouse. She left after the *bambina* was born and does not want to see any of them again." It was a painful moment for him, humiliation and anger shimmering in his dark eyes.

"Poor little *bambini,* abandoned and unwanted," Tasha said softly.

"*I* want them," Diego said adamantly. "They do not need a woman who will not love them."

12

"**W**hat is it?" It was one of the few things about being blind that made Antonietta crazy. She always had to wait for identification.

"I am sorry, *cara mia,* it is sheets of music."

Antonietta sucked in her breath. Finally, they were in the privacy of her sitting room with the doors firmly locked. Tasha had settled in for the evening to entertain the captain, and with all the other duties, Antonietta thought she would never be alone with Byron. Curiosity was slowly killing her. That, and wanting to be alone with him.

"*My* music? She was taking my music out of our home to give to someone else?" Antonietta's body didn't feel her own. Feverish. Needy. Incomplete. She moved away from Byron to keep him from noticing.

"No. It is not yours. This music is very old. I am afraid to touch it. It could crumble in my fingers."

Antonietta went very still. Her hand went to her throat. "I know what it is. How did Marita get her hands on that? It's kept locked in Don Giovanni's private safe. No one but Don Giovanni has the code. At least they shouldn't, and believe me, Nonno would never give away such a treasure. The existence of that composition is not even known outside our immediate family."

Byron leaned back in his chair and stretched his legs toward the leaping flames in the fireplace. "It is very valuable?"

"Oh, yes, it's valuable. It is genuine, the original work of the composer George Frideric Handel. As a young man, he visited Italy, and of course, he was a frequent guest here at the palazzo. Even then the Scarletti family had power and wealth and was interested in music, and he was an exceptional talent. No artist would turn down such an invitation. He stayed on and off during the three or four years he was in Italy. He left behind many notations and a journal. He also left sheets of music, of cantatas and operas, even oratorios. But our most treasured is a full opera composed by Handel for the Scarletti family. He was not happy with it. He said it lacked the fire of Italy, and he did not want it kept. Our family agreed it would never be for public use then or in the future. The Scarletti word is sacred. We have kept that vow to him for generations."

Byron whistled softly between his teeth. "George Handel. I had forgotten he stayed in Italy. It was only a short while. He left in 1710 for Hanover, as I recall, but left nearly immediately for London. His opera *Rinaldo* was produced the following year."

"You studied Handel?" She was shocked.

Byron looked down at his hands, surprised he had made such a slip. "I liked his work," he said carefully.

"So do I. He returned years later, when he was looking for artists and performers. Did you know in his later days he was blind?" She arched her back, tried to relieve some of the pressure building inside of her.

"I had heard, yes."

His voice wrapped her up in silk and satin. Antonietta shook her head. "I need to put the score somewhere safe. I'll talk to Nonno tomorrow. He's long gone to bed. I seem to be sleeping later and later every day and miss the activities." She took the package from him, avoided his touch as she did so. "I'll be right back. I'm going to put this in the vault in the passageway. I doubt Marita will find it there."

"Paul might." Byron rose, a lazy, fluid movement. He

sounded like a great jungle cat rousing itself from a warm fire. And it irritated the hell out of her. "I am coming with you."

She was already at the door to the passageway. The last thing she wanted was to be with Byron in such close quarters. "Just relax for a few minutes." She did her best to sound calm. "It won't take long."

"I do not mind. I wanted to get another look at the wall with all the carvings." His body pressed close to hers. She could feel his body heat.

Antonietta hurried forward, entering the labyrinth of tunnels without hesitation. Byron moved in his usual silent way, but she was all too aware of him. She could almost feel his muscles beneath her itching fingers. Erotic images danced in her head. She wanted him with every breath in her body. And he seemed so . . . unaware . . . uninterested.

She wanted to shred the package in her hand, rip at something with her nails. Her shoes made noise on the ancient marble tiles. Her breath seemed overly loud. Her heart was pounding, and her mouth was dry. Antonietta counted silently to herself, making each twist and turn sharply.

"Our history is very colorful." She made every attempt to carry on a conversation if that was what he desired. A *history* conversation.

Byron continued to prowl silently behind her. Breathing on the nape of her neck. Smelling good. Making his presence known by resting his hand in the small of her back. Burning right through her clothing. Branding her. Claiming her.

"I know you studied the carvings in the wall. Did you decipher the very first entry? I would think the earlier entries would be fascinating." Byron sensed her growing agitation. When he touched her mind, it was chaotic. There was no one thought. She was confused and angry. Brooding. Moody. Edgy. The gathering of a great storm. She was his lifemate, and whatever she needed he would provide. He was well aware she found the history of her family intriguing. He hoped to distract her for a time.

Antonietta clutched the package tighter to her. "I spent some time studying the first bride's entry. She wasn't alone. Her husband did his share of carving also. I think it was his idea. I think he wanted his family to know the gifts he secured for them. He was very intrigued with the idea of shape-shifting. The earlier carvings are nearly all of shape-shifters. Women and even a few men changing to the jaguar. The earlier etchings are crude, of course, but they are detailed. I think they reveal more of the secrets than the later carvings." She made herself breathe in the oppressive heat of the passageway. If only his breath didn't tease the hair on the back of her neck, she might be able to think straight.

"In the later, more modern days, was there any evidence of shape-shifting?"

She rubbed at her itching skin and stopped directly in front of what appeared to be a solid wall. Byron reached past her to run his palm over the smooth surface. Her fingers brushed his, caught, and instinctively guided his to the three shallow depressions guarding secrets. It was an admission of trust, and he knew it even before she did.

The wall slid noiselessly away to reveal the air-sealed vault. Obviously she knew the sequence of numbers on the keypad. She punched several buttons carefully. The door to the vault opened. There was no light. The passageway was pitch black, but Antonietta didn't need light. She was at home in a world of darkness. Byron was impressed with her uncanny ability to know exactly where she was in her environment.

"I didn't see any. I think the blood is too diluted."

"Could one of your cousins be capable of shifting?" Byron posed the question without inflection.

Antonietta went still, her hands hovering just inside the vault. "One of my cousins?" she echoed, the idea unsettling. "I can't think that, Byron. That one of them would be this creature tearing the throats out of innocent people. It sickens me to even imagine such a possibility."

"The smell of the cat was *inside* the palazzo. It permeated your grandfather's rooms. You say the sheets of music were kept in Don Giovanni's private safe. If a shifter was looking for them . . ."

She thrust the precious music into the vault and slammed it closed. "I don't want to think a member of my family is capable of such cold-blooded murder."

"In the body of a wild predator, it can be very difficult to control the urges. It is said that some shifters do not even recognize their human side. And some animals are much more difficult to control than others."

Antonietta bent forward to lean her forehead against the vault in guilt. "I wanted to play the music." The confession came out in a little rush. "If I hear music, no matter how difficult or intricate, I can play it, but I can't see it. I had to ask Justine to read it to me. You can imagine how difficult it was for us to decipher the entire score between us, how long it took us. Don Giovanni knew, of course; he gave it to me, but I was to guard it so carefully. Each night I returned it to his room, but anyone could have seen Justine and me working together on it."

The action of bending forward brought her buttocks in direct contact with Byron's body. He pressed against her, hard and thick and very male. Antonietta could have cried in frustration. Her skin crawled with need. Her body felt tight and alien to her. She straightened immediately to break the contact, pushing away from him to begin the walk down to the history room. She was aware of her own body. The swaying of her hips, the ache in her breasts. It was insanity that she lacked control.

"Antonietta, when I touch your mind, you are confused and distraught. I would help you, if you allow me access." Byron was going to push past that barrier if she didn't enlighten him soon. He couldn't take her being so upset. They had already exchanged blood twice. The Carpathian blood was definitely enhancing her senses, changing her, but he had no idea with her differences, what other changes the blood might cause.

"I prefer to work out my own problems," she said. "I'm sorry if I sound abrupt; everything feels like it's crashing down on me."

"In a partnership, *cara,* one shares troubles."

"I'm not used to a partnership yet." Antonietta softened her voice, not wanting to hurt him. "I'm trying, Byron. I really am. I've never had these feelings, and I've never felt so *intense* about everything. It's unsettling." *And I have never been so aware of a man before.*

Byron caught that very feminine thought. She still didn't accept the power and force of the bond between them. It was unlike anything she'd ever experienced. She was both intimidated and a bit frightened: two emotions Antonietta Scarletti was unfamiliar with. He followed her in silence to the history room.

The door slid aside, and the light automatically leapt to life, displaying the rows and rows, floor to ceiling, of pictures and words and symbols carved into the wall, much like the Egyptian hieroglyphics.

Antonietta pressed her palm over one of the etchings. "Can you imagine the time it took to do this? And it will be here for all time unless the palazzo is destroyed. Someday, perhaps a hundred years from now, another Scarletti will stand in this room and see what went before them."

Byron began reading, totally absorbed in the unfolding drama before him. Bride after bride was selected from the small village of Jaguar people. There were a few gaps, and as the generations lost touch with what the original Scarlettis intended, the brides from the village became fewer, until the bloodline was once again diluted. Many of the brides were unhappy with their husbands and the jealousies and intrigues that prevailed in the palazzo through the centuries. Some loved their husbands very much. Many had gifts of healing and telepathy. The latter stories seemed to indicate telepathy was common among the Scarlettis. "This is fascinating, Antonietta."

"I used to come here often when I was younger. I could read the wall and most of the diaries myself, even though I couldn't see, and it made me feel independent. Of course I can read Braille, but most business documents are not put into Braille for me, so I rely on Justine to read them to me."

And Justine had betrayed her. How could she ever trust her with such important and private information again? Byron rested his hand over Antonietta's. Linking them. Merging his mind with hers to feel the heart-wrenching sorrow. She no longer trusted her judgment. No longer trusted the sixth sense she used in her relationships with people. Justine had done more damage than he had first believed.

"And now you cannot rely on her."

On anyone. The words shimmered unbidden in her mind. She wiped them away quickly. "I'm not feeling sorry for myself, Byron. I learned a long time ago to pick up the pieces and move on. I just feel like I'm in quicksand, and every step I take, everywhere I turn, I'm being pulled down. I want solid ground."

He pulled her palm to his heart. "Right here, Antonietta. I am right here."

She tugged to get her hand free. "How much do I know of you? You want complete trust. You want me to change my entire life for you."

Byron kept possession of her hand. The jaguar in her was close. Wary. Wanting to run. The woman in her was feeling exactly the same way. Hunted. Under siege. She had no idea how much he intended to change her life, but she sensed he was dangerous to her. That was the jaguar's instincts, and they were strong in her.

"I want to be in your life, yes. I am not going to deny it. Allow yourself to completely merge with me. Your answers are there, in my mind."

She pulled her hand away, her heart beating fast. His words were always a temptation. His voice was sinful and filled her with a lust she couldn't seem to control. One she didn't want. "The passageway is suffocating me." Her voice was breathless, husky. She wasn't going to merge with him and let him see the images dancing in her head. It would be humiliating.

She turned abruptly and started back to her room. Byron stepped out of the history room, allowing the door to slide closed. He kept pace easily with Antonietta, his body close to hers, wanting to ease her distress but uncertain just how to do so.

The wide-open rooms were cold after the suffocating heat in the tunnels. Antonietta gave a sigh of relief, shivered, and crossed her arms to hide the way her nipples hardened into pebbles, rubbing against the lace of her bra every time she moved. She said nothing when the fire leapt to life, certain Byron had misinterpreted her gesture, mistaking her for being cold.

"Did you have the Handel score copied, Antonietta?" Byron inquired as he seated himself in his favorite armchair. Celt was curled up in her bedroom. He could see the dog through the open door. The borzoi hadn't stirred, not with Byron guarding his charge.

Antonietta stretched her arms over her head. Her body felt

heavy and sensitive. She could smell Byron's masculine scent and for some reason it called to her. She was too aware of him only feet from her. The interlude in the solarium had been brief and ferocious. And not enough. She paced across the floor, a restless, edgy mood driving her. Her breasts felt full and ached for attention. Her skin itched for relief. "I did, just to make certain it was never lost. The copy would be worth something for the score alone; it is entirely his original work, nothing borrowed from other composers, but it still would never be worth what notations in his own hand would be."

"Could Marita have the combination to Don Giovanni's safe?"

"No, he would never give it to either her or Franco. I know Nonno. He is not a trusting man, especially since Franco sold information to the Demonesini family." The fire crackled. Byron shifted, his clothes rustling. Antonietta wanted to scream. "Do you think the attack on Nonno and me the other night had something to do with Handel's composition?"

"I would think it likely. It would be too much coincidence for it to be otherwise. Those men were searching for something, and they spent a great deal of time in Don Giovanni's rooms."

Byron's voice was killing her. Stroking her skin like velvet. Like a thousand tongues. She didn't think she could stand it much longer. She tried to force her body under control. She was going to have to send him home and get distance between them. Miles would help. Oceans maybe. "The opera is not common knowledge, even among family members. Franco could have told Marita, but I've never heard of him even asking about it. Someone must have seen it when I was so insistent on playing it." With restless abandon, she pulled the pins from her hair so that it tumbled down her back, a wild display mirroring her bizarre emotions. "It's hot in here, we shouldn't have a fire."

"Come here, Antonietta." Byron said it softly, but she heard the command in his voice. It set her teeth on edge.

"Why? I say it's hot, and you want me to come to you." She paced away from him, wanting to tear at her own skin.

"You are uncomfortable."

Antonietta had a mad desire to kneel between Byron's legs

and work his trousers from his body. Her mouth would show him uncomfortable. She imagined how he would feel growing full and hard and thick. At her mercy. She would show him none, not when he was making her feel so out of control and frustrated. She kept the distance of the room between them, wary of what she didn't understand.

"Come here to me." He repeated the command, his voice coming between his teeth. Soft. Imperious. Frightening in that she wanted to obey him.

She stood her ground, refused to move. Refused to give in to whatever was happening. "What is it? What's wrong with me?" The junction between her legs burned and ached for fulfillment.

Byron touched her mind again, a shadow hiding while her mind raged and swirled with erotic images, with a terrible, insatiable hunger. "I suspect it is a combination of things, Antonietta. I do not understand why I cannot help you relieve your suffering."

"Just tell me what it is."

Byron sighed. "Carpathians must mate frequently. I have noticed you are very sensitive. I suspect between the Carpathian species and the Jaguar gene you must carry, you are feeling . . . er . . . heat."

"Heat?" She whirled around. "I am not an animal in heat. That doesn't make me feel better, thank you very much."

"Is the idea of mating with me so terrible?"

"Don't twist my words. I didn't say that. If you want to help, distract me." She twisted her fingers together in sudden daring. "I want to see, Byron. I want to see through your eyes. You said you could do it, and I want to try."

"Are you certain that is what you want? It will not be easy."

She lifted her chin. "I don't care. I want to try it."

"It will be disorienting at first. You'll have to get past your senses and hold on to mine. Your own body will fight you. The images will be in your mind. You will see things the way I see them."

"I don't care, as long as I see." There was determination in her voice.

"You will have to merge your mind fully with mine. What I see and feel, you will also. If you are uncomfortable, pull away from my mind. You will have the control to do that. Have you noticed that your power and sensitivity to the environment around you is growing?"

"Why is that?"

"You are my lifemate. As our lives merge, so do our bodies. I made my claim on you, the ritual binding, and we are tied in heart and soul." His smile was in his voice. "In this modern age, I suppose that sounds melodramatic and old-fashioned."

"Not to me." She hesitated, suddenly afraid. "What do I do?"

He went to her, recognizing she was close to tears. The intensity of her sexual need was overwhelming. Continually having to adjust the volume of hearing and coping with the separation without understanding why was daunting. He stood behind her, wrapped his arms around her waist, and held her to him.

Antonietta shivered. "You really can do this?"

He felt the small tremor that ran through her body. "I will be with you. Remember, you cannot see through your own eyes. You have to merge completely and see through mine. I can use Celt or any person I have a particular bond with to see, even from a distance. We have a strong bond. There is nothing to worry about. I can hold the merge, and you will be able to see."

"I'm not certain I understand, but I want to try." She sounded scared but determined. Her hands gripped his. "Tell me what to do."

"Let yourself reach for me. You know the path. It is the same as making love, merging minds completely. Just let it happen."

Antonietta forced air through her lungs to calm herself. She was terrified it would work. Terrified it wouldn't. Very slowly she reached up and removed her dark glasses. Her fingertips touched her eyes. She felt him. Byron. Moving in her mind. Looking into places she didn't want anyone to see. She jerked away from him.

"It is all right, *bella,* I am not looking for incriminating evidence. You are in my head as well. It goes both ways with mutual respect. Try again, and this time relax."

Antonietta dug her fingers into the back of his hand and

let go with her mind. Allowed her barriers down to merge. It was a peculiar feeling, not unpleasant, a blending of two personalities. She waited. Held her breath. Colors shimmered and danced. Raw. Vibrant. Too much so. She cried out and put a hand over her eyes. The colors didn't go away.

"Just accept them and let them go."

She tried. Her stomach roiled. She could make out something blurry in the distance. Byron was focusing on something. She strained backward, pressing against him. But she forced her eyes to stay open. She wasn't certain it was necessary to do so, she could tell the vision came from him, not her, but she wanted to feel as if she were truly seeing. The edges began to clear. Her stomach lurched again. Everything tilted and spun.

"This isn't right. I don't think I'm doing it right. Everything is moving and spinning so fast."

"Hold on tight to my hands. Anchor yourself. It is not your eyes, Antonietta. They are mine. You do not need your fingertips to tell your brain what you are seeing."

Something dark danced on the walls. She ducked to avoid it.

"A shadow, the firelight reflected on the wall. You can put your hand through a shadow. Concentrate. I am going to narrow our vision to see one thing. Celt is lying peacefully beside your bed. I want you to see him."

Antonietta fought a very real case of vertigo. She turned her head, and objects burst at her much like rockets. She cried out. "It isn't working." She pressed her hand hard against her churning stomach. "I'm going to be sick."

"No you are not. We can stop if you want." His hands held hers tightly.

"Just look at Celt. Only Celt." She was a Scarletti. Her family never backed away from a challenge. "I can do it."

She focused on the distant, blurry object. The borzoi lifted his head, and everything dipped and spun. She refused to look away. The image began to clear. Celt. Sprawled next to her bed. He was enormous, black, a noble head. She had no way of judging distances. Antonietta flung out her hand, thinking him close enough to touch.

"He is across the room."

"He's beautiful. I want to see your face. Show me your face."

He used the small mirror in the vanity, staring at his own face. Her hands went to test for herself, moving over his face, mapping familiar territory. He was far too handsome, his eyes mesmerizing, his mouth sinfully kissable, his jaw strong. She loved his hair, even pulled back the way it was and secured at the nape of his neck.

They examined a variety of objects in her room from her four-poster bed to her stained glass windows. "I do not want you to get tired. I want you to see yourself."

Antonietta shook her head. Byron was behind her, his body pressed very close to hers. She could barely breathe with wanting him. His mind was fully merged within hers, and the sensation was unlike anything she had ever experienced. She didn't know how much longer she would be able to keep her hands off him. Especially after seeing his face. And the idea of seeing herself visually was disturbing. Although she had to admit to curiosity.

"Do you know what a mirror is?" Byron persisted. "Do you recall from the days of your childhood? You can see your own reflection. I want you to look at yourself."

Her mouth went dry. "I'd rather not."

The visual belonged to Byron. Antonietta experienced her sexual reactions from touch, but he had all of his senses. He wanted her to feel what he felt simply by looking at her body. "Look at yourself, Antonietta. Do not fear who you are."

"I'm afraid. Whatever I see will be with me for the rest of my life."

"Trust me. Trust in the way I see you."

She reluctantly lifted her head and stared into the full-length mirror. A stranger stared back at her. Her hair was wild, cascading around her, shiny and black. Flickering lights from the fire put a glossy sheen in it. Her eyes were huge and black. She could see tiny white scars near the corners of her eyes when she stared long and hard. Her mouth was wide and generous, curving upward at the corners. Her skin seemed flawless, glowing even. She had a woman's voluptuous body.

Antonietta reached a shaking hand toward her reflected image. Then reached up and felt her own face in wonder.

She ran her fingertips over her face in an attempt to recognize her own features. She reached out again toward the mirror, touched the smooth, hard glass. She felt her own hair. "No one is that beautiful. I don't look like that. That can't be me."

"That is how you look to me." His voice was soft in her ear.

As deeply merged as they were, she felt his sexual excitement. The need to see her like this. He was aroused at the thought of her naked in front of the mirror. There was a heady power in the ability to make him want her so much. She was unbearably aroused already; to bring him to the same fever pitch was enthralling.

"Take off your blouse, Antonietta. See yourself the way I see you." He was temptation itself. The devil with his arms around her. She could see him in the mirror, his black hair shining in the firelight, his features hard and angular. His eyes burned over her reflection, stamped with possession and promise.

Antonietta caught the hem of her shirt and pulled it over her head and for a moment, the image in front of her wavered. She felt Byron's breath leave his body. Her full breasts were encased in lace. It was an odd thing to be looking at herself, seeing and feeling through the eyes of a man. He was violently aroused. She could feel the thick length of him pressed hard into her buttocks.

"Take off your bra."

She wanted to take it off. She wanted him to want her this way. She wanted to see him aroused, his features harsh with need and implacable resolve. Her hands went to the front clasp, her palms brushing her nipples. Lightning danced through her bloodstream at that small touch. Lace fell away. Her breasts jutted out, high and firm and tempting. Byron's hands came up under hers, pulled her hands to her aching flesh.

"Feel how soft you are. Feel what I feel when I touch you. This is you, Antonietta. Beautiful. Perfect. Mine." Her hands curved around her soft breasts, his hands holding her fingers in place. It was the most erotic thing she'd ever done.

Keeping her eyes on her reflection in the mirror, she turned her head slightly to send her long, unbound hair cascading around her bare shoulders. Byron's hands gently began to knead her breasts, using her fingers. His thumb teased and stroked her nipples into hard peaks of blatant desire. Silky hair only heightened the effect on her skin. She couldn't stop the little moan that escaped from her throat.

Byron rubbed his shadowed jaw against her neck. "Tell me you are not beautiful. You even feel that way to me." His hands left hers to drop lower to the waistband of her slacks. He kept his gaze fixed firmly on the mirror.

Antonietta watched her own hands on her breasts, watched his hands unfasten her slacks and slowly peel them from her body. He hooked her thong at the same time, stripping it away to leave her bare. She stepped out of her clothes and just looked in wonder at her legs, the curve of her hips. It didn't seem possible that that woman in the reflection could be her.

Byron stood behind her, fully clothed, his hands shaping and caressing the curve of her buttocks. His every touch sent waves of desire flooding her until she squirmed with need. She watched his hands move around her thighs, his long fingers stroking so close to that small triangle. Her muscles clenched, her knees went weak. His teeth nibbled on her shoulder, went to her neck. His tongue tasted her frantic pulse, swirled and glided. All the while his eyes were open. Watching her. Allowing her to watch.

"I am going to move around you. For a moment your vision will blur, but then my memories will be your memories, and you will see us together." His hands slid up her body to once more cup her breasts.

"Take your clothes off, Byron. I want to see you." She sounded breathless even to her own ears.

"I do not see me in quite the way I would want you to see me." There was a trace of self-mockery in his tone, but right there, in front of the mirror with her watching, he shed his clothes in the manner of his people.

Antonietta gasped. "How did you do that?"

"I am Carpathian. Clothes are fashioned from natural fibers or simply illusion, whichever is easiest."

He tried to look at himself objectively, to see his body the way a woman might see it and be pleased. His muscles were subtle but defined. His shoulders broad, hips narrow. His erection was large and thick and eager to find its way deep inside of her. There was a small silence while he waited for her response. When it came, he was unprepared for it. The flood of sexual excitement. The pouring of heat into her body, into her mind. The pleasure at seeing his naked body.

He stepped to her side, careful to keep looking at his own reflection. His fingers were long, the hands of an artist. He never noticed it before, but against her skin, he could see the shape and size.

"You're beautiful, Byron." She watched her arm go up, her fingers twisting in his long, black hair. "I can't believe I'm really seeing us. I don't want it to end yet."

"I'm moving around in front of you. Keep your eyes on the mirror and your mind firmly merged with mine. Expect the blurring and distortion, but it will not last." He moved around in front of her, watching himself over his shoulder. He saw the firm muscle of his buttocks flex and contract, felt her surge of damp heat and heightened pleasure. His gaze dropped to her breasts.

Antonietta swayed, closed her eyes, but she couldn't block out the strange, dizzy feeling assaulting her. Shadows and edges blended. She wanted to cry out a protest. His tongue lapped at her nipple. Once. Twice. He drew her breast into his mouth, suckling strongly, teasing her nipple with his tongue. Her body nearly convulsed, and she wrapped her arms around his head and stared at the gray and black shadows in the mirrors while wave after wave of sensation swamped her.

She saw them together the images so clear in his mind. Byron feeding at her breast. Devouring her body Ravenous for her and making no apologies. His hands moved over her, his fingers splayed wide to take in every bit of skin he could find. He stroked and caressed her, his hands cupping her breasts, then her buttocks, then gliding over her stomach to nestle his fingers in the tight, black curls.

"I don't care if I am a cat in heat," she said, widening her stance for him in invitation.

He spent time lavishing attention on her breasts while liquid heat trickled on the inside of her thigh. Until she was hot and wet and couldn't stop moving her hips in sheer frustration. When his mouth left her breast, she cried out a protest, but then watched, fascinated, as his mouth drifted, feathered down her body to her waist, lower still to her navel. He stayed there a few moments, his tongue lapping gently, his hand cupping the heat between her thighs.

"I can hardly breathe." She wanted him so much. Her hands moved constantly, finding every defined muscle, wanting to touch him even while her mind saw them together. "I'm burning up, Byron."

She watched as he knelt in front of her and without haste, wrapped his arms around her hips, forcing her body to him. Her mind nearly exploded with scent and taste and sensation rocketing through their merged senses, their merged brains. She heard her own small scream as his tongue stabbed deep, pushed inside of her.

Antonietta caught two fistfuls of hair, held him to her, pushed her hips into him, tears running down her face. Their shared intimacy amplified her sexual need tenfold. She felt his heavy fullness. The gathering pressure that threatened to blow the top of his head off. She felt his possessive nature. The implacable resolve to hold her to him, to bind her for all eternity. Two halves of the same whole. His hunger for her. His need of her. His need to convert her, fully bring her over.

She tried to hold on to that strange thought, but her body imploded, a vicious, wild orgasm that took her into another dimension. Her vision was gone as he swept her into his arms, carried her across the floor into her bedroom. Antonietta gasped for breath, her muscles convulsing as he thrust into her.

He filled her completely, driving deep, his hands gripping her hips, holding her still while he surged forward relentlessly, mercilessly, demanding she take every inch of him. Skin to skin. Heart to heart. He took her body and gave her his as if he were possessed. Craving her. Never getting enough. As if it could never be enough.

Antonietta didn't want to relinquish her hold on his mind. He was everywhere, in her, surrounding her, a part of her. When she was alone, in her wildest dreams, with her fingers on the keys of her piano, she allowed the intensity of her passion to pour through her, to envision such a joining between man and woman. Whatever strange needs her body had plagued her with throughout the evening, all the suffering was worth it for the time she spent in his arms.

She clung to him, held on tightly as he surged deep and strong inside of her. She wanted him deeper still where the fierce pressure gathered and built until she was burning, a firestorm she couldn't control. "Byron." She whispered his name as her muscles tightened around him, gripped convulsively. As he shuddered with the effort to hang on. One long stroke sent them both careening over the edge.

They clung to one another, fighting for air, fighting to calm their pounding hearts. Byron didn't move, his body melting into hers. They lay locked together as they were meant to be. *Antonietta. My love. I love you very much.*

She knew his face now, even more vividly than she had before. Every detail was etched in her memory, both from her fingertips and seeing him through his eyes. His whisper was against her throat. His words found their way straight to her heart. Antonietta feared she was very much in love with her dark poet. She slipped her arms around him, holding him to her, not wanting him ever to leave her. All through the night she held him close. Each time he woke her to make love to her again, she turned to him eagerly. She loved the soft whispers and shared laughter, and she didn't want their time ever to end.

13

Antonietta *woke to* the knowledge she was in danger. Tiny beads of sweat formed on her body, her heart pounded in terror. She fumbled at the nightstand for her dark glasses to cover her eyes even as her mind reached for Byron. She found a dark, black void instead of comfort. Her lungs burned for air. Where was he? And what manner of monster prowled just outside her windows, seeking a way in.

Byron. She called his name sharply. Imperiously. *Where the hell is my white knight when I'm in danger? Wake up!*

Predatory eyes watched her with a single, focused purpose. Antonietta could feel the burning malice in the stare. With a slow, unhurried movement, she sat up and swung her legs over the side of the bed. Drawing the sheet up to her chin, her hand went out instinctively to the dog. The borzoi remained absolutely silent, but she could feel the tension vibrating in the animal's body. Celt was on the alert, his posture that of a hunter. It was night, Antonietta didn't know how she knew, but it was definitely night. Once again she had slept away the day. Something terrible and dangerous prowled outside on her balcony, looking for a way into her home. A dark malevolence poured into her room.

I am with you. Stay connected to Celt. Byron sounded calm.

Something heavy thudded against the stained glass. Pushing relentlessly, steadily, scratching to get in. The dog bounded to the window, a ferocious protector rushing with teeth bared and ready. The breathing coming from behind the thick walls was a terrible thing to hear. It sounded like air rushing through a tunnel. The footfalls should have been silent, but Antonietta could hear the soft padding across the balcony, the nails scraping on her windowsill.

It's at the window, trying to get in. I can't hold Celt back. He's pacing between the windows. I'm afraid, Byron. Antonietta pulled on her robe. She smelled the pungent odor of the large, heavy cat and wanted to gag. *It wants me. Not just anyone, but me. I'm not being hysterical. I can feel it reaching for me.*

Her body itched beneath the skin, much like it had when she had been so terrified as a child, knowing a bomb was on her parents' yacht. Her senses sharpened even more. There was clarity in her mind and a tunnel narrowing to take in and amplify every sound. Colors shimmered, reds and yellows, brilliant and vivid and blinding. Antonietta couldn't shut them out. She was seeing with another part of her, not her eyes, and the colors remained in her mind. The colors took on the blurry but recognizable form of a large animal. Bright splashes of red at its chest and abdomen, surrounded by shades of orange fading to a perimeter of glowing yellow. She watched a paw print, pale yellow fade to blue and disappear and realized she was seeing body heat. Thermal images as the animal went from window to window, pawing and scratching and digging to get in.

I have it now. Jaguar. Large one. Celt is tracking its movements. Get out of the room. Go downstairs into Franco's wing and remain with him until I reach you. I am on my way.

Antonietta didn't need to be told. The sheer malevolence coming from outside the thick walls of the palazzo was alarming. She could feel black hatred. A need to rend and kill. "Celt, come with me." She yanked open the door.

The cat yowled. A nasty note that climbed to a high-pitched scream of rage. Sensing she was getting away, it slammed its body against the stained glass nearest the door. She heard the terrible thud as the heavy body rammed the glass and lead in a determined effort to gain entrance. There was the ominous sound of something cracking. Celt growled low in his throat. Antonietta heard a crunch as the borzoi closed its great jaws over something she was afraid to identify. She felt, more than heard, the dog shake its head savagely.

Get out of there. He will hold the cat at the window. Close the door behind you.

I won't leave Celt alone in here. The jaguar is evil. I feel it. She wanted to drag the dog out, but no amount of coaxing or commanding could call him from the window.

Do as I command. Byron used a soft voice, pitched low, one that cut deep into her mind and forced obedience when her entire nature insisted she couldn't leave her dog behind to face evil.

Byron exploded out of the earth, a black vapor cloud streaming relentlessly through the sky. One part of his mind followed Antonietta's progress through the palazzo, down the sweeping stairs and through the long rows of rooms toward the wing where Franco and Marita resided. Another part of him stayed connected with Celt. The borzoi locked on to the muzzle of the cat, slashed and crunched and let go, springing back. The jaguar retreated with a hideous screech of pain.

The dog tracked the cat across to the far window. Outside, on the balcony, the jaguar leapt to the roof, scrambled for purchase, and jumped up to the battlements, running across the narrow ledge to reach the tower. Celt lost sight of the cat. The borzoi tracked back and forth between the windows several times.

Go to her. I will hunt.

Byron knew he was too late. The cat had a head start. Apparently some internal warning system had alerted the creature that a predator was stalking. Byron could only hope for a lead, a small mistake to give him an idea where the jaguar's lair was. The scent and trail would be fresh. He had no choice but to uncover the newest danger to Antonietta. Why did they all want her dead?

The borzoi easily opened the door to Antonietta's quarters

and unerringly followed her scent through the palazzo, bringing a measure of relief to Byron. He turned his full attention to hunting the jaguar. The cat had to have a lair somewhere, unless it was a member of Antonietta's family. If that were the case, it might double back and enter the palazzo in human form.

If it is one of my cousins as you so clearly suspect, why wouldn't they simply shift inside the palazzo and attack me from within? And don't think you're going to get away with sending me from my room without Celt. We're going to have a long discussion about boundaries.

He ignored her comment, focusing on her intentions. *What are you thinking, Antonietta? Do not dare to search the palazzo.*

Don't you see? If the cat is out there, and my cousins are all in their rooms, it can't be one of them. I'm going to check on Franco and Marita, and if they're here, I'll check on Paul and Tasha.

Byron swore eloquently in several languages. *You will do no such thing. Where is that dog? Why is he not with you?*

He's here, and stop fussing at me. Antonietta knocked on her cousin's door. Although dark, it was early enough in the evening that everyone should be up. *Byron! For heaven's sake. Did you invite your family to the palazzo for dinner tonight?* How could she have forgotten? She had told Helena the night before but hadn't checked with her to see if everything was going smoothly.

As soon as you asked me. Do not worry. I can easily uninvite them. For all of our sakes, it may be best. I would rather your family not be exposed to young Josef.

No. Don't you dare uninvite them. I'm not going to allow a wild animal to scare me away from my chance at meeting your family.

Franco opened the door, startling her. "Have you come to see Margurite? She's better today. I brought her a computer, and I think it is the perfect idea to entertain her." He kissed his cousin's cheek as he drew her inside. "She'll love to see your dog. Both children are already wild about him."

"Where's Marita?" Antonietta asked as she waved to Vincente and crossed the room to kiss Margurite. Celt pushed his nose against the child in a display of affection.

"She's probably out looking for computer educational software," Franco said. "She's been agitated ever since she stumbled upon that . . ." He glanced down at his daughter. "You know. She's been upset."

"It was a frightening experience for her."

"And she's so sensitive and highly strung."

Volatile. The word was in her mind before she could censor it. She heard the echo of Byron's instant agreement.

"I forgot to let you know Byron's family is in the area, and I've invited them to dinner this evening. If you're able, I would very much like you and your family to join us." She caught Margurite's hand. "How are you feeling, *cara?* Does it hurt much?"

Margurite shook her head. "Byron comes in at night and does something when I'm crying, and then my leg doesn't hurt anymore. It works better than the medicine that makes me sleepy."

"I didn't know that," Franco said.

"You're asleep," Margurite pointed out with childlike candor.

"Byron is even more skilled than I when it comes to taking away pain," Antonietta explained. "I have to see to the details of tonight's dinner, but I wanted to make certain you knew we were having company."

Franco laughed. "The staff might take you seriously if you weren't in your bathrobe, Antonietta. More and more you are sleeping the day away. You artists enjoy keeping strange hours."

"So true." She kissed him lightly. "But you love us anyway."

"Yes, I do. Thank Byron for helping Margurite. And we will be at your dinner party, giving you full Scarletti support. Have no worries."

"Can Celt stay with me?" Margurite asked.

Deep inside of her, she could feel Byron still and waiting. He didn't protest. He didn't object, but she felt him hold his breath. His concern made her feel cherished. "I'll ask him if he'd like to visit a little later," Antonietta promised the child. "I need him just a bit longer." Her hand dropped to caress the dog's silky ears. The borzoi did give her more independence. She would never have entered Franco's quarters without taking him, afraid the furniture was moved in one of Marita's frenzied decorating schemes, or that the children had left their toys out. Celt simply steered her around all objects without seeming to do so.

The cat's scent is fresh in the grove. I see tracks around the garden area and the back courtyard in particular. The animal was trying to gain entry through the French doors. There is a distinct print on the door down near the bottom, as if he tried to pry it open. There are scratch marks up high on the frame.

Antonietta made her way through the long hallway separating Franco's suite of rooms from Tasha's. The sound of weeping made Antonietta frown and quickly knock on her cousin's door. Tasha could cut someone in two with her tongue, but she rarely cried.

There was instant silence. The rustle of clothes. Antonietta tried the door. It was locked. "Tasha. What's wrong?"

"Nothing, Toni, go away."

"I certainly will not. Open this door, or I'll get the master key." Alarm spread rapidly. Tasha would never lock herself in her room.

"Is anyone with you?"

"Just Celt. What's wrong, Tasha? You're scaring me."

Byron could feel Antonietta's anxiety escalating. He stayed a shadow in her mind, even as he crisscrossed the grounds for evidence of the jaguar. The cats were known for their stealth and ability to keep hidden. This one, he was certain, was far more cunning than most.

The door opened slowly. Tasha stepped back to allow her cousin entry and then shut the door firmly and locked it. "Watch the chair, Toni. Just a minute, let me push it back in. I didn't think about it being in the way."

Antonietta, sensitive to every nuance, heard the tremor in Tasha's voice, even though it was evident she made every effort to cover it up.

Something's wrong with her, Byron. She tells me everything. Every little detail. This is totally unlike her.

Direct Celt to look at her. Byron focused, using the images from the animal. Tasha's face was swollen and wet with tears. He looked closer. Dark anger swirled in his belly. *Use your fingertips, my love, someone has struck her. Her eye is swollen, and the left side of her face discolored.*

Antonietta caught her cousin's hand, drew her close. "Who dared to do this to you?" Her fingertips barely skimmed, careful of inflicting more pain. "You should have come to me immediately. I would have helped you."

"I was too humiliated." Tasha burst into another storm of weeping. "I didn't want anyone to see me, to know. And you were still in bed with . . . that man." She added the last accusingly.

"Christopher did this?"

"He came to visit today, as he does every day, with his demands. He doesn't like my clothes. He wants my hair differently. I don't know enough about art. The list of my shortcomings goes on and on, and he doesn't even know about the most damning of all." A sob escaped. Tasha wrapped her arms around Antonietta and cried into her shoulder as if her heart were breaking.

Antonietta held her. Even Celt pushed against Tasha's legs in an attempt to comfort her. "You did tell that man to go to hell, I hope."

"That's why he hit me. He was furious when I gave him back his ring. He said he refused to allow me to break the engagement. He said horrible things to me." Lifting her head, she pulled Antonietta's hand to her hip. "He hit me so hard I fell, and then he kicked me right here."

Fury welled up out of nowhere. Antonietta shook with it. She didn't know if it was her own anger or if she was so deeply merged with Byron she was feeling his anger. The combination was deadly. "I'd sell the palazzo before I would ever let that horrible man near you. Nonno would feel the same way, as well Franco and Paul. I'd like to do a little violence to Christopher myself."

She cupped the side of her cousin's face, concentrated on finding the power inside of her. *Byron, help me.* She knew he would help her, that his healing power was great, and combined, they would take away every ache. She felt him moving through her. Gathering strength, reaching for Tasha. Antonietta heard soft chanting, words in a language she didn't recognize, when she knew so many.

Tasha drew back when the terrible throbbing in her face lessened and nearly vanished. She touched her face. "It feels better. *Grazie,* Toni." She paced across the room, pushing her hand through her hair in agitation. "Christopher can make trouble for us. For Nonno. He said he'd cause a scandal. Our family can't afford any more scandals."

"Scarlettis were born to be embroiled in scandals. I think we should call your handsome captain and press charges against Christopher Demonesini. Maybe we can have the rat spend a few hours in jail."

"I just want to forget I ever had anything to do with him."

"It doesn't surprise me he was abusive. Christopher grew up thinking he was entitled to anything he wanted. I'm sorry he hurt you, Tasha, but truthfully, I'm grateful you broke it off with him."

"I wish you'd break it off with Byron. I'm not comparing Christopher to Byron, Toni, really, I'm not. But he frightens me in a way Christopher never could. I want you to promise me you'll be careful. Something's not right about him. Why don't we know anything about him?"

"His family is coming for dinner tonight. His sister, her husband, and their son. We can ask all sorts of questions."

"Tonight?" Tasha's voice rose. She covered her face with her hands. "How could this happen now, Toni?" She wailed it. "I want to meet his family. I can't very well sit at a table with my face like this. Do you have to have them for dinner tonight? Have them wait a week or two."

"Tasha, they're visiting the area. You know very well I can't ask them to wait. You always wanted to be in the middle of a drama. We should invite the captain for dinner, too. It's the perfect opportunity. And I need to get dressed. I want to look special tonight. I don't want to ask Justine to help me."

Tasha caught Antonietta's hand. "Of course I'll help you. But *don't* invite Diego. I don't want him to see me like this."

"I haven't told Paul about dinner yet, and I need to talk to Helena. I want to check that everything is perfect."

"I'll ring Helena and have her meet us in your rooms. Paul's gone. He left right after Christopher arrived."

A chill went down Antonietta's spine. *Byron?* She reached for him, needing the comfort of his presence.

I am here, cara. *I am always with you. Paul is often gone. It does not prove anything one way or the other.*

Antonietta listened to her heartbeat. The fear beating at her subsided. *Grazie, Byron. You always manage to say the right thing.*

"We'll have to hurry." Tasha took another look at her face in the mirror. "It doesn't hurt very much anymore, but it sure looks awful. Come on before I change my mind. Let's go find you the perfect outfit."

Antonietta hurried through the palazzo and up the stairs, Celt at her side and Tasha leading the way. Helena was waiting at her door, doing her best to hide her exasperation with Antonietta's interference.

"I'm certain everything is fine, signorina."

"Fine then," Tasha snapped. "She was just checking, Helena. Go do whatever it is you do."

"That was rude," Antonietta said as the housekeeper hurried away.

"She was rude. She should know you never fuss. This must be important to you, or you wouldn't be so concerned."

"I am not fussing."

Yes you are.

Antonietta opened her door warily, allowing Celt to go ahead of her. When the borzoi didn't give the alarm, she entered with more confidence. *No one asked you.*

His soft laughter poured over her.

"Toni, the window." Tasha rushed to one of the large plates of stained glass. It was pushed inward. "What happened?"

"That cat tried to get in. Byron's out looking for it now."

"How frightening. Did you call Diego?"

"No, I didn't even think about calling the authorities. I ran out of the room."

"We'll have to get this repaired. In the meantime, maybe we should have bars put up for safety." Tasha threw open the doors to the wardrobe. "Something feminine but not too sexy."

You are sexy in anything you wear.

Not tonight.

She knew she wasn't really dressing for Byron's family. She was dressing for him. She wanted to look feminine and beautiful. She wanted to look the way the woman in the mirror had looked.

"Your long skirt, the royal blue silk with the little blouse and pearl buttons," Tasha decided. "It's the perfect image. Pianist, businesswoman, and yet ultrafeminine."

Long skirt, Byron. Not sexy at all.

At dinner tonight I will be thinking of that little lace bra that does not cover a thing, and the thong. That wonderful little thong that preys on my mind my every waking minute.

You worry me. But it worries me even more that I like the way you think. Did you find the jaguar? Paul isn't here, but Tasha and Franco both are.

The cat has been prowling around the cove and down near the caves where the entrance to the tunnel is. The trail led away from the palazzo and back again. The water has removed all traces of the scent. Hurry now, and dress. Your housekeeper, by the way, is taking her ire out on the chef.

The jaguar had deliberately used the water to confuse the scent. Byron could not find a clear trail leading from the cove. Many human scents were mingled together, impossible to pick out any that might have been a shifter. He masked his presence and soared upward to Antonietta's balcony, sending a quick reassurance to Celt so the borzoi wouldn't go on guard and alert the women. The damage to one window was enormous. The jaguar had tried to force its way into the room. It had definitely wanted to attack Antonietta.

Byron gripped the balustrade tightly. Antonietta was out of time. He could no longer afford to wait when such an enemy was stalking her. She had to be with him.

What is it? You're so sad. Come to me and stop thinking about things that make you sad. Nothing happened to me, and nothing will. You gave me Celt, remember?

Her voice filled him with happiness yet tore at his heart. He had to find a way to make her understand. He wanted her to choose his life. To love him enough to choose him. Her family and her music were her world. There had to be a way to give her everything and still share in and protect her life.

Byron, what is it? I share my troubles with you. Share with me.

Hurt had crept into her thoughts. Byron straightened. *Later. After you meet my family. We will have plenty of time to talk. I'm coming.*

He used the cracks in the window to seep through, mist pouring into her bedroom and then under the door to gain the hallway so when she stepped out, he was waiting. He even remembered to dress in a suit for her.

Tasha turned her face away and for once said nothing to him. He could see the color sweep under her skin as she squeezed Antonietta's hand and then rushed away. He simply stood there, staring at his lifemate. In that moment he knew he would always feel that first moment of wonder each time he saw her. Of joy at her existence. She stood there dressed in some blue creation that clung to her curves and swirled and moved as if alive when she walked. He was speechless, unable for a moment to think.

"Is the chef really upset?"

He cleared his throat, feasting his eyes on her. She obviously had no idea how she affected him, and that might be a good thing. "Listen; you can hear him arguing with the housekeeper and his assistant."

Antonietta found she could. She simply had to want to hear it. An argument was raging in the kitchen. She sighed. "Nothing is ever easy, is it?"

Byron took her hand. Celt fell in beside her. They made their way downstairs to the large kitchen. Several workers were chopping and cutting, and the smell of bread and broth permeated the room. Everyone fell silent when they entered.

Antonietta forced a smile. "Surely there is no problem here. We have very little time to pull this dinner off. Our guests will be arriving any minute, and everything must be perfect. I sent the revised menu and asked for the Irish lace tablecloth and our best china. The palazzo must be spotless. If you have to ask the maids to work overtime, please tell them they will be compensated accordingly." For a moment she hesitated, so used to having Justine at her side taking care of details, she was unsure how to proceed. In truth, she rarely went beyond giving Helena orders.

Helena's face flushed a dull red. "I'm capable of attending to these matters, signorina." Her voice was stiff. "Have you lost confidence in my capabilities to handle the staff?"

"No, of course not, Helena," Antonietta said hastily. "It's just that this dinner is very important to me. I heard the chef possibly objected to the menu—"

Cara, bella, *truly, my family will be happy with whatever you choose to serve. It matters little to them. They are coming to meet you.* Byron rested his hand on Antonietta's shoulder, searching for a way to ease her nervousness at the idea of meeting his family. *They are so happy I found you. And they will welcome you into our family. Eleanor was so pleased when she heard we were bound.*

It matters to me. She was clearly distracted and not paying attention to him.

Byron slid his hand down her arm until their fingers tangled, intertwined.

"Signorina . . ." Helena shifted her weight nervously from one foot to the other. "The Irish lace has gone missing. Earlier I told the maids to put the cloth on the formal dining table, and they reported it is gone. The Medici lace is quite beautiful."

"Gone? What is wrong with everyone? How could the Irish lace be gone? It was my mother's."

Byron tugged until she was beneath his shoulder. She was acting out of character, fussing at her staff because she was nervous about meeting his family. And he saw immediately the importance of the tablecloth to her.

"I'm sorry, signorina, I understand, and I'll try to have it found, but if we can't, there must be something else." Helena sounded a bit desperate.

"I want everything to be perfect, Helena. I can't have Byron's family show up for dinner and not have the Irish lace tablecloth."

"I'm sorry, Signorina Antonietta, I'll check the laundry at once." The housekeeper signaled to the chef and his assistant frantically.

"This family, your special guests," Esteben said suddenly, "are they business associates or friends? Perhaps both?"

Alfredo broke into a torrent of rage, waving his arms and clipping Esteben sharply about the ears. "You never ask such a thing from the signorina."

Antonietta heard the dull thud of his fist making contact, and she winced. "Alfredo!" she reprimanded sharply. "I don't believe in striking another person. Please keep your hands to yourself in my home. Surely you know I don't allow my people to be treated in such a manner."

"I thought it would make a difference in the menu, Alfredo," Esteben apologized. Forgive me, signorina."

"There is nothing to forgive, Esteben." Antonietta put her hands on her hips. "Can you pull this dinner together for me, Alfredo? Yes or no?"

There was a distinct challenge in her voice. Byron also heard a hint of desperation. The dinner didn't matter at all to his family, but it did to Antonietta. He narrowed and focused his gaze on the chef. For a brief moment, the flames of the demon flickered in his eyes.

Alfredo looked from Antonietta to Byron. His face cleared. He spread his hands out in a passive gesture. "Of course, signorina, if you wish to change the menu, I'll be most happy to oblige."

"Good. *Grazie,* Alfredo. You have no idea how important this is to me. I'll get out of your way." She turned with a swish of her long skirt, catching Byron's hand. "I'm so glad that's settled. I'm so nervous."

Byron brought her hand to his mouth and nibbled on her knuckles. "There is no need. Eleanor will love you immediately. How could she not? Vlad is a very calm, even-tempered man. He adores Eleanor and gives her most anything she wants."

"Is he a jeweler, such as yourself? An artisan?"

"In his way. I have a special knack for finding gems, for calling them to me. The perfect gem for the piece I envisage. Vlad does not like to design jewelry. He enjoys sculpting. His work is highly prized. Eleanor was so pleased he was in the crafts. She could never have been happy with a hunter."

"Hunter? What do they hunt?"

He should have known she would catch that mistake. He was growing too comfortable with her. Antonietta was so connected to him, he hardly knew where he began and she left off. He was beginning to realize just how close lifemates were. "I should have used the term enforcer. Much like Captain Diego. I'll explain it when we have more time."

Antonietta lifted both hands to his face, her sensitive fingertips mapping his expression, feature by feature. "Yes, I think you will have to explain this to me, Byron. Not only are you frowning, but I feel your reluctance in my mind. We have a lot to talk about, don't we? Things like boundaries."

He winced. "I was looking out for your safety."

"That's not what I want to hear."

"Our mind link is becoming a nuisance."

"Only when you try to hide things from me. I can't wait to meet your family," Antonietta said. "Especially your sister. She can tell me wonderful stories of your childhood. She can tell me whether you will ever understand the term *boundary* or not."

He groaned. "Eleanor is prone to making things up."

Antonietta laughed. "You're lying to me. She probably doesn't need to make things up. I can't wait to find out what you were like as a child."

"Antonietta, I would hate to have to throw you over my shoulder in front of our two families and carry you upstairs. One mention of my childhood, and that is bound to happen."

Joy swirled in her. How had she ever managed without the excitement of sharing? Without the sheer fun of Byron in her life? "You wouldn't dare. I happen to be a famous concert pianist. I'm very respectable, and things like that aren't done."

"You happen to be a *world*-famous concert pianist, and that is exactly what will happen to you if you dare to embarrass me."

"If you're going to be a baby about it, I'll just wait until your sister and I are alone to ask her all the little humiliating details of your childhood. I'm also going to tell her your penchant for being bossy and *demanding* your way. Perhaps she will give me tips on how best to control that little flaw you have."

Byron took her hand again. He had no intentions of allowing Eleanor ever to be alone with Antonietta. "Have I told you I love the way you look in that skirt?"

"No, but you can if you'd like to. I wanted to look nice for your family."

"You look beautiful. Tempting. I could carry you off right now," he said hopefully. Deliberately, he conjured up a picture in his head, paying great care to detail: Antonietta stretched out naked on the bed, her hair a silken cloud over the pillow. His head pressed between her thighs while she writhed with passion.

Color swept under her skin. Antonietta fanned herself.

"Stop that right this minute. Your family is coming, and I have work to do."

"I thought your work was taking care of me." Under cover of the nearest piece of furniture, Byron pressed her open hand to the front of his slacks. He was already as hard as a rock.

Antonietta rubbed her palm over the thick bulge. "Poor *bambino,* so neglected. If you didn't keep running off to leave me to sleep alone, I might have more sympathy for you." Her fingers danced over the rigid length of him, a tantalizing promise. Her teeth nibbled on his chin. "As it is, I have . . . *none.*" She hurried away, laughing, her skirts swirling around her ankles. "Where's Helena gone to? She has to check that each room has been thoroughly cleaned. What if your family would like a tour of the palazzo?"

Byron found walking could be painful. "You are not getting away with torturing me, Antonietta." Her laughter was soft and so contagious, he found himself smiling. "Stop worrying. My family is coming to meet you, Antonietta, not tour the palazzo. It will not matter what you prepare for dinner. You will charm them. Trust me. I have been looking for you for a very long time, and they are thrilled I finally found you. Helena raced off to find the missing tablecloth."

He slowed the pace, walking with her through the wide hall. As they passed the music room, an object crashed on the marble tile. They could hear pieces breaking and scattering across the floor.

Antonietta turned her head toward the sound in alarm. "What is that? Surely not another crisis? Your family will be here any minute."

"No one should be in your music room. I thought that was your private domain." His voice was soft. A whisper, no more.

Antonietta stiffened. Her mind was so caught up in meeting his family, she hadn't considered that someone might be rummaging through her work. "Probably Vincente. He's so bored without little Margurite to play with." Vincente had never gone in her private music room. The room, with its perfect acoustics, was considered strictly off limits to everyone in the house while Antonietta was composing, which was nearly all the time.

"I doubt it is the boy. Stay here with Celt." Byron scanned the music room. He knew exactly who was frantically searching through the musical scores.

Antonietta gasped. "Marita." She picked the image right out of Byron's mind. "She must be looking for the Handel piece. I'm not staying here while you confront my sister-in-law. If she's betraying my family, I want to know about it."

Byron was astonished. Antonietta was moving in and out of his mind with the touch of an expert. Telepathy was natural to her. She wasn't afraid of it at all. "It sounds as if there is glass on the floor. I do not want you to be injured."

"I'm wearing shoes."

He glanced down at the smooth Italian leather. "Open-toed sandals. That does not count as shoes."

She made a small sound of annoyance. She had dressed with care, wanting to look her best for his family. Everything seemed to be going wrong. And now Marita was rummaging around in the music room.

Byron moved silently, masking their presence from Marita. He watched as the woman opened cupboard after cupboard and rifled through the contents.

What is she doing?

Searching for something. Byron reached for Marita's mind, scanning to see her intentions, merging with Antonietta at the same time.

Marita was crying softly, murmuring prayers as she rummaged through papers and musical scores.

"I have the Handel safe," Antonietta announced.

Byron hastily uncloaked their presence as Marita whirled around. She emitted a high-pitched squeak and covered her face.

"Do not cry." He ordered it, biting out the words in sheer self-preservation.

"Why would you do this, Marita? You are a Scarletti. If you and Franco needed money, why wouldn't you come to me?" Antonietta's heart was aching. "I don't understand."

"Franco knows nothing of this. He cannot know. Please, Toni, don't say anything to him of this."

The great knocker at the main entrance resonated throughout the palazzo. Antonietta clutched at Byron's arm. "They're here. We need a maid in here to clean up the glass immediately."

"What are you going to do, Toni?" Marita demanded. "If you tell Franco what I've done, you will destroy my marriage. He will send me away. You know he will."

"I can't help what Franco will do, Marita. You attempted to steal a great treasure from our family. Who were you taking it to?"

"I can't say."

The image shimmered in her mind. Loathing surrounded the image. Loathing and fear. Merged as she was with Byron, Antonietta caught the image from Marita's mind. "Don Demonesini? You were delivering a Scarletti treasure into the hands of that horrible man?"

"How could you know? I didn't say. I would never utter his name aloud, the name of the devil himself." Marita crossed herself several times.

Waves of distress and fear swamped them from all directions. Running footsteps clattered down the marble hall. "Signorina Antonietta, may the good *Dio* save us all." Helena ran into the room, her bosom heaving, her hands fluttering in the air wildly. "We've found him. We've found Enrico. He's in the laundry chute, wrapped in your good Irish lace tablecloth."

Behind Helena a young maid appeared. "I've shown Vlad and Eleanor Belandrake and their son, Josef, into the conservatory, Signorina Antonietta."

14

The silence was deafening. Byron wrapped a comforting arm around Antonietta. "I take it Enrico is no longer alive." He had a sudden urge to laugh at the ridiculous situation but was certain Antonietta wouldn't appreciate his sense of humor.

"Dead as can be," Helena admitted, pressing a hand to her mouth. "The maids went looking for the missing tablecloth, and the smell was so bad—"

Antonietta held up her hand. "Spare us, please, Helena. This can't be happening, Byron. I can't have your family for dinner with a dead body in the laundry chute. What am I going to do? Poor Enrico. He's very large. I can't imagine how he got in there."

"He's stuck," Helena reported. "I have no idea how we're going to get him out."

"I will speak to my sister and her husband, Antonietta. I am certain they will understand. Call Captain Diego and inform him we have found the missing chef." *We will discuss Marita later, when things have settled down. I'm sorry about your chef, and your mother's tablecloth.*

"We can't possibly uninvite your family for dinner," Antonietta was horrified. *Poor Enrico. He kept to himself, but he was a fixture here.*

Marita gasped aloud when Franco walked in, dressed in a charcoal gray suit. "Gossip travels fast here in the palazzo. Tasha is informing the authorities and asking them to be discreet and use the servant's entrance. Nonno is entertaining your guests in the conservatory, and you know he can be very charming." Franco squeezed his cousin's shoulder in sympathy. "We can pull this off, Toni. Don't panic. Marita, I'm allowing Vincente and Margurite a movie while we're dining. Please go quickly and get dressed. This dinner means a great deal to Toni, and we won't fail her."

"We can't possibly sit down to dinner with a dead body in the laundry chute," Marita said.

"Don Giovanni is explaining right at this moment that we've had a death in the palazzo. Enrico lived here practically his entire life. He's one of ours, and he'll be taken care of. Toni, you look beautiful. Go with Byron and meet his family. I understand there is some hysteria in the kitchen. I'll go down and see that the new chef, what's his name?"

"Alfredo," Antonietta supplied.

"I'll make certain Alfredo calms down and doesn't disgrace us. I'll take care of this, Toni. I know what this means to you. Marita, do as I say." He glanced around the room, noted the broken glass on the floor and the papers clutched in Marita's hands.

She looked desperately at Antonietta and Byron as if they might save her, then she turned and ran from the room.

"Helena, calm the maids and make certain this room is cleaned," Franco ordered.

"Yes, Signor Scarletti."

Franco took Antonietta's hand. "It will be all right, Toni. We'll get through this together, the way our family always does. Byron's relatives will be charmed by you."

"In spite of the dead body in the laundry chute, wrapped in my mother's Irish lace tablecloth," Antonietta said wryly. "I just don't believe this is happening. Poor Enrico. Who would want to hurt him?"

Byron hugged her close. "We will find out, Antonietta. I promise you. There is not much we can do for him at the moment. Come meet my family. It will not matter in the least to them if there is no dinner. They came to meet you, not to eat." Bella, *do not be so distressed. I know you held affection for Enrico, I feel it in your heart. Marita's behavior is not what it seems. I read her mind, and she does not want money. She detests and fears this man. I could not tell why. She is very emotional, and it was difficult to see past the intensity to the real reason she took the Handel score. When I have time, I will examine her memories and find out what is going on.*

Antonietta leaned her head against his chest. "I feel as if my entire life has been turned upside down. Franco, did you see Tasha's face? You've known Christopher since he was a child. Did you know he was capable of such a thing?"

Franco shook his head. "I plan on calling on him tomorrow."

"There is no need, Franco." Byron spoke low, but his voice carried power. "I will have a talk with Christopher Demonesini about how one treats a woman. You have too much to risk, while I do not have a reputation to protect."

"Neither one of you needs to be talking to Christopher about anything," Antonietta said firmly. "I think the captain should have a talk with him."

The two men looked at one another over the top of her head. Byron took her arm and strolled casually from the music room, Franco pacing beside them, just as a maid came rushing in to clean up the glass. "You know as well as I do that he has too much money for anything to happen to him, even if it was Tasha he struck," Byron said.

"Then we ruin him socially and financially," Antonietta said seriously. "Their business is already in trouble. It wouldn't take that much to tip them over the edge. No one hurts my family."

"That is a true Scarletti speaking, Byron," Franco said. "Let that be a warning to you. We seek revenge."

"Retribution," Antonietta corrected. "Justice. It isn't quite the same thing as revenge. Ask Nonno. I'm certain he'll agree." *I mean it, Byron, I feel strongly about this. How dare that horrible man hit and kick my cousin and think his life can continue without a single consequence.*

I said nothing, bella.

I just want you to know what I'm capable of. Perhaps you won't find me so appealing. She sounded very much as if she were issuing a challenge.

Byron leaned down to brush the corner of her mouth with his. *On the contrary, I think you will fit right in with my people.* There was a trace of amusement in his voice.

Franco cleared his throat. "Surprisingly, little cousin, I agree with you about retribution, too. I'm off to the kitchen to tackle Alfredo. I'll wait for the captain to show so I can talk to him without causing a scene."

"Grazie, Franco, I really appreciate your help." Antonietta reached her hand out, and her cousin caught it in a show of solidarity.

"Go enjoy yourself. Byron, see that she does."

"It will be my pleasure." Byron tucked Antonietta's fingers into the crook of his arm and walked her through the open rooms of the palazzo. "I am really very sorry about the tablecloth. When a loved one dies, we cling to the things they treasured."

"I know it's silly to feel so upset over it, with poor Enrico dead in our home." Antonietta sighed. "I feel ridiculous to even think of the tablecloth."

"I have a medallion I made for my mother. I was a boy, and I certainly would not consider it good work at all, but she treasured it. She wore it always. Even later when my skills improved, and I gave her other, much more valuable pieces, she still wore the medallion." Byron could hear his sister laughing, her voice low as she spoke with Don Giovanni. It gave him a wrenching sense of homesickness.

"Byron?" Antonietta halted abruptly, just outside the door to the conservatory. "I know I don't tell you how I feel about you, mostly because I can't put it into words, but you're very important to me." She shook her head. "That's not what I wanted to say."

She looked so close to tears, he gathered her close. "I know how you feel about me, *cara.* I feel what you feel, remember? We are connected. You do not have to say words to me. They will come in time."

"I just wanted you to know."

Byron caught her chin and tilted her face up to his. "I know." His mouth found her temple, drifted, feather light, from the side of her cheek to the corner of her mouth. He drew her closer, his arms tightening possessively, tongue teasing the seam of her lips until she opened for him. He gave her no chance to pull away, no chance for a chaste kiss. He took control with ravenous hunger. He wanted her with every fiber of his being, and he poured the intensity of his need into his kiss. He wanted her to feel loved, to feel beautiful and confident. To be confident of him and the way he felt about her.

Fire burned instantly between them. His body reacted, thickening, hardening. He ached to bury himself deep inside of her. Deep within, the ever-present beast lifted its head and roared for its mate. Demanded his rights. Byron's hands slid down her back, shaped her waist, memorized the curve of her hips and found her buttocks. She was wearing one of her sexy little thongs. There wasn't a single line under the silken material of her skirt.

Byron deepened the kiss, forgetting everything but the sheer, hot passion of her mouth. Of her body. He urged her more closely into him, imprinting the hard length of his need into her soft flesh. He held her there, took pleasure in the way her hips moved urgently against him, seeking relief. He couldn't stop kissing her, his mouth hard and hot and persuasive. *Do you want to run away with me? Right now?*

A low whistle cut through the erotic images in Byron's mind. Merged as deep as they were, Antonietta heard it, too.

Holy Smoke. Uncle Byron! Hey, Dad, check this out. He's going at it hot and heavy out there. I never thought he had it in him. I think they're going to melt right into the floor.

Antonietta pulled away with a small gasp of alarm. "Who is that, Byron, and why can I hear him?"

He stroked a small caress over her head. "That would be my nephew, the one with no manners. Are you absolutely certain you want to meet him? I can send him away," he said hopefully. "It would save me the mortification I am certain to undergo should you insist on following through with this."

"How is it I heard him in my head? He's in the conservatory, yet I heard him in the same way I heard you. I don't generally hear everyone speaking in my head." The idea clearly bothered her.

"Not in the same way. Our people are strong telepaths.

Lifemates have their own wavelength, a private path, if you will. Our minds were merged together, and my nephew spoke on the general path my people all use. You heard him through me, just as you used my eyes to see."

"That's incredible. My family are telepaths but not to such a powerful extent. Let's go in, I don't want to seem rude, now that your nephew has announced us."

"That boy needs to learn manners." Disengaging his mind from Antonietta's, he sent a private reprimand to his sister. *Eleanor, Josef is too old to act like such a child. I want a word with him later.*

He is just excited, Byron. He has not seen you in years.

Eleanor, he spoke so a human could hear him. He endangered our people by such an act. That cannot be tolerated, and you know it.

"You're muttering under your breath," Antonietta said. Her fingertips touched his lips. "And you're frowning."

"After meeting my nephew, you will be frowning, too," he predicted. With a sigh of resignation, he pushed open the door to the conservatory. His fingers twined with hers, clung, and held on.

"You're turning into a big baby," she said.

"Here she is, my granddaughter, Antonietta." Don Giovanni rose quickly. "Antonietta, our guests have arrived. Byron, how good to see you. Your sister is lovely."

"*Grazie*, Don Giovanni," Eleanor said. She hugged her brother and touched Antoinetta's hand. "You have no idea how much it means to me to finally meet you."

"My sister Eleanor, her husband Vlad, and my nephew, Josef." Byron introduced. "This is Antonietta Scarletti." Byron's tension communicated itself to Antonietta. She tightened her grip on his fingers.

"You must call me Toni," Antonietta said.

"A pleasure to meet you," Vlad acknowledged. He lowered his voice. "Josef, I asked you to remove that beret."

"She's blind; she can't see it," Josef whispered back.

My nephew is wearing one of those silly berets, a smock, and a kerchief. It is obvious he thinks he looks like a painter. Byron was very careful to keep his mental path private. The last thing he needed was for Eleanor to know he was describing her son's attire to his lifemate.

Antonietta laughed. "I'm blind, Josef, not deaf. It's good to meet you. Your uncle has told me so much about you. He's says you're very talented musically."

Mischief maker. You are going to be sorry you said that.

Antonietta heard Byron's mournful moan in her head. She had the image of him throttling her. She had to cover her mouth to keep from laughing harder. Byron made her feel so alive. His teasing, the way he shared his innermost thoughts. He was casual about their strong telepathic link.

"Josef is very talented," Eleanor agreed. "We have come to Italy, as Josef is eager to paint your beautiful country."

"I love the palazzo," Josef said enthusiastically. "I would love to try to paint it."

"Well, of course you're welcome to come anytime," Don Giovanni invited. "The courtyard would be a good place to see a good portion of the architecture."

"*Grazie,* signor, I appreciate the offer."

Byron's teeth snapped together in frustration. The last thing he wanted was for Josef to spend any more time around the Scarletti family than strictly necessary. He could hear the police downstairs, interviewing the housekeeper. Alfredo was nearly hysterical, talking so fast it was difficult to understand what he was saying. Byron was well aware his family could hear every word, but they continued a pleasant conversation with Don Giovanni and Antonietta as if they were completely oblivious to the drama unfolding in the lower regions.

He let the conversation flow around him, Eleanor trying to draw Antonietta out in vain. Antonietta was far too conscious of the police in her home. She had a vivid imagination, and the thought of Enrico stuck in the laundry chute was distressing to her.

A second disturbance at the courtyard French doors caught Byron's attention. He heard Franco's startled cry, broken off. There were hurried footsteps rushing through the palazzo, calls for Tasha. A soft scream from Justine. *Something is wrong.*

What else can go wrong? Antonietta wanted to yell in frustration.

Franco opened the door to the conservatory, smiled at their guests, and leaned close to his cousin. "You must go to Paul immediately," Franco whispered. "It's urgent, Toni, you must hurry."

Do you know what is wrong? Antonietta automatically reached for Byron.

Byron took her arm even as he smiled at his sister. "Please excuse us for a few minutes. I am certain Don Giovanni and the others will entertain you in our absence." *Paul is injured. It is severe. Franco's concern is very real, and Tasha is crying. Justine is radiating tremendous fear.* He guided her quickly from the room, and they hurried up the stairs to Paul's rooms.

They could hear Tasha's muted weeping and the murmur of voices. Justine's raised in alarm. "We have to call a doctor, Paul. You're going to die if we don't."

"Just get Antonietta. She can take care of this," Paul's voice was weak.

"You're being unreasonable. Tasha, you're his sister. Call a doctor. I swear you Scarlettis are so stubborn. Don't you understand? Paul is dying. If you let him die, I swear I'll have you all arrested."

Antonietta and Byron entered the sitting room. The door to the bedroom was wide open. Tasha and Justine hovered near the bed. *There's blood everywhere. Antonietta. If it is all Paul's, he has lost far too much.*

It was Byron's matter-of-fact voice that steadied her. Antonietta took a breath and walked with confidence to the bed. "Paul. What have you done?"

"I have to talk to you alone, Toni."

"Paul . . ." Justine protested. "Toni, please, I'm begging you to call a doctor for him. He says no, but it isn't too late. It can't be too late."

"A doctor cannot help him, Justine, you already know that," Byron said softly, his voice as mesmerizing and hypnotic as his eyes. "You must leave this to Antonietta."

Tasha wrapped her arm around Justine's waist. "Toni can help him. Let her, Justine. We're wasting time he doesn't have." She led Justine from the room, firmly closing the door behind her.

Eleanor, I need herbs now. Hurry. Vlad, I will need your help, too. Byron didn't try to keep his communication from

Antonietta. She had every right to know Paul's life was seriously at risk.

"What is it, Paul?" Her hands were already moving over his body. Byron crowded close, applied pressure to the worst of the wounds.

"He has been stabbed several times, Antonietta. He needs blood fast. I can help him. Eleanor will bring what I need."

"I need to tell you, Toni." Paul caught at Antonietta's arm.

"Don't talk until we get this bleeding under control."

"It's too late, you know that. You always know. This is important."

"Shut up, Paul," Antonietta hissed. "I mean it. You're not going to die on me. Byron, do whatever you have to do."

"I have to give him blood, Antonietta." Byron waved his hand to still Paul's struggles, continued to apply pressure to the wounds. "If I do this, we will be connected for all time. Do you understand?"

"I want you to save him. I don't care how you do it, just do it." Antonietta stroked back Paul's hair. "I love him as if he were my brother."

"You do not have to say anything else, lifemate. Lock the door. No one must come in this room. Set Celt on guard. Then open the window about two inches."

"Your sister—"

"Has her own way of getting in. She will be here soon. Sit by Paul and listen to my voice. I want you to join in. You are a strong healer."

Antonietta didn't understand, but there was an urgency about him. She trusted Byron where she might not have any other. She locked the door, gave the order to Celt, and obediently cracked open the window.

Almost immediately Byron saw mist creeping through the crack. "Eleanor. Good girl. Go around to the other side. See if you can pack the wounds. Antonietta, I am going to place your hands on him, and you have to press hard. I need my hands free." He guided her palms to Paul's stomach.

Antonietta could feel the warmth of the blood. She smelled a strange, soothing odor. She knew Eleanor was close to her. It didn't matter to her how Eleanor had gotten through a locked door or why Byron thought she could help, only that they save Paul. She merged with Byron, determined to follow his movements.

Byron was detached from his own body. She could feel his spirit soaring free. His energy, white-hot and glowing, moved toward Paul. It was strange to feel how small and huddled and tired Paul was. He was moving away from them, his energy dismally low. Antonietta's heart began to pound loudly at the realization that Paul was dying. She forced herself to remain still and quiet, to trust in Byron. She could feel determination, confidence even.

Voices began a chant in an ancient tongue. The words felt familiar to her. When she knew she had the correct pronunciation, she added her voice to the others. All the while she concentrated on sending Byron her strength. What he was doing was demanding physically and mentally. He meticulously began closing wounds from the inside out, paying particular attention to detail, removing bacteria from the gashes to prevent infection.

Antonietta felt a female presence joining them, working with Byron even as they chanted. Another joined in, Vlad, strong and sure, providing a steady flow of energy to the two working on Paul. Eleanor remained behind when Byron pulled out. Antonietta took the opportunity to wash her hands in Paul's bathroom, feeling slightly ill with so much of her cousin's blood on her. She hurried back to Byron's side.

"Antonietta. I have to give him my blood. Even a mortal transfusion would not save him. Are you certain you can live with this decision? Perhaps it would be better if you broke off the contact with me while I do this."

"I'll see it through. You're doing this for me. The least I can do is provide you with energy." She reached out her hand, finding his face unerringly. "I know you're tired, and I feel you're afraid that whatever you have to do will upset me, but it won't. I trust you, Byron."

He leaned into her, brushed her lips gently with his. She was in darkness, but she felt every sensation, as closely connected as they were. She felt the burning pain as he cut his wrist, a terrible, gaping wound. She felt the way Paul's mouth clamped on, the drawing of Byron's lifeblood from his body. Shock numbed her, protected her, just for a moment. She fought her way past that protective barrier. There was realization that Byron had used his own teeth to tear his wrist. That Paul was devouring the lifesaving blood instead of being transfused. That the smell of blood was producing a craving she couldn't understand in herself. Instead of being repelled, she was fascinated. She was also very aware that Byron was monitoring her reaction.

Antonietta lifted her chin, continued to chant, fought her human reactions, and concentrated on what they were doing, saving her beloved cousin's life. Byron had taken an enormous chance in allowing her to know what he was. He had entrusted her with a secret even larger than her own. She had Jaguar in her lineage. He was something altogether different. Something loathed and feared by humans. He was . . . vampire.

No! Byron's protest was sharp. *Never that, I am not undead.*

Deliberately, Antonietta leaned into him again, framed his face with her hands. While her cousin fed from him, she found his mouth with hers. *You amaze me, Byron.* She poured her gratitude and her feelings, as confused as they were, into her kiss, trying to tell him without words what it meant that he trusted her enough to save Paul's life in the only way possible.

Tears glittered for a moment in Byron's eyes. He had to look away from his sister and her lifemate. Antonietta had given him a gift more priceless than seeing in colors. She gave him acceptance.

"No more, Byron," Vlad said abruptly. "You are already too weak."

Antonietta felt him sway, his energy gone, his body drained of his enormous strength. He staggered and sat down abruptly, despite her trying to catch him.

"What's wrong with him? Eleanor? Vlad? Tell me what's wrong with him?" Panic rose fast, a terrible fear in her heart and lungs.

"He has not fed this night," Vlad answered calmly. "Healing as he did, holding Paul to earth while doing so and giving him blood, takes a toll. I will take care of his need. Eleanor will need help, too. You are being very brave, Antonietta."

"I haven't done anything to help at all. If Byron needs blood, he can take mine."

There was a sudden stillness in the room. Even Eleanor, deep within Paul's body, was quiet. *"Cara mia, you steal my heart with your generosity. Vlad will provide what is needed."*

"Vlad is not your lifemate. I am. I am quite able to provide for you." Her neck throbbed and burned. Her breasts ached. Sexual hunger swirled in the pit of her stomach and spread a slow, burning heat through her body. Excitement blossomed, yet at the same time she tried to analyze why she would feel such a need to provide blood for him.

Byron pulled her into his arms. "There is no other like you, *bella." In truth, just the thought of you giving me your blood fills me with a hunger I dare not name. We are not alone. Allow Vlad to give me his powerful blood, and when we are alone, I will thank you properly.*

She could hear the aching sexual hunger in his voice. "Is Vlad's blood more powerful than mine? Will it make a difference?" She tried to ignore the answering fire in her bloodstream.

"Yes, his blood will give me energy very quickly."

"What does it feel like?"

"Merge with me, Antonietta." Byron wrapped one arm around her waist and took Vlad's wrist to his mouth.

The rush hit him hard, hit her. Power pouring into his starved body. Cells and tissue, muscle and bone soaked up the life-giving fluid greedily. She tried to detach herself, to feel horror at the thought of Byron drinking blood, but she saw his power, felt his power. When he had taken what he needed, she realized she was barely breathing.

"How do you stop the blood from flowing?"

"We close the pinpricks with our tongue. The healing agent seals the wound and if we desire, the skin itself."

Antonietta felt a blush stealing up her neck and face. There had been a bite on her neck; Tasha spotted it. "You've taken my blood, haven't you?"

"Of course; you are my lifemate." Deliberately, Byron caught the nape of her neck and dragged her to him, his mouth taking possession of hers, sharing the flavor and power of Carpathian blood. His tongue swept inside her mouth, tangling with hers, a primal mating while her senses leapt to life, every nerve ending on overload.

Eleanor pulled out of Paul's body and into her own, swaying with weariness. "It is done, Antonietta. He will live."

Vlad swept his lifemate into his arms. "You are a miracle worker, Eleanor."

"She is," Byron agreed. *"Grazie,* both of you. I could not have saved him without your help."

"I guess my dinner party is thoroughly ruined. You must have such a bad impression of my family." It hit Antonietta that if Eleanor and Vlad were like Byron, they would have heard the police in the lower stories, conducting interviews with staff with sealing off the crime scene. "Poor Enrico deserved better than being shoved down a laundry chute. I have no idea what is happening in my own home."

"At least they wrapped him in the best lace available."

"That's not funny."

Vlad kept Eleanor firmly in his arms. "Welcome to the family, Antonietta. It has been our pleasure to meet you. I need to take my lifemate home and care for her."

"Grazie for all you have done, both of you. The next time we meet, hopefully things will be back to normal."

"Until then."

Antonietta listened, but there were no footsteps. She knew they were no longer in the room. "How do you do that? Just vanish into thin air? Not use doors?"

"I will teach you." He pulled a chair to the edge of the bed. "Paul will be different, more aware, as you are. His hearing, his sight, everything will be that much more acute. And I can always touch his mind. It will be a different path than ours, but the connection will be there."

"Did you pick up on what happened to him?"

"I am going to wake him briefly so we can talk. He will be weak. His body does not have the ability to heal as quickly as mine does." Byron took her hand. "I know you have many questions for me. I will answer all of them before the night is over." He brought her fingers to his mouth, nibbled on the sensitive pads. "Paul. Paul, come back to us now. You can rest soon, but you need to speak with Antonietta. You want to tell her something. It is very important to you to tell her the truth."

Antonietta heard the compulsion buried in his voice, was

astonished that she recognized it for what it was. "Your voice is hypnotic, isn't it?"

"Yes, when I choose."

Paul stirred, moaned softly. "Toni?"

"I'm here, Paul." She tugged her hand free to rest her palm on her cousin. "You're going to live, but you mustn't move around too much."

"I had strange dreams."

"I know. It can happen that way, Paul. How did this happen? Tell me. We need to talk to the police."

"No. You can't do that, Toni. Promise me. Please promise me you won't go to the police." His agitation rose sharply.

Byron rested a hand on his shoulder, calming him instantly. "Tell us, Paul. We will handle whatever it is together." *Do not mention the authorities again. He will undo all we have wrought.*

"I know you thought I was stealing from the family, Toni. I don't blame you for believing that. I wanted you to think I was gambling again."

"Why, Paul?" There was hurt in her voice, pain in her heart.

Byron's fingers curled around the nape of her neck, began a slow, soothing massage to ease the tension out of her.

"I went to a party a few months ago on a yacht. The owner had a priceless painting on display. It was one of ours, Toni. I went immediately to the police, and they told me they had been investigating the theft of treasures from prominent families for months. I knew someone in our family had to be helping whoever was behind the thefts. No one knew the way to the vaults, let alone the codes to get in, except you, Nonno, and Justine. I knew you and Nonno would never sell out our family. So I volunteered to help the police find the thieves."

"Paul, what were you thinking?"

"I was perfect for it. I already had the bad reputation. I always needed money. I was believable. It was easy enough to start paying attention to Justine." Paul's voice was weak, his breathing labored. "She was under suspicion, the one person who would have access to all the security codes. And she would know the way to the art rooms and the vaults."

"This is too hard for you," Antonietta said. "We'll talk later when you're stronger."

Paul's hand covered hers. "I fell in love with her, Toni. I know you're angry with her, and she probably deserves to be in jail, but I'm asking you to let her go. Tell her to go back to America. Just don't put her in jail."

Byron shook his head. *She is not involved in any conspiracy other than trying to help Paul find a way to pay off his gambling debts. She has never stolen anything from the Scarletti family. Unlike your family, Justine is easy enough to read.*

"I would never believe such a thing of her. After all these years, why would she suddenly decide to steal?" Antonietta asked Paul.

"It has to be her. There is no one else," Paul said. "She had access to everything. She's the one who drew me a map to the vault and gave me the access code."

"You were willing to die instead of going to a hospital so she wouldn't go to jail? Lie and take the blame for missing objects, for Justine? Paul, you aren't thinking clearly. You should have come to me with this immediately."

Antonietta, Justine did not steal. She regretted giving Paul the codes and the map. She wanted to give him money, but he refused. She believed he was in trouble and wanted him to tell you, but he refused that option. He convinced her he would be in danger from the men he owed money to. It is clear he thought she would involve him in the theft ring, but she did the only other thing she could. She gave him a map and the codes. I felt it was a betrayal of your friendship. But that is all it was. She is not involved in any theft ring.

"I'm not going to turn Justine over to the police, Paul. But you need to tell me who did this to you. They have to be dealt with."

"Stay out of it, Toni. These people play for keeps."

He did not see his attackers. There is nothing he can tell us about the men who assaulted him. The thing uppermost in his mind is protecting Justine.

"Send him to sleep. I'll let Tasha and Justine in to watch over him tonight. Nonno must have been informed by now; I can't see Franco keeping it from him."

You know Marita is more likely to be the person stealing and handing the goods over to someone else. And it was the elder Demonesini she was going to meet with the Handel score.

Franco will be devastated if it is so. She made her way to the sitting room while Byron issued the order for Paul to sleep. Tasha and Justine practically fell into the room with Franco and Don Giovanni on their heels.

"He is alive," Antonietta reported. "Just barely. He needs sleep. And plenty of liquids. Can you clean him up and fix the bed? We're both exhausted. Byron has a talent for healing much greater than mine, and he did most of the work."

"I would like to take Antonietta to my home where she can rest," Byron added.

I can't go anywhere.

Paul will not wake until we return. Just enough for them to give him fluids.

Too much is happening.

I need you this night, Antonietta.

"Your family excused themselves," Don Giovanni explained. "They could see we were uneasy. I'm afraid we didn't make much of an impression on them, my boy."

"They understood," Byron assured. "Have the police left?"

"They've questioned everyone but Paul and the two of you. We said Paul was out, and you two would be available tomorrow," Franco said.

"Grazie, Franco," Antonietta said, "I doubt if I could sit through more of their questions."

Byron took Antonietta's hand firmly in his. "Good night everyone, we will return tomorrow evening."

15

"What are we doing?" Antonietta lifted her face to the wind. She hadn't been out on the battlements in years. It was far too dangerous. Even with Byron, she was afraid. It would only take one careless slip, and she would fall to her death. When she inhaled, she could scent the faint odor of the cat's presence lingering. The idea that the jaguar could be near, could be watching them at that very moment, was terrifying.

"I am going to take you flying. You said you wanted to try. The sky is clear, just a trace of fog rolling in. I think you will enjoy it after such a difficult evening."

She studied his voice not the words. "What is it, Byron?"

He pulled her to him, buried his face against her neck. "You are in my keeping, Antonietta; always your safety comes before all else. Your acceptance of what and who I am means everything to me. I want to give you something special. Something you will always remember."

Her fingertips moved over his face. Byron found it curiously intimate each time she read his expression. There was a caress lingering on his skin whether she knew it or not. He knew she was reading his apprehension of what was to come. She was too connected to him. So much had happened from the moment she awakened, so much more would be demanded of her.

"If flying is so memorable, why are you afraid for me?"

For the first time he caught her wrists and pulled her hands from his face, cradling them against his chest. He leaned his forehead against hers. "I have to talk to you tonight about what I am, about what being my lifemate means to both of us."

"And you're afraid I can't accept you? I've already done that. I won't say I don't have a million questions, Byron, but how can I be afraid of what you are, if you aren't afraid of what I am, especially now when some jungle cat is killing people? I feel the jaguar in me sometimes. My skin literally itches to change. Or are you afraid for me because you think the killer is someone in my family, perhaps Paul?"

"It is not Paul. Or if it is, he has no memory of taking the shape of a jaguar."

She sagged with relief. "I was so afraid. I don't know what to think about Paul and his bizarre behavior. Why would he think he could help the police uncover a professional theft ring? Believe me, I know Paul; he's not the undercover type. It's just like him to be stabbed and come here instead of going to a hospital and to manage to convince everyone he can't go. All to save Justine from prison." She shook her head. "Nonno would never leave Paul in charge of the shipping business, no matter how astute he is. When it comes down to it, he'll make an emotional decision every time."

"You do not want the business." Her hair was soft. Her skin too tempting. He removed her dark glasses to allow freedom to his lips to drift over her eyelids.

"No, I'm an artist. I want to compose my music. I'm selfish, I guess. I really don't enjoy stopping what I love to attend endless meetings. Paul has the ability but not the personality for it."

His hand cupped her chin, lifted her face to his. "I love kissing you. I could spend a lifetime or two just kissing you."

"Funny, I feel exactly the same way." She opened her mouth to his, let the magic take hold. The breeze coming off the sea was crisp and cool, but it only acted as a counterpoint to the flames leaping between them.

A shadow passed over them, a brief gray over the moon. Byron was aware instantly they were no longer alone. He whirled around, sweeping Antonietta behind him. *Do not move; do not make a sound.*

What is it?

I do not know yet. On the alert now, he scanned the surrounding areas for signs of an enemy. There was no sign of the vampire and no scent of the jaguar. The disturbance came from above him on the turrets and tower looming above their heads.

Byron narrowed his vision to search, his gaze moving continually, restlessly, working every inch of the eaves and rooftops. He caught a slight movement out of the corner of his eye and froze. The gargoyle crouched just above his head stared down at him with red, burning eyes. There was a loud creak as the giant sculpted head turned slightly, and the wings spread outward a good six feet in preparation for flight.

Antonietta's fist tightened in his shirt at the small of his back. She immediately merged with him. She couldn't see what he was seeing, but she had the sharp impression of it. *That's impossible. Those gargoyles aren't alive. Their eyes are stone. There aren't even gems in them to capture or reflect light. And they can't spread their wings or turn their head.*

You are so right, Antonietta. The grim note in his voice sent a shiver down her spine. *I only know one person who would dare to try to play such a joke on me.*

Byron concentrated on the gargoyle. The head turned further, facing back toward the rooftop. As the head swung around, the giant mouth yawned open, and huge teeth filled the jaw. The mouth snapped closed, a vicious bite of warning. Josef yelped, scooting out where Byron could see him.

"You almost took my leg off," he accused.

"That was the idea," Byron replied calmly. "Next time you try to sneak up on me, I will make certain the gargoyle takes a chunk out of you."

Josef sat on the back of the gargoyle, dejected. "I can't get it right. No matter how many times I try to make an inanimate object move, it's always clunky. If it had been smooth, you wouldn't have known it was me."

Antonietta put a restraining hand on Byron when she felt him gathering himself for a lecture. "It sounds difficult to do, Josef. I think anyone would have trouble making a sculpture of a gargoyle move."

"I thought you were blind," Josef said.

"I'm not nearly as blind with Byron around. I catch images through him, at least awareness of what's happening around me. You shouldn't be out this late. I don't know if Byron warned you, but there's a jaguar out killing people. I'm serious. I don't think your mother would want to lose you."

"I can take care of myself," Josef assured. "Do you shape-shift yet?"

"I can't shape-shift, but it sounds fun."

"It's hard to do on your own. I practice a lot, but I still get it wrong sometimes. Why haven't you tried it yet?"

"I'm not like you."

"Yes, you are. You're Byron's lifemate. You're—"

"Josef." There was a distinct warning in Byron's voice. "Enough. You get back to the villa. Antonietta is right; it is not safe out here for you." *Although I think it is more likely he would come to harm through me rather than another source.*

He is just a boy.

So Eleanor keeps reminding me.

"Can't I go with you, Uncle Byron? Mom won't let me do anything. I was scaling the wall of the villa, and she just about screamed the house down. I can get a running start and leap pretty high, but then I can't quite get the hang of going up a vertical wall. I have to use toe- and fingerholds."

Byron sighed. "You are trying to use your body. Use your mind. You are too aware of your physical body."

Antonietta shivered. The wind could be biting cold. Byron immediately removed his suit jacket and wrapped her in it. She was surprised it was so warm.

"Go on back to the villa, Josef. I will work with you tomorrow on some of these things, although you have to remember you are not supposed to use these gifts or discuss them outside of our people. The idea is to blend in." Byron did his best not to sound as long-suffering as he felt.

"No one else is around. You were so busy kissing Antonietta I thought I could sneak up here and play a joke."

"You are very lucky I did not zap you with a lightning bolt. Go home. I want to be alone with my lifemate."

Josef sighed heavily. "I never have any fun. I don't think it's fair the way I'm always told I have to wait to learn anything."

Enough! Byron bit the silent command out between bared teeth. *Do as I say.*

Josef stood up, looking extremely petulant. He shimmered several times but nothing happened. Byron closed his eyes and sent up a silent prayer for patience. "Josef, you hold the image in your mind."

"Dad always does it for me."

"Then how did you manage to get up there in the first place? If I do it for you, you will never learn."

Antonietta leaned into Byron. "If you're going to take me flying, we could escort him home, couldn't we?"

Byron kissed her temple. "You are a very understanding woman."

"*Grazie* for noticing." Antonietta waved in the direction she knew Josef to be. "Come with us. Byron's going to take me flying. I've never been before."

"I will take the shape of a dragon with wings. That way I can hold you close to me. If you become alarmed, I will know, and we will go back to earth immediately."

"Will you have scales?"

"Yes, I can do scales."

"Can I have any color?"

Byron laughed. "What color do you want?"

"When I was a little girl, my mother always read me a book where the dragon had beautiful iridescent blue scales. I loved the sound of that. I still picture the dragon shimmering with watercolor blues, just like in that book. It's a very vivid memory."

"Then your dragon will be iridescent watercolor blue." He held her close to him, nuzzled her neck.

"Why can't I ride on the dragon's back? In all the books, a rider was on the dragon's back. Only the idiot who was going to be eaten was clutched in the dragon's claws." Antonietta could feel his teeth scraping back and forth across the pulse beating strongly in her neck. Her entire body tightened in response. There was something mesmerizing and erotic about the motion. His teeth nipped, sending darts of fire racing through her bloodstream. His tongue swirled over the ache.

"I do not want to take a chance that you could fall." The words were whispered against her neck, his breath warm on her cold skin. His teeth closed over her pulse, teased gently while desire burned hot in her deepest core.

"I won't fall, Byron. I'll hold on tight. Please let me do this."

How could he deny her anything, her slightest wish, when he knew what was in store for her? "I will be most unhappy with you should you slip, Antonietta."

"You do growl like a bear sometimes, Byron."

"I want to be a dragon, too," Josef called. "I've never done anything like that before. That would be too cool."

Byron threw his hands up in the air in defeat. "Hold the image that you find in my mind, Josef. Make certain you are able to maintain it before you step off that roof. You cannot be distracted. This is a large beast, quite unlike a bird. It is not as easy because it is unfamiliar. Study the details in my mind, and hold that image at all times. I want you to stay close to me in case you get into trouble."

"You really are a sweet man, Byron." Antonietta smiled at him.

"You cannot do that, *cara,* I have trouble thinking when you smile at me. If one hair on Josef's head is damaged, my sister will rip my head off. And if anything should happen to you, I do not know what I would do."

Her laughter at his suffering tone drifted up to the clouds. "I'm excited. Be my dragon, and let's go flying."

He didn't wait. He was afraid he would change his mind if he thought too much on what could happen. He shifted his shape, holding the detailed image of the iridescent blue dragon in his mind for his nephew. Carefully, so as not to knock into Antonietta accidentally, the huge dragon lowered itself so she could climb onto its back.

Antonietta let out her breath slowly and reached out to the great bulk so close to her. The huge back was cool, scaled, and felt much like a large python she had once touched. "Oh, Byron, this is unbelievable." She felt tears burning in her eyes at the unexpected gift. In her wildest dreams, she never imagined such an opportunity. She took her time, feeling her way over the great hulk, the neck, even the wedged head, seeing with her fingertips. "It's beautiful. Perfect. I'll never forget this moment."

She stepped up on the offered leg. It took several tries to make it onto the back. There was a small saddle for her to fit into, stirrups for her feet. Her heart turned over at his thoughtfulness. Byron seemed to think of the smallest detail to make everything easier for her. She leaned forward and wrapped her arms around the dragon's neck, the reins tight in her hands. "I'm ready, Byron. Go."

The dragon rose with great caution, fearful of jarring his rider. *Josef? Are you ready?* The smaller dragon, crouched upon the roof of the turret, unfolded its wings, and shook them experimentally.

Antonietta laughed as she felt the rush of air on her body. She felt Byron extend his wings. Again he used the same careful movements, but the dragon was large and the wings enormous. When he launched himself from the battlement, into the air, she was unprepared for the way the pit of her stomach dropped away. She clutched at the dragon's neck convulsively, the air slamming out of her lungs.

I can hold you, cara.

She forced her body to sit up, to find the motion of the beast between her legs. Antonietta lifted her face to the sky. *No, you can't. I'm going to fly by myself. I love this.* And she did. It was exhilarating to be moving through the sky, great wings flapping, roiling the air so that she was aware every moment of the mythical dragon with its iridescent blue scales beneath her. It was a fairy tale come to life. *Can you breathe fire? We could sweep over the Demonesini palazzo and singe Christopher's hair.*

Byron felt her laughter right through the dragon's body. Through his body. Deep within the dragon, Byron felt elation sweeping through him.

Joy burst through Antonietta. The wind blew her hair in every direction, rushed at her face, robbed her of speech, made her eyes water. She couldn't see the night sky, but she could imagine stars sparkling over her head like gems. She leaned over the dragon's neck, urging him to fly faster.

Watch this, Uncle Byron.

Josef attempted to spin around, the body of the smaller dragon coming dangerously close to the larger one so that Byron had to perform a quick maneuver to avoid a collision in midair. Antonietta clutched the reins as her hips rose away from the dragon's back. Byron rose with her, reseating her before she could slide off. She clamped her legs as tightly as possible, her heart pounding. *I'm fine. This is great. I feel so alive.* She said it hastily as she felt his rising ire at his nephew.

Josef didn't seem to notice what he'd done. He continued with his antics, dropping fast toward earth and pulling up sharply, nearly somersaulting. He was instantly disoriented. Vertigo hit hard. Panic replaced the image in his head. He plummeted toward earth.

Byron, great wings laboring, put on a burst of speed, dropping below the youth. *Watch yourself, Antonietta. He is falling, coming from above you. I will try to catch him and hold him in my claws. The idiot should be eaten.*

Byron reached for the falling boy. Josef saw the huge, wedge-shaped head, the mouth filled with sharp teeth, and he panicked. He punched the dragon on the snout, kicked viciously at the reaching claws, driving his body away from the dragon.

Byron swore and dropped hard and fast, coming up under his nephew. *I will direct him toward the tail section. Try to help him, but do not fall yourself.*

Josef hit the dragon's back, careened downward toward the dragon's tail. Antonietta had already dropped the reins and reached instinctively behind her. She brushed Josef's shirt, caught, and hung on. His weight nearly pulled her from the dragon's back, but Byron, inside the large bulk, adjusted his body to help her stabilize and keep from rolling off. Josef clung to the dragon, digging his heels in hard.

He pulled himself up behind Antonietta, wrapping his arms firmly around her waist. She was shocked at his size and strength. It didn't feel as if a boy were behind her. He felt like a grown man.

How old is your nephew?

In human years, he is twenty-two. In our years he is considered a fledgling. A child still learning our ways. Shape-

shifting is difficult. Most parents hold the image for the child over and over until the child learns to pay attention to detail. You have to operate on several levels at the same time. When you learn to do this, I will be the one to hold the image for you.

I don't have the ability to shape-shift, Byron. I really don't. I feel the jaguar close at times, it is in me, but I can't make the change, not even when I try.

Antonietta was grateful for Byron's jacket and the perpetual warmth it generated as they soared through the sky. She felt the dragon circling, spiraling in long, sweeping circles, until it hovered in one spot, wings flapping ferociously. Josef slipped off onto the balcony of the villa where he was staying. The dragon immediately streaked skyward.

Antonietta leaned forward and wrapped her arms around the dragon's neck. "I don't want this ever to stop. I think we should fly all night."

Byron was grateful Eleanor had thought to secure a second smaller and much more secluded villa for her brother and his lifemate. He didn't want to take Antonietta to a cave deep below the earth and explain his life to her. Explain what her life was to become. He wanted a beautiful setting where she might feel comfortable and completely at ease. He sent his sister his silent thanks for her thoughtfulness. He didn't know how she had accomplished it in so short a time, but Eleanor was always efficient.

The dragon settled on the wide verandah overlooking the sea. Antonietta waited while the wings folded against the great body before she felt around for the extended leg. Her feet found firm ground as Byron shifted into his human form. She laughed and threw her arms around him. *"Grazie.* You have no idea what that meant to me. I could learn to love flying."

His fingers curled around the nape of her neck, drew her to him. "I will have to teach you."

"I still don't understand why it is so difficult for Josef, yet you have no trouble shifting. I saw the image clearly in my head."

"Because I was holding it for you. It is much like breathing. You do not think of the mechanics of breathing, your brain tells your lungs, and everything just works in the background as you go through the day. Shifting is different. You have to control it even as you do other things. The details have to be uppermost in your mind no matter what else is going on. Carpathians have to think on several levels at the same time, and our children must learn this; they are not born knowing how. Of course, some have more ability than others. And we have our geniuses."

His fingers were massaging her neck. There was possession in his touch. Antonietta brought her hands up to catch his wrist. He had given her the most extraordinary experience of her life. She fit her body into his, turning her face up to his with trust. With love and acceptance.

Byron groaned softly and lifted her, cradling her against his chest. "I want to make love to you more than anything in the world right now."

"You say that as if it's a bad thing. I want it, too." Her fingertips caressed his finely chiseled lips. She loved his mouth, the shape and texture. The way he tasted. Every nerve ending was alive after her wild ride through the sky. She wanted him every bit as much as he could possibly want her.

Byron carried her into the villa. Eleanor assured him one room was reasonably safe to use as a sleeping chamber. He moved unerringly through the furniture as if he had been there numerous times, finding the winding stairs to the luxurious bedroom belowground. The windows were heavily covered with rich velvet drapes. The room was large, with an expanse of thick carpet underfoot. A step down led to a large sunken marble Jacuzzi, tiled with an intricate mosaic pattern.

"This is your home?" She was puzzled by his sudden reserve. So used to his continual presence in her mind, his withdrawal was distressing to her. "I don't have Celt with me, so show me the layout of the room. I memorize rather well, and it will cut down on the accidents. I've never liked falling over chairs. It's very undignified."

Instead of laughing, Byron's tension level seemed to increase. He lowered her feet to the floor, beside the bed. She felt the thick quilt with her palm.

"I would never allow you to fall." He immediately provided the map of the room for her.

She deliberately smiled at him. "No, of course you

wouldn't. Nice room. I wouldn't mind sitting in the Jacuzzi after being in the night air. How about you?"

Byron raked his hands through his hair and obligingly turned on the water spigots before seating himself on the edge of the bed.

Antonietta studied the map of the room in his head, then slowly walked around, feeling her way down the single step until she could seat herself on the edge of the Jacuzzi. "Why are you so troubled, Byron?" She didn't have a sense that he wanted out of their relationship, more than he feared she might want out. "Is it because of the way you had to give blood to my cousin?" She shrugged out of his jacket, folded it neatly, and set it away from the filling tub. "You may as well talk to me. You want to, you just are having trouble figuring out how to explain everything to me. Am I that difficult to talk with? I was there. I recall I begged you to save Paul. Do you think I'm going to quibble over how you managed to do the impossible?"

Byron lifted his head to look at her. "I do not know what I ever did to deserve you, Antonietta. You are truly remarkable."

Her soft laughter was inviting, a sultry siren teasing him with the sexual allure of her voice. He was instantly mesmerized as he watched her slowly slip her sandals from her feet. There was something very feminine about the way she ran her hand over her nylon-encased feet. "Does any man deserve a woman? I'll have to give that some thought. But you're definitely my choice." She leaned toward the sound of running water, dipped her hand in to test the depth.

"My people exist on the blood of others. It is how we feed. Food makes us ill, particularly meat. We can force ourselves to eat, but it is uncomfortable. Most of the time, we give the illusion of eating. If we do consume food, we have to rid ourselves of the contents as soon as possible." He tried to keep his voice matter-of-fact, but his gaze burned over her face, watching her closely for the smallest reaction.

"I see. You really were telling the truth when you tried to assure me your family wouldn't care what I served. I was anxious for no reason at all." A small, self-mocking smile curved her mouth. "That does put things in perspective, doesn't it?"

Byron kept his touch in her mind light, a mere shadow monitoring her reaction. She absorbed what he said without judgment. She tapped her fingernail on the marble. "So you have fangs? Like a vampire in the books?" Antonietta held her palm over the pulse on her neck.

"When I need to feed, yes, my incisors lengthen." He didn't take his eyes from her face.

Antonietta turned off the water. "Do you have music in this room?"

The question was so unexpected, he was startled. "Did you hear what I said?"

"Of course I did. Here's the thing, Byron. Before we take this any further, I need to know some important things about you."

"The fact that I have fangs might be considered important by some people, Antonietta," he said patiently, wondering if he was losing his mind. He was beginning to feel frantic. She was so beautiful to him, so courageous. He ached to hold her. He had carefully planned the way he would break his heritage to her, the way he would lovingly reassure her, yet she didn't seem to be in need of reassurance.

"I suppose so, but I'm more concerned with your choice of music. I can live with some things, but music is my life. If you had atrocious taste, I don't know, I'd have to reconsider this entire affair."

He pushed his hands through his hair again with growing agitation. "That is another thing. We are not having an affair. In the eyes of my people, in my eyes, we are husband and wife. More. We are bound for all eternity. The binding ritual has already taken place."

She turned her head then, her eyes finding his face unerringly, as if she could see him. "Where was I during the binding ritual? Because I don't actually recall such a thing. And while you're at it, you might explain it to me."

Her direct gaze shook him. She looked serene sitting there on the edge of the Jacuzzi in her stocking feet and long skirt. "A female is bound to her lifemate when he recites the ancient bonding words. The power of those words is imprinted on every male of our species before his birth. We are two halves of the same whole. When the words are said, the souls become one as they are meant, and neither can be apart for long without the other."

"And this can be done without her knowledge or consent?" Her tone was mild. She dipped her hand in the water, created swirling patterns.

"We have few women. Our race is nearly extinct. We found that a few rare women who possess psychic ability are born the other half of a Carpathian male."

"So without their knowledge or consent, you bind them to you," she repeated.

"The male has little choice in the matter if he chooses to survive. She is light to our darkness. We cannot feel emotion or see in color without her influence. Too many of our males have turned vampire or walked into the dawn because they could not find their lifemate. It is our duty to see that our species survives. Lifemates belong together."

She nodded her head, but he caught the flash of anger in her mind. "A male has a choice, Byron. There is always a choice. The reason I don't wake up until the sun is down is because of you, isn't it? And the reason my hearing and my ability to smell is so acute is also due to you."

"We exchanged blood twice. Lifemates often exchange blood during lovemaking."

"Am I like you? Is that why Josef was so certain I could shift into a different form?"

"Not yet. It takes three blood exchanges to convert a human. The human must be psychic. You are far more sensitive than most."

"But that's why you brought me here tonight. You intend to convert me to be like you are. That's why you're so troubled."

"I wanted to wait, Antonietta. I wanted it to be your decision."

"What changed your mind?" She stood up, drew the silk blouse over her head in one motion. There was curiosity in her voice but no real censure that he could detect. And no real fear. In fact, she seemed very sure of herself. She folded the blouse and set it on top of his jacket, facing him in her blue lace bra, long swirling skirt, and stocking feet.

Byron was distracted by her mild reaction. By her full breasts, a temptation in nearly transparent lace. He watched as she pulled the pins from her hair and shook the long rope free. Her breasts moved in invitation.

"Byron? What changed your mind? Why did you decide to bring me here tonight and convert me without my knowledge or consent?" Antonietta shimmied out of her long skirt and stood in her stockings and tiny thong.

It took him a moment to find his voice and sort out his thoughts in between the lust rising so sharply. "The jaguar this evening. I was not there to protect you. I gave you Celt, but it is not good enough to rely on the borzoi. I need to know you are completely safe." Even to his own ears his voice sounded strangled. He held his breath as she peeled the nylon stockings from her legs.

"Why can't you just stay with me at the palazzo?"

"We do not sleep in the same way. I would appear dead to the world and to you. If you woke and thought me dead to you, your grief could be life threatening. You had a small taste of it when Paul shot me. I am also very vulnerable during the daylight hours. I could not adequately protect you or myself at the palazzo."

His heart nearly stopped when she turned her back on him, bent at the waist to step out of the small thong. He had no conscious thought of moving, but he found himself across the room, his hands smoothing her firm buttocks.

Antonietta rested both hands on the tile, pushing back against his hand, arching like a cat. "So you think converting me to what you are would make me safe from the jaguar?" His hands roamed over her body, slipped into secret hollows, turning her insides to a pool of lava.

Byron leaned forward to press a kiss in the small of her back. "I know you would be safe, Antonietta."

There was absolute conviction in his voice, in his mind. His hand slipped between her thighs, urging her legs farther apart. His clothes rubbed against her sensitive skin. Antonietta obligingly widened her stance. "Do you like the taste of my blood?"

His entire body hardened, thickened, became painfully full. "You are trying to seduce me, Antonietta."

"I'm so glad you noticed, Byron. I would hate to think you brought me here with only the intention of saving me from a wild cat." She pushed back against him, rubbed her bottom with delicious slowness over the thick bulge in the front of his trousers. A soft moan of pleasure escaped as his finger found her feminine channel and pushed deep.

His teeth teased her buttocks, small, little nips, his tongue lapping gently.

"I want you to take my blood now, Byron. And I want to feel it this time."

The husky note in her voice as she uttered the enticement was the most sexually exciting thing he'd ever experienced. Very slowly he withdrew his finger and straightened her, turning her to face him. "Do you mean it, Antonietta? You are not afraid?"

"I don't want an exchange, only to see what it's like. To be honest, the idea excites me, and I don't know why. I should be grossed out. I was upset that Vlad gave you blood. I wanted to give it to you. I felt like I should be the one to give you whatever you needed." Antonietta slid her hands under his shirt. "Get rid of your clothes. All of them. We really don't need them, do we?"

"No." Byron caught the back of her head and fastened his mouth to hers as he shed his clothes. They were skin to skin. He found he was ravenously hungry, his body tied up in knots. He fed on her mouth ruthlessly, Antonietta matching him heat for heat. Tongues tangled and dueled. Hands went everywhere, touching, exploring, claiming. Desperate for the feel and taste. On fire.

When his mouth left hers to trail kisses down her throat to her breast, she threw her head back, her body arching into his mouth eagerly. Byron knew he was on the edge of control, his incisors already lengthening, so he had to be careful as he suckled and teased her nipples into hard peaks. He kissed the swell of her breast, her collarbone, pressed a kiss into the hollow of her throat.

She caught fistfuls of his hair, breathless with need, with anticipation. Her body pulsed with hunger, with heat. His breath on her neck made her muscles clench in anticipation. Her breasts ached, her womb throbbed. His tongue touched her skin. His teeth scraped gently. Tenderly.

Byron shifted her into his arms. Held her body in the shelter and protection of his. "Antonietta. You are certain this is what you want? I can protect you from the experience if you are afraid."

"Do I feel afraid? I need this as much as you need it. I ache for you, Byron. I think about you every minute I'm awake. I want to know everything about you. I want to see what my life would be like. You're offering me things I can't fully comprehend." Her fists tightened in his long hair. Her entire body vibrated with sexual tension.

His teeth found her pulse, his tongue swirling over the spot so that she caught her breath. He found love welling up, swamping him, mixing with lust, with erotic hunger. "I love you." He whispered the words to her and sank his teeth deep.

16

Antonietta *cried out*, her legs nearly giving out as white-hot pain whipped through her body, then gave way immediately to a burning pleasure. Byron's mind was fully merged with hers, and she felt his reaction to her blood. The hot taste. Sating a hunger that was nearly impossible to sate. Lightning danced through their bloodstreams, long whips that crackled and sizzled and set them on fire. She held him possessively. She *had* to have him, had to feel his body beneath her fingertips. Had to have him buried deep inside her.

Do not. I am already at the end of my control.

He didn't have to warn her; she knew. She didn't want him in control. She wanted him to burn the way she was burning. She wanted him to *need*. To hunger. To be so aware of her that nothing else mattered. Her hands slid over his broad shoulders, mapped his chest, his belly. Found the thick length of his erection.

She felt the jolt go though his body, through hers, at the touch of her fingers. The intensity of his desire shook her. She stroked, massaged, teased, her fingers danced over the velvet head until she felt the fire roaring in his belly.

He swept his tongue over the pinpricks, caught her chin, and welded their mouths together. She tasted the hot, sweet spice of blood, the passion in his kiss. Then they were feeding off each other, so frantic to get close, Byron drove her backward against the wall, pinning her there, his hands everywhere. She curled one leg around his hip, fighting to align their bodies perfectly, fighting to get him inside of her.

There was never enough. The storm raged ferociously, wild and out of control and so hot they had to feed each other air. She wanted to share his skin. She needed him in her body. He had to touch every inch of her, hear her gasp, the soft little cry that escaped when his hands found every spot that sent her reeling with pleasure.

Outside the wind lashed the windows of the villa. Lightning streaked across the sky, and thunder cracked and boomed, shaking the earth. The dark sky lit up with fiery sparks, a shower of star gems, raining from the sky into the churning sea.

Byron took her to the carpet, unable to make it to the bed with his body raging at him and his mind swamped with her hunger. Immediately he indulged his need for intimate exploration, leaving the haven of her mouth to rain kisses over her breasts and stomach, teasing her navel, lifting her hips and plunging his tongue deep.

Antonietta screamed, her orgasm so intense her hips bucked. He rode it out, holding her in strong arms, laving and teasing, working carefully around her hottest spot until she pushed hard against him, squirming for more. The instant he touched her, her body spiraled out of control again, even wilder than before.

Byron dragged her hips close to him, pressing tightly against her wet, slick entrance. He could hear her heart pounding. She writhed against the thick carpet, pushing into him, trying to impale herself, seeking relief. He wanted the image in his mind for all time, her black hair a stark contrast to the white carpet, her body sprawled out, flushed with excitement, her breasts a tantalizing sight, and the soft demand in her voice as she ordered him to take possession of her.

He surged forward, a hard, deep stroke, filling her with the thick length of him, just for the joy of hearing her scream again. She was always uninhibited with him, wild and passionate, wanting him with every fiber of her being. With their minds so deeply merged, he could feel her hunger for him. He knew exactly what she wanted, thrusting deeper with every stroke. The carpeted floor had no give to it, so his body pounded into hers and still it wasn't enough.

Antonietta clutched him to her, dragging him even closer, lifting her hips to meet him in a wild, sensual ride. She couldn't tell where one orgasm left off and the next one started. A tidal wave swept through her body that went on and on, each stronger than the last, yet never enough. Her appetite for him seemed insatiable. Her fingernails dug into his skin, dragging his hips into her while her entire body rose up to meet his, bucking beneath him in the thrall of total pleasure.

Byron reveled in the way she gave herself completely, without reservation, to him. His body swelled beyond his expectations. There was a roaring in his ears, a dark storm of sensual hunger overtaking him a rush. *I want you to hear the words, cara mia, to know what I am giving you, what you give me. This is the mating ritual. The words that have the power to restore the two halves of our souls to one. I claim you as my lifemate. I belong to you. I offer my life for you. I give you my protection, my allegiance, my heart, my soul, and my body. I take into my keeping the same that is yours. Your life, happiness, and welfare will be cherished and placed above my own for all time. You are my lifemate, bound to me for all eternity and always in my care.*

Her feminine sheath was tight and hot, a velvet friction driving him utterly mad. He felt the fiery blast start somewhere around his toes and drive up through his body with the force of a battering ram. Antonietta took him deeper, driving her hips up to meet the fury of his body so that they were welded together in the midst of explosion. He thought he might have disintegrated, holding fast to Antonietta and his sanity.

Antonietta lay beneath him, clinging to his arms, fingertips rubbing at his biceps, exploring the shape and definition of his muscles as she tried to regain her ability to breathe and her equilibrium. Byron buried his face against her neck, his lips soothing on her pulse, his body so deeply buried in hers she was certain they were locked together forever.

"Do you think we know the meaning of the words *take it easy* and *slow?*" There was humor in her voice. "I thought we were going to set the room on fire."

"My skin is scorched," he said. He propped himself up on one elbow to take some of his weight off of her, his other hand shaping her breast.

Antonietta felt the ripple of reaction through her entire body. "Don't even breathe on me. I've melted into the carpet." Her lashes drifted down. "I'm going to go to sleep right here on the floor, and I want to wake up with you still inside of me." She sighed blissfully. "You may just be the greatest lover in the history of the world."

He bent his head to the temptation of her breasts, his tongue swirling around her nipple. The way her body tightened around his made him smile. *"May* be the greatest lover?" He sucked hard on her breast to punish her, laughed when her hips thrashed again, the rippling of an orgasm washing over her. "You respond so beautifully, Antonietta." She was soft and giving, her body so welcoming of his.

She tangled her fingers in his hair as his mouth worked greedily at her breast. "Do you plan on spending the night lavishing attention on my breast? Not that I'm complaining, but you're making me crazy. I can't afford to get any hotter. Now I know why there are rare cases of spontaneous combustion."

"I was thinking I might spend the night chewing on other parts of your anatomy," he answered. "I have decided I want to try every way in the world there is to make love to you. What is that famous book with all those intriguing positions and ideas?"

Her fingers caressed his hair, laughter bubbling up so that her muscles clenched around him intimately. "Well, not tonight. Tonight you are somehow going to figure out how to get me from here to the Jacuzzi without both of us falling in a heap on the floor."

"We are already on the floor. In any case, it would require me removing my body from yours, and I think I have found a home. You are the hottest thing on the face of the earth. I am staying right where I am."

"Lazy man. I promise to make love to you all night, but if I don't get into some soothing water, I might not be able

to keep that promise. We were a bit on the vigorous side."
For a moment she held his head to her breast, allowing waves
of pleasure to wash over her. She felt cocooned in sensual
delight.

He kissed her nipple with a soft sigh of regret. "I suppose
you are right, but I want you to know, I was enjoying myself."

"When we go to bed, I'll let you have all the fun you
want. You can indulge your every fantasy." She had been in
his mind; she saw each fantasy and was excited with the
knowledge of his intentions. "I wish I had your stamina, but
I don't. I need to rest. I don't want to be sore."

"My saliva contains a healing agent. We do not have to
worry about that. I will not allow you to feel discomfort."
He slowly began to withdraw from her body. Her muscles
reacted, gripping at him, trying to hold him to her. Byron
kissed her throat. "See how you are? Even your body does
not want us to separate."

"Don't listen." She wrapped her arms around his neck
when he scooped her up to cradle her against his chest. "I
can't move. I may not ever again."

The water in the Jacuzzi was hot and foamy, bursting
around her and against her most sensitive parts. Even that
sensation seemed to be highly erotic. Antonietta sighed blissfully. "This is perfection. Do you have candles?"

"If you want them."

"I can't see them, but if they're scented, it's always nice."

Almost at once the room was filled with the fragrance of
honeysuckle and rain. Antonietta smiled and allowed her legs
to drift to the surface, her arms spread wide to embrace the
atmosphere. "My very own sorcerer."

Water washed over her breasts, across her belly button,
over the triangle of dark curls and the shadow between her
legs. Byron leaned back and watched her, a peculiar emotion
stabbing at the pit of his stomach. She was so tightly bound
to him, so entrenched in his heart and soul, he wasn't certain
how it happened. Just looking at her sent a spear piercing
his body. It was a strange sensation, a physical pain, aching
with love when he looked at her.

"So what kind of music do you like?" Antonietta floated
in the gently rippling water, her hair spread around her like

so much seaweed. Her head bumped against Byron's chest. His arms locked around hers to hold her in place while the water bubbled and fizzed over her sensitized skin.

"Josef sings a particularly interesting version of rap," he said.

Her mouth opened wide in a gasp of alarm. She slid beneath the water as she spluttered a protest. He caught her and pulled her to the surface, his soft laughter mocking. "I have all your music," he assured.

"That was really mean," she said. "In retaliation, I might point out we didn't use birth control. I don't even think about birth control when I'm around you, which is silly, because I'm always responsible. I can't see your face, and I hope you're frowning."

He took her hand, brought her fingertips to shape his mouth. "Does it feel as if I am frowning?"

She snatched her hand away. "You are impossible to upset. You'd probably be thrilled if I got pregnant, which isn't logical at all."

"I would prefer you wait until I convert you."

Antonietta sat up, scooted to the small hollowed-out seat beside him. "All this talk of conversion sounds suspiciously like a vampire. What's the difference?"

"A vampire is wholly evil. Carpathian males lose emotions around two hundred years when they are fully adults. At that time, the lure of power begins to work at them, whispers to feel the rush of the kill. We are predators, with some animal traits. We can be dangerous when provoked, but we do not kill indiscriminately. A vampire lives to bring pain and torment and ultimately death to others. We take blood but do not harm those we take from. A vampire kills for the adrenaline in the blood and also the rush of power, a momentary thrill, when he kills. It is the duty of our hunters to bring these males to justice and protect our species by concealing their existence."

"That was what you meant by a hunter. A vampire hunter."

"Yes, among other things. I have done so, but it is not my calling."

"For which I'm grateful. How long do you live?"

He shrugged, a lazy shift of his shoulders causing the water to wash over her skin. His hand caught her foot, pulled it into his lap so his fingers could massage her. "Unless there is a mortal wound and no one to supply blood, we can live as long as we wish."

"So if I became as you are, I would live, but I would watch my family die, and eventually even their children."

"Unfortunately, that is one of the difficulties we all face. We have people we lose, but then, everyone does. Don Giovanni is not going to live forever. You will have to face his death, no matter what. And young Margurite could have been killed when the shield fell. Anything can happen in life." His fingers moved up to her calf.

Antonietta slid down further beneath the water to extend her leg to him. "That's true; I can't argue with that. I wouldn't be able to be awake during daylight hours?"

"No, and you would have to acclimate your skin to the early morning hours slowly before you could be out during that time."

"But I would have you."

"You are my lifemate, Antonietta. You will always have me."

"Men leave women all the time, Byron. You're asking me to change my entire way of life for you. I love my family. I love the palazzo. I don't want to leave my home. And I don't want to quit my career. Music defines who and what I am."

"It is impossible for lifemates to leave one another. I have not asked you to give up your career or to leave your home. There are some Carpathians who live with humans, and it works out very well."

"How does conversion work?"

"We exchange blood three times. The blood works on your organs, reshaping and changing you to what you should be. Already there are signs of it."

She idly flicked the surface of the water, popping bubbles as they churned around her. "What about my eyes? The strangest things have happened lately. I've seen flashes of light, shadows, even colors, as if I'm seeing body heat. I thought it was because we're so closely connected."

Byron turned the information over in his mind. "I saw color through Jacques. It was not my memory I was tapping into, but his vision of his lifemate. That is unusual. We tap into memories to feel emotion, but it does not work that way with vision as a rule. Perhaps there is something in my lineage that allows for such a thing. I would think your sight would be restored as the blood heals and reshapes. Our eyes are different, more functional for night vision. Is the thought of seeing again more tempting than choosing to be with me?"

Antonietta laughed. "You are such a male. That's such a little-boy thing to say."

He tugged on her foot until she slid underwater. Antoinetta pulled her leg away from him and reversed direction beneath the water to bump her head against his stomach. She circled his waist with her arms to anchor herself and rested her head in his lap, her mouth closing over his floating penis.

Byron looked down at the wealth of silky hair floating in the churning water. Her mouth provided a strong suction that brought him to instant attention. Her tongue danced and teased and stroked until his body trembled and hungered all over again. She seemed to be pulling a volcano from the very center of his being. His blood thickened and pooled, and his every nerve ending seemed to be centered where her hot, passionate mouth was working. The breath slammed out of his lungs. She came up for air, a water nymph laughing at him.

"Come here, you crazy woman." He reached for her, pulled her to him. "We will live in your house with your family. You will travel the world playing your music for people, and I will once again make art from the gems I call to me. Live your life with me. I cannot bear to be without you. Lifemates are for eternity, Antonietta. We can be married in the way of your people and live and seem to age. At times we may have to go away, but we will always return if that is your wish."

She tilted her head, a small siren's smile playing around her mouth. "Can you really make it so I'm not uncomfortable and we can make love all night?"

"Absolutely."

"I think I need proof before I commit to any more biting."

In answer, he lifted her, seating her on the rim of the Jacuzzi, parting her thighs wide enough to allow his broad shoulders between her legs. "A challenge I cannot resist." He bent his head to her, teeth nipping gently on the insides of her thighs, his breath warm on her most vulnerable entrance.

His hands gathered her hips and simply slid her into his mouth so that she cried out, grabbed fistfuls of his hair for an anchor.

Antonietta allowed her head to fall back. Her breasts seemed to ache with fullness. Every muscle in her body went taut. His tongue did incredible things, caressing, and stroking, and probing. Everywhere he touched, he soothed and heightened her pleasure. Her body coiled tighter and tighter, winding like a spring. She was wet and hot and impatient for him. She wanted to cry with the wonder and beauty of the way he could make her feel. And yet she needed. And hungered. For him.

Byron lifted his head, brought her mouth to his, sharing her taste, his tongue teasing hers before he spun her around and bent her over the edge. "Is that enough proof? I can give you more." His hands cupped her breasts while he pressed against her buttocks, deliberately showing her the fullness of his desire. "Do you need more?"

She reached back in an effort to guide him into her. Byron avoided her hand, rubbed again, his teeth nipping her firm bottom. Antonietta began to turn around, determined two could play. Byron held her against the rim, caught her hips, and pushed into her tight sheath with exquisite slowness. "You want slow and easy, remember?"

He was so thick, she could feel him stretching her, pushing his way into her folds, the slow friction driving her to the edge of madness. "I didn't say that. I'm sure I didn't say that." He was very strong, holding her with a gentle but completely unbreakable grip, all the while moving with leisurely, long strokes. Each surge forward made her shudder with pleasure. She had to remain completely still while he did the work.

She stopped trying to struggle back into him, just allowing the pleasure to wash over her in waves. Her breasts tightened, and Byron's every movement enhanced her experience, just as he meant it to. Antonietta reached for his mind to share her every orgasm, the beauty of giving herself up to heat and fire. To him. She could feel his growing exhilaration as her body became more and more stimulated, gripping him tightly and taking him with her right over the edge.

When she could breathe again, Antonietta found herself

laughing as he stepped carefully backward, taking her with him into the bubbling water. "Are we permanently stuck together? My legs are going to give out, and I didn't do any of the work." The water bubbled over her buttocks, fizzed between their bodies, and teased her feminine core. "I hope you know you're never going to persuade me using sex. You can try, I hope you do try, but I'm going to make a decision based on other things. Important things like your choice of music." The laughter faded from inside of her. Antonietta went very still.

Byron slipped out of her body, turned her around to face him, his hands resting lightly on her hips. "What is it, Antonietta?"

"Do I have a choice, Byron? Are you asking me if I want this conversion or telling me about it because you intend to convert me, no matter how I feel?"

Her fingernails dug into his arms. He could feel the beat of her heart, hear the steady, frightened rhythm. Byron curled one hand around the nape of her neck. "I brought you here with every intention of converting you." His voice was very low. "My first duty to you and to my people is to protect you."

"I need to sit down." Her breath was trapped somewhere in her lungs, and her legs were rubbery. She felt behind her for one of the seats. Byron helped her to sit in the foaming water. "Turn off the jets."

He did so, and the room was suddenly quiet. She drew up her knees, wrapped her arms around them. "Do you have any idea how vulnerable a woman can feel? I'm a strong woman and not afraid of most things, but I'm intelligent enough to stay in an environment that works for me. I have managed to do most things I've wanted, but I've always made certain that I surrounded myself with people I trusted. Being blind makes me even more vulnerable. I can't slap your face and walk out of here like a drama queen. If I fell over a chair, it would ruin the effect."

"Do you want to slap my face?"

She pushed her wet hair from her face. "No, I want you to let me make my own decision. This isn't a small thing you're asking of me. This is even bigger than marriage, and I was never going to get married."

"Why wouldn't you marry, Antonietta?"

She shrugged her shoulders. The water held heat, and right now she needed heat. "How would I ever know a man wanted me for me? I'm not how you see me at all. I'm overweight, and I do have scars; not like Tasha led me to believe, but they're there. I've seen firsthand how damaging a wrong marriage can be. Paul and Tasha suffered so much. You have no idea. Their father was such a womanizer." She rubbed her hand over her face. "He was with every maid in the palazzo and every other woman he could charm. He was in all the tabloids. He didn't care where he was or who would see him. He was capable of having sex with a woman in front of the Paul and Tasha and laughing about it. He was abrupt and disapproving with Paul and showered Tasha with presents and little else."

"He had no honor, Antonietta. I do."

"Aunt Selena knew about all the women. She drank so she could pretend otherwise. There was a rumor that one of his women had his baby." Antonietta rubbed her hand across her mouth as if trying to wipe away a bad memory. "Aunt Selena died one day under what the authorities claim were suspicious circumstances. She and Anton were in the tower. There was a terrible fight. Nonno went up and tried to calm her and get her to come down. Even Helena tried. Selena fell or was pushed. It was a horrible time in our lives. If there ever was a baby, Uncle Anton paid the woman off, and she aborted it, because it was never mentioned again. He went on with his life as if nothing happened."

"How did he die?"

"A car accident. He was drinking and went off the road." She leaned the back of her head against the rim of the Jacuzzi. "Tasha's been married. Both times her husband cheated on her. Franco is married, and his life is miserable. The few men I've dated that seemed a reasonable partner ended up wanting my money and/or the Scarletti business."

"Is that what you think I want, Antonietta?" His voice was very quiet.

She shivered despite the heat of the water. "You want me to be a creature, another species that needs blood to survive. You want me to change what I am for you."

"Would you prefer me to walk away from you?"

The moment he said the words, she felt a wrenching panic inside of her. "I thought you said lifemates could never be apart."

"Do you want me to leave you? Do you want to go on with a life that does not include me in it? That is the question, more than any other, for you to decide."

"I want out of here." She stood up, the water pouring off of her.

Byron was there instantly, lifting her out of the Jacuzzi and wrapping a soft towel around her. Antonietta clutched it to her and made her way to the bed, using the map in Byron's mind. "Then there is a choice. You brought me here to convert me, but you're giving me a choice."

"You would never be happy or trust me completely if I made such an important decision for you, Antonietta. I know that much about you. I want your trust. And I want you to choose me. I do not want it to be because you are my life mate, or because you might regain your sight, or even because we have good sex. I want you to say yes because you feel the same way about me as I feel about you. I want you to know you love me that much."

"Great sex," she corrected softly. He was tearing her up inside. If he had tried to force her, she would have fought him at every turn, but he was asking her. More than just asking her. He was stripping away his pride and laying his feelings at her feet. "Byron, if I ask you to live with me at the palazzo, the two of us together, married in my way, and we could find a way to be safe, would you do it if I didn't follow through with the conversion?"

"You are my lifemate. I would choose to live with you and grow old with you. I would end my life when you died."

Antonietta heard the ring of truth in his voice. She curled up on the bed, her head on the pillow. "Come keep me warm, Byron."

He went to her immediately, just as she knew he would, fitting his body around hers, his arms drawing her close, wrapping around her so that she felt safe and warm.

"I want a family wedding with Tasha standing up for me. And I want you to make peace with her."

"She is determined to have Captain Diego throw me in prison."

"She'll stop when you're family. We protect family, and that will include you."

"You are asking a lot of me, but I suppose for you, to keep you happy, I will find a way to get along with your provoking, impossible cousin."

She turned in his arms, found his face with her fingertips, moving her hands over it to take in every detail. She touched his lips, his teeth. "I choose you, Byron. I want to spend my life with you. So let's get to it."

He leaned into her, kissed her on her mouth. Her lips were trembling beneath his. "I want you to be certain. There is no going back. Once we do this, I cannot undo it."

"I would never say yes if I didn't mean it."

He kissed her again with such tenderness her heart somersaulted. He held her with such care, his enormous strength leashed. Even in the throes of wild passion, he was careful with her. She felt his breath, the soft velvet of his lips, the gentle tug of his teeth as they scraped back and forth in a mesmerizing rhythm over her skin. There was white-hot pain giving way immediately to pleasure. Whips of lightning danced in her veins. Antonietta wrapped her arms around Byron's head, her fists tangling in his hair. She felt his tongue, heard his soft whisper, words she didn't catch.

She felt him shift her in his arms, hold her close to his chest. She ran her hands over his body. His hand moved to the nape of her neck, pressed her mouth just above his heart. There was power and heat. Her body flooded with energy. Fire blossomed in her belly, in her breasts, between her legs. His body was over hers, surging into hers with the same fire and power. There was a dreamlike quality to their lovemaking. The taste in her mouth was hot and tangy. Salty. His hands were gentle, shaping her body, holding her close. His lovemaking was tender and gentle, completely unlike his earlier passion, making her feel cherished and precious. With every movement of his body, she felt the tension wind tighter and tighter, felt him rising with her. Their release rocked them both, yet left her exhausted, resting against him, limp and drained but filled with a strange peace.

She snuggled against him, burrowing against his shoulder, closing her eyes. *I'm so tired, Byron. I don't think I can stay awake. If anything momentous is happening, don't wake me up; just let me sleep through it.* She wasn't altogether certain if she had dreamt their joining. If she really had taken his blood. Her mind felt hazy, her body so limp she couldn't move.

"Why did you say yes to me, Antonietta?" He kissed her eyelids, the corners of her mouth. "Why would you choose something so unknown over a life you enjoy that is familiar? Your courage is terrifying."

She rubbed her face against his shoulder like a contented cat. "I think everyone wants to be loved, Byron. All of my life I dreamt of meeting a man who would really love me and want to share his life with me. I need to be loved. I look into your mind and I see that same need in you. It isn't so courageous to grab hold of life's opportunities when they come your way. Life is meant to be lived. I don't want to sit on the sidelines and watch it go by. I never have. Being blind has taught me to take the opportunities I can, the moment they're offered. With you it is easy. I see into your mind, and the way you feel about me is shattering." Her soft laughter played over his skin. "It's unrealistic, but if you want to view me as beautiful and wonderful, that's okay with me."

He wrapped his arms more closely around her, his touch possessive. "You already have certain abilities, and you are extraordinarily sensitive. It will be interesting to see how your gifts develop over the coming years."

"But we will live at the palazzo," she reiterated, wanting reassurance. "Nonno would not want me to leave. And no one understands Tasha."

"She never says what she means. Most of the time I would scan her mind and read her intentions, not paying any attention to her words, but your family and even some of your servants have those strange barriers."

"Will I be able to do that, too?"

"Yes. But in the case of your family, they would realize what was happening, and you would have to remove the memory. You learn, over time, it is better, if possible, to allow people the privacy of their own thoughts."

"I found it intrusive and a bit frightening when I realized you could read my mind. Thoughts come and go randomly at times. I wasn't sure I wanted you to see what I was really like."

He laughed softly, feathered little kisses into her hair. "I find it better to scan Josef at all times, and you might want to remember to do the same. He looks innocent enough, and sounds it, but in truth he is a holy terror."

"Do you think I'll really be able to see?" She drew up her knees. There was a strange burning in her stomach. With each passing minute it had increased until it was painful. Moving her legs didn't seem to help.

Byron slid his hand to her belly, fingers splayed wide to take in the expanse. His touch should have been soothing, but sharp spears of pain shot through her abdomen and down her spine.

"Byron?" Sweat broke out on her body. Cramps gripped her muscles. "What's happening to me?"

"The conversion is taking place." He merged fully with her, tried to shield her from the pain. No matter how hard he tried to block it, the burning ripped through her body. A convulsion lifted her up and slammed her back into the mattress, in spite of his restraining arms.

She felt something alive racing beneath her skin, itching horribly, trying to force its way out of her pores. She thought she screamed, but no sound emerged. A noise boomed in the room, annoying, hurting her ears. She couldn't seem to adjust the volume.

Jacques. Jacques, what should I do? Byron reached for the one man who he knew had been through such an event. The one man who might aid him in helping to shield Antonietta from the worst of the pain. It was easy enough to allow Jacques to share knowledge of what was happening to Antonietta.

There is little you can do until her body is rid of all the toxins. Then you must send her to sleep and give her body time to heal in the earth. It is a difficult time, Byron. If you should need aid in any form, I am here.

Antonietta gasped as another wave of fire burned through her body, burst over her heart and lungs and gripped every muscle in her body. She forced air through her lungs, realized Byron was breathing for both of them. She reached out blindly for his hand. Byron tightened his grip on her, wanting to hold her to him.

A thousand needles stabbed her eyes; fire burned her eye sockets. The ends of her fingers went numb, then burst, hooked claws emerging, then receding. Byron was forced to let her hands go to keep from being ripped open. Her body convulsed again, arcing, stretching, contorting. She was slammed back to the mattress.

"I had no idea, Antonietta. I would never have asked you to go through this."

She rode out another wave, tried a small smile, but her face felt like it was lengthening. "Labor should be a piece of cake to Carpathian women after this." Her voice was constricted, not her own. A soft growl accompanied her words. The noise in her ears increased to a deafening roar. "I'm going to be sick. Get me into the bathroom."

Byron scooped her up, moving quickly. Tears burned in his eyes. Guilt rode him hard. "I should have known about this. Before I asked such a thing of you, I should have known what I was getting you into. I am sorry, *cara*." He held her hair out of her face as she vomited repeatedly.

Byron had no idea how much time passed. It seemed hours. Endless. He was shocked at the pain, the terrible burning, a blowtorch assaulting her insides. He was grateful she couldn't see as something raised her skin rushing through her body time and again. Several times he was forced to restrain her when she would have ripped her skin from her bones or torn her own eyes from her face. He tried everything he could think of to lessen her suffering, but all he could really do was hold her to him and watch that she didn't harm herself. Exhaustion helped more than anything so that she rested between the waves of pain, holding his hand, keeping her mind carefully blank.

Byron was grateful the moment he sensed it was safe to send her to sleep. He issued the merciful command ruthlessly, and she succumbed without a murmur.

17

Byron *carried Antonietta* from deep within the healing soil back to the bed in the villa. He made certain there was no evidence of having spent the day in the ground as he laid her on the sheets and curled up beside her. His heart was pounding, and he actually tasted fear in his mouth. Framing her face with his hands, he kissed her mouth. "Wake for me, Antonietta. Wake and embrace your new life."

She stirred, her lush body moving beneath his, her breasts pushing into his chest, her hips providing a cradle for his. Antonietta stretched leisurely and opened her eyes.

She screamed and covered her eyes. "Something's wrong, Byron. This can't be right. Something went wrong."

Byron tried to read her mind, but panic was uppermost. "Let me see. I do not understand what is wrong, Antonietta. You just woke up, there should not be pain. Are you in pain?"

Her stomach churned. "I came awake all at once and could hear things outside the walls of the villa. I could feel you, your skin, your body, and I immediately wanted you. I was thinking of making love, how beautiful it would be and how wonderful it is to wake up in your arms. I opened my eyes, and everything went crazy."

Byron breathed for both of them, slow and steady until her wild heart was back in rhythm, and the chaos of her mind was under control. He examined the memories in her mind. The room tilting. His face shooting at her, distorted. Blurring. Light coming in from all directions. It was a dizzying kaleidoscope of images and color. Pain shot through his head, his stomach lurched.

"Can we fix it?" Antonietta wrapped her arms around Byron's neck and hung on, her eyes closed tightly. "That was scary."

He kissed the corner of her mouth, nibbled at her chin, his mind racing as he sought answers. "My friend Jacques has a lifemate, Shea, a doctor before her conversion, now a valued healer. Let me see if I can show him what is happening. She might be able to tell us what to do."

It was his continual display of affection, the little love bites, the way his lips feathered over her skin as absorbed as he was in the problem that provided her with reassurance. Antonietta relaxed completely under him, the tension draining out of her. The moment she did, she became aware of the way his body was hard and thick and ready for hers. Sliding her hands over his back, she allowed her mind to become fully engaged in the definition of his muscles. With her eyes tightly closed, shutting out the unknown, she could concentrate on what she knew best, the texture and feel of Byron's very masculine body.

Byron reached for Jacques. *I need help once again. Have you seen this before? Has Shea? Antonietta cannot open her eyes.* He shared the dizzying vision with Jacques. *Her conversion was difficult, and there were obvious signs of the Jaguar's presence. Her entire family has strange barriers, shields preventing scans. Is it possible her genes have in some way contributed to a vision problem?*

There was a short silence while Jacques obviously conferred with Shea. *It is so good to know you have found your life mate, Byron.* Shea's soft voice was in his mind. *She seems a remarkable woman, and we are anxious to meet her. Do you have plans of a traditional human wedding? I caught glimpses in her mind of staying with her family.*

She wants a wedding, and of course, we will have one. If Jacques can make it, I would want him to stand up for me.

That goes without saying. I think the problem with her eyes is twofold. She hasn't seen in years. The connections to the brain aren't there and in proper working order. Time will fix that. She should try to rely on her other senses and give her eyes a break. Short practice without moving so she doesn't add to the chaos she experiences. The heat images are more than likely her Jaguar genetics. She is far closer to the species than we've ever encountered. Cats, like us, have a layer of reflecting tissue which reflects back all external light. They also have binocular vision. Without moving their heads, cats can detect motion over a visual field of two hundred and eight degrees. The things happening to her that you shared with Jacques during her conversion were not normal.

Byron's heart jumped. *You should have told me.*

It was too late to stop it. In truth, we have no idea what the conversion will do. Again, a guess would be the enhancement of her natural abilities. We know she is compatible. The eye problem is a drawback, Byron, but with time and practice, she should be able to reestablish connections. This is unknown territory.

We thank you both. Byron broke the connection, leaned down to kiss Antonietta's throat. "Your skin is amazingly soft. I love the way you feel. Did you get all that? We are breaking new territory."

"I just have to keep my eyes closed?"

Byron rolled over, bringing her on top of him. "That is the idea, although she said practice. Without movement. Maybe you should sit up there, just straddle me, and look around without moving."

She laughed softly. "You always make me feel beautiful, Byron. No matter what, around you, I feel happy." His hands cupped her breasts, his thumbs sending a shiver of excitement down her spine.

"Make me happy and give this a try."

She found his heavy erection, took her time settling over him, gasping as he filled her, her tight muscles giving way to allow him deep inside of her. "You think I can just sit here without moving?"

He laughed, lifting his head to lap at her nipple. "Just think of the rewards." He lay back and clasped her hands tightly in his. "Just look at the wall. It is dark in here, very little light can penetrate through the heavy curtains."

Antonietta deliberately wriggled, tightening her muscles around him, and lifted her hips to ease back over him in a slow, teasing slide. "You want me to hold still?" She lifted herself again, used her muscles to contract around him, slid back and squirmed.

"Very still."

She had the impression of white teeth bared. "Well, if you really insist." She tightened her fingers around his, trying not to be afraid. Very cautiously, she opened her eyes. The room lurched and spun. Images leapt at her from every side. She concentrated on the way Byron felt, filling her with his thickness, stretching her muscles. The heat and fiery friction that could be hers with a simple thrust of her hips. She allowed the images in her mind to wash over her and retreat. Feeling mattered. Byron mattered. His body, so masculine, so hard. His mind with such wicked, erotic ideas. Just the thought of his fantasies flooded her body with a need for instant relief. She deliberately picked one out of his head, a particularly graphic picture of her exploring his body, her mouth wrapped tightly around him.

Byron groaned aloud. "You cannot think about things like that. Concentrate on your vision."

She laughed, careful of moving. She didn't want to blink; too many images leapt at her. "You're the one with all those pictures in your mind. I had no idea you were so set on that. I would have been most happy to oblige. I think it would have been far more fun than staring at the wall."

"Are you able to see anything? If you do not, I swear I might explode." He had no idea it could be so erotic to lie perfectly still, connected together, surrounded by heat and fire. Her breasts were tempting, begging for his attention, but all he could do was lie passively while she stared at the opposite wall.

"I can't judge how far away it is, but I can bring the Jacuzzi into focus." There was excitement in her voice. "I am seeing it through my own eyes, aren't I?" She shifted, a slight, languorous movement that brought beads of sweat to his brow.

"Yes," he bit out between his teeth. Fire raced through his bloodstream. She was doing something with her muscles that wasn't fair. "You are not supposed to be moving."

Antonietta closed her eyes. "I wasn't moving." She leaned back slightly, her hair sliding over his thighs as she began to ride him. "This is moving. There's a big difference. And let me show you this." She sped up, hard, fast strokes designed to massage and caress. To drive him wild.

He reached up to capture her breasts, watching the sultry expression cross her face. She always gave herself completely to him, every bit as passionate or more than he. It only added to the dark intensity of his sexual hunger for her. His hands slipped lower to her waist, lifting her in time to his thrusting hips. He was close, so close. He caught her hair in his hand, dragged her to him as he half sat. "Take my blood, Antonietta. I feel your hunger beating at me." The idea of it excited him so that he swelled even more, so that he throbbed and burned.

He felt her body ripple with life at his husky plea. Her arms circled his neck. Her tongue lapped at the seam of his lips. Touched his throat. Found the spot on his chest. White-hot pain flashed through his body, whips of lightning broke over his skin. His hips thrust wildly, over and over, pumping into her, his body exploding with pleasure so intense it shook him, left him trembling with the force of their combined orgasm. Her mouth was a brand, claiming him, locking them together. The beauty of it took his breath away.

Byron wrapped his arms around her and simply cradled her to him. When her tongue closed the tiny pinpricks, he rocked her gently. *"Grazie,* Antonietta, for your generosity. I cannot believe you are real at times. Years ago, I was captured by a vampire and given to humans so they could torture me and lure others of my kind into a trap. I tried to get past the pain by imagining what having a lifemate would be like. I did not even come close to the real woman."

She kissed him. She had no other way to answer him, to show him what he meant to her. She poured her feelings into her kiss, came up for air laughing. "I can't possibly keep my eyes closed all the time. What are we going to do about this?

I'm kissing you, lift my head, and accidentally open my eyes. You have three heads, and one of them is whirling around on your neck. Another appears to have some sort of strange bonelike thing running through the middle of your forehead. You don't really look like that, do you? If so, you might have warned me that handsome man in the mirror you showed me was a complete figment of your imagination."

Laughing, he rolled over so she was flat on her back. "We have to have very dark glasses that do not allow you to see at all."

"In the meantime, shall I wrap my head like a mummy?"

"I doubt your family will find the humor in it. Tasha would think I had you wrapped up to ship off to Egypt. I think you better wear your own glasses until we can get others. They should help." He handed her the familiar pair.

"*Grazie,*" she murmured and slipped them on.

He stood up. "Picture being completely clean and showered. See if you can build the image."

She stood up, stretched, her arms over her head. "I can't wait to see poor Celt. He must have been so lonely. Can he stay with us from now on? I know he didn't like being alone." Antonietta did her best to hold a picture of herself, fresh from the shower, uppermost in her mind. "What do you do for clothes when you shape-shift?"

"I will make certain you have clothes, *cara.*"

"Did you touch Paul this evening? Is he going to be all right?"

"Yes, he is weak and in pain, but he will heal. Tasha and Justine spent the night with him. At the moment he is resting. We will attend him when we reach the palazzo. We should go. We must tell Don Giovanni we are to be married immediately. I think it will be better if I ask him for your hand in marriage. While I am doing that, you can tell Tasha. I am certain she is bound to throw things, and it will be better if I am not present."

"Coward." The smile faded from her face. "Before we do anything else, we have to talk to Marita. I can't have her in the house, even if she is Franco's wife, if she's involved in some sort of theft ring." Antonietta shook her head, touching her dark glasses to make certain they wouldn't come off. "If she's involved in some way, the children and Franco are going to be devastated."

"Marita is easy enough to read, Antonietta. And it is time we push past some of these barriers to see just who has been adding poison to your meals. It has to be someone in the house. As much as I know you want the culprit to be someone other than your family, few outsiders have access to your food."

Antonietta turned away from him. She couldn't bear to think that a member of her family would try to kill her, let alone Don Giovanni. He could be stern and even at times seemed unforgiving, but she knew he was a loving, generous man whose life revolved around his family.

"Are you ready to try shape-shifting? Something easy. A bird, something familiar to you." Byron captured her hand, wanting to take her mind off her fears and give her something to anticipate.

"I've been ready since I woke up."

Byron bent his head to kiss her. "I knew you would say that."

It was all she could do not to jump up and down on the bed like an eager child. She knew exactly how Josef felt. "Tell me what to do."

He led her out to the verandah overlooking the sea. "Merge completely with me. I will hold the image of the owl in your mind. At first you will be caught up in the beauty of flying, but you have to work at remembering to hold that image yourself. It takes years of practice to perfect it. And the actual shifting feels strange. You are submerging yourself, the essence of who you are, into another creature, another form. You have to control that form and all of its urges."

"Do the other women who have been converted have help?"

"From what I understand they do, they just accept it without question. I am not certain they even realize the image and control is being held by their lifemate. We stay merged so much, can you always tell who has the first thought?"

She nodded. "Let's do it then."

The detail of the bird was amazing. She studied it carefully, paying attention to every curve, every feather. She caught the first shimmer of awareness in her mind. Her skin prickled. She kept her eyes closed tightly and let it happen, allowed her body to change while somewhere inside she felt the entire process. She stayed very still, afraid if she moved she might make a mistake. Afraid it wouldn't happen.

Try your wings.

Cautiously, she stretched the layers of feathers to their full length and fanned the air experimentally. Joy burst through her. *I'm an owl.*

Stay very close to me, Antonietta. Keep that image uppermost in your mind.

You have to provide a map. If I try to open my eyes, I'm disoriented.

Just stay close. When we get to the palazzo, we can practice shielding our physical bodies from the sight of others.

Oh my gosh! Like an invisibility cloak. The invisible man. This is so fantastic.

That is later. This is now. Really concentrate, Antonietta. You can get in trouble and fall from the sky. Hop up here to the banister, and we will launch out over the sea.

So if I crash, I'll just fall into the sea and drown as opposed to hitting the ground at record speed and breaking every bone in my body.

That will not happen. I can carry you again if you prefer.

Antonietta, deep inside the bird's body, sniffed her disdain of his idea and hopped up beside him on the wide railing. Before she could talk herself out of it, she leapt off the ledge, wings spread wide. The wind caught her, lifted her up, ruffled her feathers. The feeling of flying was even more intense when she was the one actually doing it. Antonietta forgot everything Byron told her. The sheer exhilaration of soaring in the heavens with the wind and the clouds filled her with joy.

Byron flew close to her, holding the image in her mind, shifting to place his body slightly below hers to keep her from falling when she became too exuberant. He didn't reprimand her. Her joy flooded him with memories of his first experiences. They approached the palazzo from the seaside, dropping down in the cover of the maze.

Antonietta landed hard on her bare bottom, was shocked when Byron thrust clothes into her hand. "I'm not going to ask." She was trying hard not to laugh, rubbing her posterior. "Was that the very worst landing you've ever seen?"

He framed her face with his hands and fastened his mouth to hers. "You are a miracle, Antonietta, and you do not even realize it." He watched her pull the soft moss-green trousers over bare skin and shimmy into the matching silk blouse.

Leaves rustled, a twig snapped. The soft murmur of voices in the distance alerted Byron and Antonietta to the others walking in the maze. They could also hear Don Giovanni singing softly under his breath as he puttered around the courtyard, checking his beloved flowers.

The voices were hushed but angry. "That's Christopher Demonesini," Antonietta said. She shoved the dark glasses onto her nose, so upset she didn't ask where Byron got them. "How dare that man show his face in our home? Franco should have thrown him out immediately."

Byron put a restraining hand on her arm. "Let me give you the rules of invisibility, Warrior Princess. You do not get to go wielding your broadsword and driving the enemy from your property. You are invisible. You gather information, and the most important of all things is not to react to what you hear. No reaction. That is the key." He pulled her closer to him as the footsteps continued to approach and the voices became louder.

Wrapped in Byron's restraining arms, Antonietta did her best to simply listen when every instinct she possessed told her to confront Christopher.

"I don't care who you are or what power your family has, Demonesini. You can fill the Scarletti palazzo with a million roses. It won't make up for what you did." Diego's voice was a whip of contempt.

"This is none of your business," Christopher contradicted. "Natasha is my fiancée, and what happens is between us."

"Not anymore. She broke the engagement, and she asked you very politely to stay away from her. Your calls and flowers aren't wanted."

"I don't think you know who you're talking to. I can have you dismissed from your job. You might remember that the next time you decide to stick your nose in my business. Get the hell away from me and stay away from Natasha." Christopher laughed. "You probably think she'll look at you next, but a woman like Natasha Scarletti would never stoop so low."

"I don't think you quite understand what I'm saying to you." Diego stopped walking and turned toward Christopher only feet from where Antonietta and Byron were standing. Antonietta could easily see the images in Byron's mind. Diego's hand shot out and caught Christopher by the throat. "Your money doesn't impress me. You can threaten me with dismissal from my job, but it won't stop me. Leave her alone." His fingers threatened to crush Demonesini's larynx. "She doesn't want to see you again. She doesn't want to hear your voice. Stay away from her, because if you don't, you'll be looking over your shoulder for the rest of your life. Have I made myself perfectly clear?"

Diego let go of Christopher, who staggered and coughed, massaging his throat. The captain walked away, disappearing behind the tall hedges.

Can you read his mind?

I thought you did not approve of reading minds.

Maybe he's the jaguar. He's always been a smug little brat, even when we were kids. He hasn't improved with age. I should have known he was capable of beating a woman. His father certainly is.

He has the same barrier all of you have, so the Jaguar genetics run deep in him. Byron materialized in front of Christopher Demonesini, waving his hand for silence and staring deep into the man's eyes. Antonietta, merged so deeply with Byron, received the flow of information as Byron extracted it.

Christopher Demonesini lived with a monster. His father was ruthless with his fists and ruled his household as a dictator. There was no memory of a jaguar or killing people, but his father had ordered him to marry Natasha Scarletti-Fontaine. It seemed to be part of a plan for a merger of the two shipping businesses. Christopher was afraid of his father and would go to any lengths to prove himself to the man.

Byron moved some distance away, veiling Christopher's sight and removing all traces of his memory of sharing his thoughts. Christopher shook his head repeatedly, cursed as he rubbed his throat, and hurried back through the maze, retracing his steps.

Antonietta leaned against Byron. "How awful to grow up like that. I'm ashamed of myself for disliking him so intensely. He had little chance to be anything but like his father."

"Tasha is not like her father. We all have choices, Antonietta. At some point we have to take responsibility for our own lives. Christopher is capable of becoming a monster every bit as ugly as his father. Diego will have to watch himself in his career. Christopher will never forget what happened here today. Still, as much as I wish to have found it, I could see no trace of the jaguar in him, although the genetics are clearly present as they are in you. How strong, I do not know. We cannot rule him out as the animal, but I detected no conspiracy for murder or even for theft."

"His father is a horrible man. I can remember him coming to visit when I was a teenager. Our families travel in the same social circles, so he was often at parties and charity events. He always touched me. Brushing his hands accidentally against my breasts. Standing behind me and pushing against me, rubbing his body against mine. He made me ill. If I said anything, he always acted as if I were a child, misinterpreting what happened. Accidents, you know, and I was blind and couldn't see what happened. Then he actually tried to court me. I had such an aversion to him, I wouldn't even stay in the same room alone with him. I made poor Tasha stay right by my side every second. Tasha never let me down. Not once. The don would do his best to get her out of the room, but she stuck like glue." A shudder ran through her body. "I always know when he comes in a room. Every hair on my body stands up, and I get that strange itching under my skin I always associate with the jaguar wanting to come out."

Byron smiled. She had the instant impression of teeth bared. "I look forward to meeting Christopher's father. He should meet a real monster and learn the rules of the jungle."

Antonietta wrapped her arms around Byron's neck. "I don't want you to do anything at all. I have you, and his family can't hurt us. They're desperate for a way to save their business, but it won't be through a Scarletti."

His kiss was tender, loving. "I want to speak to your grandfather and arrange our wedding immediately."

"He'll ask you to sign a prenuptial agreement."

"I am a gem-caller, Antonietta. I find rare gems. I do not need nor want the Scarletti fortune. You do not need it either. What I have is yours. I will be more than happy to sign whatever agreement your grandfather deems necessary, as long as he has it drawn up immediately." He took her hand as they made their way through the twists and turns of the maze.

In the courtyard, Josef stood before an easel gazing up at the battlements. He wore his beret at a jaunty angle and a bright kerchief tied around his neck. Splashes of paint dotted his face and were smeared on his smocklike shirt. *He is clearly in his painter period.* Byron was sarcastic. *He seems to go through stages like no other child in history.*

Antonietta studied the painting. *Actually, he's not bad. He has talent.*

Of course he has talent. Eleanor raised him. She would make certain he had every opportunity to develop whatever gift he had. He is just such a . . .

Boy? Antonietta laughed softly in Byron's mind. *Isn't he supposed to be one?*

Josef put down his paintbrush and went over to the side of the palazzo, studying the smooth walls, the wealth of sculptures and stained glass. For a moment his form shimmered, wavered, then he was crouched on the side of the palazzo, clinging with hands and feet, a human spider dressed in black with a webbed mask over his face.

What in the world is he doing?

Byron scanned his nephew's mind and sighed loudly. *Vincente and Margurite shared an American comic book with him. He is Spiderman, racing up the side of the building to rescue the maiden in distress.*

What maiden?

Tasha. She just does not know she is the figment of his boyish dreams. It is not dark enough for him to be trying such a stunt, and he is not able to do more than one thing at a time, so he cannot cloak himself from human eyes. Your grandfather is in the courtyard looking at his flowers. All he has to do is look up, and he would see Josef.

Antonietta studied the images in Byron's mind. Josef moved up the side of the second story, much like Dracula in the movies. His form shimmered, shifted, went from webbed mask to startled horror. He slid down the sheer wall, bumped a window ledge, and plummeted to the courtyard below.

Swearing, Byron bounced airwaves, cushioning the boy's fall. Josef landed hard enough to knock the wind out of him but obviously wasn't seriously hurt. Don Giovanni heard the impact as Josef crashed through a low shrub, breaking several branches.

"What happened, young Josef? Did you trip? Are you hurt?"

Josef climbed gingerly to his feet, rubbing his posterior as he did so. "Just my pride. I can't seem to get anything right these days."

"I had a good look at your painting a few minutes ago, and it seemed quite good to me. I don't know all that much about art, but Tasha does. She'll have to take a look at it for you."

Josef followed the older man over to his easel and picked up a brush. "Do you really think she'll like it?" He splashed more paint on the canvas, choosing a bright, vivid red for droplets that ran over the entire painting.

Don Giovanni frowned and studied the work from various angles. "The picture was very authentic until you did that. What is the reasoning behind the red?"

Oh no. Byron groaned and covered his face. *Do you mind very much if I strangle the kid and stuff him in the laundry chute?*

Antonietta did her best not to laugh. Practicing to maintain invisibility and then giving the entire thing away by laughing wouldn't earn her too many points. *You said the key was not reacting to anything.*

That was the rule before Josef came into the world. Now it's kill or be killed, the way of the jungle.

"It's blood, of course. See up here, looming over the palazzo, the eyes of a predator? That's the vampire cloaked in darkness. He's made his kill up on the battlements."

Don Giovanni struggled to keep his face blank. "Very imaginative. I have seen few villas with vampires on the battlements."

Josef shrugged his shoulders. "The hunters do a fairly good job of keeping the numbers down. I would make a great hunter, but my mother won't hear of it." For a moment he stared deliberately at Don Giovanni, his eyes glowing red, his face contorting into a mask of evil.

Don Giovanni took a step back, blinked to bring Josef back in focus, and saw only a grinning, boyish face.

Byron waved his hand to veil Don Giovanni's mind, holding him still within a thrall. Positioning himself in front of his nephew, he shifted the shape of his head.

Don't do it. Antonietta cautioned, pressing a hand to her mouth to keep from laughing. *It's so undignified to stoop to his level.*

Josef reached up with his paintbrush to add a finishing touch to one of the droplets. The muzzle of a wolf came at his face, bared teeth, dripping with saliva, snapped, eyes red and wicked, glowing in the dusk. Josef stumbled backward, stabbing at the wolf's head with his paintbrush as he did so, tripped over his own feet, and fell to the lawn screaming, crab-walking backward.

In the blink of an eye, Byron disappeared, and Don Giovanni was staring down at Josef with a strange expression. "You need to get off the drugs boy, no good comes of using that stuff. You have a good family. You don't want to bring them sorrow."

Josef looked around himself cautiously. "Has my family been here? My father or my uncle?" He dusted off his clothes meticulously.

"Not yet, but they'll probably come soon. You should think about what I said, Josef. Take it from an old man who has lived a long time. Drugs tear apart families."

"Yes, sir." Josef said politely, "you're absolutely right."

Byron and Antonietta strolled out of the maze, hand in hand. "Good evening, Don Giovanni, Josef." Byron's white teeth flashed. "How is Paul this evening?"

"He woke only a short time ago. He slept all day and is still refusing to have us call a doctor. He said he would wait for you and Antonietta. He looked pale to me, but he isn't running a temperature, thank the good *Dio.*" Don Giovanni took Antonietta's hand and drew her to him. "You look lovely, my dear. Byron is good for you."

"I would like to speak to you about my feelings for Antonietta," Byron said. "Would you mind walking with us?"

The older Scarletti lifted a hand toward Josef even as he retained possession of Antonietta. "You're thinking of stealing my granddaughter from me."

"Never that, old friend. She would be far too unhappy away from you. I can do my work here as well as in my homeland. Short trips away only. I would like your permission to marry her. More than anything, we would want your blessing."

Don Giovanni tucked Antonietta's hand into the crook of his elbow. "This is what you want? You're certain?"

"Absolutely, Nonno. We're good together. I trust him completely, and I'm very much in love with him."

"Where would you live?"

"I've asked Byron to live here at the palazzo, and he agreed."

"We can maintain more than one residence. I will have to make trips to my homeland, but the palazzo can be our main residence. I would prefer and would insist on a ground-floor suite of rooms. And we hope to marry as soon as it can be arranged."

"The lawyers will demand a standard prenuptial agreement, stating everything belongs to Antonietta."

"I expected no less. I will not ask one of Antoinetta in return. What is mine, I share with her. We have no need of her money, but she will want it for the children." In his mind Antonietta gasped. Byron grinned boyishly. "Should there be any."

"I had hoped you two would fall in love." Don Giovanni hugged Byron, kissed him on either cheek. "I will arrange it. I'm grateful you aren't taking her away from me. I hope to live out my years with her close."

"I'll always be close," Antonietta assured him.

"That dog of yours has been pacing for the last couple of hours. He was fine with Vincente and Margurite, keeping them company, and then just about sunset he seemed agitated. Even Marita seems to like that dog. She didn't say a single word when the dog showed up in their rooms and stayed close to the children."

"Is Marita home, Nonno?"

"Yes. She seems different. Sad. She went to the small chapel right after dinner was served and remains there. I haven't heard her speak a single word all day. The police captain has been here asking more questions. Alfredo took to his bed, and that young man in the kitchen had to try his hand at cooking. What's his name? He prepared a very passable meal, although with Paul so ill, no one felt like eating."

"Esteben. He's related to Helena. She's always good in a crisis, so he must get it from her. I'll have to thank her for recommending him."

"The house is filled with flowers from Christopher. He's been calling for hours and begging to come over to speak with Tasha. I hope she has better sense than to take him back. She threw the first six bouquets away, but after that she gave up getting rid of them. The palazzo smells like a garden."

"At least the man has good taste in flowers," Antonietta said. "I need to speak to Marita. Would you mind telling Tasha I'll be in a little later?"

"Tasha will want to hear your news right away. She's been anxious about you. Between her and that dog, I haven't had a moments' peace."

Antonietta kissed Don Giovanni's cheek. "I'll be right in, I promise."

18

Shadows filled the chapel. The only light came from the flickering candles in a small alcove. The dancing light washed over the sculpted face of the Madonna recessed into the wall above the rows of candles. Marita was seated in a pew in front of the life-sized sculpture, weeping softly, a rosary wrapped around her hands. Tears poured down her face. Byron thought she looked haunted.

Byron and Antonietta slipped into the pew beside her. She kept her head down. "I knew you would come today. I knew you would have to come." Her voice was very low. "I was going to leave this morning, but I knew I owed you an explanation."

"Marita, this is your home. No one has asked you to leave." Antonietta searched carefully to find the right words. "We're family. Whatever is wrong, tell us and let us help you fix it."

"It can never be fixed. *Never*. I can't undo what happened, and no matter what, Franco will never forgive me."

Antonietta reached for Marita's hand. In the dark of the chapel, through the dark glasses Byron had given her, she could see the tear-ravaged face of her sister-in-law. Lights burst around her and made her stomach lurch, but she concentrated on Marita, willing herself to get past the dizzy shapes coming at her and see only her cousin's wife. "Let me help you, Marita. I'm asking you, one sister to another. I love Franco and the children. They need you. Going away isn't your answer, and I think you know that."

"Margurite is not Franco's child." The confession burst from Marita, horror she could no longer contain. She erupted into another storm of weeping, burying her face in her hands, sobbing as if her heart were breaking.

Antonietta tried not to show her shock. It was the last thing she expected from Marita. "That can't be. It's not possible."

"Years ago at a party at the Demonesini palazzo, Don Demonesini raped me. I was thrilled to be invited." Marita shook her head. "I don't know how it happened. I don't remember much at all. Don Demonesini paid me so much attention. He gave me drinks. I wasn't drinking alcohol, so I don't even have that excuse. I remember him taking me to a room. I tried to say no, I tried to push him away, but I couldn't stop him. I couldn't move. He did horrible things to me. There was someone in the room with us, someone taking pictures. It was a nightmare that will never go away."

"Why didn't you tell us?" Rage swept through Antonietta, a violent swirl of emotions. She couldn't tell if it was her feelings or Byron's, but a demon lifted its head and roared for release. For retribution.

"How could I tell anyone? I was so ashamed. My head hurt for days afterward, and I was sick to my stomach. And a month later I was late with my period. I didn't make love to Franco for a couple of weeks after the party, I couldn't bear him to touch me. I felt filthy. How could Margurite be his? He loves her so much. He was so happy when I was pregnant with her. I couldn't tell him. I couldn't break his heart."

"Marita, it wasn't your fault," Antonietta said. "There are tests to determine paternity."

"No! I won't do that to her. Margurite loves Franco, and Don Demonesini is a monster. I will never, never let her know she is his."

"I do not think she is Demonesini's child," Byron said.

Margurite's thought patterns are the same as yours and that of your cousins. Christopher's barriers were a bit different as are some of your servants. Helena's thought patterns are closer than Christopher's. I do not think it is possible Margurite is a Demonesini.

"Does Demonesini know you suspect Margurite is his child?" Antonietta asked.

"He's mentioned her age numerous times and says she has Christopher's eyes. I lied and said I went to a doctor and made certain there was no baby, but I didn't. I didn't." She pressed a trembling hand to her mouth. "He had the pictures of me. He threatened to sell them to a tabloid. It would ruin Franco. You know it would. And the children would see—"

"So he told you to talk Franco into giving him the information he wanted to underbid us on the contract with the Drange Company five years ago," Antonietta guessed.

"Franco would *never* have given them the information. Never, ever in a million years. He lied to protect me. I went to his office and I found the papers Demonesini told me would be there, I copied them and took them to him." She slumped back in the pew. "He knew, when it all came out, Franco knew I had to have done it. He lied to the family, and I let him. I let you all think he was a traitor to his own family. You should have seen his face when he found out, the way he looked at me." She covered her face with her hands again. "I broke his heart."

Antonietta shook her head. "What reason did you give Franco for doing such a thing?"

"I was hysterical when he confronted me. I was certain he would find out about the rape, and Demonesini would sell the photographs. I think he was afraid he would have to put me in a hospital. Franco just stopped questioning me and told me not to say anything no matter what happened."

"And the Handel score?"

"I thought if I could give Demonesini something worth a lot of money, he would give me the pictures."

"Did you take anything else from the palazzo to give him, Marita?" Antonietta's tone was very gentle, but Byron could hear the compulsion already buried deep within her voice.

Marita shook her head. "No, I don't know why I thought of the Handel score. I heard you working on it with Justine, and the idea suddenly came to me. I just waited until I had the opportunity to visit Don Giovanni and I asked him to put my necklace in his safe. He opened the safe with me standing right there. Trusting me." She pressed her hand to her temple. "I'm glad you caught me. I'm glad you found out the truth. When I leave, you can tell Franco about the pictures. Don't tell him about Margurite. It would break both their hearts, and if Don Demonesini insisted on his rights, poor little Margurite would be in his hands."

She is telling the truth. She is not part of a theft ring, she knows nothing about it.

"Demonesini will never get near Margurite. You have to tell Franco about the photographs. You're a strong woman, Marita. You're a Scarletti, and we don't back away from trouble or even scandal. If he wants to incriminate himself by selling those pictures to a tabloid, let him try. Franco will see him not only ruined but jailed. You don't know Franco if you think he will let Demonesini get away with this. Trust him. Tell what happened. Tell him everything. Let him decide if he wants or needs a paternity test. Once you tell Franco, Demonesini has lost his hold on you."

"I'm so afraid," Marita said.

"If you tell him, there's a chance he will accept everything and work with you to find a way out of this mess. If you sneak away and leave him and the children, all of you will be miserable, and you'll never know what his reaction really would have been."

Marita squeezed Antonietta's hand in gratitude. *"Grazie,* Antonietta, for making me feel like I'm truly family."

Antonietta hugged her hard. "You *are* family, Marita. Go make peace with Franco so you can dance at my wedding."

Marita cried out. "You are really getting married? Nonno has given his blessing?"

"Yes, he's happy for us. We're going to tell Tasha and Paul."

"Paul's not well, Antonietta, but he still refuses a doctor. He's been sleeping most of the day, so much so Justine was alarmed, but he woke around sunset."

Antonietta stood up. "Go to Franco, Marita. Go somewhere quiet and pull the teeth from Demonesini. If Franco becomes enraged, and he will, it will be at that horrible monster, not at you."

"The pictures are graphic."

"Have courage."

Marita nodded and slipped away. Antonietta sat for a long moment in silence. The flickering candles set bizarre shapes dancing in front of her eyes. "How sad that she didn't tell her husband immediately." She leaned her head against Byron's shoulder. "Why is it I keep getting glimpses of Don Demonesini lying dead on the floor and you standing over him with sharp teeth and demonic eyes? Surely you aren't thinking of harming him in any way."

"You are not?"

"Not quite in the same way. You seem a bit violent and earthy. I prefer sophistication. Taking apart his empire and exposing him for the monster he is."

"That still leaves him to prey on other women. He drugged her. You know that. He drugged her, raped her, and blackmailed her."

She heard the bite to his voice. This time she knew the demon roaring for release was in him. She felt the slow unfurling of claws, the lengthening of fangs, the snarl of rage at a monster of a man who could torment a woman in an attempt to ruin her family life. *Byron. You can be a very scary man.*

Never to you, cara. He leaned down and kissed her on her mouth before taking her inside the palazzo.

Celt greeted Antonietta in his dignified but obviously affectionate manner, falling in at her side to guide her up the stairs to Paul's room.

Tasha turned quickly from her vigil by the bed and threw herself into her cousin's arms with a glad little cry. "I was so worried about you, Toni. No one was with you. You were gone so long."

"I was with her, Tasha," Byron said quietly. "I can make you a sincere promise that nothing will ever harm her when she is with me."

"He took wonderful care of me, Tasha. How is Paul?" Antonietta kissed Tasha's cheek and hurried quickly to Paul's side. She had to keep her eyes tightly closed or she became disoriented and suffered vertigo. If she were still, she could use her eyes if she remained cautious and concentrated. *I hope your friend is right about my eyes. It is difficult to remember to keep them closed. Even with the dark glasses, I still see objects that aren't there.*

We will find a way to fix this problem, Antonietta. I know it is disorienting for you and nearly impossible to keep your eyes closed.

"Paul slept all day. He just woke a couple of hours ago." Tasha stroked back her brother's hair. "Justine and I have been taking shifts. We kept up on the fluids."

Paul is pale and weak, but he will live. We need to reduce his pain.

"That's good, Tasha." Antonietta laid her palm on Paul's brow. "I saw Christopher in the maze earlier."

Tasha sighed. "He pounded on the door. I was afraid he would break it down. I couldn't get him to go away, but then Franco came with Nonno, and they told him to leave. I'm not altogether certain he would have, but Diego arrived, and Christopher left."

"Not exactly," Antonietta said. "Diego had a short talk with him out in the maze. Christopher threatened to ruin his career and said a woman like you would never stoop to looking at a man like Diego."

Tasha pressed her hand against her mouth. "No. How could he say that?" Her voice was strangled. "Christopher is very vindictive. He might really do something to ruin Diego's career. Why? We've only talked a few times. It's not like I've slept with Diego. He's a very nice man with children to think of. I wouldn't involve him in a scandal, and Christopher would make it one."

"Diego didn't seem very afraid. Or maybe your protection mattered more than his career, because he grabbed Christopher by the throat and told him to leave you alone."

"He didn't?" Tasha looked to Byron for confirmation. "He grabbed him by the throat? For me?"

"He was very angry with Christopher for striking you." Byron shrugged. "If Diego had not made it very clear to Christopher that he was not wanted here, Franco or I would have." When Paul stirred, he placed a restraining hand on the man's shoulder. "Or Paul when he recovered. The nice part about having family who loves you, is they protect you when it matters."

"Byron asked me to marry him, and I said yes," Antonietta announced as she seated herself on the bed beside Paul. She tried to sound casual and matter-of-fact, but there was a tremor in her voice.

Celt pressed close to her, put his head in her lap to show camaraderie. Byron laid his hand gently on Antonietta's shoulder, his dark gaze on Tasha, willing her to say whatever Antonietta needed from her.

There was a short silence, a stilling of the air as if everyone held their breath. "What did Nonno say?" Tasha asked.

"He gave us his blessing," Antonietta said, rubbing Paul's arm. "How are you feeling, Paul? You're drinking plenty of fluids, aren't you? Do you need me to take away the pain?"

"Grazie, Toni, I was hoping you'd offer. Congratulations, Byron. There's no one in the world like our Toni. You'd better take good care of her."

"You do not have to worry, Paul. She will always be my first priority."

Antonietta waited for Tasha to say more. When her cousin remained silent, Antonietta turned her attention to directing healing energy to Paul. She could feel the steady flow Byron fed her, but he stayed in the background, allowing the actual healing to come through her.

When it was obvious Paul was more comfortable, not moving restlessly, Antonietta handed him a glass of water. "Drink this. Did you talk to Justine about your absurd suspicions? Because she is not part of a conspiracy to steal. She isn't, Paul. I can't tell you exactly how I know, but I do."

"Then who is selling our things? I saw the painting. The one my mother loved so much. It was moved down to the temperature-controlled room with the filtered air to preserve it until we could remodel the art room." He eased his body into another position. "I loved that painting. There's no mistake, and I'm going to get it back." There was determination in his voice.

"Then I'll ask Justine to take an inventory to see what else is missing."

I thought you were going to fire her.

Paul's in love with her. He was willing to die to keep her out of jail. I can't very well fire her. If he feels that strongly about her, hopefully she feels the same way about him and thought she was saving his life.

You are far too softhearted. I cannot imagine what our children will be like. Josef is thoughtless because he has been spoiled. Can you imagine ten Josefs running around the palazzo barefoot and clinging to the sides of the walls and making the gargoyles come alive? Singing rap music? What have you gotten me into?

I can't imagine ten of anything, let alone ten little Josefs. And they will sing opera. How did I become responsible?

You walked onto the stage looking so beautiful and courageous, you stole my heart.

Antonietta burst out laughing. There was a sudden silence in the room. "I'm sorry, I know we're discussing a serious subject. I just . . ." She trailed off, mentally kicking Byron in the shin.

The strange phenomenon of objects rushing at her face had lessened enough that if she held her head very still, she could see through the heavy black lenses. Tired of closing her eyes and anxious to see her family members, she stared toward where she knew Paul's face would be and lifted her lashes.

"Someone in this house is stealing," Paul reiterated. "The police know it, Interpol knows it, and no one but a family member would know the way through the passageway. Who else but Justine?"

Antonietta's heart gave a funny jump when Paul's face stopped moving. The blurred image cleared, and she was staring at her cousin. "Paul." She breathed his name softly. Reached out to brush at the hair spilling across his forehead. There was a curious burning sensation behind her eyes. *He looks just like I remember my father looking. Tell me where Tasha is. She's so quiet I can't tell exactly.*

Byron shifted closer to wrap his arm around her shoulders. "We do not know who could be doing this, Paul, but we believe you. If it is someone living in this house, it should not be that difficult to find out who it is." *Tasha is standing to your left.* He gave Antonietta the mental image of height to her face.

Her heart pounding, Antonietta closed her eyes and turned her head carefully to stare up at Tasha. She pressed back against Byron for comfort and opened her eyes. For a moment Tasha swam in front of her, distorted and out of focus. Antonietta persisted, forcing her brain to connect with her eyes. Tasha stared back at her. Antonietta couldn't prevent the small cry of joy.

Tasha's eyes widened in shock. "You can see me. *Dio,* Toni. You can see me. That's not possible. How can you see me?"

Antonietta burst into tears. Tasha immediately began weeping with her. Byron looked at Paul helplessly.

"Is it true?" Paul asked as his sister and cousin clung to one another. "It was you, wasn't it, Byron? You are like she is, you have the gift."

"She has to be careful of light and movement, but we are hoping it will improve for her. Most of the time she keeps her eyes closed or she feels sick," Byron explained.

"Have you told Nonno?" Paul asked the inevitable question.

Before Byron could answer, Tasha flung her arms around him. "I don't care if you scare me to death. *Grazie* for this. You can't imagine how much I'd hoped we could find a way to restore Toni's sight. Our money seemed so useless at times. She's always been so patient, but there were so many times she wanted a particular book and she couldn't get it right away. . . . So many things. Just *grazie,* Byron."

He could feel the genuine love and gratitude pouring out of Tasha, and it made him feel humble. Antonietta's family relationships were very complex, not at all black and white like his world seemed to be for so long. He thought in terms of enemy or ally. They were far more than that. There was so much joy radiating from Tasha and Paul at the knowledge that Antonietta might be able to see, that Byron wondered how he could have ever suspected either of them of conspiring to kill her, yet he felt he had to be certain. He couldn't afford to take a chance with Antonietta's life.

Tasha and Antonietta began to laugh together, sitting on Paul's bed, holding hands. "I think they're hysterical," Paul commented.

Byron waved his hand to still the room.

"I think you are right." Byron glanced at Antonietta. *Forgive me,* cara mia, *I feel I have no choice but to be certain.*

I am certain. Her protest was instant and adamant.

Byron ignored her and leaned down to stare into Paul's eyes. He did the same to Tasha. Antonietta pulled out of his mind, her anger nearly tangible. "Neither is involved in the thefts or the poisonings, and if they can shape-shift, they are not aware of it. I do not like the way Tasha feels to me. I want to examine her. Merge with me."

They found traces of poison in Tasha's cells. Antonietta was outraged. "Who could be doing this? Christopher? He was often at dinner with us. He could have slipped something into Nonno's drink or food. I can't see, so it's possible he could have with any of us, and I wouldn't have known. Get rid of it, Byron. I know you did for me, so get it out of her. Hurry. It makes me sick to think she has that in her."

"Paul did not eat anything today. We need to check the others. Even the children. Someone is introducing poison into food or drink." Byron closed his eyes and sent himself seeking outside his body and into Tasha's. Antonietta merged with him, watching how he separated body from spirit, became a bright ball of pure energy, and meticulously went through Tasha's body, examining every cell, muscle, and tissue.

He showed her what to look for, how to maintain outside his own body while he worked, and the intense concentration it took. He seemed much weaker when he was through pushing the poison from Tasha's body, staggering a little as he reentered his own body.

"What's wrong with you?" Antonietta asked, alarmed.

"I have not fed this night, and we have used a tremendous amount of energy." He added a command to her cousins to forget his invasion into their thoughts. *Your family has tremendous barriers. It requires a powerful command to keep them from knowing we have intruded. If you have no choice but to read them, remember to remove the memory.*

I told you they weren't involved. His weariness was beating at her. She couldn't help herself. She laid her hand on his arm. *Go find whatever you need to be strong again. Or use me.*

He laughed softly and leaned down to kiss her on her upturned mouth. *Thank you for the invitation, but I cannot touch you in front of your family. I would want to retire to your bedroom.*

It was his voice, a velvet-soft symphony of seduction, that teased the color into her face. Before she could respond, Tasha hugged Antonietta again, completely unaware of the interruption. "Are there things you can do to help you see better? Glasses? Maybe an operation? The laser techniques are supposed to work miracles."

"I've had my miracle," Antonietta said. "Byron, you have that one thing to take care of. If you want to do that now, I'll sit up here and visit with Paul."

My tyrant lifemate. He was secretly pleased that she was worried enough to be insistent he feed.

Antonietta tried to watch him leave, but the room spun, and the strangely shaped objects flew at her eyes. She closed them tightly. "Movement makes it more difficult. I have to look at something stationary to really see it. We think that will change with time and a little practice."

"Antonietta." Paul reached for his cousin. She responded immediately by threading her fingers through his. "Please make peace with Justine. I know you're hurt by what she did, but I told her they were going to kill me. I laid it on pretty thick. She begged me to go to you. She begged me to lay low until she could get the money together herself. We had a terrible fight about it. I felt like such a lowlife, but I was certain she was involved in the theft ring."

"Have you told her what you thought? Does she know you nearly died coming here and not going to a hospital? I couldn't have saved your life, Paul. Byron was the one who worked on you and managed to keep you alive."

"I feel different. And it's strange, Toni, but I swear there was a noise this morning, this weird whirring sound. Justine tracked it all over the bedroom. It turned out to be a bug, and the noise was its wings. I just feel more alive, even though I hurt like hell most of the time." He rubbed his shadowed jaw. "Justine is going to marry me. She was pretty angry with me, especially that I would think she would sell out our family, but I convinced her. It helped that I look pathetic right now."

Antonietta sighed. "She really hurt me, Paul. I trusted her, and I depended on that trust for my confidence. She took that away from me."

"I took it away. You know how I am. Tasha, talk to her, she always listens to you. This is important."

Antonietta felt Tasha's sudden stillness. "You do, Toni. You do listen to me. I always matter to you."

"Silly. Of course. I love you. Your opinion has always mattered to me. You know how I think and feel. You know what's important to me. What would you do? I love Justine, but I don't know if I can forgive what she did."

Tasha laughed softly. "Toni, don't be an idiot. You forgive *everybody, everything*. That's just how you are. You couldn't carry a grudge if your life depended on it. Not with family. Whether you like it or not, Justine falls under the family umbrella, so no matter what, you're going to forgive her. You're hurt, not angry. There speaks undoubtedly the voice of true wisdom." Tasha sounded self-mocking.

"Great, Tasha, you're not entering in the spirit of the thing. I wanted to wallow in self-pity, and you're not letting me."

"It isn't your style."

"I'm going to ask you both a crazy question. Do either of you ever feel strange, like there's a beast inside of you, trying to get out?"

"Like a cat," Paul said. He rubbed his arm. "Sometimes I itch, and I feel an incredible power."

"And all your senses come alive," Antonietta added.

"I don't feel that way," Tasha said, "but I can speak to Paul telepathically. We've done it ever since we were children. I can't with anyone else but him."

"You never told me."

"Only because I didn't want you to feel left out." Tasha sighed softly. "Do you really love Byron, Toni?" There was a catch in her voice.

"More than I ever thought possible. I can't imagine my life without him."

"Where does he want to live? What does he do? Do you know anything at all about him?"

"He works with gems. He has his own money. We will have to take trips to his homeland, but we'll reside here at the palazzo. He can make his jewelry here. He'll travel with me when I tour."

"How did you know for certain? Aren't you afraid?" Tasha looked down at her hands. "I always marry the wrong man."

"You marry for the wrong reasons," Antonietta replied softly. "You know going into the marriage it's wrong for you."

"I really like Diego. I really do, Toni. He makes me laugh, and I feel good about myself. He talks to me like I have a brain. We've spent quite a bit of time together, just talking. I'd like to meet his children. But what if I can't be married to a man like him?"

"You mean a man who isn't wealthy?"

Tasha waved her hand exasperated. "It isn't the money. I'll have plenty of money in time. I can borrow money from you if I don't have it. He would expect me to be a wife and mother. Full-time. I've never done anything full-time."

Antonietta laughed. "Tasha, you don't have to be anything but yourself. You spend most of the day with Margurite and Vincente. You watch Nonno like a hawk, even when it makes him crazy. I hear you pushing chairs in when I'm walking because someone else was careless and left them out."

"I *detest* giving orders to the servants."

"I doubt if Diego has servants."

"I *have* to have servants, Toni. Certainly he wouldn't expect me to do the laundry." She shuddered. "The thought of touching dirty, smelly clothes is awful. But I did love cooking. I took that gourmet course, and I was really good. Cooking was fun. Sometimes Enrico let me cook in the kitchen, but I know Alfredo would never let me."

"For heaven's sake, Tasha," Paul burst out. "Afredo doesn't own the kitchen, we do. If you want to cook, tell him to get out and leave you to it."

Justine knocked on the door politely as she entered. "Paul, you're looking so much better."

"Byron and Toni worked their magic on me." Paul held out his hand to her. "Come and join us. I told Tasha and Toni I badgered you until you agreed to marry me. Toni has *big* news. Even bigger than ours." He didn't wait to see if Antonietta would relate the information. "Byron was able to heal her eyes enough that she can see."

"That's impossible. Toni saw every specialist possible, and

they all said it couldn't be done." She turned to her employer. "How could he have healed your eyes?"

"He has the gift. It isn't perfect, Justine. My brain doesn't have the connections it needs between sight and objects. I try to keep my eyes closed most of the time and rely on my other senses. It's much easier. If I have my eyes open, and whatever I'm looking at moves, I feel very sick. Sometimes I see strange shapes and objects, like I'm connecting with the wrong image. It's weird."

"But exciting," Justine said. "Toni, I know you're very angry with me. I know I deserve it, but I don't want to lose our friendship. This is my family. I love you very much. It was wrong of me. I can't change what I did, as much as I'd like to, but I'd like to find a way to show you how sorry I really am."

"I'm hurt, Justine, not angry. I'm trying to understand."

"I'm going to stand up for Toni on her wedding day," Tasha announced, "so there's no need to get all buddy-buddy, you two. And Marita can forget it, too."

"Well, of course you'll stand up for me, Tasha, but there's room for Marita and Justine, too."

"You're really limiting your colors, Toni," Tasha warned. "Marita looks awful in pastels, and Justine is so pale—"

"Tasha." Paul reprimanded.

Celt suddenly lifted his head from Antonietta's lap. His entire body tensed alertly. Antonietta moved uncomfortably, her skin itching, her stomach doing a strange flip. Dark dread gathered in the pit of her stomach. A shadow seemed to pass through the room. It was more in her mind than in reality. An ominous warning.

"Toni," Tasha rubbed her arms as if suddenly cold. "What's wrong?"

"I don't know. Do you feel something odd?"

Paul slumped back against the pillows, his hand in Justine's, his eyes closed. Justine shook her head for both of them. "Everything seems fine to us, Toni."

"The dog is acting funny," Tasha reported. "He looks dangerous."

"Stay with Paul," Antonietta said. "I want to check on Nonno. Celt can go with me. He's a good guide."

"Do you really think something's wrong? I can call Diego," Tasha offered.

Antonietta didn't answer. She didn't bother to try to use her eyes. She needed speed, and it was so much easier to rely on Celt. He paced at her side, his body maneuvering her around every obstacle in the hall and down the stairs. *Byron.* She connected instantly with him. *How far away are you?* She sent the impression of the dark shadow. Of impending danger. Of dread.

Stay inside the palazzo. I will come to you immediately, and Eleanor and Vlad are on their way. I have tried to touch Josef, but he is not responding or is incapable of it. Vlad says the same.

He was with Nonno in the courtyard.

Stay inside, Antonietta.

"As if I would," she muttered rebelliously. "Franco!" She raised her voice, something she seldom did, hating to interrupt what she knew was an important talk, but needing him. "Helena! Come out to the courtyard and help me find Nonno." She leaned down toward the dog. "Celt, I'm counting on you. We don't want anything to happen to Nonno or young Josef. She pushed open the French doors leading to the terrace that opened into the courtyard.

Celt didn't growl, but a nearly inaudible sound rumbled in his throat. His body seemed to vibrate with tension.

Antonietta inhaled deeply and caught a pungent odor. Something wild. Something deadly. She hung on to Celt. "Find Nonno, Celt. Show me where he is."

"What is it, Signorina Scarletti?" Helena asked, coming up behind her.

"Have you seen my grandfather?"

"Don Giovanni was out in the garden as he is most evenings. That young man, Josef, was with him. They must have walked into the maze."

"Please tell Franco to follow me. I'm going to look for Nonno."

"Yes, of course, I'll tell him immediately. Do you need me to help you?"

"If you would get Franco and tell him to be careful," Antonietta said, "that would be wonderful." She didn't want Helena exposed to any danger. Cautiously she stepped down the terrace stairs into the courtyard. "Find him, Celt, find Nonno."

The dog fairly shook with the effort to contain his need to hunt. He started off toward the maze, but just feet away from one of the entrances, he stopped and swung back toward the palazzo.

Antonietta released her hold on the dog and opened her eyes very slowly. It was dark enough and with the glasses, the terrible lurching and flashing lights didn't intrude. She looked up toward the battlement, trying to focus on one of the gargoyles, just to get her bearings. It took a few moments for the image of the sculpture to clear. She saw the wings spread wide as if about to launch into the air, teeth bared, eyes wide open and staring. Her breath caught in her throat when she saw the body of young Josef lying motionless, his beret hanging off the gargoyles' wing tip. Crouched over him was a large spotted cat. The cat turned its head and looked down at her, malice in its eyes.

19

Byron. Quickly, I need the image of an owl. Hold it for me. Antonietta waited a heartbeat, an eternity, and then the image was there for her. Thankfully, Byron didn't make the mistake of asking questions or chastising her. He caught the terrible sense of urgency and provided the data she needed. Her skin prickled, her body compressed. She closed her eyes tightly as she shifted into the shape of the night predator.

It was much more difficult to launch from the ground, but she managed. As she leapt, a great gust of wind swept under her to aid her in rising. She flew straight up to avoid having to open her eyes until the last possible moment.

Link with me. The command was impossible to ignore. There was a mixture of fear and anger tinged with respect, but Byron's tone held a compulsion Antonietta had to obey. She felt him take her mind completely, force her eyes open. She waited for the strange, disorienting sickness, but it didn't come. She realized he was using her eyes and making the connections himself. He understood what he was seeing, and he instantly translated.

Fog rolled in, unexpectedly, from the sea. It was so thick, wisps seemed to hang in the sky like a barrier. The owl flew silently, stealthily, using the fog as cover. It took only seconds to make its way over the battlements and drop like a stone at the cat as it bent its head to Josef's exposed throat.

Antonietta was startled when she heard a far-off scream of anguish followed by the echo of a male voice crying out his promise of retribution. Razor-sharp talons ripped at the eyes of the jaguar, slashing and digging, driving the cat backward away from its prey. The wind howled, nearly drowning out the snarl of the beast. It spat and swiped with its paws, then whirled and ran, leaping easily over a multitude of gargoyles to race along the banister toward the far side of the tower.

The owl settled down close to Josef, shifting back into human form. Antonietta bent over the young man. There was a terrible gaping wound on his throat. He had bled profusely. She couldn't get a pulse. *Byron. Is he dead?*

Black threads swirled and spun overhead. Lightning raced across the sky. Thunder boomed, shaking the palazzo. Dark cauldrons of clouds boiled and seethed, spitting out rage and anger and a terrible grief that was hardly to be borne.

Antonietta fought past the weight and intensity of the storm of emotion raging in the heavens. Her hands covered the wounds as she attempted to assess the damage done to his body.

Josef shut down his heart and lungs when the blow was struck. Byron hoped he was telling her the truth. Josef was young for his people. Shutting down completely after suffering a mortal wound was not an easy task.

Eleanor and I have him now. His life force is weak. Holding him to earth will slow us down. Byron heard Vlad's voice, filled with fear and determination. *I cannot help you track the cat and hold our son to us.*

I will get the cat, Vlad, just keep him alive.

Where is the jaguar now? Antonietta sought for a way to close the wound. *Nonno is in the courtyard, and Franco is coming to look for him. Hurry Byron. The cat came here with the intention to kill.*

Byron burst out of the darkness, a creature of power, hurtling past Antonietta to follow the cat. She felt the brush of his hand on her face. *You know what to do.* His voice was very soft. Filled with complete faith.

She had to take the boy to the ground below. She needed the soil and her own saliva. Byron didn't tell her, but somehow she gleaned the knowledge from his mind. She was up on the battlements. *Do you see Celt or Nonno? Or even Franco?* Franco could carry Josef down to the garden.

Byron flew out toward the cove. The cat would go for the water to cover its scent. *I do not see any of them.* He reached for the dog, a connection he had established weeks earlier. For a brief moment, Byron caught glimpses of shrubbery, a bench, Don Giovanni sitting on a bench, trapped and unable to leave, with Celt pacing around him. Byron sent the reassuring image to Antonietta and dropped down closer to earth under cover of the fog.

The danger hadn't passed. Antonietta wanted to rush to Byron, make certain that he was safe. Her skin was crawling with the need for change. Inside the pit of her stomach, darkness spread, every bit as black as the clouds spinning over her head. She sighed Byron's name, wanting to warn him of the danger, afraid she would distract him at the wrong moment.

Antonietta caught the whisper of cloth brushing against one of the sculptures. She turned her head toward the sound and inhaled. "Helena. Thank the good *Dio*. Please find Franco at once. We need to get this poor boy some help. He was attacked by a wild cat. The same one that made a kill the other night."

"Are you certain it's the same one, Signorina Scarletti?"

Antonietta opened her eyes cautiously, trying to focus on her housekeeper. The woman continued to move toward her. Antonietta couldn't tell how close she was. The body was distorted, rippling in a sickening way. Spots leapt at her eyes, flying at her face. Colors shimmered. Reds, yellows. A dark blue. She dug her fingernails into her palm for an anchor and kept her eyes trained on Helena, willing herself to see. "I doubt there are two cats, Helena. Please get Franco. We need to save this boy's life."

Helena just kept coming. Faster now, her face lengthening until she appeared to have a muzzle, her body contorting, bending, until she was on all fours.

Antonietta waited, timing the cat's leap, throwing herself to one side, using her new abilities to take her over the jaguar and land on the edge of the battlement. The jaguar snarled, shifted into half-human form. Helena bent over Josef, all the while keeping her eyes focused on Antonietta. There was hatred there.

"Why would you do this, Helena?" Antonietta asked, her voice gentle. The wind lashed at them, ruffled the fur on the large cat, and tore strands of Antonietta's hair loose from her braid to whip across her face.

"Signorina Scarletti." Helena spat the words at her. "How I hate that name. Your precious family. It should have been my family. I belonged, but none of you wanted to see it. I was right there under your noses, but you all refused to see."

Antonietta strained for sight. Helena was shifting her weight, rumbling with rage and hatred. One clawed hand reached down to push Josef's body toward the edge of the battlement. Antonietta didn't stop to think; she launched herself, kicking hard, connecting with Helena's startled face. Her momentum carried her beyond her housekeeper. She tucked and rolled, coming back onto her feet facing Helena, shocked at her own agility. She didn't hesitate, leaping back toward Josef, planting another kick squarely in Helena's face, knocking her off the battlement.

Helena twisted in midair, shape-shifting completely, landing on all fours on the rolling lawn. The jaguar lifted its muzzle toward the palazzo and snarled. The cat immediately leapt into a nearby tree, using the branches as a highway, rushing toward the ramparts with deadly purpose.

Antonietta dragged Josef from the edge of the battlement, picking him up, cradling his leaden body to her as if he were a baby. As the jaguar gained the first-floor balcony, Antonietta jumped from the battlement to the ground below, landing in a crouch, in the shadow of the palazzo. She sprinted, under cover of the thick fog, to the garden. She knew how many steps it took, and she counted as she ran, her eyes closed tightly.

"Toni? Are you out here? Where's Nonno?" Tasha called from the terrace overlooking the courtyard. "Can you believe this fog? It was supposed to be clear tonight."

"Tasha, hurry, get over here," Antonietta said softly. Her

voice sounded strange and muffled in the swirling mist. She laid Josef in the garden bed, uncaring that she squashed her grandfather's flowers. There would be only minutes to do what needed to be done. Scooping up handfuls of the rich soil, she mixed her own saliva and packed the wounds carefully.

Tasha came out of the eerie fog, looming over them. "What in the world are you doing, Toni?" She crouched down, saw the thick congealed blood shining black in the mist, and covered her mouth. "Good God, are you crazy? You'll kill him putting dirt in his wounds like that."

"Don't ask questions, just help me. The jaguar did this. It's hunting us now."

Tasha dropped to her knees, scooping up the dirt, glancing around warily. The fog was too thick to see much. "Shouldn't we get him inside?" She kept her tone low.

"His mother and father are coming to help him. I just have to keep the jaguar off of him. Nonno is in the maze with Celt."

It didn't make sense to Tasha, especially with Antonietta's sight problems, but she leaned over Josef protectively. "He's a nice kid, a little young for his age." She shivered in the howling wind.

"It's Helena." Antonietta rose, placing her body between her cousin and the expanse of lawn. "The jaguar is Helena. She can shape-shift."

"That's not possible, Toni." Tasha spoke very distinctly, as if to a child.

"Yes it is. I'll explain later, but I saw her. Why would she hate us so much? She said she belonged, and we didn't see it. I don't understand. How could she be a Scarletti?"

"She was the one. It had to be Helena."

"The one that what?"

"Don't you remember? When we were children? My father carried on with every woman in sight. Helena was so beautiful. Of course he would have chased after her. She must have been the woman who became pregnant. Remember she was gone for months taking care of her father when he was ill. She could have been pregnant then."

"She was friends with our mothers," Antonietta protested. "She was family to us."

"I was never friends with your mothers." Helena limped out of the fog, her face bloody, her nose crooked. Her eyes glowed strangely, much like a cat. She was across the lawn, and the mist clung to her, curling around her legs and body. "We were lovers. He should have married me. We could have had it all. With Antonietta and her parents out of the way, he would have inherited so much. He talked to me about it, but I was the one who did something about it. What did he do to repay me? He refused to get rid of his wife. He despised her, a weak woman, but she clung to him. I had to take care of her, too. He knew I loved him. I had his child inside of me. I would do anything for him, but he wanted me to get rid of it. He called my son a *bastard*."

"That was wrong of him," Antonietta said. "Very wrong of him. He should have been proud of his child." Her hand behind her back, she signaled Tasha to silence.

"He deserved to die. Out with his whores, refusing to marry me, refusing to claim his son, even when I freed him from his miserable marriage. It was so easy with him drinking the way he did. I didn't even feel bad about it." Helena's voice vibrated with a strange, raspy growl.

Lightning ripped across the sky, slammed to earth very close, shaking the ground beneath their feet. The howl of a predatory cat accompanied the sound of thunder. Helena smiled. "My son. Esteben. He is killing Don Giovanni. Soon there will be no one left to inherit but my son."

The cat screamed again. An orange-red fireball broke off from a dancing whip of lightning overhead, streaking to earth, disappearing in the thick fog. The silence was deafening. Antonietta strained to keep Helena in focus. "You sold Scarletti possessions, didn't you?"

"Esteben is a Scarletti. We took what belonged to us. What should have been ours. If he had done as I said, in the kitchen, we would have been rid of most of you, but he wanted accidents. Poison works just as well, and we could have blamed Enrico." She moved slightly, her body contorting.

"Enrico found out, didn't he? That's why you killed him." Antonietta forced her eyes to stay focused on Helena. Her arms were becoming mottled, fur racing over her skin, the spots dancing and leaping at Antonietta.

She took a breath, let it out. *Byron? You killed Esteben, didn't you? Nonno and Celt are safe?*

So are you, my love. Stay away from her.

It's easier for me to fight with my eyes closed and rely on my other senses.

There is no need.

Tasha gasped in alarm. Antonietta didn't dare take her eyes from Helena's body, now half human and half cat. "What is it, Tasha?"

"Aside from the fact that our housekeeper is a demonic murdering psychopath, and is, at this moment turning into some kind of possessed, twisted half-human killer, I would say Byron's sister and brother-in-law appeared out of thin air and startled me."

"Step back, Antonietta," Vlad cautioned. "We need you here, to save our son. Byron will handle the cat. *Grazie,* for protecting Josef."

"Tasha, maybe you should go back inside."

"And miss all the drama? Not a chance. I can spit as well as the next person. I think." Tasha tugged on Antonietta's hand until she knelt beside her. "Tell me what to do to help."

Byron walked out of the fog, a tall, dark figure with flowing hair and power clinging to him. Mist curled around his legs, touched his broad shoulders. The wind whispered to him, carrying a million secrets. In the distance the sea rose up, crested and foamed, crashing and booming in a rhythm as old as time. He seemed part of nature, his features timeless, his eyes old. Antonietta saw him clearly in spite of his moving. He raised his hand to the sky, and lightning forked, jumped from cloud to cloud.

"Antonietta, we need you." Eleanor's voice was a soft hiss of anxiety. "Just as we did with Paul, I will enter and heal. Vlad will hold him to earth. You must chant and provide us with energy. The healing gift is strong in you. Your cousin's voice is a gift also. Teach her the words and have her join with us."

"No one has ever called my voice a gift before." Tasha's gaze was fixed on Byron. He was facing a full-grown jaguar. The animal lowered its head, eyes focused on its prey, the body crouched low in preparation of the attack. It was mesmerizing, so much so that Tasha held her breath.

Byron's lifted hand opened, palm facing the sky. Threads of orange red broke from the sizzling bolts of lightning, spinning tightly into a ball at a twist of his fingers.

"Antonietta?" Don Giovanni stepped from the maze, Celt at his side.

Instantly, the jaguar rushed, not at Byron, but at the head of the Scarletti family. Byron moved so quickly, his body was a mere blur, crossing the distance in the blink of an eye to reappear in front of the don. The orange-red ball of flames whistled through the dark sky, leaving a trail of sparks that lit up the night before burning out. The jaguar leapt at Byron's throat. The fireball intercepted the cat's body in midair, driving through it, leaving a wide, cauterized hole through the middle. The cat dropped lifeless to the ground at Byron's feet.

He barely glanced at it. Don Giovanni appeared so shaken, Byron gathered him close and assisted him to the nearest bench close to where Josef lay so still. "Let me help them with Josef, Don Giovanni, and then I will take you in."

Antonietta and Tasha's voices were soft and melodious, filling the night with the healing chant. Ancient words that sped up the healing process and provided the healer with energy and a soothing atmosphere to work in. Byron joined in the chant, feeding his sister energy. She worked slowly and methodically, making certain to close and begin the healing of every wound from the inside out. Time meant nothing to a healer. She worked until she was certain she had repaired every gash and every tear. When she merged back into her own body, she swayed with weariness. Vlad immediately slipped his arm around her.

Tasha tried to see them through the swirling mist, but the thick fog cloaked their bodies. "We should transport Josef to a hospital." The boy was still not moving. "And Nonno should be inside out of the weather."

Byron glanced up at the sky, noticing for the first time the wind and storm. At once the wild winds calmed, and the roiling clouds began to dissipate. *Antonietta, I must give blood to Josef. Will you take your family into the house?*

Of course. Where is Esteben?

The other cat? He is dead in the maze. He tried to attack your grandfather. Celt has a couple of scratches on him, nothing serious, but we should heal them to prevent infection. He sent her waves of love and warmth. *I want you to notice how restrained I am being. I do not recall that going outside was part of our conversation at any time. Or fighting off jaguars or leaping from buildings.*

If you have the ability, why not use it? Antonietta tried not to feel smug. There were so many other emotions to be feeling. As long as Antonietta could remember, Helena had been a large part of her household. As far back as when her mother was alive. Could Helena have really planted a bomb on her parents' yacht? It didn't seem possible. And what of Tasha's parents? Had she really arranged both of their deaths? Esteben or Helena could easily have poisoned their food or drink. And both had access to any of the cars. She let out her breath and swept a hand through her hair. To her surprise, she was shaking in reaction.

"How are we going to explain any of this to Diego?" Tasha asked fearfully. "He'll think we're crazy talking about our housekeeper and kitchen boy becoming wild animals." She didn't want to think too much about Esteben being a half brother.

I am going to incinerate the bodies and bring a lightning bolt from the sky. The cats, Esteben, and Helena, will all meet with a tragic accident at once.

With today's forensics . . .

Have no fears. I am certain the DNA will show both human and cat if there is anything left to find. A tragic event. The thefts from the palazzo will stop. No more poison will be fed to your family, and I will not have to worry day and night that someone is attempting to harm you. Diego will be given credit for finding out about Estaban and Helena. He will think he has discovered these things through investigation.

Antonietta took Tasha's hand. "Let's get Nonno into the house."

"Will Josef be all right?" Tasha clung to Antonietta as they hurried to Don Giovanni. The wind died down, but it was still cold, the sea thundering and spraying water into the air. They wrapped their arms around their grandfather's waist and walked him away from the body of the jaguar.

"Yes, his family will see to him. Don't worry about him."

Antonietta didn't look back. Her eyes were already burning from overuse. But she knew exactly where Byron was. She had the impression of him gathering his nephew gently in his arms. She felt the tear in Byron's wrist as he opened his own vein. Felt his skin pressed tightly to Josef's mouth as Eleanor and Vlad awakened him with a strong command to feed. She felt the flow of Byron's life force passing into his nephew, replenishing starving, shriveled cells.

Do not forget to feed. I do not want you to come staggering into the house weak and useless.

Soft laughter greeted her. *You are getting to be very good at nagging.*

I'm good at everything. She snapped her fingers. "Celt, come with me, boy. *Grazie,* for watching over Nonno." The borzoi ignored the dead cat now that it no longer presented a threat and fell into step beside Antonietta.

I hope you are good at sitting through an all-night lecture on staying safe. I cannot be in two places at one time.

Why not? You can do just about everything else. Haven't you learned that yet? She conjured up the image of wrapping her arms around him and holding him close to her, sent him waves of warmth and love.

Don Giovanni staggered as they opened the terrace door. Behind them, a bolt of lightning crashed to earth, and black smoke rose, taking the smell of burning flesh into the clouds. Tasha glanced back and winced as she saw the black ring on the lawn where the jaguar had been. Eleanor, Vlad, and Josef were nowhere to be seen.

Tasha and Antonietta helped Don Giovanni to his room. He waved them away. "I'm not on my deathbed. I have no idea what happened tonight, but I'm cold, not hurt."

Antonietta kissed his cheek. "Of course, Nonno, we'll explain everything tomorrow. Sleep tonight."

"It's late for an old man," he conceded.

As Antonietta and Tasha stepped out of Don Giovanni's bedroom, Marita hurried up to them, her face tear-streaked and pale beneath her olive skin. "He's gone after Don Demonesini. I told Franco everything. *Everything.* I thought he might throw me out, but I never once thought he would go crazy and go after the don. Demonesini will kill him. You know he will. Franco is a gentle man. What was he thinking?" She wrung her hands together in agitation. "We have to stop him."

"Franco is a Scarletti, Marita. Demonesini hurt you. Of course Franco would go after him. I should have been prepared for that," Antonietta said.

"He took a gun."

Antonietta's fingers curled in Celt's silky fur. "That's not good."

"Shall I call Diego?" Tasha asked. "Maybe he could stop Franco before he gets into trouble."

"No, don't do that," Antonietta said hastily. "Franco could be arrested and charged just for going over there with the intent to do bodily harm."

"Ask Byron to go," Tasha said. "Franco would listen to him."

"Please, Toni, please ask him. Franco is a businessman, not a gangster. He can't go threatening Don Demonesini." Marita looked down at her hands. "What if something terrible happens? What if Franco gets hurt or is arrested?"

Byron. Franco has gone to confront Don Demonesini. I know I can take apart their business. I can ruin them financially, and I should have told Franco my plans.

It would not have been enough. Demonesini touched Franco's beloved wife. He tormented her for years. Your cousin needs more than stripping his enemy of his money.

Will you go and make certain nothing happens to Franco? I know you're tired and you need to feed, but I have to ask you.

There is no need to ask. The jaguar is dead. Have Tasha call Diego and tell him there were two cats, not one. I will talk to him myself about what happened.

Byron looked up at the clouds. He was weary, and he did need to feed, but more than that, he needed to make Antonietta happy. She had gone through so much and handled it in her usual self-assured, unruffled way. It made him smile each time he thought of the way she had become distressed over a simple dinner when she took jaguar attacks and flying on dragons in stride. He would not allow Demonesini to hurt her family again.

Byron took to the sky, the fastest and most direct method of travel for one of his kind. The fog bank he had so carefully constructed had nearly dissipated, leaving him a clear vision of the city below. The Scarletti estate was enormous, encompassing the area surrounding the palazzo, up to the cliffs and in the other direction, going up into the mountains. The city was some distance away, and the Demonesini villa was built on the edge of the sea, right in the center of the most prominent villas in the city.

The water gleamed like glass, a silver layer over black obsidian. Byron reveled in his ability to see colors. Without conscious thought, he reached out to share his joy with Antonietta. *You gave me this,* cara mia. *I will always remember the bleak days and know what you have done for me.*

Her soft laughter washed over his skin like a caress. *Diego is here. He's searching Helena's room and then will search Esteben's room for evidence of involvement in the theft ring. He's hoping to find names.*

The villa's lights were just below him. Before breaking contact, Byron sent Antonietta kisses, enough to tide her over until his return. The verandah circled around the entire house. Byron shifted into human form and walked around the porch until he found an unlocked door. He entered the villa boldly, striding through the long hallway in the direction of the raised voices.

"I'll bet the little whore told you she was innocent." Don Demonesini laughed, a wicked, ugly sound. "Look at these photos. She begged to pleasure me. Begged for my attention. Nothing could satisfy her." He threw the pictures in Franco's face. "Your Madonna, the mother of your children, with her legs spread for another man. Crawl on home, Scarletti, and be a man for once in your own home. Throw her out in the street where she belongs."

Byron could feel the viciousness in the man. There was a gloating triumph, much like the feeling of a vampire, evil and empty and filled with malevolence. Don Demonesini was a man who hated. The hatred ran deep, was embedded in his heart and soul. He enjoyed power and domination over others. His main purpose seemed to be the misery and ruination of others.

Franco radiated rage. He didn't so much as glance at the pictures strewn around the floor at his feet. "You belong in jail." His tone dripped with contempt. "How many other women have you raped and blackmailed? There must have been more than my wife."

"Your whore you mean," Demonesini goaded.

Byron realized Demonesini's intention. He wanted Franco to lose his temper. There was a weapon hidden beneath the desk, Demonesini's hand gripping it, waiting, hoping to be able to kill a Scarletti. He would claim Franco came at him and he was forced to defend himself. The pictures would be proof to the world, and he would have the added satisfaction of exposing the graphic photographs and further embarrassing the Scarletti family. It was a perfect plan.

Byron stepped into the room, baring his teeth, his dark eyes glowing with the beast struggling for supremacy. "Good evening, Don Demonesini. How good to see you looking so healthy. I feared for your well-being and thought I would drop by to check on you." He didn't wait for Demonesini to respond but looked him straight in the eye, pushing hard past the barrier. The very core of Demonesini was corrupt, evil. He wouldn't respond in the normal way to hypnotic suggestion.

Byron didn't wait. He simply leapt across the desk, catching Demonesini's wrist, preventing him from bringing up the gun. Holding the don still with his enormous strength, he bent his head to the pulse beating strongly in the side of the neck and drank.

Franco gasped. Keeping a wary eye on Byron, he gathered the photographs. He could only stare at the incisors buried in Demonesini's neck.

Byron drank his fill and shoved the man across the room with a casual flick of his hand. "Where are the negatives and all the copies you made of these pictures?" He spoke very low, his voice velvet soft, but it carried such power the walls in the room seemed to expand and contract. "I want you to get them right now and hand them to Franco."

Demonesini slowly picked himself up from the floor, backing away from Byron, his eyes wide with terror but holding the cunning of a cornered animal. Once his gaze shifted to the gun Byron had tossed so carelessly aside. When the don hesitated, Byron shrugged and studied his hand. One by one, his fingernails lengthened into razor-sharp talons. He smiled down at the curved claws before raising his gaze to Demonesini. "I am not going to make the request twice."

The don used a key to unlock a cupboard and pull out a drawer. Byron glimpsed several files in the drawer. Demonesini tugged one folder free of the others.

"Just put them all on the desk, close and lock the cupboard."

Demonesini hesitated. A soft growl spurred him to action. He piled the manila folders on the desk. "These are private files."

Franco flipped one open and swore under his breath. "Photographs of another woman, Byron."

"I suspected as much. Make certain Marita's negatives are there."

Franco thumbed through the folders, distaste evident on his face. "Everything is here, Byron."

"Take them and go, Franco. If you meet Christopher or anyone else in the house, stop and have a pleasant chat with them. If they ask you about the folders, tell them Demonesini gave them to you for a private project. Then walk away and do not look back. When you get home, burn those files without looking at the rest of them. I am certain you will know more than one of those women socially."

"I came here to rid the world of him."

"I know. I am family. Trust me to do what is necessary." Out of the corner of his eye, Byron could see Demonesini edging closer to the gun lying on the floor on the other side of the desk.

"Since you're family, I'm not going to ask you about anything I saw here tonight. And don't bring it up later. In return, I won't tell you about jaguars and how close our family is to them." Franco gathered the stack of files into his arms. His gaze, filled with contempt, flickered to Demonesini. "You deserve whatever you get."

The don made a dive for the gun. Byron closed his fist hard, staring at Demonesini's chest. The man went rigid, his face twisted with pain.

Franco hesitated. "Keep going," Byron said softly, his gaze fixed on the don. "Walk away, Franco."

Don Demonesini clutched his chest, falling to his knees. His color was mottled, his eyes bulging.

Franco left the room, the manila folders safe in his arms.

He didn't look back. Not even when he heard the sound of a body falling to the floor. He hurried through the villa, trying to look as casual as possible, but he was grateful he didn't run into anyone. His car was parked beneath the shade of several trees, a short distance from the circular drive and the wrought-iron gates. He hastily stuffed the folders into the trunk of his car and yanked open the driver's-side door, sliding behind the wheel.

His heart slammed hard in his chest when Byron materialized beside him. "Are you trying to give *me* a heart attack? Don't do that!"

Byron grinned at him. "I thought we should talk about the fact that you think I am a vampire. I know you said you would prefer not to, but I am going to marry your cousin, and it is best to clear the air."

Franco sat for a moment and then leaned forward to turn the key. "You're saying you're not a vampire?"

"No, I am not. I am something altogether different. If you wish to keep this knowledge, I would have to take your blood. Otherwise, I will have no choice but to remove your memories of this encounter."

Franco drove through the streets with more speed than vision. "You can remove memories? *Dio,* Byron, does Toni know what you are?"

"Of course." His tone lowered an octave. "You cannot betray us for any reason, Franco. If you did, I would know, and I would have no choice but to protect my people."

Franco glanced at him, noted the hard lines etched into Byron's face. "You mean it, don't you? I understand loyalty, Byron." A small grin spread across his face. "Once you marry Toni, we'll be family. I don't think it'll be so easy to harm me."

"It wouldn't be so easy now, Franco. Make your choice."

"I like knowing you have certain abilities. They may come in handy sometime. I know Toni doesn't really want to run the family business. Sooner or later, Nonno is going to have to turn it over to me. I think having you at a board meeting would be very helpful."

"Helena had an affair with Tasha and Paul's father. Esteben was her son, not her nephew. Helena thought she deserved the Scarletti fortune. I believe she was responsible for the deaths of Antonietta's parents and even Tasha and Paul's parents. Esteben probably killed Enrico. Helena and Esteben arranged accidents for Don Giovanni and fed poison to members of your family. They were both able to shift into the form of a jaguar. They were the ones killing the locals. They probably could not control the urges of the beast when they were in the form of the cat."

"You are telling me something."

"Do not shift into the form of a jaguar and expect to stay in control. It is dangerous."

"How did you know?"

"You accepted my differences far too easily."

"I would never have suspected Helena. She seemed so much a part of our household. What a waste. Had she just gone to Don Giovanni and told him about Esteben, they would have been welcomed into the family." He parked the car in the large garage. "Marita doesn't believe Margurite is my child."

"What do you believe?"

"She is a Scarletti through and through. And I love her. She's my daughter, and she'll always be my daughter, no matter what a paternity test says."

"She is a Scarletti." Byron smiled. "There is no mistaking the scent and thought patterns of your family."

Franco leaned back in his seat and smiled. "*Grazie,* Byron. Do whatever you think necessary to protect your people. Your family is tied to my family now. It is what any of us would do."

And hurry please. I am lonely for you. Antonietta startled him. She learned fast, staying a shadow in his mind even when he was no longer aiding her.

I am coming. He sent his assurance to his lifemate.

20

"**I** *do not* believe this. Byron, you are nervous." Jacques Dubrinsky clapped Byron on the shoulder as he circled around his friend to check that the tails on the suit jacket were straight.

Byron glanced quickly at the other occupants of the room. Eleanor and Vlad grinned openly at him while Shea, Jacques's lifemate, tried to hide her smile.

"I am not nervous. Why should I be nervous? Antonietta is my lifemate. We are already tied together. This is just a ceremony to please her family." Byron straightened his tie and ran a finger under the collar of his immaculate white shirt. "Why are these things always so tight, like a noose around one's neck?"

Jacques laughed at him. "The noose has been there for some time. You just now are feeling it?"

Shea delivered a solid punch into Jacques's arm. "Ha-ha. You think you're so funny. His sense of humor is warped, Byron, don't pay him any attention. Your bride looks beautiful. I took a peek at her as her cousin helped her dress."

"*She* is nervous. Antonietta is so peculiar. She chose to

convert without batting an eyelash. She was willing to fight off a dangerous jaguar. She walks blind onto a stage to perform in front of forty thousand people, but she's so nervous marrying me, she is making me nervous." Byron glared at Jacques as he said the last.

"Or perhaps it is the other way around," Jacques pointed out. "I think you are sweating."

"Don't listen to him, Byron. Jacques is the one nervous. You know how he just loves crowds." Shea gazed at her lifemate with love. "How's Antonietta's vision, Byron? Is she coping any better?"

"She has learned to understand what she sees but often the thermal images superimpose themselves over her normal vision, and she still has difficulty with depth perception. She also remains highly sensitive to the emotions and electrical currents around her." There was a note of worry in Byron's voice.

"Bring her back to the mountains as part of your honeymoon," Shea suggested. "The soil may speed the process up a bit. I've suspected for a while that many of the human life mates who display psychic abilities may be descendents of the Jaguar race, not all of them, but at least a substantial majority. Antonietta's the first with such a strong Jaguar genetic code. I'm very interested in seeing how the conversion enhances her natural abilities."

Byron's eyes darkened. "She is not an experiment."

"Of course not," Shea laughed lightly, even as she put a restraining hand on Jacques's arm. "I do tend to talk in medical and researcher terms, don't I? Antonietta is a delightful, courageous woman, and she brings with her a rich history. I suppose you noticed this region has several humans with strong barriers to mind scanning."

"That has to be the Jaguar influence. Franco actually is capable of shape-shifting, which would lead one to believe his genetic code is mainly Jaguar, yet he has a tremendous sense of family and is a good father and husband," Byron said.

"I've talked to him," Shea admitted. "He's promised to allow us to witness his shape-shifting. It will be interesting to see the differences."

Byron looked up quickly. "He did not say a word to me.

I have serious reservations about that. I'll take you to the history room. Antonietta has agreed it is very important to us all. But I do not want Franco shifting."

Vlad nodded his head in agreement. "I have to go with Byron on this. The natural inclinations of the Jaguar seem difficult to control."

"It's important," Shea reiterated. "Franco, especially with his strong sense of family and yet the ability to shift, is important. He's been wonderfully cooperative. Antonietta, too. Both understand the importance to our people of unraveling the mysteries."

"What if he makes a kill while in the jaguar form?" Byron asked, turning to face her. "Franco also has other Scarletti traits. He is capable of violence; do not think he isn't. He wouldn't forgive himself if he harmed an innocent person while in that form."

"The Scarlettis are your family, Byron," Jacques said, his voice, as always, low but impressive. "Mikhail has accepted them under our protection for that reason, and all of us here have done so because of the strength of your feelings for them. I have found them to be just as loyal to you in return. Franco wants to help us with this. He cannot possibly escape the control of three fully mature male and three female Carpathians."

"If I can witness the differences during a shifting," Shea said, "I should be able to figure out how to better help Antonietta with her vision problems. The Jaguar genes are very strong in this family. This might be our only chance to really find out the information we need to help our people with so many things, Byron."

"I'll have to speak with Franco again about this. I would want him to understand the risks before he does it," Byron said.

"Of course," Jacques agreed. "And do not forget, he has shifted more than once, and he did not make a kill."

"He does not remember," Byron pointed out, "that is not the same thing as knowledge. He obviously did not have control of the beast; it controlled him."

Shea paced across the room, halted beside the stained glass window to touch the intricate artwork. "I know you're worried about Franco, Byron, but I'm really not as clinical as I sound. I appreciate that these people not only are loved by your lifemate but are family to you. I also appreciate that they accept us and our differences. I would never put one of your family members in jeopardy for research, no matter how important it is to our race. I just wouldn't do that."

Jacques went to her immediately and drew her into his arms. "No one thinks you would, Shea."

Byron shook his head. "I just have a difficult time understanding genetics. My expertise is elsewhere, and I can never figure out how something like watching Franco shift into a jaguar as opposed to watching Jacques shift could be of use."

"It is rather fascinating," Vlad said. "I watch poor little Josef working at shifting, and one time half his body will be a bird and the other half something else. He doesn't remember to hold one image."

"It's such a matter of focus," Shea said. "For me, because we have such a tremendous problem having children, genetics is a primary concern."

"I am grateful, too," Eleanor said. "Our women have just about given up all hope of successfully carrying children or keeping them alive beyond the first year."

"And yet we have had a success or two," Shea pointed out. "The Carpathian who fascinates me most, though, is Gregori's brother, Darius. He accomplished things as a boy that no one else ever has. I'd love to study him under a microscope." She laughed when Jacques nudged her. "I know, there I go again. I'll stop now."

"Actually, Vlad and I were discussing Darius just the other day. Josef is still struggling to learn these skills, yet Darius was able to hold images for not only himself but other children as well. We don't have the luxury of time for our children to learn the necessary skills," Eleanor said, "and the old ways don't work in this era."

"I am grateful I am a gem-caller rather than a healer," Byron said. "It is far too complicated to figure out."

"Speaking of which," Jacques said, "Mikhail is looking forward to your return. He wants to give Raven a special gift and was hoping you would put your gem-calling skills to use. He would have come himself, but Raven recently miscarried."

There was a short, shocked silence. "Please give my sympathies to your brother, Jacques," Byron said.

Vlad took Eleanor's hand. "As well as ours," he added.

They regarded each other with shared, heartfelt sorrow. It wasn't just the fact that the child belonged to the prince of their people, it was the fact that every child lost brought their race closer to extinction.

"Is Raven all right?" Eleanor asked.

"She was depressed, of course, but physically, she is fine. They'd been trying for another child for a long while, and they feel the loss tremendously," Shea said with a small sigh of regret. She pressed both hands over her womb protectively. "Whatever has affected our people's reproductive abilities must be in our blood or in the soil itself. I have my theories but nothing substantial yet."

"I never considered that by converting Antonietta, I would be asking her to cope with the sorrows of losing a child. Raven successfully gave birth to one child; I just assumed she would easily have more."

"Raven has Carpathian blood flowing in her veins, just as the rest of us," Eleanor said. "All of us hoped it wouldn't happen with her as it did with the rest of us."

Byron swept a hand through his hair. "Antonietta went through so much already just with the conversion. I should have thought this all the way through before I brought her fully into our world. I do not want her to have to face losing children." He remembered Eleanor's deep anguish as she lost baby after baby. And Diedre, Vlad's sister, suffering such depression after the losses.

"I don't want to give Antonietta false hope that we may have children. I always thought if I found my lifemate I would have children, but she's accepted the idea she never would have a family because she didn't believe she would ever find a man to share her life. I don't want her hoping for children only to lose her baby."

Eleanor sighed softly. "I have lost many children over the years, Diedre more than I, yet we tried over and over. Not, as many think, for the good of our race but because a child is a treasure we cherish, a gift unequaled on this earth. Tell Antonietta the truth, and allow her to choose for herself."

Byron? Do you need me? Why are you so sad? This is our wedding day.

Antonietta was there in his mind instantly, a warm, loving presence. *I will always need you. Are you nervous?*

She laughed softly, the sound playing over his skin, tugging at his heart. *I'm afraid not; that's you, not me. I feel wonderful.*

Do not be late and leave me standing there looking like an idiot.

I cannot imagine you looking like an idiot. Antonietta laughed softly and turned away from the mirror. Her room seemed crowded with her family members all helpfully gathered around her. Even little Margurite, dressed in her finest, had been allowed to join them. Franco had placed her carefully in the most comfortable chair.

"Are you talking to Byron?" Tasha asked curiously. "He's telepathic, too, isn't he? Diego isn't at all. I've tried, but he's not originally from this area and has no telepathic ability whatsoever. You said you didn't mind if I invited him, and I've asked him to bring the children. I want everyone to meet them."

Antonietta kissed Tasha's cheek. "This is the perfect day for all of us to meet his children. I want all my family around me and, of course, everyone they love."

Franco reached out to touch a tendril of his cousin's hair. "This is what you really want, Toni? This man is for all time."

"I'm absolutely certain, Franco." Antonietta could feel happiness spilling out of her. "He's exactly right for me. Everything I've ever wanted. Is this the way you feel about Marita?"

"I knew from the first moment I saw her that she was my other half. I gave her no chance to get away from me. I spent weeks courting her. I think I frightened her with my intensity." He turned his head to look at his wife.

Her answering smile was tentative. She was busy fussing over Margurite's hair. Celt kept pressing his nose into the little girl's lap. Marita didn't scold, allowing Margurite to scratch the dog's silky ears.

Antonietta lowered her voice. "I know we took a loss undercutting the Demonesini company on the last three bids, Franco, and that you're worried about it, but you needn't be. It forced them to sell their stock in hopes of recouping the loss of revenue, and Nonno has been quietly buying it. We're taking that company down piece by piece. I didn't want to say anything to Marita because she seems as if she's finally happy again. What a terrible experience for her to endure."

Franco kissed his cousin, mindful of her clothes. "*Grazie,* for your compassion. We are together, and we will always remain so." He, too, kept his voice low. "The additions on the lower floor have been completed to Byron's specifications. Paul and I will see to it that your orders are always carried out, Toni. You and Byron will be fully protected during the times Byron says you are most vulnerable."

There was no way she could express her joy, so Antonietta didn't try. It was so much easier for her three cousins to know the truth of what she was. She knew Byron had given them the choice and that he could monitor them at will, but they had accepted that condition readily. She hadn't lost her family or the life she loved so much.

Byron? If I haven't said so this evening, I love you.

He was there for her immediately. His warmth surrounded her, held her close. *I feel you laughing. What are you doing on this solemn occasion?*

Antonietta's teasing voice spread warmth through Byron's body. *We are talking about Josef. Vlad caught him trying his Spiderman routine again. He was not very successful and fell into a flowerpot. As he was recouping, I think Eleanor grounded him.*

That sounds like our Josef. They are telling me I have to go to the chapel. See you soon.

Our Josef. Byron liked the sound of that. Somewhere along the line, his horror of his nephew's antics had turned to genuine amusement and affection. He didn't know when or how it had happened.

Eleanor rose from the chair by the window and kissed Byron's cheek, startling him, bringing him out of his thoughts. "In all the excitement and trauma, I honestly do not remember if I thanked Antonietta for saving Josef's life. He is fully recovered and is up and about again."

"Is the world safe?" Byron teased.

Jacques suddenly laughed. "I will never forget his performance in front of my brother. It was all I could do not to fall down laughing watching Mikhail's face when Josef sang his rendition of rap."

Vlad covered his face. "Do not remind me."

Byron nudged Jacques. "Antonietta has a sound room. I bet we could persuade Josef to cut an entire rap CD for Mikhail. I would not mind a copy for myself, just to put on every once in a while to watch Antonietta's face when she hears his lyrics."

"A brilliant idea," Jacques agreed. "Just the thing for that brother of mine."

"Byron! Jacques!" Eleanor was horrified. "Do not dare encourage Josef."

Byron wrapped his arm around her. "I think encouraging art is a wonderful trait."

"You will answer to me if you do such a thing," Vlad said in his severest voice.

Byron and Jacques exchanged a quick grin. Shea hid a knowing smile, shaking her head at their antics, pleased they were falling back into their old camaraderie.

A single knock sounded on the door, and Franco stuck his head in the room. "It's time, Byron."

Byron took a deep breath. "Has anyone noticed it's hard to breathe in here?"

Eleanor kissed him. "Do not disgrace us by being a baby about this. I will see you in the chapel."

"No running away now," Shea cautioned. "Your lifemate looks unbelievable." She followed Eleanor out.

Byron looked at Jacques. "There is something about standing up in front of a crowd. Why do women like these things?"

"To torment us," Jacques said.

"You have that right." Vlad opened the door and waved his brother-in-law through.

The night was crystal clear, the calm sea gleaming like glass. Night flowers bloomed along the pathway, bringing bright colors to light the way. The chapel sat in the midst of a small grove of trees. Lit from within, Byron could see the stained glass windows in all of their vivid beauty. The breeze touched his face, cooled his skin, carried with it the smell and taste of the sea. He inhaled deeply, appreciating that Antonietta had chosen a setting close to nature, close to his world. The three men wound their way through the gardens to the entrance that would lead them directly to the altar.

Byron walked in through the side door, Jacques and Vlad at his side. Hundreds of candles set the chapel softly aglow.

They were all there. Her family. His family. The people he had grown to care about. Franco with Vincente and Margurite. Eleanor sat beside the two children, whispering something in Margurite's ear. Diego sat with his young children, staring enraptured at Tasha, who was already at the altar with Marita, waiting for the bride. Paul and Justine held hands. Byron was especially pleased to see that Shea was sitting very close to Josef, and whatever she was saying to him wiped the wicked, teasing grin from his face. Byron's heart contracted at the sight of them all sitting together with no separation between them.

There was music, but Byron could only hear the wild thunder of his heart. He stood, his hands folded in front of him. Waiting. There was a soft rustle at the entrance to the chapel. A second heart found the perfect rhythm of his. He turned as their guests rose to their feet.

Antonietta stood at the back of the church, one gloved hand tucked into the crook of Don Giovanni's arm. She wore exquisite Italian lace, a dress that clung to her enticing curves and fell in graceful folds to her ankles. Her abundance of hair was swept up in some intricate knot with curling tendrils everywhere. She looked straight at him and smiled.

His heart stuttered. His breath caught and was trapped in his lungs. For one moment he was certain he was locked in a dream. She couldn't be real. Couldn't be his. Music filled the chapel. Byron locked his gaze with hers, willing her to come to him. Time stopped for him. The world forgot to turn. He felt Jacques's restraining hand and realized he had started to move toward her. And then Antonietta started up the aisle toward him. His pounding heart returned to its natural rhythm. The air moved through his lungs.

Jacques. Do you have the ring? Byron spent hours in secret, fashioning the perfect ring of rubies and diamonds, using an ancient threading technique. The setting was unique, made just for Antonietta and her sensitive fingertips. Feeling was more important to her than vision, and he had formed a ring of texture in hopes of pleasing her.

Jacques patted his pockets, looked alarmed, then laughed softly. *Of course I have the ring, you dolt. Shea would have my head if I messed up.*

I'm listening. Antonietta reminded, her smile widening.

So am I, Shea added.

Byron stepped forward to meet his bride. Don Giovanni kissed his granddaughter and placed her hand in Byron's. "I give her into your keeping."

"And she will always be safe," Byron promised solemnly.

Byron turned back to the altar and, together with Antonietta, faced the priest, his heart swelling with joy. He had found his lifemate, a woman of courage and compassion who would spend eternity at his side.

The marriage ceremony was solemn, the priest's words eloquent. Byron felt the words in his heart and in his soul. He knew it was right that they had married in the way of her people. They were blending two worlds together, and each mattered equally. He spoke his vows in a clear voice, meaning every word. Antonietta's voice was low and played over his skin like a caress.

"I love you, Byron Justicano. I will always love you," Antonietta whispered softly as he placed his ring on her finger.

The priest pronounced them man and wife.

Byron bent his head to hers as she lifted her face. Her expression of love was so passionate, his heart moved in his chest. He kissed her with exquisite tenderness. *I have always loved you, Antonietta.*

And I, you.

"I give you Signor and Signora Justicano."

Byron and Antonietta turned and faced their families together, hand in hand. The roar of happiness and joy spilled out of the chapel to reach up to the heavens and down to the sea.

*C*aptain *Ryland Miller* leaned his head against the wall and closed his eyes in utter weariness. He could ignore the pain in his head, the knives shredding his skull. He could ignore the cage he was in. He could even ignore the fact that sooner or later, he was going to slip up and his enemies would kill him. But he could not ignore guilt and anger and frustration rising like a tidal wave in him as his men suffered the consequences of his decisions.

Kaden, I can't reach Russell Cowlings. Can you?

He had talked his men into the experiment that had landed them all into the laboratory cages in which they now resided. Good men. Loyal men. Men who had wanted to better serve their country and people.

We all made the decision. Kaden responded to his emotions, the words buzzing inside Ryland's mind. *No one has managed to raise Russell.*

Ryland swore softly aloud as he swept a hand over his face, trying to wipe away the pain speaking telepathically with his men cost him. The telepathic link between them had grown stronger as they all worked to build it, but only a few of them could sustain it for any length of time. Ryland had to supply the bridge, and his brain, over time, balked at the enormity of such a burden.

Don't touch the sleeping pills they gave you. Suspect any medication. He glanced at the small white pill lying in plain sight on his end table. He'd like a lab analysis of the contents. Why hadn't Cowlings listened to him? Had Cowlings accepted the sleeping pill in the hopes of a brief respite? He had to get the men out. *We have no choice, we must treat this situation as if we were behind enemy lines.* Ryland took a deep breath, let it out slowly. He no longer felt he had a choice. He had already lost too many men. His decision would brand them as traitors, deserters, but it was the only way to save their lives. He had to find a way for his men to break out of the laboratory.

The Colonel has betrayed us. We have no other choice but to escape. Gather information and support one another as best you can. Wait for my word.

He became aware of the disturbance around him, the dark waves of intense dislike bordering on hatred preceding the group nearing the cage where he was kept.

Someone is approaching . . . Ryland lifted his head, abruptly cutting off telepathic communication to those of his men he could reach. He remained motionless in the center of his cell, his every sense flaring out to identify the approaching individuals.

It was a small group this time, Dr. Peter Whitney, Colonel Higgens and a security guard. It amused Ryland that Whitney and Higgens insisted on an armed guard accompanying them despite the fact that he was locked behind both bars and a thick glass barrier. He was careful to keep his features expressionless as they neared his cage.

Ryland lifted his head, his steel-gray eyes as cold as ice. Menacing. He didn't try to hide the danger he represented. They had created him, they had betrayed him, and he wanted them to be afraid. There was tremendous satisfaction in knowing they were . . . and that they had reason to be.

Dr. Peter Whitney led the small group. Whitney, liar, deceiver, monster-maker. He was the creator of the Ghost-Walkers. Creator of what Captain Ryland Miller and his men had become. Ryland stood up slowly, a deliberate ripple of muscle, a lethal jungle cat stretching lazily, unsheathing claws as he waited inside his cage.

His icy gaze touched on their faces, lingered, made them uncomfortable. Graveyard eyes. Eyes of death. He projected the image deliberately, wanting, even needing, them to fear for their lives. Colonel Higgens looked away, studied the cameras, the security, watched with evident apprehension as the thick barrier of glass slid away. Although Ryland remained caged behind heavy bars, Higgens was obviously uneasy without the barrier, uncertain just how powerful Miller had become.

"Good morning, Captain Miller," Peter Whitney said pleasantly. "How are things with you this morning? Did you sleep at all?"

Ryland watched him without blinking, tempted to try to push through Whitney's barriers to discover the true character hidden behind the wall Whitney had in his mind. What secrets were hidden there? The one person Ryland needed to understand, to read, was protected by some natural or man-made barrier. None of the other men, not even Kaden, had managed to penetrate the scientist's mind. They couldn't get any pertinent data, shielded as Whitney was, but the heavy, swamping waves of guilt were always broadcast loudly.

"No, I didn't sleep but I suspect you already know that."

Dr. Whitney nodded. "None of your men are taking their sleeping meds. I noticed you didn't either. Is there a reason for that, Captain Miller?"

The chaotic emotions of the group hit Ryland hard as it always did. In the beginning, it used to drive him to his knees, the noise in his head so loud and aggravating his brain would rebel, punishing him for his unnatural abilities. Now he was much more disciplined. Oh, the pain was still there, like a thousand knives driving into his head at the first breach of his brain, but he hid the agony behind the façade of icy, menacing calm. And he was, after all, well trained. His people never revealed weakness to the enemy.

"Self preservation is always a good reason," he answered, fighting down the waves of weakness and pain from the battering of emotions. He kept his features totally expressionless, refusing to allow them to see the cost.

"What the hell does that mean?" Higgens demanded. "What are you accusing us of now, Miller?"

The door to the laboratory had been left standing open, unusual for the security-ridden company, and a woman hurried through. "I'm sorry I'm late, the meeting went longer than expected!"

At once the painful assault of thoughts and emotions lessened, muted, leaving Ryland able to breathe normally. To think without pain. The relief was instant and unexpected. Ryland focused on her immediately, realizing she was somehow trapping the more acute emotions and holding them at bay, almost as if she were a magnet for them. And she wasn't just any woman. She was so beautiful she took his breath away. Ryland could have sworn when he looked at her, the ground shifted and moved under his feet. He glanced at Peter Whitney, caught the man observing his reaction to the woman's presence very closely.

Ryland's first thought was embarrassment that he had been caught staring at her. Then he realized Whitney knew the woman had some kind of psychic ability. She enhanced Ryland's abilities and cleared out the garbage of stray thoughts and emotions. Did Whitney know exactly what she did? The doctor was waiting for a reaction so Ryland refused to give him the satisfaction, keeping his expression totally blank.

"Captain Miller, I'd like to present my daughter, Lily Whitney. Dr. Lily Whitney." Peter's gaze never left the Captain's face. "I've asked her to join us, I hope you don't mind."

The shock couldn't have been more complete. Peter Whitney's daughter? Ryland let out his breath slowly, shrugged his broad shoulders casually, another ripple of menace. He didn't feel casual. Everything inside of him stilled. Calmed. Reached. He studied the woman. Her eyes were incredible, but wary. Intelligent. Knowledgeable. As if she recognized him, too, in some elemental way. Her eyes were a deep startling blue, like the middle of a clear, fresh pool. A man could lose his mind, his freedom in eyes like hers. She was of average height, not tall, but not exceedingly short. She had a woman's figure encased in a gray-green suit of some kind that managed to draw attention to every lush curve. She had walked with a decided limp, but when he looked her over for damage, he could see nothing to indicate injury. More than all of that, the moment he saw her face, the moment she entered the room, his soul seemed to reach for hers. To recognize hers. His breath stilled in his body and he could only stare at her.

"Captain Miller." Her voice was soothing, gentle, pleasant. Sexy. A blend of smoke and heat that seared him right through his belly. "How nice to meet you. My father thought I might be of some use in the research. I haven't had much time to go over the data, but I'll be happy to try to help."

He had never reacted to a voice before. The sound seemed to wrap him up in satin sheets, rubbing and caressing his skin until he felt himself break out in a sweat. The image was so vivid for a moment he could only stare at her, imagining her naked body writhing with pleasure beneath his. In the midst of his struggle to survive, his physical reaction to her was shocking.

Color crept up her neck, delicately tinged her cheeks. Her long lashes fluttered, drifted down and she looked away from him to her father. "This room is very exposed. Who came up with the design? I would think it would be a difficult way to live, even for a short period."

"You mean like a lab rat?" Ryland asked softly, deliberately, not wanting any of them to think they were fooling him by bringing in the woman. "Because that's what I am. Dr. Whitney has his own human rats to play with."

Lily's dark gaze jumped to his face. One eyebrow shot up. "I'm sorry, Captain Miller, was I misinformed, or did you agree to volunteer for this assignment?" There was a small challenge in her voice.

"Captain Miller volunteered, Lily," Peter Whitney said. "He was unprepared for the brutal results, as was I. I've been searching for a way to reverse the process but so far, everything I've tried has failed."

"I don't believe that's the proper way to handle this," Colonel Higgens snapped. He glared at Peter Whitney, his bushy brows drawing together in a frown of disapproval. "Captain Miller is a soldier. He volunteered for this mission and I must insist he carry it out to its conclusion. We don't need the process reversed, we need it perfected."

Ryland had no trouble reading the colonel's emotions. The man didn't want Lily Whitney anywhere near Ryland or his men. He wanted Ryland taken out behind the laboratories and shot. Better yet, dissected so they could all see what was going on in his brain. Colonel Higgens was afraid of Ryland Miller and the other men in the paranormal unit. Anything he feared, Higgens destroyed.

"Colonel Higgens, I don't think you fully understand what these men are going through, what is happening to their brains," Dr. Whitney was pursuing an obviously long-standing argument between them. "We've already lost several men . . ."

"They knew the risks," Higgens snapped, glowering at Miller. "This is an important experiment. We need these men to perform. The loss of a few men, while tragic, is an acceptable loss considering the importance of what these men can do."

Ryland didn't look at Higgens. He kept his glittering gaze fixed on Lily Whitney. But his entire mind reached out. Took hold. Closed like a vise.

Lily's head snapped up. She gasped out a soft protest. Her gaze dropped to Captain Miller's hands. She watched his fingers slowly begin to curl as if around a thick throat. She shook her head, a slight protest.

Higgens coughed. A barking grunt. His mouth hung open as he gasped for air. Peter Whitney and the young guard both reached for the colonel, trying to open his stiff shirt collar, trying to help him breathe. The colonel staggered, was caught and lowered to the floor by the scientist.

Stop it. The voice in Ryland's mind was soft.

Ryland's dark brow shot up and his gleaming gaze met Lily's. The doctor's daughter was definitely telepathic. She was calm about it, her gaze steady on his, not in the least intimidated by the danger emanating from him. She appeared as cool as ice.

He's willing to sacrifice every one of my men. They aren't expendable. He was just as calm, not for a moment relenting.

He's a moron. No one is willing to sacrifice the men, no one considers them expendable, and he isn't worth branding yourself a murderer.

Ryland allowed his breath to escape in a soft, controlled stream, clearing his lungs, clearing his mind. Deliberately he turned his back on the writhing man and paced across the cell, his fingers slowly uncurling.

Higgens went into a fit of coughing, tears swimming in his eyes. He pointed a shaky finger toward Ryland Miller. "He tried to kill me, you all saw it."

Peter Whitney sighed and walked with heavy footsteps across the room to stare at the computer. "I'm tired of the melodrama, Colonel. There is always a jump on sensors in the computers when there is a surge of power. There's nothing here at all. Miller is safely locked in a cage; he didn't do anything at all. Either you're trying to sabotage my project or you have a personal vendetta against Captain Miller. In any case, I'm going to write to the general and insist they send another liaison."

Colonel Higgens swore again. "I'll have no more talk about reversing the process, Whitney, and you know what I think about bringing your daughter on board. We don't need another damn bleeding heart on this project, we need results."

"My security clearance, Colonel Higgens, is of the highest level and so is my commitment to this project. I don't have the necessary data at this time, but I can assure you I'll put in whatever time necessary to find the answers needed." Even as she spoke, Lily was looking at the computer screen.

Ryland was "reading" her. Whatever was on the screen puzzled her as much as what her father was saying, but she was willing to cover for him. She was making it up as she went along. As calm and as cool as ever. He couldn't remember the last time he had smiled, but the impulse was there. He kept his back to the group, not certain he could keep a straight face while she lied to the colonel. Lily Whitney had no idea what was going on, her father had given her very little information and she was simply winging it. Her dislike of Higgens, compounded with her father's unusual behavior had left her firmly in Ryland's camp for the moment.

He had no idea what Whitney's game was, but Peter Whitney was buried deep in the mire. The experiment to enhance psychic ability and bring together a fighting unit had been his project, his brainchild. Peter Whitney had been the man to persuade Ryland the experiment had merit. That his men would be safe and that they would better serve their country. Ryland couldn't read the doctor as he could most men, but whatever Whitney was up to, Ryland was certain it wasn't anything that would benefit him or his men. Donovans Corporation had a stench about it. If there was one thing Ryland knew for certain, Donovans was about money and personal profit, not national security.

"Can you read that code your father uses for his notes?" Higgens asked Lily Whitney, suddenly losing interest in Ryland. "Gibberish if you ask me. Why the hell don't you just put your work in English like a normal human being?" He snapped the question at Dr. Whitney irritably.

At once the captain swung around, his gray gaze thoughtful as it rested on the colonel. There was something there, something he couldn't get hold of. It was shifting, moving, ideas formulating and growing. Higgens's mind seemed a black ravine, twisted and curved and suddenly cunning.

Lily shrugged. "I grew up reading his codes, of course I can read it."

Ryland sensed her growing puzzlement as she stared at the combination of numbers, symbols, and letters across the computer screen.

"What the hell are you doing getting into my private computer files, Frank?" Peter Whitney demanded, glaring at the colonel. "When I want you to read a report, I'll have the data organized and the report will be finished and up-to-date, neatly typed in English. You have no business in my computer either here or at my office. My research on many projects is on my computer and you have no right invading my privacy. If your people go anywhere near my work, I'll have you locked out of Donovans so fast you won't know what hit you."

"This isn't your personal project, Peter." Higgens glowered at all of them. "This is my project too and as the head of it, you don't keep secrets from me. You don't make any sense in your reports."

"I want something done about Miller," Higgens said, acting as if Ryland couldn't hear him.

I'm already dead to him. Ryland whispered the words in Lily Whitney's mind.

All the better for you and your men. He's pressing my father hard about pushing this project forward not terminating it. He isn't satisfied with the findings and doesn't agree it is dangerous to all of you. Lily didn't look away from the computer or give away in any manner that she was communicating with him.

He doesn't know about you. Higgens has no idea you're telepathic. The knowledge burst over him like a light from a prism. Brilliant and colorful and full of possibilities. Dr. Whitney was hiding his daughter's abilities from the colonel. From the Donovans Corporation. Ryland knew he had ammunition. Information he could use to bargain with Dr. Whitney. Something that might be used to save his men. His flare of excitement must have been in his mind because Lily turned and regarded him with a cool, thoughtful gaze.

Peter Whitney glared at Colonel Higgens, clearly exasperated. "You want something done? What does that mean, Frank? What do you have in mind? A lobotomy? Captain Miller has performed every test we've asked of him. Do you have personal reasons for disliking the captain?" Dr. Whitney's voice was a whip of contempt. "Captain Miller, if you were having an affair with Colonel Higgens's wife, you should have disclosed that information to me immediately."

Lily's dark eyebrows shot up. Ryland could feel the sudden amusement in her mind. Her laughter was soft and inviting, but her features gave nothing of her inner thoughts away. *Well? Are you a Romeo?*

There was something peaceful and serene about Lily, something that spilled over into the air around them. His second-in-command, Kaden, was like that, calming the terrible static and tuning the frequencies so that they were clear and sharp and able to be used by all the men regardless of talent. Surely her father hadn't experimented on his own daughter. The idea sickened him.

"Laugh all you want, Peter," the colonel snapped, "but you won't be laughing when lawsuits are filed against Donovans Corporation and the United States government is after you for botching the job."

Ryland ignored the arguing men. He had never been so drawn to a woman, to any individual, but he wanted Lily to remain in the room. He *needed* her to remain in the room. And he didn't want her to be a part of the conspiracy that was threatening his life. She seemed unaware of it, but her father was certainly one of the puppet masters.

My father is no puppet master. Her voice was indignant and faintly haughty, a princess to an inferior being.

You don't even know what the hell is going on so how do you know what he is or isn't? He was rougher than he intended but Lily took it well, ignoring him to frown at the computer monitor.

She didn't speak to her father, but he sensed her movement toward him, a slight exchange between them. It was more felt than seen, and Ryland sensed her puzzlement deepen. Her father gave her no clue, but instead, led Colonel Higgens toward the door.

"Are you coming, Lily?" Dr. Whitney asked, pausing just inside the hall.

"I want to look things over here, sir," she said, indicating the computer, "and it will give Captain Miller a chance to fill me in on where he is in this."

Higgens swung around. "I don't think it's a good idea for you to stay alone with him. He's a dangerous man."

She looked as cool as ever, her dark brow a perfect arch. Lily stared down her aristocratic nose at the colonel. "You didn't ensure the premises were secure, Colonel?"

Colonel Higgens swore again and stomped out of the room. As Lily's father started out of the room, she cleared her throat softly. "I think it best we discuss this project in a more thorough way if you want my input, sir."

Dr. Whitney glanced at her, his features impassive. "I'll meet you at Antonio's for dinner. We can go over everything after we eat. I want your own impressions."

"Based on . . ."

Ryland didn't hear a hint of sarcasm, but it was there in her mind. She was angry with her father but he couldn't read why. That part of her mind was closed off to him, hidden behind a thick, high wall she had erected to keep him out.

"Go over my notes, Lily, and see what you make of the process. Maybe you'll see something I didn't. I want a fresh perspective. Colonel Higgens might be right. There may be a way to continue without reversing what we've done." Peter Whitney refused to meet his daughter's direct gaze.

"Do I need to leave an armed guard in this room with my daughter, Captain?"

Ryland studied the face of the man who had opened the floodgates of his brain to receive far too much stimuli. He could detect no evil, only a genuine concern. "I'm no threat to the innocent, Dr. Whitney."

"That's good enough for me." Without looking at his daughter, the doctor left the room, closing the door to the laboratory firmly.

Ryland was so aware of Lily, he actually felt the breath leave her lungs in a slow exhale as the door to the laboratory closed and the lock snicked quietly into place. He waited a heartbeat. Two. "Aren't you afraid of me?" Ryland asked, testing his voice with her. It came out more husky than he would have liked. He had never had much luck with women, and Lily Whitney was out of his class.

She didn't look at him, but continued to stare at the symbols on the screen. "Why should I be? I'm not Colonel Higgens."

"Even the lab techs are afraid of me."

"Because you want them to be and you're projecting, deliberately enhancing their own fears." Her voice indicated a mild interest in their conversation, her mind mulling over the data on the screen. "How long have you been here?"

He swung around, stalked to the bars and gripped them. "They're bringing you on board and you don't even know how long my men and I've been locked up in this hellhole?"

She turned her head, tendrils of hair swinging around her face, loose from the tight twist at the back of her head. Her hair, even in the muted blue light of the room was shiny and gleamed at him. "I don't know anything at all about this experiment, Captain. Not one small fact. This compound is the highest security clearance this corporation has and while I have clearance, this is not my field of expertise. Dr. Whitney, my father, asked me to consult and I was cleared to do so. Do you have a problem with that?"

He studied the classic beauty of her face. High cheekbones, long lashes, a lush mouth—they didn't come like this unless they were born rich and privileged. "You probably have an underpaid maid whose name you can't even remember, who picks up your clothes when you throw them on your bedroom floor."

That bought him her entire attention. She moved away from the computer, crossed the distance to his cage in a slow, unhurried walk that drew his attention to her limp. Even with her limp she had a flowing grace. She made every cell in his body instantly aware he was male and she was female.

Lily tilted her chin at him. "I guess you were brought up without manners, Captain Miller. I don't actually throw my clothes on the bedroom floor. I hang them in the closet." Her gaze flicked past him to rest briefly on the clothes strewn on the floor.

For the first time that he could remember, Ryland was embarrassed. He was making an ass out of himself. Even her damn high heels were classy. Sexy, but classy.

A small smile curved her mouth. "You're making a *total* ass out of yourself," she pointed out, "but fortunately for you, I'm in a forgiving mood. We elitists learn that at an early age when they put that silver spoon in our mouths."

Ryland was ashamed. He might have grown up on the wrong side of the tracks in the proverbial trailer trash park, but his mother would have boxed his ears for being so rude. "I'm sorry, there's no excuse."

"No, there isn't. There's never an excuse for rudeness." Lily paced across the distance of his cage, an unhurried examination of the length of his prison. "Who designed your quarters?"

"They constructed several cages quickly when they decided we were too powerful and posed too much danger as a group." His men had been separated and scattered throughout the facility. He knew the isolation was telling on them. Continual poking and prodding was wearing, and he worried that he could not keep them together. He had lost men already, he was not about to lose any of the others.

"Your men are all in similar cages? I wasn't given that information." Her voice was strictly neutral, but she didn't like it. He could feel the outrage she was striving to suppress.

"I haven't seem them in weeks. They don't allow us to communicate." He indicated the computer screen. "That's a constant source of irritation to Higgens. I bet his people have tried to break your father's code, even used the computer, but they must not have been able to do it. Can you really read it?"

She hesitated briefly. It was almost unnoticeable, but he sensed the sudden stillness in her and his hawklike gaze didn't leave her face. "My father has always written in codes. I see in mathematical patterns, and it was a kind of game when I was a little girl. He changed the code often to give me something to work on. My mind . . ." she hesitated, as if weighing her options carefully. She was deciding how honest to be with him. He wanted the truth and silently willed her to give it to him.

Lily was quiet for a moment more, her large eyes fixed steadily on his, then her soft mouth firmed. Her chin went up a miniscule notch but he was watching her every expression, every nuance and he was aware of it, aware of what it cost her to tell him. "My mind requires continual stimulation. I don't know how else to explain it. Without working on something complex, I run into problems."

He caught the flash of pain in her eyes, fleeting but there. Dr. Peter Whitney was one of the richest men in the world. All the money might have given his daughter every confidence, but it didn't take away the fact that she was a freak . . . a freak like he was. Like his men were. What her father had made them into. GhostWalkers, waiting for death to strike them down.

"So tell me this, Lily Whitney, if that code is real, why can't the computer crack it?" Ryland lowered his voice so that anyone listening wouldn't hear his question, but he kept his glittering gaze fixed on hers, refusing to allow her to look away from him.

Lily's expression didn't change. She looked as serene as always. She looked impossibly elegant even there in the laboratory. She looked so far out of his reach his heart hurt. "I said he always wrote in code, I didn't say this one made any sense to me. I haven't had a chance to work with it yet."

Her mind was closed so completely to him that he knew she was lying. He arched a dark brow at her. "Really. Well you'll have to put in for overtime because no one seems to be able to read how your father managed to enhance our psychic abilities. And they sure can't figure out how to make it go away."

She reached out, gracefully, almost casually, naturally, to grip the edge of a desk. The knuckles on her hand turned white. "He enhanced your natural abilities?" Her mind immediately began to turn that bit of information over and over as if it were the piece of a jigsaw puzzle and she was finding the proper fit.

"He really let you walk in here blind, didn't he?" Ryland challenged. "We were asked to take special tests . . ."

She held up her hand. "Who was asked and who asked you?"

"Most of my men are special forces. The men in the various branches were asked to be tested for psychic ability. There was a certain criteria to be met along with the abilities. An age range, combat training, working under pressure conditions, ability to function for long periods of time cut off from the chain of command. Loyalty factors. The list was endless, but surprisingly enough, we had quite a few takers. The military issued a special invite for volunteers. From what I understand law enforcement branches did the same. They were looking for an elitist group."

"And this was how long ago?"

"The first I heard of the idea, was nearly four years ago. I've been here at Donovans's laboratory for a year now, but all the recruits that made it into the unit, including me, trained together at another facility. As far as I know we were always kept together. They wanted us to form a tight unit. We trained in techniques using psychic abilities in combat. The idea was a strike force that could get in and out unseen. We could be used against the drug cartels, terrorists, even an enemy army. We've been at it for over three years."

"A wild idea. And this is whose baby?"

"Your father's. He thought it up, convinced the powers that be that it could be done and convinced me and the rest of the men that it would make the world a better place." There was a wealth of bitterness in Ryland Miller's voice.

"Obviously something went wrong."

"Greed went wrong. Donovans has the government contract. Peter Whitney practically owns this company. I guess he just doesn't have enough money with the million or two in his bank account."

She waited a heartbeat. Two. "I doubt my father needs any more money, Captain Miller. The amount he gives to charities each year would feed a state. You don't know anything about him so I suggest you reserve your opinion until all the facts are in. And for the record, it's a billion or two or more. This corporation could disappear tomorrow and it wouldn't change his lifestyle one bit." Her voice didn't raise in the least, but it smoldered with heat and intensity.

Ryland sighed. Her vivid gaze hadn't wavered an inch. "We have no contact with our people. All communication to the outside must go through your father or the colonel. We have no say in what is happening to us at all. One of my men died a couple of months ago and they lied about how he died. He died as a direct result of this experiment and the enhancement of his abilities. His brain couldn't handle the overload, the constant battering. They claimed it was an accident in the field. That's when we were cut off from all command and separated. We've been in isolation since that time." Miller regarded her with dark, angry eyes, daring her to call him a liar. "And it wasn't the first death, but by God, it's going to be the last."

Lily pushed a hand through her perfectly smooth hair, the first real sign of agitation. The action scattered pins and left long strands falling in a cloud around her face. She was silent, allowing her brain to process the information, even as she was rejecting the accusations and implications about her father.

"Do you know precisely what killed the man in your unit? And is there the same danger to the rest of you?" She asked the questions very quietly, her voice so low it was almost in his mind rather than aloud.

Ryland answered in the same soft voice, taking no chances the unseen guards would overhear the conversation. "His brain was wide open, assaulted by everyone and everything he came into contact with. He couldn't shut it off anymore.

We can function together as a group because a couple of the men are like you. They draw the noise and raw emotion away from the rest of us. Then we're powerful and we work. But without that magnet . . ." He broke off and shrugged. "It's like pieces of glass or razor blades slashing at the brain. He snapped, seizures, brain bleeds, you name it. It wasn't a pretty sight and I sure didn't like the glimpse of our future. Neither did any of the other men in the unit."

Lily pressed her fingers to her temple and for just a moment, Ryland caught the impression of throbbing pain. His face darkened, gray eyes narrowing. "Come here." He had an actual physical reaction to her being in pain. The muscles in his belly knotted, hard and aching. Everything protective and male in him rose up and flooded him with an overwhelming need to ease her discomfort.

Her enormous blue eyes instantly became wary. "I don't touch people."

"Because you don't want to know what they're really like inside, do you? You feel it too." He was horrified to think her father may have experimented on her too. *How long have you been telepathic?* More than that, he didn't want to think about never touching her. Never feeling her skin beneath his fingers, her mouth crushed to his. The image was so vivid he could almost taste her. Even her hair begged to be touched, a thick mass of shiny silk just asking for his fingers to toss away the rest of the pins and free it for his inspection.

Lily shrugged easily but a faint blush stole along her high cheekbones. *All of my life. And yes, it can be uncomfortable knowing other people's darkest secrets. I've learned to live within certain boundaries. Maybe my father became interested in psychic phenomenon because he wished to help me. For whatever reason, I can assure you, it had nothing to do with personal financial gain.* She let out a slow breath. "How terrible for you, the loss of *any* of your men. You must be very close. I hope I can find a way to help all of you."

Ryland sensed her sincerity. He was suspicious of her father in spite of her protests. *Is Dr. Whitney psychic?* He knew he'd been broadcasting his sexual fantasies a little too strongly but she was unshaken, handling the intensity of the chemistry between them easily. And he knew the chemistry was on both sides. He had a sudden desire to really shake her up, get past her cool demeanor just once and see if fire burned beneath the ice. It was a hell of a thing to think about in the middle of the mess he was in.

Lily shook her head as she answered him. *We've conducted many experiments and have connected telepathically a few times under extreme conditions, but it was sustained completely on my side. I must have inherited the talent through my mother.*

"When you touch him, can you read him?" Ryland asked curiously in a low voice. His attraction to her was raw and hot and beyond any experience he'd ever had. And she knew it. Unlike Ryland, she appeared to be cool and unaffected, while he was shaken to his very core. She carried on their conversation as if he weren't a firestorm burning out of control. As if his blood wasn't boiling and his body hard as rock and in desperate need. As if she didn't even notice.

"Rarely. He is one of those people who have natural barriers. I think it's because he believes so strongly in psychic talent where most people don't. Being aware of it all the time, he's probably built up a natural wall. I've found many people have barriers to varying degrees. Some seem impossible to get past and others are flimsy. What about you? Have you found the same thing? You're a very strong telepathic."

"Come here to me."

Her cool blue gaze drifted over him. Dismissed him. "I don't think so, Captain Miller, I have far too much work to do."

"You're being a coward." He said it softly, his hungry gaze on her face.

She lifted her chin at him and gave him her haughty princess look. "I don't have time for your little games, Captain Miller. Whatever you think is going on here, is not."

His gaze dropped to her mouth. She had a perfect mouth. "Yes it is."

"It was interesting meeting you," Lily said and turned away from him, walking without haste away from him. As cool as ever.

Ryland didn't protest, instead watched her leave him without a single backward glance. He willed her to look back, but she didn't. And she didn't replace the glass barrier around his cage, leaving it for the guards.

A new Carpathian novel from

CHRISTINE FEEHAN

DARK POSSESSION

MaryAnn Delaney is well aware of the aggressive instincts of Carpathian males—but she has no idea of the trap awaiting her. She's been lured to South America by her destined lifemate, Manolito De La Cruz, who has seductive plans for the irresistible human female.

Once there, she'll be his. Once his, she'll never be released. She is his dark possession.

IN STORES NOW

penguin.com
AD-014782